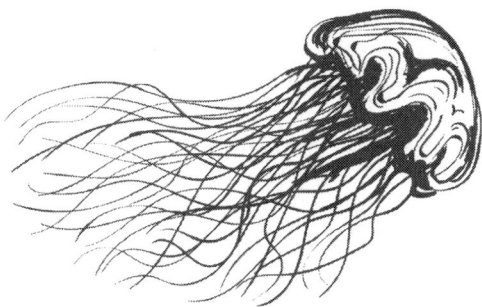

VENGEFUL MAGIC

WHITE HAVEN WITCHES

BOOK EIGHT

TJ GREEN

Vengeful Magic

Mountolive Publishing

Copyright © 2021 TJ Green

All rights reserved

ISBN 978-1-99-004719-0

ISBN Paperback 978-1-99-004720-6

ISBN Hardback 978-1-99-004788-6

Cover design by Fiona Jayde Media

Editing by Missed Period Editing

www.tjgreenauthor.com

www.happenstancebookshop.com

Contents

One

The smell of sizzling meat drifted through Avery and Alex's walled garden, and their guests chatted and laughed as they filled their plates with the food spread out on the patio table.

It was a Saturday night in early June, and they had gathered to celebrate Cassie, Dylan, and Ben finishing their post-grad studies, and Dan completing his master's degree. The White Haven witches, plus Newton, Sally, and Shadow were there too, the drinks were flowing, and the weather was balmy.

Reuben was wearing his loudest pink Hawaiian shirt that clashed with his yellow board shorts, and despite the fact that his clothes were partially covered by an apron stuffed with barbeque tools, Avery still winced when she looked at him.

"Who wants more sausages?" he asked, as he placed another dozen on a plate and ferried it to the large wooden table, setting them down next to some steaks and chicken wings.

"Good grief, Reuben! Are you trying to fatten us up?" Cassie asked.

"Don't complain!" Dylan said, already leaning forward to top his plate up. "This is brilliant! You're doing a great job!"

Reuben grinned and pulled up a chair. "I aim to please. Besides, it's the least I can do, since I'll eat most of it."

Alex raised his beer bottle. "Cheers, Reuben. Saves me some work, seeing as I've been slaving away all afternoon!"

Avery just looked at him, knowing he'd spent a couple of hours on the preparations, at most. "Exaggerator! Besides, you were enjoying yourself. I could hear music blasting!"

"It's still work, Ave!" Alex leaned over and kissed her cheek, looking very smug, and eased back in his seat again. "So now that your studies are over, what's the plan?"

Ben groaned. "A couple of weeks off would be nice. I'm knackered!"

"I wish," Dan said, laughing. "Avery is a hard task master."

"I'm not," she said, mock-outraged. "I'm very generous! If you want a holiday, just say so!"

He winked. "I'm kidding! But maybe in early July, before the school hols begin and the place is inundated with hoards of kids."

"Yeah, I might need some time off for the school holidays," Sally said. She raised an eyebrow at Dan. "Are you going away with Caroline?" She was referring to Dan's girlfriend of only a few weeks.

Dan winced. "Maybe? It might be too soon."

"Why didn't you bring her tonight?" Shadow asked, finishing her conversation with El. They had been leaning close in an animated exchange, and Avery wondered what they had been talking about. "I was hoping to meet her!"

"That's precisely why I didn't bring her. The poor woman would have been interrogated by all of you! Besides, I haven't shared some of the more *interesting* things about you yet, so I wasn't sure it would be wise."

Briar laughed. "Did you think we'd get a bit witchy and start casting spells? We're very discreet, you know!"

Dan gave Shadow a knowing look. "It was more Shadow's habit of pulling a knife at any minute that had me worried."

Shadow looked affronted. "I don't attack people at random!"

"But you do carry weapons—always!" Dan pointed out. "Regular people don't do that."

She shrugged, a mischievous glint in her eye, and a ripple of glamour made her hair shimmer. "I like to be prepared. Besides, they're hidden, most of the time."

"That's worse," Briar said. "You whip them out of thin air. It's so unnerving!"

Newton just shook his head. He was sitting next to Briar, and Avery was pleased to see their old friendship had resumed. "Twelve months ago I can honestly say I didn't think I'd be sitting at a barbeque with five witches, one fey, and three paranormal investigators." He shot Sally and Dan a grateful look. "Thanks for being normal!"

"I hate to break it to you, Newton," Sally said, smiling, "but seeing as you're the head of paranormal investigations for the Devon and Cornwall Police, you're not that normal anymore."

"Yeah, well, I keep trying to forget about that." He looked at Shadow. "Your friend, Maggie Milne, has phoned a couple of times."

Shadow looked suspicious. "Maggie is *not* my friend! Was she asking about me or the boys?" By 'boys' she meant the Nephilim—and they were far from boys.

"No, don't worry. Whatever you've been up to lately seems to have escaped her. Although, she did mention something about a missing necromancer."

Shadow shuffled uncomfortably in her seat. "He's dead, not missing, and we reported that."

"*Dead*?" Avery asked, shocked. "A necromancer? Did one of his demons kill him?"

Shadow looked up at the darkening sky where the faint pinpricks of stars were already appearing, and grimaced. When she looked at Avery again her eyes were wide. "It's sort of complicated—but essentially, it was a test of sorts and he failed."

Avery crossed her arms, sensing more to this story than Shadow was sharing. "Ah! That's the thing you needed Alex and El for, in the Mendips!"

She nodded. "We were on the trail of an unusual tomb. He was the competition."

Cassie leaned forward, intrigued. "What sort of tomb?"

Alex gave a short laugh. "They were hunting for angels."

"*Angels?*" Cassie's face filled with disbelief. "I know we've been busy swotting, but how did that happen?"

"Long story," Shadow explained, "to do with lost maps and weird visions, and Harlan's boss." By now, the clusters of separate conversations had dwindled as everyone looked at Shadow, and she appeared uncomfortable as everyone watched her. "What? The necromancer's death had nothing to do with me! But, there are many, many occult organisations out there." She gestured wildly. "Far more than I thought. No wonder Maggie is kept busy in London. You've got it easy here, Newton." She took a slug of her beer as she watched his reaction.

"Depends on your definition of busy," Newton said, caustically. "But Inez's brother-in-law works with Maggie, so I know what you mean. Besides, Maggie has a bigger team than me. She certainly needs it."

Shadow nodded. "I remember him. He took my statement."

Ben, Dylan, and Cassie glanced at each other, clearly baffled, and Ben said, "I feel we have some catching up to do!"

"So, now that you're going full-time with the business," Reuben said to them, "what are you going to call yourselves?"

Cassie groaned. "Don't ask. We can't decide. Ben wants to keep it simple, but I think it should have more of a ring to it!"

Ben glared at her. "We don't want to put people off by having them think we're fruit loops! We need to sound professional."

"But we don't want to sound boring!" Dylan put in.

Reuben laughed. "Is Ghostbusters too obvious?"

El rolled her eyes. "Yes!"

"I thought you had a name?" Avery asked, confused. "You set up last year, didn't you?"

Dylan shrugged. "Sort of. We capitalised on the Walk of the Spirits," he said, referring to Samhain. "But we still didn't really name ourselves, and of course now we have to for what is essentially our re-launch."

"Are you still based out of your flat?" Alex asked. Ben and Dylan were renting together in Falmouth, and they had moved all of their equipment there the previous year when they could no longer use the university campus.

Dylan nodded. "Yep. I think we need to clean it up over the next couple of weeks, sort out an office for clients."

Cassie sniggered. "And maybe just stop living in squalor?"

"It's not squalor!" Ben said, crossly. "It's just slightly messy!"

"Yeah right," Cassie said, shooting Avery an amused look.

Avery laughed. "So, you're still living with your friends in Harbour Village, Cassie?"

"Yep. They've got local jobs, so that works out for me."

Briar sipped her wine and said, "I can give you some hours in my shop again, if you need extra money."

"Cheers, I might take you up on that," Cassie said gratefully. "I take it things have settled down here after all the excitement of Beltane?"

The witches glanced at each other, relieved, as Alex said, "Yes, fortunately. The Goddess seems to have gone, and we're just left with the Green Man doing his usual thing."

Dylan topped up his plate and asked, "What do you consider *usual*?"

"I guess my definition would be that he's a regular presence now," Briar explained. "I feel him all the time, especially in all the green spaces, and particularly in Ravens' Wood. Although, thankfully, that place doesn't feel anywhere near as weird as it did on Beltane." She turned to Shadow. "I keep meaning to ask—did you go that night?"

Shadow looked wistful as she turned her beer glass in her hand. "I did...on my own. It was both amazing and heart-breaking."

"What else did we miss?" Ben asked, confused.

"The Otherworld was allowed through—but I couldn't cross." Shadow shrugged, frustrated. "It was a taste of home. But, I can't complain. This is home now. It's different, but it's fun." She grinned mischievously and winked. "Very fun."

"Don't tell me anything else," Newton warned her as he put his empty plate on the table. "The less I know, the better."

Shadow had a fixed smile on her face. "You really need to learn to trust me!"

"No, I really don't." Newton's phone started to ring, and he groaned. "Damn it. Excuse me."

He stood and walked to the far side of the garden, and Avery watched him with a sinking feeling. He'd said he was off that night, but she knew that meant nothing. If something really odd happened, he could get a call. With luck, this call wouldn't be the police.

They all fell into an easy conversation while Newton was absent, and Avery started to stack the plates. It was fully dark now, and the fairy lights that were strung around the trees and the candles she'd placed in lanterns gave them enough light to chat by. Reuben had lit the fire in the small brazier at the centre of the gravelled area, and Alex added some logs, sending the flames flaring. They all rearranged their chairs as they topped up drinks, and settled themselves closer to the fire.

"What will you do for the Litha celebrations?" Cassie asked, as she took a sip of her wine.

El spoke up first. "We're celebrating with the coven at Rasmus's place in Newquay." She looked a bit guilty. "We sort of blew them off for Beltane."

"Yeah," Briar grimaced. "We should keep our coven happy. Besides, it was fun with them at Imbolc."

"As long as I don't have to run around a circle with a broom," Reuben complained.

Avery was so busy laughing at her memory of Reuben holding a besom broom she almost didn't notice the faint shimmer of movement at the edge of the seating area. She turned to look at it, wondering if she'd had too much wine, and with horror realised the disturbance in the air was expanding.

"Shit!" she shouted. "Something's coming!"

She dropped the plates on the table and raised her hands, summoning her magic, and heard the clatter of chairs as the others turned to look.

Alex started to speak. "Avery, what are—"

A wave of power flashed out from the centre of the disturbance, and *something* flew at her.

Avery sent a blast of air ripping through whatever was manifesting, and the window in her shed beyond smashed with its impact. But whatever it was counterattacked, knocking Avery off her feet.

With lightning-quick reflexes, she threw air around her, cushioning the impact so that she floated rather than crashed into the ground, and simultaneously heard a disembodied shout. A shower of coins rocketed towards her, bouncing off Avery's protection and ricocheting across the garden, and then a face emerged in the darkness.

Helena.

Two

Alex jumped to his feet, overturning his chair, and ran to Avery's side, ready to join her attack, but whatever had manifested out of the darkness had gone.

He hugged her as she lowered herself gracefully to the ground. "Are you all right?" He examined her swiftly for signs of injury, but although she was pale, and her hair streamed across her shoulders from the wind that had buffeted around her, she was otherwise unharmed.

"I'm fine," she said, but she was already distracted, her eyes turning to the dark corner of the garden. "Did you see that?"

"I saw something! What the hell was it?"

"And what is *this*?" Shadow asked, holding up a golden coin, her knife in her other hand. She was already standing by the shed, and Alex blinked. He hadn't even seen her move.

By now the others were on their feet, Reuben and El already heading purposefully to where Avery had directed her magic, while Briar scanned the garden with narrowed eyes.

"Is that a coin?" Cassie asked, looking confused. She crouched and picked up something shining in the gravel. "Look, here's another!"

"Bollocks!" Ben said, looking annoyed. "Why the hell didn't I bring my EMF meter?"

"It's in the van!" Dylan said, already running out of the gate.

Sally, wide-eyed with shock, grabbed Dan's arm. "What happened? I don't understand. And Avery flew!"

Of course she was shocked, Alex realised, suddenly feeling very sorry for Sally. She knew they were witches, but she'd never been this close to any action before. Even when they rescued her from Caspian, she'd been in the cellar, well away from the fight.

Avery looked guilt-stricken. "Yes, sorry, I do that sometimes. Just ignore me."

Dan helped Sally to a chair again. "I'll get you another drink."

Sally nodded, her face vacant, as Newton emerged from the garden.

"I've been away for minutes only!" Newton said, shocked. "What the hell has happened?"

Avery shook her head. "I'm not exactly sure, but I think I saw Helena."

Alex thought he was surprised before, now he was doubly so. "Helena! Where?"

Avery gestured to the area that Reuben and El were investigating. "There! I don't know how to explain it, but the air sort of shimmered, as if something was manifesting." She looked frustrated. "Sorry. That sounds ridiculous, but that's what I saw!"

Shadow reassured her. "I saw it too, but I couldn't make out anything in it."

"But you saw Helena," Alex persisted.

Avery grimaced. "Yes. Initially, it was just swirling darkness, but right at the end, for just a split second, I saw her face."

Alex's anger was building. "I knew we should have banished her! I'm going to do it—tonight!"

"*No!*" Avery turned to him, alarmed, her hand restraining his arm. "I think she was in trouble!"

"She attacked you!" Alex had always been frustrated by Avery's inexplicable loyalty to Helena. He understood family ties, but she had tried to kill Avery. "We can't trust her!"

Her mouth was set in a stubborn line. "But she's helped us, too—you know that! And besides, she wasn't attacking me."

"How could you possibly tell that in a split-second?"

Briar had joined them, and she shot Alex a warning look before speaking in her gentle, reasonable tone. "Why do you say that, Avery? I think we're all a bit confused right now."

Avery took a deep breath and exhaled heavily. "I think there was something else there with her. Did you hear the shout?"

Alex met Briar's worried gaze and glanced at the others, who all shook their head. "No, we didn't," he said. "What did it say?"

"Nothing! It was just a scream, or a cry," Avery said crossly, "and I'm pretty sure it was female. What if she's in trouble?"

At that moment, Dylan came running, the EMF meter in one hand and his camera in the other. He thrust the meter at Ben. "Quick, we might get residual readings!" He took in their tense faces. "What did I miss?"

"Nothing but confusion," Alex said, resigned. "Whatever you can get will be great." He turned to Avery, knowing she was annoyed with him. "Come on, let's sit and talk while these guys do their thing."

"Yeah!" Shadow said. She and Cassie were now striding around the seating area, collecting coins. "Let's talk about these, too!"

Newton rubbed his face with his hands, his mood clearly growing grim. "Not me, I'm afraid. I have to go. There's been a death in Fowey—a suspiciously paranormal one, obviously."

Not something else, Alex thought as he asked, "How weird this time?"

"A body was found on the beach just beside the town, close to the mouth of the estuary." Newton's mouth was set in a thin line. "Every bone in his body was broken. Every one! That's not normal!"

Briar frowned. "But the cliffs are high there. He could have fallen. Surely that would explain it?"

"Maybe, but I have a feeling there's more to it." Newton looked at everyone's tense faces. "I hate to leave after this, but I can't wait. I'm sure you'll be hearing more from me about this. Is there a witch based there?"

Alex shook his head. "No, but Oswald and Mariah are close. I suggest dealing with Oswald, if you need to. He's a good man."

"But we're happy to help," El said quickly. "Fowey is really not that far."

Newton nodded. "Thanks, but perhaps you've already got your hands full." He met Alex's eyes, a knowing look in them. "I'll call you tomorrow."

Alex watched him go, a sinking feeling already settling into the pit of his stomach, and then encouraged Avery into a chair, the others sitting next to them, while Ben and Dylan started their investigation.

"All right," Alex said, forcing himself to be patient. "What did you think you saw?"

"I didn't *see* anything—I felt something. Something malevolent."

"A demon?" El asked.

"No, I don't think so. Although, it was sort of portal-like."

"A spirit, then," Reuben said, catching Alex's eye.

"Maybe." Avery looked frustrated. "I couldn't tell. It was just the feeling of *something*—and Helena's face. But she didn't look evil, or mean. If anything, she was appealing to me."

"But you only saw her for a moment!" Alex reminded her.

"That was enough!" Avery told him. "And we haven't seen her for weeks! Not since before Beltane. I've actually been worried about her. Where has she gone?"

Sally shook her head as she clutched her wine like her life depended on it. "Do you need to worry about Helena? She's a spirit."

"Yes!" Avery said forcefully. "She's my relative, and she could still be influenced by other spirits!"

"Okay!" Sally held her hand up, palm outwards. "Just a question!"

Alex looked at Avery, surprised. Something had touched a nerve with her tonight. She wasn't normally this tetchy. "Maybe I should try and summon her, see what I can find. Not tonight, obviously, but tomorrow? If you think she's in trouble, then I'm willing to help her. I guess I could consider entering the spirit realm, if I can't summon her."

Avery smiled at him, and he felt his heart catch. "Would you? That would be great!"

"Whoa!" Reuben said, alarmed. "If there's something malevolent, you need to be careful, mate! You shouldn't walk in there alone. I could help."

Alex shook his head. "No, it's easier on my own, and I'm pretty good at this. No offence to you, but you're not as comfortable with the spirit realm as me."

"I could be your anchor, here."

Alex had often used the other witches for their power, and to ground himself while he communicated with spirits. "Okay, let me think it through and I'll let you know."

"And now," Shadow said, a clutch of coins in her hand. "What about these?"

El reached over and took one from her. "Gold coins! Wow. These look old. Are they English?"

Shadow shrugged. "They're not fey!"

"Unfortunately," Cassie said, holding one up to the firelight, "I know nothing about coins, but these must be valuable."

She started passing them around until they all had one.

"How many have you found?" Dan asked, squinting at his coin.

Cassie and Shadow did a quick count, and Cassie said, "We're pretty much all holding one—about a dozen. Not many."

"We should take these to an expert," Dan suggested. "Get them valued, and maybe find out some history on them."

Shadow shook her head. "Oh, no. You'd have to declare them and everything! How are you going to explain that they came from some weird, ghostly portal?"

Dan's face fell. "Good point. Is there someone we can trust?"

El grinned. "Dante! He might know. And if he doesn't, we'll rethink."

"He owns a forge! That doesn't make him a coin expert," Reuben pointed out.

"But he studied art history, and worked in a museum, a million years ago," El said. "It's worth asking him."

Briar had fallen silent as she examined her coin, but she finally spoke. "I think the most important question is, why are they here? Are they a warning to us? A clue to finding Helena? Or something else entirely?" She looked at them all one by one, as the whine of the EMF meter finally fell silent. "What has the power to carry a physical object in the spirit realm and then eject it? Whatever these mean, it isn't good."

Ben and Dylan joined them, Ben looking grim. "I agree with you, Briar. I may only be picking up residual energy patterns, but they're strong. I'll analyse them properly tomorrow, though."

"What about you?" Alex asked Dylan. "Anything in thermal imaging?"

"Nothing," he said, looking disappointed. "But again, I'll look properly tomorrow. Maybe we should take a coin—run that through some tests, too."

"Great idea," Alex said, passing him his. "And now I think I need a beer. I'm hoping that's the end of our excitement for the night!"

Reuben laughed. "Yeah. This time last year we were battling demons. I really hope we're not in for a repeat of that."

"True." Avery looked as if she was starting to relax, and she leaned back in her chair and sipped her wine. "We were still hunting for our grimoires then."

"And Newton hated us!" Reuben reminded her.

"And we," Dan said, gesturing to include Sally, "had no idea how powerful your magic was. This year has been quite the ride! And tonight, Avery," he said looking at her pointedly, "was quite the demonstration!"

"Sorry." She looked chastened. "I didn't mean to scare you. It was instinctive."

He smiled. "That's okay. I'd rather you did that than get injured. What we all need after a nasty shock is sugar. Didn't you say you'd made some cake, Sally?"

Sally groaned. "Some things do not change. Yes, I did. It's on the table."

"Allow me," he said, leaping to his feet as he headed to get everyone a slice, and Alex was suddenly very grateful for Dan's affability.

Alex took a deep breath, relieved that some normality seemed to be descending on their evening again. But nevertheless, he couldn't really relax now, and neither could anyone else. An air of watchfulness had settled on them all, and expectation. And what about Newton's dead body? Alex feared that whatever had happened tonight was just the beginning.

Three

Newton looked at the body at his feet and inwardly groaned. *Christ.* The man was smashed to a pulp. It didn't look as if there was a single bone in his body that wasn't broken.

Moore's deep voice rumbled next to him. "A few kids spotted it while they gathered firewood." He gestured to where the remnants of a fire smouldered a short distance away among the rocks at the back of the beach.

"Bloody hell. How old?"

"Mid-teens. At least they weren't younger."

"Could the fall have done this?" he asked, studying the cliff top above them.

"I doubt it...not unless he bounced off every single rock on the way down."

Newton grimaced as he crouched to examine the dead body. The man's limbs were splayed awkwardly, and his head was an odd shape, partially crushed on one side. Newton had a hard stomach, but he could feel his recently eaten food rising and he quickly stood and took some deep breaths. "Who was first on scene?"

"PC Marshall." He gestured to the officer on the edge of the beach a few minutes' walk away, where the path led from the car park. "The kids were good. They called it in and said they hadn't touched the body."

"Are they the ones I saw on the car park?" Newton had parked and headed to the crime scene quickly, nodding to Inez who was talking to three boys.

"Yeah. Coroner and SOCO will be here soon."

"I thought they'd have been here before me."

Moore ran his hand through his red hair. "Saturday night. There was a stabbing in Helston."

Newton nodded, distracted. "Any ID?"

"I waited for you."

Moore had recently been promoted to sergeant and seemed wary of overstepping his bounds, which was unusual. Most newly promoted officers couldn't wait to flex their new powers. Newton pulled his gloves from his pocket and, crouching again, felt in the man's pockets, finally pulling a wallet free. He quickly found the driver's license.

"Miles Anderson, twenty-eight years old, with what looks like a Carlyon Bay address."

Moore frowned. "Not far from home, then."

Carlyon Bay was about 15 minutes from Fowey. He could have been there visiting friends, or a girlfriend. "We need to search along the cliff top," Newton said, quickly assessing their options. "Let's see if there's any sign of a struggle." Newton squinted up again, but it was too dark to see anything. "The light will be poor. Is the coastal path close?"

"I think it's set further back from the cliff top at this point," Moore speculated, "but I'm not sure. It could be hazardous now. St Catherine's Castle is on that point, too."

Newton nodded, remembering the ruined castle on the headland. "We shouldn't wait. We'll seal off the path and get lights up there so we can start looking straight away." Every minute lost meant evidence could be lost too.

Moore folded his arms, his face grim. "So, if it's not an accident, what kind of supernatural creature could do this?"

"It might not be one," Newton said cautiously.

"Oh, come on, Guv. Have you seen the look on his face? I know he's badly damaged, but he looks terrified!"

Newton followed the line of Moore's torch and realised he was right. He hadn't taken much notice of the man's expression until now, but his face, what was left of it, was frozen in horror.

"Fair point," Newton said, nodding. "I have no idea, but I'll probably consult with our friends on this."

Moore knew exactly who Newton meant. "Good. They're useful. Does Inez know much about them?"

"Not yet. Although, I'm sure she suspects," Newton said. "I suppose I should share their unique abilities with her. She has been on the team a couple of months now."

Moore laughed. "She suspects, all right. She's on the team for a reason, Guv."

"True." Newton still felt he needed to protect the witches, wanting to keep their abilities known only to a few, but Moore was right. Inez was on the team now, and wasn't going anywhere. Part of his reticence was to protect himself, too. "I'll inform her tomorrow." More torches flashed at the end of the beach, and Newton sighed with relief. "SOCO is here. With a bit of luck, we might get some sleep tonight."

★·❂·◊·✶·❂·◊·✳·❂·◊·✶·❂

Alex rolled over in bed the next morning, and grinned. Avery was half-hidden under the duvet, her red hair sprawled across the pillow, snoring softly. He leaned forward and kissed her outstretched arm, and her eyes fluttered before she settled into sleep again.

Avery was not an early riser, especially after a late night, so rather than make her grumpy, he rolled out of bed, pulled his shorts and a t-shirt on, padded across the bedroom, and headed down to the kitchen to make coffee.

Circe and Medea, their two cats, circled his ankles, threatening to trip him up on the stairs, and he hissed at them. "Bloody hell, kitties, if you kill me, you starve!"

As usual they took no notice of him at all, and he fed them first before making his drink. He headed to the balcony, throwing open the French doors to a pale blue cloudless sky, and sat at the small table to enjoy the early sunshine. It was going to be another warm day; there was hardly any wind, and the sea was calm and flat for miles. It was probably already busy on the seafront, despite the early hour. Some of the boats would leave early to take visitors on day trips, depending on the tide. He sighed, wishing he could take the day off, but he had to head to his pub for the afternoon shift, and he had a feeling it would be busy.

Alex put his feet up on the chair opposite him and wondered if they'd hear from Newton today. If the death reported last night was suspicious, what type of creature could break every bone in someone's body? It was more likely that Briar was right about the fall, but maybe Newton knew something else he hadn't told them yet. He grabbed his phone and pulled up the local news, seeing that the death had already been reported on, but the coverage was light on details, not surprisingly. The only thing it said was that the victim was a young man.

They had speculated on it the night before after Newton had left, but without any details to go on it had been fruitless. Fortunately, the mysterious swirl of energy that had manifested hadn't returned, either. They ended up suggesting ridiculous names for the three parapsychologists' business, before they'd finally all headed home in the early hours of the morning.

His phone rang, jolting him out of his reverie, and he answered it quickly. "Hey, Newton. I guess this is bad news."

"You could say that. They weren't joking about this poor guy's state. He was pulp." Newton sounded cranky.

Alex groaned as a horrible image entered his mind. "Shit. Not a fall, then?"

"He'd had have to have fallen from a plane to be so injured."

"Shit," he repeated, wondering what might follow, because he doubted this would be an isolated incident. "Have you been up all night?"

"No, fortunately, but I've been at the station since six this morning."

"We were talking about it last night," Alex said as he made himself more comfortable, "but have no suggestions as to what could do this, I'm afraid."

"That's okay." Newton sounded distracted and his voice muffled for a moment as he turned away. "Sorry about that. We did find something odd, though. The victim had an old gold coin in his mouth."

"What? Placed there?"

"I reckon...like a warning."

Suddenly, Alex wasn't seeing the view anymore. He was picturing the gold coins that had spread across the gravel in the garden the previous night. "I hate to say this, but two appearances of gold coins in one night is not a coincidence! What kind of coin?"

"A very old one. A doubloon."

Alex nearly spat his coffee out. "Isn't that Spanish?"

"Yep. Maybe it's pirate gold. Don't ask how it came to be there, because I don't know! What were yours?"

"Honestly not sure, but English, we think."

"Mmm," Newton mumbled. "It would be good to know. I wonder if they're related?"

"Herne's balls," Alex said, using Shadow's favourite curse, which seemed to have caught on. "Is this to do with smuggling?"

Newton sighed. "Maybe. Look, I don't need you to do anything right now. I just wanted you to know."

"What about the victim?"

"His name is Miles Anderson, he's twenty-eight, and he lived in Carlyon Bay. But we haven't announced that yet, so keep it quiet."

"Of course."

"Anything else happened with you after I left?"

"Nothing, fortunately."

"Well, that's some good news," Newton said, obviously relieved. "I have to go, but I'll call you later if I find anything else. Let's hope this isn't the start of some summer madness."

He rang off abruptly, and Alex finished his now cold drink. A doubloon? This was going to require more coffee.

★ ❂ ⬦ ★ ❂ ⬦ ✶ ❂ ⬦ ★ ❂

By the time Avery woke up, the scents of bacon and coffee were drifting through the house. She stretched, easing the kinks from her neck, and wished she'd had a better night's sleep.

Dragging herself out of bed, she wrapped a light summer robe over her long t-shirt and shorts and then padded downstairs, smiling at seeing Alex cooking at the hob, the radio low in the background. She walked up behind him and wrapped her arms around him, leaning into his back.

"Something smells fab. Is there enough for me?"

"Of course!" He twisted around to kiss her. "Egg and bacon sandwich on crusty bread sound good?"

"Perfect!" She headed to the coffee machine and made herself a drink, but Alex was watching her with a worried expression on his face.

"Did you sleep okay after last night?"

She nodded. "I did, eventually, other than a few weird dreams. I am really worried about Helena."

"I know. I have to work this afternoon, but I can search for Helena afterwards. I find that communing with spirits is more effective at night."

She smiled. "Do they have a night?"

He laughed, a little ruefully. "I don't think so. I think it's better for me, not them." He paused, a wary look on his face, as he said, "I didn't mean to doubt you last night, or piss you off."

"You didn't," she said, knowing he'd been concerned about her welfare, and understanding his feelings about Helena. "I was just worried...and a bit shocked. That attack came from nowhere. In our garden!" She shook her head. "Something punched straight through our protection spells. That will be one of my jobs today—I'll reinforce them."

"Just promise me you won't try to find Helena on your own!"

"Witches' honour!" Talking to spirits was Alex's specialty, not hers. "Any news from Newton?"

"'Fraid so. The guy was pulverised." He updated her while he cooked, and then steered them both to the outside table with their breakfast.

Avery brushed her hair back from her shoulders as she settled at the table. "I feel I should have lost my appetite, but I'm afraid I'm still starving." She took a bite, swallowed and said, "Do you think a witch attacked him?"

"It's possible, I guess. It would have to be a pretty nasty spell to break every bone, and I can't see it being one of the Cornwall Coven, but we shouldn't rule it out."

Avery shuddered. "I just hope his death was sudden. I hate to think he'd have suffered. But the doubloon is odd!"

"The Spanish attacked Mousehole and a few other towns farther along. Not the Armada...it was a few years later than that. I looked it up after Newton phoned."

"Wow. That's like over five hundred years ago!"

"It's even weirder when you consider the gold that was thrown at you last night. We've still got a coin here, so I'll see if I can get a timeframe on it."

"They have to be connected, surely," Avery reasoned. "We all know how popular smuggling was in Cornwall years ago. It makes me think they must be part of a treasure hoard."

"Maybe more than one," Alex suggested. "Newton was very sure his coin was Spanish, but if ours is English, are they from the same place?"

"And why would the Spanish hide their own gold?" she asked, puzzled, before taking another bite and speaking through a mouthful of food.

"Shouldn't they have been stealing it?"

"In theory, yes. But they burned entire towns then—Mousehole was completely destroyed, except for the pub."

"Wow. They burned everything?"

He nodded. "And then moved on to Newlyn, Penzance, and Paul. A few locals were killed, and they took prisoners. Fortunately, they were released unharmed when they left."

Avery finished eating and pushed her plate away. "So there were a lot of them?"

"Four galleys, according to what I read. They were planning to take England, eventually." He laughed and sipped his coffee. "But failed."

"I guess trade would have meant their coins would have been circulating here too." Avery groaned. "So many questions for a Sunday morning. One night and everything changes!"

"Typical White Haven."

Avery tried to dispel her worry, especially about Helena. "With any luck, this is just a horrible one-off."

He grabbed her hand and kissed her fingertips. "Ever the optimist! I hope you're right. Apart from doing protection spells, what are you getting up to today? You know I'm working later."

"Gardening, I think. Going to take advantage of this beautiful weather."

He grimaced. "Great!"

She laughed, knowing he hated gardening. "Grinch."

"Like you want me grumbling around you," he pointed out.

"Ha! True." As much as she wanted to disagree with him, he was right. Once she was in the garden, she lost hours, just as Briar did.

"I shall do something useful and clean the attic!" he said, rising to his feet. "We've been making a lot of mess lately, practicing our spells."

Avery drained her cup. "Deal."

✦·✹·✧·✨·✹·✧·✳·✹·✧·✨·✹

By the time Alex arrived at The Wayward Son at just after one in the afternoon, the pub was already packed, and his staff were busy.

Alex didn't waste time, heading into the kitchen to see how everything was going. His head chef, Jago Hammet, a big burly man in his late thirties, was generally good-humoured and loved his work, in a sharp-tongued way. He had a quick wit and was very impatient, and although he was inclined to shout when busy, the other staff loved him. He looked up as Alex walked in, a cloud of steam billowing around him. "He finally arrives! About time!"

"Cheeky sod," Alex said, nodding in greeting to the other three staff that were busy preparing the meals. There was a young man barely out of his teens called Jake, Georgie, who was in her mid-twenties, and the sous chef named Larry who had four kids. He constantly looked knackered, and Alex wasn't sure if it was the job or the kids. He suspected the kids. "How's it going?" he asked them.

"Like clockwork, of course." Jago glanced outside at the weather. "The sun always brings the punters out in force. Doesn't stop them from eating acres of roast beef, though."

Alex winked. "It's Sunday lunch! Not the same without it." He inhaled deeply. "Smells amazing."

"That's because it is." Jago never doubted himself. "Tell Anna out there to get a move on—and that bloody big unit, Zee. Next lot of food is up."

Alex nodded and left them to it, narrowly avoiding Anna as she swung through the door as he exited. She'd been working at the pub for a few months and was a good find. Dark-haired and feisty, she was a single mother in her thirties with teenage sons. She worked hard and was reliable. "Hey, boss. Newton is in. You in trouble again?"

"Funny," he said dryly. Everyone knew Newton by now. He made himself comfortable at the bar and watched the football if Alex wasn't around, and Alex was pretty sure if he focussed less on the match and more on his surroundings, he might actually get a date.

"And Reuben's here, too." She lowered her voice and looked hopeful. "Is he still with El?"

"Of course."

"Damn it. A girl can hope. That big hunk of muscle." A dreamy expression passed across her face, and then she disappeared to grab the plates on the counter.

Alex shook his head as he headed into the bar, half wondering why Zee wasn't on her hit list. If she wanted 'a big hunk of muscle,' Zee was it. He banished the thought from his mind, vowing never to refer to his friends like that again. Instead, he thanked the Gods that his employees were cheerful and upbeat, which made his life easier. He often envied Avery for her small number of staff; running the pub was hard work and usually busy, and sometimes the bar staff turned over quicker than he liked. He was lucky with Simon, his manager. He was calm and organised, which allowed Alex time to pursue some of his more unusual activities. He spotted Zee further along the counter and went to relieve him, nodding to Kate, his barmaid, as he passed her.

"Hey Zee, finish this order and then head to the kitchen. I'll cover this."

"Sure thing," Zee said as he finished pulling the pint, placed it on the bar, and took payment. As soon as the customer had gone, he said, "Shadow said there was a problem last night."

"That's one way of putting it." Alex reminded himself he shouldn't be surprised by Shadow's masterful understatements. He lowered his voice. "They found a man dead on the beach by Fowey last night. It's been on the news. And it's probably paranormal. Hopefully Newton can tell us a bit more today."

Zee nodded. "Good, keep me informed."

He disappeared into the kitchen to start carrying dishes as Alex continued to work, finally making his way to Reuben and Newton's spot on the bar.

"Didn't expect to see you today, Newton. Do either of you need another pint?"

"Not for me," Reuben said, wiggling his half-full glass.

"Just a coke, please," Newton said. "I needed a break, and time to think, and the drive has given me that." He checked his watch. "I'd better be getting back, though. I've just told Reuben we can't find anything on the cliff edge."

Reuben's eyes were narrowed as he watched Newton. "The cliff path isn't close at that point though, is it?"

"No. There's a patch of open ground and a few stunted trees, all sloping towards the edge—but the ground is undisturbed." Newton shook his head, perplexed. "It doesn't make sense. We should have found *something*!"

"He wasn't washed ashore?" Alex asked.

"No. The victim was bone dry. Time of death is estimated to be between eight and ten last night."

Reuben sipped his pint. "I take it you searched a good distance?"

"Yep, on the beach and the cliff top, a half a mile on either side. There's no sign of a scuffle, or his car."

"The cliff path runs a long way. Maybe it was parked further than you think."

"Maybe." Newton sipped his coke and grimaced. "Not quite Doom, is it? Anyway, with luck we'll find his car today somewhere."

"Has he got family?" Reuben asked.

"An older sister who lives in Penzance, and parents who live in St Ives. I went to see them this morning." He frowned. "Unfortunately, they can't tell us anything. They have no idea what he was doing there. He lives with his girlfriend, so I really need to find her, but so far she's not at their house, or answering her phone...and that's worrying."

"Do you think they've been up to something dodgy?" Reuben asked.

"Possibly. He had a very unpleasant death." Newton stared into his drink. "Something feels off. I don't suppose you've thought of anything that could smash someone to a pulp?"

Alex shrugged. "Not really." He looked at Reuben. "I guess this could be demonic?"

"It's possible," Reuben said, nodding. "They are violent!"

Newton groaned. "I hope it's not! We might find something useful when we search his house. I'm heading there now." He drained his glass. "I had to get the identification confirmed first. His father did that. His mother was hysterical. Horrible."

Newton rarely shared the details of his job, and Alex suddenly felt sorry for him. He'd never even considered the things such as victim identification. "Sorry, Newton. What a crap way to spend your day."

"You never get used to it," he said sadly. "Anyway. Must go, and I'll keep in touch."

Reuben and Alex watched him leave, and Reuben said, "Demon is a good suggestion."

Alex felt a heaviness settle in his stomach. "But that means someone is controlling it. I'm really hoping it's something else."

"Like what? An angry spirit? A poltergeist?" Reuben looked uncertain. "Sounds dubious. And I can't see it being anything to do with a witch."

Alex glanced down the bar to make sure no one was waiting to be served, and with relief noticed Zee was back, serving again. "No, hopefully not."

Reuben pushed his empty pint glass to Alex, and he topped it up absently, saying, "I think we should call Oswald. He's a bit closer than us. We can see if anything odd has been happening up that way. I'll ask Avery to call him, she'll have time."

"*I've* got time!" Reuben said, looking slightly affronted.

Alex slid his pint in front of him, and laughed. "Well yes, but you don't have Avery's winning ways."

"Are you saying I'm not charming?"

"You know exactly what I'm saying," Alex said, deciding to lay it out. "Your dry sarcasm and general scepticism doesn't always win friends and confidences."

Reuben gave him a sly grin. "I suppose when you put it like that, maybe Avery should call him." He paused for a second and then asked, "How is she today? She was a bit...*sensitive* last night."

"I guess sensitive is one word for it," Alex admitted, unwilling to criticise Avery but also feeling the need to confide. He wiped the counter down, even though it was perfectly dry, and saw Reuben still watching him. He gave up. "She's unreasonably protective of Helena. I don't get it! I'm glad to see the back of her! Damn spooky ghost just manifesting around the flat. And I'm used to spirits!"

"I'd hate it, too," Reuben admitted. "And Helena did try to kill her. I'm with you. I'd put my foot down with El if she had a spirit lurking around."

Alex gave him a long look. "You say that, but I think we both know where she'd tell you to get off. We are both blessed with feisty women."

Reuben grinned. "Well, yes, but you do live there, too!"

"It's not that simple though, is it?" Alex said. "It would be like suggesting I get rid of the cats. I can't! Helena isn't just any spirit, and she has this odd sentience, too."

"So did Kit, but you got rid of him well enough!"

"Yeah, well, he was actively hurting people. And Avery has a point. She has helped us in many ways since. I guess I was hoping she'd just quietly disappear, but now it seems as if she's trapped in some kind of spirit prison." He rolled his eyes. "Just my bloody luck! It's like having to rescue my mother-in-law!"

"Ha!" Reuben threw his head back and laughed. "Let's hope you get rewarded for your services."

"But seriously, what's with the gold coins? What is this, some kind of smugglers' revenge?"

They both stopped laughing then and Reuben's eyes widened. "Maybe

Helena's past needs more investigation."

"The smuggling was well after her time!"

"But were the Spanish?"

Four

A very finished weeding her herb beds with the aid of a little magic and stepped back, pleased with her progress.

In the last couple of weeks, since the risk of frost had gone, she'd planted lots more annual herbs, trimmed the existing ones, and had harvested some to dry. A trug was on the gravelled path next to her, filled with cuttings. She filtered through her favourite gardening spells, decided on one that was best for this occasion, and said it softly under breath. Her magic rolled around her, and she smiled as she saw her plants respond.

Satisfied, she headed back to the patio table where they had partied the night before, pulled the phone from her pocket, and called Oswald, as Alex had asked, smiling at hearing his warm but slightly old-fashioned mannerisms.

"Avery, I'd like to say this is a pleasure, but I sense trouble."

"You do?" she asked, surprised.

"I have a sixth sense for these things sometimes, especially when I'm relaxed. Which I was. And besides, you don't normally phone for a chat."

Avery felt horribly guilty for disturbing his afternoon. "I'm so sorry Oswald, but we thought you should know about the death they reported this morning."

He groaned. "The young man found on the beach outside Fowey? Go on."

Avery updated him as succinctly as possible, but as soon as she mentioned the doubloon, she felt Oswald's excitement. "A *what*? How very unexpected, but exciting too! Terrible though this death is, the doubloon does lend an air of intrigue, and the suggestion of smuggling, dare I say!"

"I guess so," she said, surprised by his response. "I must admit, we thought of smuggling, too."

"It's a natural assumption when you hear of treasure, and a doubloon is undoubtedly just that. We all love a pirate story, and there's plenty of smuggling tales around here, too!"

Avery leaned back in her chair, looking over her garden, but not really seeing it anymore. "Well, true, but a doubloon is from a couple of centuries before the smuggling industry became really big in Cornwall."

"But it doesn't mean they're not connected in some way." He fell silent for a moment and then said, "I'm going to have to do some smuggling research."

"But how could that be connected to the poor man's death? It was so violent!"

"Early days for that, Avery, but I'll have a think. No sign of any more treasure?"

"Well, actually yes," she confessed, relating the events of the night before.

After a moment's shocked silence, Oswald said, "That's fascinating. And your ancestor?"

"I got the impression she was in trouble."

"Well, I have no idea what to do with that," he murmured.

"Nor us, but we were wondering if you've noticed anything odd in your area lately?"

"Nothing, but you can be sure I'll be keeping a close watch from now on. I'll tell Ulysses, too."

After they said their goodbyes, Avery headed up to the attic with her herbs, surprised by how clean it now was. Alex had done a good job, and he'd opened the windows, allowing a light breeze to drift through the room. She placed her herbs on the table, and took her time tying them together before hanging them from the rafters overhead. Then she turned to her bookshelves, looking for something on supernatural creatures.

She pulled one book after another, but frustrated at having nothing really suitable, decided to search her shop instead. Rather than walk downstairs, she used witch-flight, and materialised in the occult section.

It was hot and stuffy in Happenstance Books; dust motes hung in the sunshine that slanted through the windows, and yesterday's residual incense mixed with the scent of old and new books. Avery searched the magic section, noting the new books that Sally had ordered in. There were lots of new spell books, and books on the history of witchcraft, and they continued to add to their selection regularly. Ever since Rupert had started his occult tours, they had increasing interest in witchcraft and had decided to capitalise on it. However, there was nothing that listed supernatural creatures specifically, and instead she decided to check the shelves stocking books on myths and legends, pleased when she found a few about Cornish folklore. "Bingo," she said softly, as she pulled them from the shelves.

Then she felt a breeze across the back of her neck, and the temperature around her dropped.

Avery whirled around, her hand raised, ready to either defend or attack. "Helena? Is that you?"

A shimmer in the air to her left had Avery turning swiftly, but nothing appeared, and the cold air disappeared as quickly as it had arrived. *That was odd*. Was Helena trying to contact her again, or was it something else? One good thing, she reflected, was that at least nothing had been thrown at her. But where the hell was Helena?

At six that evening, after a couple of hours of research, Avery arrived at The Wayward Son and found that Reuben, El, and Briar were already in the back room at the pub, chatting over drinks. She grabbed a glass of wine at the bar, unable to see Alex, who she presumed was in the kitchen, and joined them.

The small room at the back of the pub was, as usual, quieter than the main area, spelled by Alex to only encourage locals to loiter. The patio doors were open, and a warm evening breeze flowed inside, carrying the sounds of voices and laughter from those seated in the courtyard garden.

"Hey, guys," she said, sipping her wine and taking a seat. "I hear Newton has had an interesting twenty-four hours."

Reuben nodded. He had a half-empty pint glass in front of him, and his arm was slung across the back of El's chair. "Yeah, unfortunately. We haven't heard from him since lunch, though. I guess he's very busy."

Avery frowned at him. "Have you been here all afternoon?"

"No! I've been surfing, obviously! Trying to clear my head after a few too many beers last night."

El laughed. "Like that ever puts you off. You're a freak. What have you been up to, Avery?"

Avery reached into her bag and withdrew a small, slim book with a few pages marked, placing it on the table. "I've been doing some reading this afternoon, and have a few ideas of what could have caused that man's death."

"Have you?" Briar asked, looking hopeful. "I've been completely tied up with making new stock for my shop."

"I have news, too," El confessed, looking pleased. "I've been at the forge with Dante for a couple of hours. The boys want enhanced weapons, so I've been working on them in my downtime."

Avery was momentarily sidetracked. "As in the Nephilim?"

"Yeah—I'm making swords and daggers with enhanced powers. They've all decided they want some. Nahum wants throwing knives, so that's a challenge." She grinned. "Fun, though. Anyway, while I was there, I showed him the coin...but you first!"

"I've been reading up on piskies, púcas, spriggans, and other Cornish creatures, trying to decide if they have something to do with that man's death, but to be honest, I'm a bit bewildered," Avery said, her hands idly flicking the pages of the book. "I need to chat to Dan. There are so many legends to consider."

"That's a good idea," Briar agreed. "Reuben said you were going to phone Oswald. Did you ask him about supernatural creatures?"

"No, actually," she said, telling them what they'd discussed. "But he will keep an eye out for anything odd."

Reuben pulled the book towards him and started leafing through it. "What sounds most likely then, according to this?"

Avery frowned. "Púcas are a possibility—they have a reputation for being menacing. Or, more likely, spriggans."

"Like what our beach is named after?" Reuben asked.

She nodded. "Among the many stories about them, they apparently hang around old ruins and cairns, guarding buried treasure. They can become very mean when disturbed."

El looked baffled. "Aren't they supposed to be like little old men?"

"Yes, though that doesn't sound particularly threatening," Avery confessed.

Briar rubbed her face, bemused. "This is a crazy conversation to be having—and I know that I've been possessed by the Green Man—but this just sounds mad!" She leaned forward. "Are we actually entertaining this discussion?"

Reuben tutted. "Briar! Of all the people who should be the most accepting of this! You go out with a shape shifter! How is he, by the way? He hasn't been down for a few weeks."

"He's fine," she said, a flush colouring her cheeks. "Just involved with pack business. And I know exactly what you mean. It's just that piskies, of all things, and other little creatures sound, well, make-believe!"

"You're right," Avery admitted. "I've been wrestling with this for the last couple of hours, persuading myself that I'm already mad just thinking about it."

El laughed. "You live with a ghost, and we've banished mermaids, spirits and demons, *and* seen the Raven King! Surely it's not that far-fetched?"

Her finger tapped her pint glass. "Maybe we should speak to Shadow. She's fey, and might know far more about them than what's written in that book."

"I hadn't considered that," Avery said, nodding. "By the way, talking of ghosts, I had another odd experience this afternoon." She started to relay what had happened in the shop, and Alex arrived halfway through, taking a seat opposite her.

Once she finished, he frowned. "But you didn't actually see Helena?"

"No, not this time." Avery took another sip of her wine. "But I'm even more worried about her now."

"I wish I could say I miss her," Alex said, "but I don't. However, I will look for her tonight, as agreed."

"Thank you!" Avery hadn't wanted to make such a big deal about it, but now that he'd offered, she couldn't wait to see what he found. Realising he hadn't heard her update about Oswald, she said, "And I spoke to Oswald. He's going to make inquiries, but there's nothing much going on that he's noticed."

"Well," Alex said, looking pleased with himself. "I've found out that our very own White Haven Museum has a new exhibition on smuggling. It starts next weekend, and is only open for a short time, but it will be worth seeing."

"I've never been in there at all," Reuben confessed, slightly sheepish.

Alex laughed. "Well, that's not surprising. You're not exactly known for your love of museums and research."

"I could be persuaded to go, though," he said, "if there's a pub lunch at the end of it."

"I'm sure we could manage that," Avery reassured him. "I wonder if there'll be something about the West Haven tunnels there?"

The passages they had found that led from Rupert's House of Spirits connected to a network of tunnels, and they hadn't followed most of them, focussing only on finding vampires.

El looked thoughtful. "I'd love to know how far they go. There are smuggling tunnels all over Cornwall. But where has that doubloon come from?"

"And what's its message?" Briar asked. "It would have been better off leaving the man dead with no doubloon. Now we have a clue!"

"Is it, though?"Reuben said, ever sceptical. "Or is it a diversion?"

"So, what have you found out about our coins?" Briar asked El.

"They are guineas, British, and the one I have is eighteenth century—King George, I think Dante said, though not sure which George." She shrugged. "But guineas were made in the seventeenth century too, so we may have a mixture."

"Are they worth anything?" Alex asked.

"Sure! Not millions or anything," El said brightly, "but a few hundred pounds, depending on the guinea. The quantity of gold in them varies, apparently, and they're worth more than their value to a collector."

"So," Avery reasoned, "these are obviously a very different timeframe to Spanish doubloons. I guess the question still is, are they connected? Is the death of the man in Fowey and Helena's odd appearance connected?"

"Surely, they have to be!" El said, appealing to them all.

The others looked around the table blankly, and Avery realised that with so little to go on, they were speculating wildly. But at this stage, there was nothing else they could do.

"If we're going to look into smuggling," Briar said, interrupting her train of thought, "we should go to Bodmin and see the Jamaica Inn Smuggling Museum, too. That's supposed to be good." She rose to her feet wiggling her glass. "Another drink, everyone?"

Five

A lex sat in front of the fire in the attic, in the centre of a circle of protection, with a single candle burning in front of him. Avery sat opposite him, cross-legged. She'd watched his preparations silently, her lips pressed tightly together.

He tried to reassure her. "Avery, I'll be okay."

"You don't know that! You've never done this before!"

She was right, and he was worried, too. He had just spent the last hour trying to summon Helena, seated outside a summoning circle, but she had failed to appear. He'd sensed some kind of block, and unable to work out exactly what it was caused by, he'd opted to travel into the spirit world to find her.

He squeezed Avery's soft, warm hands that were in his own. "My own magic is now stronger than it ever was."

"I know. So, I just ground you—give you some power, like when you spoke to the Nephilim in All Souls' Church?"

"Sort of. Just remember, I might take quite a while, but don't freak out."

The candlelight flickered across Avery's face as she nodded, the rest of the attic in complete darkness. The potion he'd drunk to help him enter the necessary mental state was already taking effect, and as he started to utter the spell that would bring him into the spirit realm, the darkness seemed to get more absolute. Within seconds, Avery's face disappeared completely, and he was surrounded by a shadowy void.

Alex felt weightless, his body left behind, but still he felt Avery's warm presence, like a kiss on his consciousness. But she wasn't just there to support him; she was there to help him find Helena. Whatever he thought about their connection didn't matter; the important thing was that their connection was strong.

He'd noticed similarities in their looks, around the eyes and slim build, not to mention a certain stubborn set to their features, but there was more than that. Helena was of a similar age to Avery when she died, something that had upset Avery more than anything, especially as she had two young children. But where did she go when she wasn't in Avery's flat? And how had she corralled so many spirits on Samhain to walk through the town? Helena was unusual in that she wasn't a spirit at rest; she still visited the real world, and had managed to retain some kind of control of her actions.

For a few moments Alex tried to orientate himself, and felt a tremor of unease as he realised that was impossible. There were no landmarks here, just shadowy presences that he sensed rather than saw. He was in a grey void. Was this what spirits saw? Or only him, as a live being moving in a place where he probably shouldn't be?

Enough. Time to move. He willed himself forward, feeling presences brush past him, mostly harmless and curious. But the further he travelled, the stronger their curiosity grew. His spirit was bright in their realm, like a beacon. He paused, trying to detect Helena's presence, calling out to her with his spirit voice, but he couldn't feel her at all. Every now and again he felt an echo of her presence, but still pushed on, frustrated at her nebulousness.

Something wasn't right, he knew it. He was deeper now, and the atmosphere had changed. Spirits fled before him, but with a flash of recognition and a feeling of victory, he picked up Helena's energy—but following it was like following a fine thread. She was so elusive.

And then he felt something else, something that watched him, waited for him. No, there was more than one presence—there were many more—and he picked up a distinct feeling of resentment from them. He ignored them and called for Helena, projecting his power outwards, and finally heard a cry. A glimmer of light flashed from what seemed to be a long way away before vanishing again.

He was close, he knew it, and he continued on, regardless of the brooding menace of those watchful presences that were too close for comfort. Then he summoned his magic. Using magic here was very different to using it on the Earthly plane. Spells didn't work as effectively, but his power would be visible to those around him. He flexed it now, so that it pulsed as a warning to others, and then pushed on, Helena's presence growing closer.

Out of nowhere, something hit him, like a punch to the gut. It sent him spinning away, leaving him confused and disorientated—and feeling smothered.

And worse still, Avery's presence had vanished.

Alex tried not to panic; that was the worst thing to do. Getting lost in the spirit world was a sure way to die, but the feeling of being restrained was stronger now, as if a bag had been thrown over his head. He was suffocating—which should be impossible—but it was happening.

It was a trap. Was this Helena's doing?

Anger surged through Alex and he flexed his power again, feeling a wave of magic roll around him. For a moment, he could breathe, just before he felt rough hands on him and smelt something sour and fetid. Alex fought back, desperately trying to break free, but with every struggle, his bonds grew stronger.

What the fuck was happening?

Real panic kicked in then. Something malevolent was here with him, gleeful with his capture. Alex's spirit struggled wildly, his magic now rolling off him in waves, but nothing seemed to work. He was stuck, and the sour smell returned, thick and oily, filling his mind with death.

And then he felt someone else, someone so familiar that he almost forgot the trouble he was in, and a wave of different power flashed from a point close by. The hands that restrained him weakened, and Alex broke free.

"*Alex*," the presence whispered in his ear.

Alex jerked back. "Gil? Is that you?"

Gil's shimmering face appeared before him, its kind, comforting lines so familiar to him that Alex could have cried.

"*It is, old friend. You have ventured too far, Alex. It's dangerous here. Go back.*"

"But why? What's happening? How did you find me?"

Gil glanced behind him, at nothing that Alex could see, but a hardened resolve appeared on his face. "Another witch, strong like you, has walked these paths, but whoever it was knew exactly where they were going. They've been helping old spirits who want revenge. They're the ones who attacked you. Let's go.*"

Gil sent another flash of power behind him, and then before Alex could comprehend what was happening, Gil propelled them both away. They were travelling swiftly now, streaking through dark, shadowy realms he hadn't even realised he'd passed through, and so fast that Alex was dizzy and sick by the time they finally stopped. He felt Avery again, a candle in the dark.

Gil looked around once more. "We've lost them for now—but you have to go!*"

"What witch? Tell me. It's important."

"*I don't know who it is. I can't even tell if they were male or female! It was just their energy that made them stand out.*"

"You're sure it's not the spirit of a witch?" Alex asked, desperate for answers before he left. "I'm looking for Helena—Avery's ancestor!"

"*Helena?*" Gil gave a hollow, empty laugh, his eyes filled with a mixture of sorrow and joy. "*Why are you looking for her?*"

"It's a long story, but ever since we regained our grimoires, she's been with us...until recently."

"*No wonder she feels different,*" Gil said, nodding as if things were making sense to him. He looked behind him again, fearful of pursuit, and then focussed sharply on Alex. "*Yes, I have felt Helena, but she's trapped, and you won't get her free—not yet.*"

"And you're sure she's not the witch you sensed?" Alex was confused now.

"No. The other witch was as real as you are, not a spirit. Causing trouble with the ones who attacked you. You were far deeper than you realised—and you don't know this place like I do. Skilled though you are, you travelled too far." *Comprehension dawned.* "Helena was a lure. You must go—they're getting closer*!" Gil's spirit pushed Alex again, shepherding him away, and Alex felt desperately sad; he didn't want to leave Gil so soon after finding him.*

"But Helena!" Alex persisted. "I can't leave her trapped."

"You must leave her to me, and instead deal with the witch in your world. I'm just sorry I can't tell you more." *Gil gave him one final push.* "Go! Give my love to the others, especially my brother.*"

And then he vanished.

For a moment, Alex hung in the dark, and then feeling the vengeful spirits once more, he returned to his body with such speed that his breath left him. He opened his eyes to find Avery staring at him with surprise and relief.

"Thank the Gods!"

But there was no time to rest. "Something's coming!" Alex leapt to his feet—or tried to. His legs felt numb, and it was more of stagger, but he stood in the dark attic, lit only by the flickering fire and single candle. "Don't move from the circle!"

"Why?" Avery asked, standing as well and raising her hands, magic balling in her palms.

The words had barely left Avery's mouth when a whirling object appeared out of nowhere, clattering against their wall of protection and falling to the floor. It was followed by a hollow-eyed spectre wearing rags, and then another, and another. Instead of attacking them, they ransacked the room, causing mayhem.

Alex cast his strongest banishing spell, and with a crack like thunder and flash of white light, he sent them back to the spirit world. For what seemed like endless minutes, they stood there, waiting, just in case something broke through again, but when nothing happened, Alex dropped his hands, satisfied that the door to the Otherworld was sealed.

He turned to Avery and sighed. "Well, that was all kinds of unexpected."

She looked at him with utter shock. "*Unexpected*? What the hell happened in there? You've been gone for almost two hours!"

Exhaustion hit him as his adrenalin ebbed, and breaking the circle, he dropped on the rug in front of the fire.

Avery sat next to him, her hand resting on his arm. "Alex, what happened?"

He lay flat, his chest heaving up and down, and reached for her hand. There was no way to sugar-coat what had happened. "I saw Gil."

Avery froze, her eyes wide, momentarily silenced. Her mouth worked as she tried to form words, finally saying, "*What*? How?"

His heart was filled with sorrow it could barely contain. "Come here."

She lay next to him, and he pulled her close, glad of her vibrancy, and immensely grateful she was part of his life. Her arms trembled and he kissed her forehead.

"Was he okay?" she mumbled into his chest. "Sorry—that's a stupid question."

"It's not." Alex's breathing had settled, and she placed her hand on his chest as he said, "He seemed well, for a spirit. But it was a shock to see him."

Avery propped herself on her elbow, watching him. "I don't really understand how the spirit world works. Why haven't you seen him before?"

"It has never crossed my mind that I should even try to contact Gil. It seems wrong somehow. But," he admitted, feeling guilty, "I travelled too far into the realm, deeper than I realised. I was so intent on finding Helena, I didn't stop to think. I guess I was too sure of myself, too. I got into trouble."

"Alex! I trusted you. You could have died!"

"I'm sorry. It won't happen again. But I found her—sort of. She's a prisoner. Don't ask me how, because I've no idea. They used her to lure me to them."

Avery was clearly more confused than ever. "What do you mean? Who are *them*?"

"Whoever those spirits are who followed me here." He rolled over to face her. "Gil said they're seeking vengeance."

"On you? Us?"

"I don't know, and neither did Gil. But he said another witch has been there, strengthening them...stirring their anger." He lifted his hand and ran his fingers across her cheek. She was so precious to him; he hated to see her upset. "Gil sends his love."

Avery's tears welled up. "It's almost a year since he died. I can't believe it. What happened in there?"

"The spirits who have trapped Helena tried to trap me—or kill me. Gil saved me." The feeling of being lost filling him with horror, but he tried not to show Avery that. "I had no idea how far I'd travelled. I'd lost sight of you. I was an idiot. And what's worse is that I didn't even tell Gil how much I missed him. I was so focussed on Helena. What a jerk."

"You're not a jerk, and Gil knows that. I will be forever grateful that he brought you back to me. But what about Helena? I don't want you to go back there again—obviously—but how do we rescue her?"

"Gil said to leave it to him. We have another job to do. We need to find the witch who travelled there."

Six

Behind the counter in Happenstance Books the next day, Avery was enjoying a mid-morning coffee and biscuit while updating her friends on Sunday's activities.

"What do you mean, you were attacked by ghosts?" Sally asked, horrified.

"They whirled around our attic, making a bloody mess," Avery said crossly. "It annoyed the crap out of me!"

Dan looked at Sally, and then back at Avery. "They followed Alex? He actually walked in the spirit realm?"

"Well, not exactly *walked*, but I know what you mean." Talking to Dan and Sally in the cold light of day, the enormity of what Alex had done hit her. "It was nuts, really. I get so used to the odd stuff we do that I didn't even worry too much." She looked at their expressions of disbelief, and tried to explain. "I mean, I know it was dangerous, and I *was* worried, but not much. I trust Alex's power!"

Dan lowered his voice. "It's the realm of the dead, Avery! I didn't even know that was possible!"

"Mediums do that kind of thing all the time!"

"No, no, no!" He wagged his biscuit. "They summon spirits to them—in *this* world. They don't enter another! That's very different."

"He's right, Avery," Sally agreed, looking at her like she'd grown two heads. Actually, Sally had been looking at her like that all morning, and Avery had the feeling that was because she'd seen her float during the barbeque. "I don't think you realise quite how unusual your life is—compared to us mere mortals, at least!"

"Don't be ridiculous," Avery said. "I'm a 'mere mortal' too, I just happen to have a few special skills. And besides, I can't do what Alex did!"

"We're getting side-tracked," Dan said, breaking up what could have become an argument. "Who were they?"

"We don't know! But Alex banished them pretty quickly."

"Interesting," he said, nodding abstractedly. "Why are they targeting you?"

"They're not!" Avery said. "Not really."

Dan rolled his eyes. "Avery! Something appeared in your garden and threw coins at you. They lured Alex away by using your ancestor! I don't think that's a bloody coincidence."

That reminded her of something else. "They threw something else yesterday—an old dagger. Fortunately, it hit our wall of protection, but that was worrying."

"A dagger!" Sally said, almost squealing. A few customers turned and stared, and Sally immediately lowered her voice. "How can an object materialise out of nowhere?"

Avery shrugged. "We've been debating that for hours, but think it's because they're abnormally strong."

"Good grief, Avery!" Sally said crossly. "Your capacity for trying to make *nothing* out of *something* is amazing!"

Avery looked at Sally with alarm. She really was cranky. But once again Dan waded in, asking, "How old was the dagger?"

"Not sure, but it looked very old. I'm going to ask El to take it to Dante."

He nodded. "To return to my previous point—this must be connected to Helena or you."

"But Helena has been gone for weeks!" Avery pointed out. "I think her disappearance was something entirely separate—for a while, at least."

"Huh!" Sally grunted in a very un-Sallylike way. "Tenuous, at best!"

"Whatever it started as," Dan said, "you are now connected to it—big time."

Avery groaned. "I know. It's really messy. Gil said another witch had walked the spirit realm, too—a mortal, not a dead one. He suggested they were deliberately stirring up the ghosts who had imprisoned Helena, however that works!"

Dan and Sally exchanged worried glances as Dan said, "That's quite an important point, Avery, because it absolutely suggests you *are* being targeted. Who have you pissed off?"

"No one!"

"Oh, come on! I thought there were a couple of witches in the Cornwall Coven who resented you being there?"

Avery sagged in her seat. "Yes, there's Zane and Mariah, but just because they don't like us doesn't mean they would act against us!"

"Well, someone is!"

Avery wanted to change the subject. It depressed her to think that another witch was responsible for Helena's capture and the attack on them. "I need your brains, Dan."

He nodded encouragingly. "Of course. With what?"

"I've taken some of those folklore books off our shelves. I was trying to find out about supernatural Cornish creatures that could kill or cause mayhem. What about Púcas or spriggans?"

"Well, they're about as Cornish as you can get! Like any fairy-style myth, the creatures are untrustworthy, mischievous, and sometimes deadly. But why them?"

"The man that died had every bone in his body broken. It could be spirits—the ones we've encountered this weekend are particularly violent—but we're considering other options. And," she added, "spriggans are said to guard buried treasure and burial sites."

Dan looked thoughtful. "Well, that's true, and spriggans are also said to be the ghosts of giants, so are very strong."

"Giants?" Sally's voice rose again. "Now that sounds like a fairy story!"

"But Cornwall is renowned for its giants!" Dan reminded her. "Jack the Giant Killer is supposedly based on a Cornish giant."

Avery blinked. "Hold on—did you say ghosts of *giants*?"

"I did." He scratched his chin thoughtfully. "It's like the essence of a giant has been distilled into the wizened form of a grumpy old man."

"Well, whoever killed that man would have been very strong," Avery reasoned. "So maybe our vengeful spirits—whoever they are—are working with them, or at least one of them." As weird as that idea was, Avery felt a glimmer of intrigue. "Is there such a thing as a pack of spriggans?"

Dan laughed. "I hope not, but I wouldn't put it past you to find one. I think they should have a better collective name, though."

Sally looked disbelievingly between them both. "I can't believe you're making light of this! A man is dead...pulverised. It's horrible!"

"Yes it is," Avery said quickly. "Sorry, Sally. I'm not making light of this, but all of this is really odd!"

A fire began to smoulder behind Dan's eyes. "And you said there was a doubloon in the dead man's mouth?"

"Yes!"

"And you had guineas thrown at you, and a dagger...maybe the dead guy actually found buried treasure, and someone's not happy about it."

"That's why we're going to look into smuggling," she admitted. "It must be related. We thought we'd take a trip to Jamaica Inn, and our very own White Haven Museum."

"Of course," Sally said. "They have a new display. It doesn't open until the weekend though, so you'll have to wait."

"That's okay," Avery said, nodding. "We've got plenty to keep us going."

"What are you going to do about Helena?" Sally asked.

"I don't know. I hate the thought of her being trapped, but equally I'm terrified that Alex could be, too. I guess at the moment I have to trust that Gil will help."

Sally crossed her arms. "And will you tell Reuben about Gil?"

Avery nodded nervously, knowing how upset Reuben would be. "Yes. We're inviting the others around tonight. I don't want to tell him in the pub."

"Maybe you should be a little less blasé when you tell him," she said, before draining her coffee and marching across the shop, leaving Avery looking after her, dumbstruck.

★·✹·◌·★·✹·◌·✳·✹·◌·★·✹

Reuben looked at Avery and Alex and felt a lump forming in his throat. "You saw my brother? In the spirit realm?"

Alex nodded at him, his eyes narrowing with concern. "Yes. It was completely unexpected. I promise I didn't go looking for him, he just swept in to save me."

"Are you sure?" Reuben asked, suddenly suspicious. "Because when I offered to help you, you refused. Was this why?"

Alex jerked back in his seat like he'd had an electric shock. "Of course not! Bloody hell, Reuben. I would never summon Gil to do my bidding!"

Reuben felt sick and suddenly hot, and he stood up abruptly, almost upending his chair as he stalked to the small balcony off Avery and Alex's living room. It was Monday evening, and they had just eaten dinner together, but for the last hour he thought they looked worried about something, and he couldn't work out what. Now it was obvious.

He leaned on the balustrade, taking deep breaths and trying to blink back tears. He'd done enough crying over Gil's death, and didn't think there could possibly be any more, and yet...

El appeared at his side, sliding under his arm and wrapping hers around his waist. "Are you all right?"

He looked at the sea in the distance, the waves sparkling in the evening light, but he wasn't really seeing them. Instead he was seeing Gil's broken body on the ground in the cave on Gull Island.

"Reuben, please talk to me," El said softly.

He blinked away his tears and looked down at her. "Sorry. I'm in shock."

"Don't apologise. You have every right to be upset." She reached up and kissed his cheek, and the warmth of her skin and familiar scent of patchouli and musk steadied him. "But equally, you know Alex would never use Gil like that. I'm upset, too, and so are the others."

He nodded, unable to speak. *Great.* He'd just accused one of his best mates of being a dick. *He could make such a mess of things sometimes.*

El continued, her tone light. "I'd hoped he was sipping Mai Tais on a beach somewhere in the spirit realm."

He laughed, despite the situation. El could always cheer him up. "There's a beach there? And Mai Tais?"

"There better be! I'm banking on it."

"Maybe he does that in his downtime." He kissed El's forehead and then rested his cheek against her silky hair. "It's been almost a year, El. I thought his spirit would be at rest. I wanted it to be."

"And maybe it is," she murmured. "Maybe it was just Alex being in trouble that attracted him. But isn't it lovely to feel that he's out there, watching for people...like with Shadow and Gabe beneath your family's mausoleum?"

"I guess so." He grunted. "He's like some avenging angel."

"Maybe he's in Valhalla—a hero!"

"He *was* a hero. Bloody Caspian." And suddenly, all of Reuben's hard-fought magnanimity came crashing down as his anger surged. "Fucking Faversham bastard. It's his fault."

El squirmed in front of him, her back to the railing as she gripped his arms tightly and stared at him. She was so tall that she was almost at his eye level, and her blue eyes challenged him. "No. Don't go there. He apologised, and then saved me—don't forget that."

"Gil was too sodding young to die, El."

"Of course he was. But Caspian said he didn't mean it! It was a horrible accident, and a warning to us all to be careful of our magic. We take it for granted," she said, trying to appeal to him. "We're powerful witches! Caspian unleashed his strength in his effort to get our grimoires, and so did we when we retaliated."

Guilt hit Reuben like a punch. "And I have squandered my magic. Gil wouldn't have."

El looked confused. "You don't squander it!"

He met her gaze belligerently. "Yes, I do. I don't practice my magic, or use it half as much as you do."

"You use it more than you used to. You wield it more confidently now. You know you do."

"Not like you, or the others."

"But you can, when you try." She cupped his face in her hands. "Remember the wall of mist you conjured behind the Crossroads Circus? That was brilliant. And how you found the mermaids' cave. Stop doubting yourself!"

She was humouring him, and he dismissed her comments. "You know I'm right."

"All right. I admit you don't use it as much as we do, but that's because you choose not to! And that's okay. You're ambivalent about it, and we're not. But you always help, and we—*I*—can always count on you!"

Reuben suddenly felt incredibly weary as his normally enormous amounts of energy seemed to drain from him. Gil's reappearance had hit him hard, and so close to the anniversary of his death. It made him realise how very little real progress he had made with his power. "I need to go home and think."

Concern flashed across El's face. "Think about what?"

"Me. My future and my magic and my place in this coven."

El gripped him with surprising strength. "You'll always have a place in this coven. You're part of us. Don't you dare think that you're not!"

"I'll think what I need to," he said, gently but firmly. "I'm going home now—to my home—and I'll call you tomorrow."

He turned, but El didn't let go. "You shouldn't be alone tonight."

"That's exactly what I need to be." Reuben extricated himself from her grip, lifted her hands, and kissed them. "Don't worry. I'll be fine. And no, I won't try to drown myself doing some kamikaze-surf thing."

El's eyes filled with tears and Reuben felt horrible that he'd upset her, but he knew he'd be awful company that night.

He entered the large, open living area of Avery and Alex's flat, and found that they and Briar were sitting on the sofa, talking quietly. All three looked up at him, obviously worried, and he smiled wanly. "I'm heading home, guys. I just need to think." He could feel El at his back, and he couldn't look at her, so he headed to the stairs, grabbing his jacket on the way.

They leapt to their feet, Briar saying, "Don't go, Reuben. Stay and talk."

"You talk. You can fill me in another time." He didn't wait, and almost ran down the stairs and out of the back door, pausing to take a deep breath in the lane behind the house, but within seconds, Alex was next to him.

"Reuben, I meant it. I didn't do it deliberately."

Reuben looked at his old friend, similar to him in so many ways, and noted the lines of worry etched around his eyes. They had grown up together, but had never been as close as they were now, partly because Reuben had ignored his magic for years and kept apart from the witches in White Haven. "I believe you—sorry about earlier. I was shocked. But I just need to go home now."

"I'll call you tomorrow, then?"

"Sure." And with that, Reuben walked away, feeling Alex watching him until he turned the corner.

Seven

"I feel like shit," Alex said to the others when he re-entered the living room.

The girls sprang apart from where they had been conferring, heads together on the sofa, as Avery said, "So do we."

Alex continued through to the kitchen. "I need beer. Anyone else?"

"Me, please," El called.

When he returned, carrying two open bottles, El was pacing, and she gratefully accepted the drink. "Thanks. Now I'm going to be worried about him all night."

"Sorry," Alex repeated, feeling doubly guilty. "I swear I didn't summon Gil."

"I'm not blaming you, you twit! Gil was always generous and helpful. It makes sense he still would be after death. But this has just brought everything flooding back for Reuben."

"Of course it has," Avery agreed. "For all of us! I dreamt about Gil last night. Just weird, random stuff. And I know it's unexpected, but I'm so grateful that he helped Alex."

Alex dropped into the squishy armchair. "I'm sure Reuben needs time—just like he said. We need to respect his space. In the meantime, we've got plenty to think about. Like who our mysterious spirits are, and who the witch could be." He looked at Avery. "Any news from Oswald?"

"Not yet. We should go to the Jamaica Inn Smuggling Museum. I'd actually love to know a bit more about smuggling. I've lived here all my life and heard so much about it, but I know so few details!" She flopped back, huffing. "What a day. You know, I upset Sally today, too. She looked so cranky about Gil."

"It's hardly surprising though, is it?" Alex said, wishing they could change the subject. "It's one thing to meet with a random spirit, but it's totally different to hang around with someone you know!"

Avery looked offended. "She said I was blasé! I was anything but!"

"We do take this stuff for granted," Briar pointed out, and then added hurriedly, "not that you did it intentionally, I'm sure!"

El clapped her hands like a tour guide, as much, Alex thought, to distract her than anyone else. "Come on! Let's make a plan. That will cheer us up. Tomorrow is Tuesday, and I can definitely spare a few hours to go to Bodmin." She looked at Avery hopefully. "Shall we go together? It's only half an hour to get there."

"Absolutely! We can grab lunch, too." Avery turned to Briar and Alex. "Do you two want to come?"

"Not me, sorry," Briar said, shaking her head.

"Nor me," Alex replied. He groaned at the thought of his busy day. "I'm interviewing a couple of new bar staff with Simon, just to tide us over the summer."

El winced in sympathy. "Ooh, fun."

Briar settled herself into the corner of the sofa. "You know, you haven't shown us the knife that came out of the spirit world. I'd like to see it."

"Great idea," Alex said, rising to his feet. "It's upstairs, give me a sec."

He bounded up to the attic, grabbed the knife and quickly returned, examining it again before handing it to Briar. It was made of a dull metal, with two sharp edges, and a bone hilt with no discernible markings on it. "Here you go. It doesn't give us a clue as to where it came from, unfortunately."

"I don't feel any magic in it," Briar said as she examined it. "Looks horribly sharp, though. El?"

She held it out and El took it from her, heading to the window to see it better in the fading evening light. "It's simple and cheap, so clearly not belonging to a rich man. And it's quite dirty. Would you mind if I cleaned it up?"

"Not at all," Alex said. "Whatever you can find out about it would be good."

El wrapped it up in her cotton scarf and tucked into her leather bag, while Briar asked, "Did the spirits do much damage?"

"Everything was tossed off the shelves," Avery said, still cross. "Fortunately, nothing was broken, but some of our books were damaged. Bloody heathens! At least the grimoires were too heavy to be lifted by them."

Briar cradled her glass of white wine, rolling it between her hands. "And you said they wore rags?"

Alex tried to remember what he'd seen as they whirled around the attic. "I think so. I'm pretty sure they were male, and I think they wore long, loose trousers—"

"No," Avery interrupted. "A couple had three-quarter trousers, and one wore a kind of bandana."

"How many were there?" El asked.

"Four," Alex said, very sure.

"They looked unkempt," Avery added, "with long hair and scraggly beards. I mean, Helena always looks clean and wears her long dress, despite the manner of her death, so I presume this means they were unkempt in life?" She wrinkled her nose. "Am I making assumptions?"

Briar laughed. "Maybe. But the three-quarter trouser is interesting. They could be sailors."

"True! That would fit with smuggling!" Avery agreed.

"Or it could be that they were wrecked sailors, killed by pirates, who are seeking revenge," El suggested. "Yes! Maybe they are seeking revenge on the townsfolk who abandoned them and let them die!"

Alex tried to recall what he'd sensed of them in the spirit realm. "They smelt sour—like I could smell their breath. That was horrible, actually. I could feel them pressing around me."

"Ugh!" Briar shuddered.

Alex rubbed his cheek, feeling his stubble and realising he needed a shave. It felt more like a beard. "I can't see how one spirit can imprison another, but I guess it comes back to the other witch who walked the spirit realm."

Avery looked distracted and worried. "Dan said I should consider Zane and Mariah, seeing as they are openly resentful of us."

"Unfortunately," Alex said, hating to admit it, "I think he's right."

★·۞·۵·★·۞·۵·✳·۵·✳·۵·★·۞

"I bet it's freezing here in the winter," El said to Avery as she exited her Land Rover on Jamaica Inn's car park.

Jamaica Inn was actually a collection of grey stone buildings in the middle of one of the highest points of Bodmin Moor, situated on the main road with a large car park and a sign with a scowling pirate on it. Outside the main pub was a cobblestoned area filled with tables and benches, and hanging baskets were overflowing with flowers, bright against the grey building. It was full of 'olde world' charm, and huge cartwheels were propped in plant beds to add to the theme, as well as a set of stocks.

Avery nodded. "Yeah, I bet the wind howls over the moor."

"It's very atmospheric. Maybe I should persuade Reuben to stay here one night." She said his name lightly, but she was actually worried sick about him, and didn't want Avery to know. They had avoided the subject in the car, talking about anything else.

"Have you heard from him?" Avery asked.

"Just a text," she admitted. "Saying he's fine. I'm just giving him some space."

"That's good." Avery hugged El briefly as they found the entrance to the museum. "It was inevitable he'd take it hard—especially considering the timing."

"I know."

El was grateful she didn't ask any more questions. They headed through Pedlars Restaurant to get their tickets, and she admired the low roof with dark timber beams and stone walls. It was cosy, and because it was mid-week, not too busy.

"Did you know it has a farm shop," El said, "and a gift shop, too? We must go before we leave. And get a pub lunch, of course!"

Avery laughed. "I'm sure we can manage that. They're advertising cream teas, too!"

The museum focussed on the smuggling scene of the late 1700s and early 1800s, and was filled with wooden and glass cases displaying weapons, examples of smuggled goods, and even small scenes depicting wrecking crews. For a while they split up, and El drifted around on her own, fascinated by the displays and the history. Smuggling was a cutthroat business. While it may have originally been opportunistic, started by looting wrecked ships on the shore, it quickly escalated, and soon looters were luring ships in with false lights instead. El shivered to think of the poor men drowning or being murdered by the bootleggers. But, she had to admit, it was a hard life. The crown had increased taxes on brandy, gin, tea, silks, and salt in order to fund expensive wars, and it came to a point where ordinary folk couldn't afford them. The museum also had old wanted posters on the wall, and a couple caught her eye. They mentioned the names of bootleggers who were wanted, and rewards were offered, but from what El could tell, most of the locals were involved.

She found a display about the Carters of Prussia Cove, and she called Avery over. "Have you seen this?"

Avery nodded and started to laugh. "John Carter, the King of Prussia! Self-styled, I guess. He and his brother, Harry, really put smuggling on the map here. They had two huge ships, and plenty of crew. I wonder if these could be our spirits?"

El shook her head. "Doesn't sound like they came to a sticky end, though, so maybe not." She moved on to another display. "What about this guy? Cruel Coppinger. His gang was ruthless, and his ship was called Black Prince." Her eyes widened as she scanned the text. "Wow. He sounds like a nightmare. There aren't many details here, though."

Avery took her phone out and snapped a few pictures. "Something to look into though."

"And this inn was the central hub," El said, "to store all smuggled goods before they were moved out of Cornwall. Apparently, they estimate that there were potentially a hundred hidden routes to get here from the shore."

Avery's mouth dropped open in shock. "A hundred!"

"Yep. It was totally isolated in the eighteenth century, and the moor was boggy and wild. Can you imagine how dangerous this place would be?" El had a vision of the moor under moonlight, clouds scudding across the sky and the wind flattening the heather as men made their way with their goods. Were they excited or scared? Did their blood race, or were their feet like lead in their boots, the threat of pursuit ever present. "And the inn is rumoured to be haunted. Why the hell don't I come here more often?"

"Good question," Avery had to acknowledge.

El spun on her heel, looking around the room. "This has been really fascinating, but I don't feel any closer to finding out about any mysterious buried treasure."

"Me neither." Avery pointed to Daphne Du Maurier's memorial room. "Come on, let's have a look at that before lunch. I love the book, *Jamaica Inn*."

"I love *Rebecca* more," El admitted, heading across the room. "Lots of gothic mystery!"

She was almost on the threshold when she realised she'd lost Avery. El turned, wondering where she'd gone. Avery was staring at a poster and plaque on the wall, and El hurried to her side, curious as to what had caught her attention.

"What's up?" And then she too stared at the picture of a middle-aged man standing next to a familiar figure, and her mouth fell open in shock.

"El, it's Mariah! And that's Ethan James, the man who had oversight of the modernisation of the museum!"

El was still reading the text. "It says that Mariah donated an old ledger that belonged to Zephaniah Job, the smugglers' banker." She scanned the room again. "I saw those, but didn't see Mariah's name." She grabbed Avery's arm, tugging her to where a collection of papers were displayed in a glass cabinet, and squinted at the writing on a card. "No wonder I didn't see her name. The writing is tiny."

"According to this," Avery said, reading it too, "Job was based in Polperro, and most of his records were burned after his death. No wonder they were excited to find one of his ledgers."

El straightened up, biting her lower lip as her mind raced with possibilities. "Intriguing. This was several years ago, but it means Mariah has a link to smuggling that we can't ignore. Come on, let's see this memorial room and then have lunch. I can't think on an empty stomach."

Almost two hours later, after they had eaten lunch in the Smugglers Bar, stocked up on local produce in the farm shop, and indulged in the gift shop, where Avery bought a couple of interesting-looking books on smuggling, they headed home, still musing on their findings.

Avery's phone rang, and she quickly answered it. "Hi Oswald, any news?"

El focussed on the road, half listening to Avery's conversation, and half wondering if Reuben was feeling any better. She'd wanted to call him many times but had resisted, knowing that Reuben hated being crowded, and she was desperately trying to respect that. But she also knew that underneath his devil-may-care exterior he could be incredibly vulnerable, and she hated knowing that he thought he was letting them down. She was glad when

Avery broke her train of thought.

"Oswald said there have been some unusual incidents around Fowey lately. Strange, paranormal events such as lights on the moor and unusual noises," she told her without preamble. "Some of the older folk are talking about piskies and spirits haunting the town, too."

"For how long?"

"Just the last few weeks, from what he could tell." Avery laughed. "Good old Oswald. He just sat in a pub and started chatting. He said the locals were intrigued, especially the older ones, thinking it was part of Cornwall's charm, but they do admit something odd is happening."

"I guess the advantage of being old is that you can gossip with impunity!" El said. She noted the moors streaking past, still wild and remote once away from the road. "And what about the death?"

"The victim had been spotted in the area a lot, hanging around St Catherine's Castle with another man who no one has seen in days."

"Wow." El glanced across at her. "That's great. Any local theories?"

"He said that everyone knew about the doubloon, and they reckon he'd found a hoard of gold that had been cursed. No specific spot was suggested, though."

"Ha! More gossip!"

"They found the victim's car, though. Did you hear?"

"No. Where?"

"On the National Trust car park, just out of the town. The Goddess knows why he ended up on the beach," Avery said, and she fell into a thoughtful silence, allowing El to start worrying about Reuben once again.

Eight

A very wound through the stacks at Happenstance Books, greeting some of the regulars, before heading to the counter to talk with Dan and Sally.

"Hi guys, anything thrilling happen while I was away?" she asked.

"Haven't you heard the news?" Sally asked, surprised. "There's been an incident in Looe."

"Looe?" Avery shook her head. "We weren't listening to the radio. What happened?"

"There was a cave-in on the cliffs above the town—"

"A sinkhole, really," Dan corrected, and Sally shot him an impatient look.

"Whatever. Anyway, it's lucky no one was killed, because this massive area just collapsed, revealing this huge cave beneath."

"Oh, wow! Was anyone hurt?" Avery asked. Looe was a beautiful Cornish town situated on the south coast, further north than White Haven. It was a popular spot for tourists, too.

"Fortunately not," Dan told her, "but it was what they found at the bottom that had more interest."

There was a speculative look on his face that worried Avery, and warily she asked, "What?"

He raised his eyebrows. "Three skeletons, rotting casks, and a few empty chests."

"Holy shit! Smugglers' remains?"

"Looks like it!"

"Well let's hope so, or it could be their victims," said Sally. She still looked disgruntled, but Dan was trying to suppress his excitement—probably so as not to annoy Sally.

Avery sank onto the spare stool as she considered the implications, and it was Dan she addressed next. "Do you think this is linked to—"

Dan didn't even wait for her to finish. "Absolutely! Something has been set in motion, Ave!" He lowered his voice. "*Something wicked this way comes!*"

"Oh, good grief!" Sally said, exasperated. "How can you be excited about potential disaster?"

Dan just rolled his eyes dramatically, and Avery had the feeling she had arrived in the middle of a bigger discussion. "Get over it, Sally! A man died in Fowey! Horribly, yes, but why? What was he doing? He—and others—are meddling in something that should have been left alone." He crossed his arms like an old fish wife. "You mark my words."

Now it was Sally who rolled her eyes. "Drama queen."

"Slow down, you two," Avery said, interrupting their squabble. "When did this happen?"

"Middle of the night, apparently," Sally said. "Not far from the coastal path."

"The police and the council have been onsite to secure it," Dan added. "Once they made sure it was safe, a couple of climbers headed down there. But guess what was more interesting!"

"There's more?" Avery said, surprised.

Dan nodded. "Oh, yes!"

Sally butted in, her excitement now clearly overriding her irritation. "Someone was in there recently! It looks like whatever was stored down there had been recently stolen."

"But how can they tell?" Avery asked. "Surely the fall of rock and earth would have covered up all the evidence."

"Something about specific damage to the chests," Dan said. "They were to the side of the cave, beneath an overhanging bit of rock, so they were relatively protected. And there's a passage leading off the cave that shows signs of recent use."

"Wow. I wonder why the cave suddenly collapsed?" Avery mused on her earlier conversation. "You know, Oswald phoned me this afternoon. Apparently, Fowey has been experiencing paranormal events recently. I wonder if Looe is as well."

Sally opened the drawer and pulled a pack of biscuits out, took one, and then offered them around. "Is there someone representing the council in Looe?"

Avery knew she meant the Witch Council, and nodded as she accepted a cookie. "Mariah. She's a sour-faced puss. Well, with me at least."

"One of Caspian's old cronies?" Dan asked.

"Yes. And a friend of Zane from Bodmin. He hates us, too." Avery crunched her biscuit. "We did find out something interesting about her this morning, though! She donated one of Zephaniah Job's accounting books to Jamaica Inn!"

"Bloody hell!" Sally said. "That's an impressive name. Who's he?"

"He was the smugglers' accountant. Got very rich himself, too. He was based in Polperro."

Dan's eyes lit up. "Fowey, Polperro, Looe. They are all very close, and very entwined in smuggling back then. How did she find the ledger?"

"In old family papers, apparently. Not that her family was in any way linked, of course!" Avery laughed. "The museum was very keen to point that out."

"Doesn't mean she's not your spirit-walking witch though, right?" Dan said softly.

Avery nodded. She'd been debating that since finding out, but didn't want to accuse her just yet. She didn't like Mariah, but that was no reason to vilify her unjustly. "Nothing supernatural reported on the news, I presume?"

"Nope," Dan said, having a second biscuit.

Avery thought for a moment, and then said, "I'll wait, see if Newton or Genevieve call, and if not, I'll call them."

They paused their conversation when Mary, one of their older regulars, appeared at the counter with a stack of books. She smiled apologetically. "Sorry to interrupt your chat, but I'm just topping up my romance selection!"

"You never interrupt us, Mary," Sally said, starting to serve her. "That's what we're here for! We're just gassing about Looe."

Mary's hand flew to her chest. "Such a terrible thing. That poor man!"

Confused, Avery asked, "What poor man? I thought there'd just been a cave collapse?"

"Didn't you hear the lunchtime news? A man was walking his dog along the cliff path this morning and never came back. They found his body just before lunch." She lowered her voice conspiratorially. "He'd had his throat cut!" Despite Mary's age and very proper appearance—her blue-grey hair was rigidly set in a perm that hadn't changed in decades—she looked morbidly fascinated. "Ear to ear! It almost beheaded him!"

"Bloody Hell!" Dan exchanged a nervous glance with Avery. "That's terrible."

"I know. My cousin is in a right old flap about it. She lives close to the coastal path, at the top of Looe. Heard the big rumble in the night, and a very strange, bloodcurdling cry."

By now, all thoughts of the sale had vanished as Mary leaned forward on the counter, eager to impart gossip. She was quickly joined by Fred, another local who was a very similar age.

"You talking about the murder, Mary?" he asked, leaning in next to her. "Bad business, that. Very bad. Doesn't do to go disturbing smugglers' remains. They'll have their revenge, they will!"

Avery could barely believe her ears, and she almost stumbled over her words. "Well, dead men can't kill people. Someone else must have killed that poor man."

Fred fixed her with his steely blue eyes. "You should know better than that, my dear! You more than anyone!" He wagged a finger. "Spirits are walking this coast now. Two deaths in two days. Won't be the last of them, either!"

"Be away with you, Fred," Sally said impatiently, her accent broadening as she chatted.

Mary chimed in, settling shoulder to shoulder with Fred in solidarity. "Don't be so foolish, girl. These are smugglers we're talking about. They lived violently, and they died violently. That makes for a restless spirit. Mark my words, there's more to this than meets the eye." She raised an eyebrow at Avery. "You need to look after White Haven. We had our fair share of smugglers; one of Coppinger's places, this was." She shuddered. "We don't want him back. Evil bastard. Anyway," she smiled at Sally. "Ring me up dearie."

Coppinger. Avery had read his name only hours ago.

"You free for a pint of stout down at the Bootleggers Arms?" Fred asked Mary as Sally fumbled through the sale, obviously flustered. "We can catch up on some gossip."

"Sounds lovely," she said, handing Sally some cash, and then turning to Avery, she waved her hands above her head in some vague gesture that encompassed the room. "Mind what I said, now. Whatever it is you do, do it bigger!"

And then she and Fred cast beaming smiles at them before heading out the door together.

Avery's head was swimming. What had just happened? Was she just outed as a witch by two of her most regular customers?

Dan grinned. "Your face is a picture."

"I'm glad you find it funny," Avery said crossly. "'Whatever it is you do, do it bigger!'"

He shrugged. "I keep telling you, people love you for it."

"Aren't we missing the point here?" Sally reminded them, her tone sharp. "Another man is dead. Spirits are walking the coast—horrible, vengeful, restless spirits!"

"That settles it," Avery said decisively, "I'm calling Genevieve."

★ ⊙ ◌ ☆ ◉ ◌ ✳ ◉ ◌ ☆ ◉

Newton's hands were on his hips as he surveyed the coastline below him. Looe was to his left, and it looked bright and welcoming in the afternoon sunshine. Further along on his right was the crime scene where the man had been found, and now the whole area was crawling with forensics.

Boats bobbed on the sea, white freshets breaking its smooth expanse, and he had a sudden longing for an ice cream. That, however, would have to wait. *Another coastal town, another violent death.* He sighed heavily, and then turned to survey the expanse of green behind him, unable to see from here the deep pit that had opened in the night. "Bollocks," he muttered to himself.

"What was that, Guv?" Inez said, as she finished her phone call and joined him.

"I'm just swearing. Bloody paranormal bullshit."

Inez laughed, her wide smile illuminating her face. "You could always apply for a transfer. But once you know this stuff, you can't un-know it."

"I know. And to be honest, I'd rather deal with this than some snivelling little thief or sex offender."

"Oh, I'm sure restless spirits or other paranormal creatures could be those things, too." The victim's body had already been removed, but Inez gestured to where the white suited team, tiny from this distance, searched for clues. "Are we sure this is supernatural? It could just be a vicious murder."

"It could. But it's close to the cave, and the coroner reckons he was already dead before his throat was cut."

"Does he? Why?"

"Very little bleeding. There should be arterial spray everywhere, but there isn't. Maybe a heart attack?"

Inez was shorter than Newton, and she squinted up at him now, shielding her eyes from the sun with one hand and restraining her hair from whipping around her face with the other. "Well, that could be natural!"

"Then why slit his throat? And did you see the look on his face?"

She winced and nodded. "Just like the other victim. Horrified."

Newton recalled the wide-eyed stare and silent scream frozen on the man's face. "And there was rust in the very ragged wound."

"A dodgy knife. That happens." She paused at Newton's sceptical expression. "I'm playing devil's advocate here."

"He's the last thing we need." Newton looked inland again. "Come on, let's see this cave again."

Inez fell into step beside him and they walked across the springy turf on the cliff top. "Where's Moore?"

"Interviewing the victim's wife, but I doubt if he'll find much out."

"Is the dog okay?"

He smiled as he cast her a sideways glance. "He's upset. We found him whimpering at his master's side, but is otherwise unharmed."

Within minutes they ducked under the police tape and after a short walk reached the sinkhole, looking down the rubble-filled sides. The whole area was an uneven circle with a sheer drop on some sides, but in front of them was a gentler gradient, allowing for a safer descent to the cave itself. On the far side was the section that had been least affected because of the over-hanging rock that sheltered the remains and the old chests.

The area had been thoroughly checked that morning and declared safe—to the police, at least—which was why a couple of police climbers had descended to investigate. A safe route had been marked out, and Newton glanced at Inez. "I'm heading down there."

"Newton! There could be a bigger collapse."

"Maybe, but I want to see it for myself. Stay here if you want."

"I don't think so!" she declared, gesturing to her trainers and jeans. "I can manage."

Inez Walker dressed smartly most of the time, but Newton noticed she had a distinct leaning towards jeans, trainers, and sweatshirts whenever she could get away with it. That was fine with him. If he weren't the inspector, he'd be more informal, too.

"All right—after me. And be careful!"

They both edged their way down the rocky slope, gently testing their way, despite the assurance of the marked path, and Newton sighed with relief when he reached solid ground. The cave was a decent size and about fifty feet down from the surface, well above the shoreline.

Inez examined the cave with a critical eye and pointed at the rubble they had descended. "Do you think there's a passage here from the beach, hidden under that?"

He nodded. "This coastline is riddled with tunnels from smuggling days, so there must be. But," he pointed to the other side, "there is one leading away from here." He made his way carefully across the debris to a narrow tunnel entrance. Extracting a torch from his pocket, he illuminated the darkness.

"You're not going down that, surely?" Inez asked, startled.

"Nope. Not yet, anyway, but I'd love to know what's down there."

"Me too," she admitted, "but death by suffocation doesn't appeal to me."

Newton wondered how safe it would be. The tunnel looked clear—from here, at least, the ground churned up around the entrance. But Inez was right; being buried alive under a mountain of earth was not appealing. However, he had other options. "I might try it with one of our friends."

"I presume you mean *your* friends, the witches?"

"No, I meant *ours.*" Inez looked amused at his response. "What? They are. They have been very helpful to our investigations."

"I know they have, but they are good friends of yours, too. Personally, I mean. And there's nothing wrong with that."

When he'd told Walker about the witches a couple of days ago, she had taken the news quite well. "I take it you don't object to witches, then?"

She shrugged. "It depends on the witch. I've only come across a couple with real power and haven't really liked them, but your guys seem okay."

"Where was that?"

"The witches? Brighton."

Newton wasn't usually so chatty with his work colleagues, but now he was intrigued. He leaned against the rock wall. "Really? Did you meet them with a case?"

"Yes, but they weren't helpful. They were on the periphery of an investigation into illegally shipped items, but it turned out they weren't involved."

"And you came here after Brighton?"

She gave him a tired smile. "I'm going through a divorce. Getting away from Brighton seemed like a good idea. This job came at the right time."

"Oh," Newton said, genuinely surprised. "I had no idea. Does your soon-to-be ex work in paranormal policing, too?" Newton, for some reason, presumed her husband was a policeman.

"Ha! No. He's hates it—calls it mumbo-jumbo! Only Ted does that. Mike works in drugs."

"Well, I'm sorry to hear about your divorce." Newton turned away to walk back to the broken wooden chests. "Any kids?"

"No, thank God. It's complicated enough." Inez followed him, crouching down to move the shattered wood of the old chests, pulling aside earth and stones. "Damn it. There's nothing left in these. Do you think they'll find prints on the old locks?"

Newton knelt next to her, sifting through the rock. "Maybe, but I doubt we'll be so lucky." A couple of hours ago, they had removed the old, broken locks from the two chests that provided evidence they had been forced open recently, and they were being processed by the lab. But this wasn't urgent, and they couldn't really connect it to the murdered man on the path. They had also removed the skeletal remains for examination, certain they were very old. "I'd love to know where that passage goes, though. From the churned up ground, I think they had to have come in that way!"

"So, it should be safe—in theory," Inez said. She sounded excited, and looked at him with a hopeful expression.

"I thought you said going down there was a mad idea?"

"I've changed my mind! Woman's prerogative. What do you say?"

"We haven't got hard hats or anything sensible!"

"We've got brains and a torch, and if the tunnel forks, we head back. We can't risk getting lost in there."

Newton had to admit that now that they were down here, it seemed stupid not to head into the tunnel, at least for a short way. He grinned. "All right. You text Moore and let him know what we're doing, and I'll call Alex."

Nine

A very leaned against the doorframe and looked out onto the lane behind her shop while she talked to Genevieve, enjoying the warm breeze that lifted her hair and caressed her cheek as if it knew her.

In the end, she hadn't had to phone Genevieve; she had instead called her, just as she arrived in the back room. It was uncanny.

"This situation could get a lot worse," Genevieve admitted, sounding more exasperated than worried. "The spirits of bloody smugglers sounds annoying! And I'm trying to plan Litha!"

"And of course two people are dead," Avery reminded her.

"Of course," she answered crossly. "I can hardly forget that!"

Sounded like she had. "So, what now?"

"We meet at eight tonight, at Oswald's. I doubt everyone will make it, but I've let them all know—or left messages, at least." She hesitated a moment, and then said, "Would you try Caspian again for me? It's so unlike him not to answer, and I've called three times already."

"Of course I will," Avery answered, feeling uneasy. It was unlike Caspian. He was a very reliable communicator. "I can even head to his house if he doesn't answer. Have you tried his work?"

"No, actually. Could you? I need to pick the kids up from school and I'm running late already."

The idea of Genevieve, their statuesque High Priestess, doing the school run was so incongruous that Avery almost laughed, but instead she said, "No problem."

As soon as she rang off, Avery called Caspian, hoping Alex wouldn't complain. His phone rang and rang before his voicemail kicked in, and she left a message before ending the call. Straight away she called his office, asking to be put through, but was told he was working from home due to office renovations. Maybe he was just busy, she reflected, trying to quell her concern. And besides, his sister would be around, or his uncle. He *must* be fine.

Heading into the kitchen, Avery filled the kettle and turned it on to make tea, but she couldn't dispel the niggling thought that something was wrong. If Caspian was at home, she could check on him. Without waiting to question the wisdom of her decision, or whether Alex might be upset—she was, after all, seeing Caspian on her own, and she knew Alex's opinion on that—she summoned air, and using witch-flight was in his extensive front gardens in seconds.

Caspian's velvety lawn stretched ahead of her, the borders bursting with summer flowers. More importantly, no one was in sight. Avery headed to the front door and knocked, gently at first, and then with increasing strength, ringing the doorbell, too. It echoed through the house, but no one responded. He could be at his warehouse, or maybe even the docks. Avery recalled that Shadow and Gabe said that he was very hands-on with the business.

She waited by the front door for a few moments more and then strolled around the house; on such a warm day, maybe he was in the back garden. She headed to where Caspian's study was, and paused. The house was ominously quiet. There were no open windows or doors, and peering through his study window, she noted it was empty. But something felt weird.

Avery stepped back and looked at the upper floor. She remembered Caspian's bedroom from when she was practicing witch-flight and had accidentally ended up there. She could head straight there. Or, she chided herself, use witch-flight to cross the short distance to the study—if she could get through his protection spells.

And that's when it struck her. She couldn't detect any spells on the house at all.

Something was very wrong.

Without a second thought, Avery manifested into Caspian's study and paused, listening. The house was utterly silent. Keeping her power raised and magic crackling at her fingertips, she walked into the hallway, following it to the main reception area. She couldn't detect any other energy, but why wasn't the alarm on, and why couldn't she feel any spells?

"Caspian!" she called out. But her voice echoed around her. She knew it was unlikely his sister would be here, but... "Estelle?"

Still no answer. Tempting though it was to go upstairs on her own, if Caspian had been injured in some way, whatever had hurt him was clearly very strong. If the house were empty, she'd feel like a bloody fool. She pulled her phone from her pocket and quickly called Alex. He answered straight away. "Alex, I'm at Caspian's, and something is wrong."

"What the hell are you there for?"

She explained the call from Genevieve and how Caspian hadn't answered his phone.

"For fuck's sake, Avery. Come and get me. Now."

"What?"

"Come to my flat, pick me up by witch-flight, and take me back there with you."

"But—"

"Do it." And then he hung up.

Half annoyed, and half relieved, Avery flew to Alex's old flat, and within seconds the door burst open and he was there, his lips pursed as he stared at her. "I can't bloody believe you went there alone."

"There are no protection spells on his house, Alex, and he's not answering his phone. It's odd!"

"Why are you phoning him?"

"I told you! Genevieve asked me to. There's a meeting tonight, and she can't get hold of him."

He gave her one final, impatient look, stepped behind her, and wrapped his arms around her waist. In seconds, Avery had flown them back to Caspian's hall.

In the brief time since she had left, nothing had changed, and after a few deep breaths to control his nausea, Alex straightened and looked around, his annoyance disappearing.

"I see what you mean. Have you checked the ground floor?"

"Not that half," she said, pointing to the other wing of the house.

"Call him again, while we search." Alex marched down the hall, but Avery waited for a second, hoping Caspian would answer or she'd hear the phone, but neither happened, and she hurried after Alex.

"He's still not answering."

"What's worrying me," Alex said, pausing on the threshold of a large lounge, "is that I can't even feel any residual magic. What if he's..." He looked at her, his gaze serious.

"Don't even suggest that," Avery said. Not feeling any remnant of magic might mean Caspian was dead, and Avery didn't want to entertain that thought at all—and she was glad to see Alex didn't, either. For all that Alex resented Caspian flirting with her, he would never wish him ill.

By now they were almost running through the ground floor of the enormous house, and they raced upstairs, finding the next floor as quiet as below. But this level was cold; far colder than it should be on a warm June afternoon, and they paused on the landing, wary of what they may find.

"Something's here," Alex whispered. "Something is watching us."

Avery felt a prickle down her spine and a cold draft on her neck, and she whirled around, hands raised, to find a knife whirring towards her. She batted it away with her magic, shouting, "Alex—duck!"

The dagger smashed into the wall, but it was followed by more, shooting out of nowhere like darts. She ducked and rolled, and immediately smelt brine and seaweed as a shower of coarse sand hit her, almost blinding her.

A wave of Alex's magic rolled above her, and she heard him cast a banishing spell. But he couldn't finish it. A dark, shadowy figure hit him, throwing him to the floor, and together they rolled down the hallway, smashing into the wall and upending furniture.

Avery leapt to her feet, bewildered as to what to do. If she mistimed a fireball, she could hit Alex, and she wasn't even sure if it would be effective against spirits. And then icy cold, wet hands slipped around her throat, and started to choke her.

She used witch-flight and manifested behind the spirit, just in time to see the shade of a ragged-clothed man spin and jab at her with a knife, a rictus grin revealing blackened teeth and vacant eyes. She leapt back and smacked it with a lightning bolt of energy. It sizzled through the spirit, hitting the wall behind with a burning smell, and the spirit vanished.

Hoping there weren't many more ghosts to contend with, she raced down the hall to where Alex was still fighting. She could see the figure clearer now. Like the other spirit, it was wearing old-fashioned, ragged sailor's clothing. He sat on Alex's chest, pinning him to the floor. His arm was across Alex's neck, and Alex struggled to get his hands free. Without hesitating, Avery propelled a powerful wind at the spirit, picking it up like driftwood, and tossing him down the hall. Alex leapt to his feet, and with a sure and commanding voice, banished the spirit into the void.

For a few seconds, they both stood there poised for further attacks, but an eerie silence descended on the house.

Alex swept his tangled hair back, and glanced at her. "Are you okay?"

"Yes, you?"

"A bruised ego, but that's all." He rubbed his throat. "He felt all too real."

"I know. I was attacked, too, and I'm not entirely sure that it's gone." Avery headed to the closest door, nudging it open to check the room beyond. It was a bedroom, but no one was in there. "Empty," she said, relieved. "I'm really worried, Alex."

"Me too," he said, already checking the room closest to him.

Avery headed down the passage, giving the rooms she passed a cursory glance before rushing to Caspian's room, Alex right behind her.

"This is his room," she told him, summoning her courage before she opened the door.

Alex froze and his eyes hardened. "How do you know that?"

She knew that admission would make him suspicious and she laid her hand on his arm to reassure him. "When I practiced witch-flight I accidentally ended up here. That's all."

He nodded, his expression relaxing. "Yes, of course. Sorry."

Avery opened Caspian's door, peering inside cautiously, and saw a crumpled heap next to the bed. "Alex! He's hurt!"

They both ran in, Avery abandoning all caution as she raced to his side. Caspian was lying on the floor wearing track suit bottoms and a dirty, sweat-soaked t-shirt. His face was bloodied and bruised, and she only saw the knife in his side once she was kneeling next to him. Blood pooled on the floor, already thick and sticky.

"He's been stabbed!" She reached for his pulse, his skin cold beneath her fingers, and relief swept through her as she felt its faint, thready beat. "He's still alive, just barely. I have to get him to a hospital!"

Alex knelt next to her, half watching her, and half scanning the room. He laid a calming hand on her arm. "Briar first! You know she's better."

"But—"

Alex's phone was already in his hands and he called Briar, while Avery gathered her power. Alex was right, but Caspian might need a blood transfusion, or surgery, or... She could barely think straight, and was hardly listening as Alex summarised the situation before hanging up.

"Take him to the back room of her shop, then come back for me later. I'm going to search the house."

For the first time since she had entered the room she took in the damaged furniture that indicated a chaotic fight, terrified that the same fate could befall Alex. "It's not safe for you on your own."

"In that case, don't be long." He kissed her cheek. "Go!"

Ten

B riar watched Avery manifest in the middle of her herb room situated at the rear of her shop, and hurried to Caspian's inert, pale body lying twisted on the floor, quickly assessing his condition.

"By the Goddess!" she said, falling to her knees and examining his wound. "He's lost a lot of blood!" She held his wrist, feeling for his pulse.

"He's been stabbed by a ghost!" Avery looked beside herself, her green eyes wide with shock. "How can a spirit do this, Briar?"

"I'll worry about that afterwards. I want him on the table. Can you lift him?" She needed to keep Avery focussed.

"Yes, of course."

They both stood as Avery summoned air, sending it under Caspian and lifting him gently until he was deposited in the middle of Briar's large, wooden table that she'd dragged to the middle of the room. Avery had arrived so quickly that Briar had only had time to boil water, but she had more than enough herbs to deal with this situation. She rolled him gently onto his back and eased his t-shirt out of the way to inspect the wound. The knife was still embedded in his side.

"It's an old knife. It has a weird hilt," she observed.

"But his wound? Is it deep?"

Briar glanced up at Avery's pinched expression. "It's hard to say until the blade is out."

It was low on his left side, and caked in blood, but there was only one stab wound. He was lucky there weren't more. But as her eyes travelled across his hard, muscled physique, she noted a myriad of cuts and bruises across his chest and face. He'd been beaten severely.

She pointed to his throat. "Finger marks. It tried to strangle him, too." That was odd. "I don't understand why they left him alive."

Briar heard the door open and shut as Eli came in, crossing quickly to her side. "I've locked up," he said, his tall frame dwarfing her. "What do you want me to do?"

"Make a poultice using yarrow and shepherd's purse," she instructed him. "When I pull the knife out, I want to be able to fill the wound with it. Avery, pour some hot water from the kettle into a bowl, grab the cotton gauze, and bring it here."

Within moments, the hot water appeared next to her, but rather than use it straight away, Briar wanted to scan Caspian's body first and assess his energy levels. However, Avery's anxiety was washing off her in waves, and Briar looked at her, perplexed. She knew her and Caspian's relationship was complex, and respected her silence on it, and her wish to keep Caspian as a friend. It was pretty obvious to all of them that Caspian wanted more than that. But Avery's mood wasn't helping now.

"Where is Alex?" Briar asked her.

"Still at Caspian's. I need to get back to him."

Briar smiled. No wonder she was anxious. She was worried about Alex, too. "Go. I have Eli now, and we'll be fine."

"Are you sure?"

"I'm sure."

After a moment's hesitation, in which Avery cast another worried look at Caspian, she disappeared in a swirl of witch-flight, and Eli crossed the room to stand in her place. Eli was one of the seven Nephilim, with honey brown hair and gentle brown eyes, and was charm personified. He was also a very good apothecary, and had taught her things about herbs that had long been lost to time. That was one advantage of working with millennia-old Nephilim. He was also calm, competent, and kind.

He reached for Caspian's wrist, taking his pulse. "It's weak. He could have internal bleeding. I'll prepare a herbal drink when we've finished."

Briar nodded, pleased with the suggestion. "I'm going to scan him now."

She held her hands over Caspian's abdomen. She could feel his blood flow as well as energy levels, but she needed to concentrate, and she fell silent for a few minutes as her hands travelled across him, inches above his skin. He was covered in a sheen of sweat, his breathing shallow and quick. She detected swelling around his windpipe, and could feel the sluggish flow of blood around the wound where it had already clotted. His energy was low, too, his natural magical powers stunted somehow, and that was just as worrying as his physical injuries.

She dropped her hands as she glanced across at Eli. "He's weak, but I don't think the wound is deep." Briar dipped the cloth in the hot water and started to wipe the blood away. "I don't understand why the spirit attacked him, and once it did, why it didn't kill him. From what Alex told me, it sounded like he'd been lying there for hours—with the spirit still there."

"It is odd," Eli admitted. "Maybe it's a warning." He took the bloodied cloths from Briar, and moved next to her to inspect the wound. "It's a dirty knife, too—old and tarnished."

Suddenly fearful for all of their safety, she asked, "Do you understand how a spirit can manifest with a weapon?"

He shook his head. "I can only presume it's very powerful." He must have picked up on Briar's hesitation because he looked at her, eyes narrowed. "Why don't I pull the knife free? I've done this before."

"You have?" Briar prided herself on being level-headed, but she also hated violence, and the thought of pulling the knife out of flesh and muscle made her feel nauseous.

He was already gripping the bloodied hilt. "Too many times. You stand ready with the poultice."

"Okay, but I have a spell to say first. Wait one moment." Briar dipped her hands in the bowl of hot water, cleansed them with a spell, and then placed them either side of the knife. "I'm ready."

As Eli carefully withdrew the knife, Briar uttered a spell to clean the wound and reduce inflammation, speeding up the healing of flesh and damaged blood vessels. The knife was about four inches long with wicked-sharp edges that had been buried to the hilt, and she sighed with relief that it was a short blade. Fresh blood welled as the blade exited the wound, but Briar continued the spell, watching as Eli pressed hard with thick cotton cloths. They both worked calmly, full of intent, and when Briar nodded to say she'd finished the spell, satisfied that flesh had started to knit together, she reached for the poultice and filled the ragged hole. Then, for the next half an hour, they worked on Caspian's neck, reducing the swelling there before moving on to the other cuts and bruises covering his battered body. Eventually, they both sighed and stood back, Briar happy to see that Caspian already looked better.

She gave Eli a grateful smile. "Thank you. You were fantastic. Can you carry him to the sofa?"

She had a small couch in the corner of her room, under the window where it caught the afternoon light, and Eli nodded, scooping their patient up effortlessly and then gently positioning him. Briar wrapped a blanket around him, anxious to keep Caspian warm, before turning to boil the kettle once more. She leaned against the counter, watching Eli clean his hands at the sink, his shirtsleeves rolled up to his elbows.

"Caspian is a powerful witch, Eli. He has strong protection on his house. This shouldn't have happened."

Eli shrugged. "We're all caught unawares sometimes. Maybe he has a weakness that someone knew about."

"Maybe. Mind you," she said, recalling the events at the barbeque, "it happened at Avery's place, too. A spirit appeared in her garden, bursting through the protection spells."

Eli dried his hands and threw the cloth into the basket of dirty laundry. They were both scrupulous about cleanliness. He leaned his hip against the counter, mirroring her actions, and folded his arms across his chest. "Sounds to me like the ghost—or ghosts—have something to prove." He jerked his head at Caspian. "He's been beaten up! I think whoever did this wanted him to remember it."

"Like a warning?"

"Exactly. Maybe there's more violence to come." Eli's gentle eyes darkened. "Maybe he'll target someone close to him next. His sister? Avery?"

"Avery's not his girlfriend, Eli."

"But he loves her."

Briar jolted in shock at his words. "I'm not sure it's love."

"You're brighter than that, Briar. Of course it's love—as much as he tries to hide it and she tries to ignore it. I've seen enough of that in my lifetime. But, we should warn Estelle." And then he grimaced. "We need to tell her about Caspian's injuries, too. She might want to be here."

"I haven't got her number," Briar admitted, now worrying about Estelle, even though she didn't like her.

"We do. I'll get one of my brothers to call her. But what are we going to do with him?"

"I'll stay here for a few hours," Briar said, watching Caspian's deepening breaths. "I think he's stable, but even so..." She looked at Eli to find that he was staring at Caspian, too. "You can go. I can get Avery to take him to my spare room later."

"Oh, no," he said, grabbing some cups and starting to make tea. "I won't let you wait alone. I'm waiting, too. But I'll call Gabe first. He can have the pleasure of finding Estelle."

Briar smiled, relieved. She was used to being the healer in the coven, and was happy to do it. It gave her great satisfaction to make someone well, and she enjoyed drawing on the Earth's power to do so. But, it was nice to have someone to bounce ideas off. "All right, thanks Eli. I hope you're not disappointing any ladies tonight," she added, teasing him.

He winked. "Absence makes the heart grow fonder."

★·❂·◌·✦·★·❂·◌·✦·✳·❂·◌·✦·★·❂

Reuben stood at the threshold of the cave beneath Gull Island, his heart pounding, as he wondered what had possessed him to come *here*.

His mouth was dry and he felt dizzy suddenly as grief threatened to overwhelm him. Almost one year ago they had been searching for his family grimoire when Gil died. No, when Gil had been killed by Caspian Faversham.

Reuben's legs buckled beneath him and he collapsed in a heap as he surveyed the gloomy cavern. He'd thrown a couple of witch-lights up, and they faintly illuminated the old crates stacked at the side of the cave and the stones strewn across the hard ground. Opposite was the lip of rock that hid the entrance to the passage leading to the narrow rocky strip of beach on the far side of the island.

He leaned back, feeling the cold stone behind him, and remembered how optimistic he had been when they first arrived here, sure that he and Gil would find their grimoire and their old family spells. Instead, there had been disaster and death, and his life had changed forever. Now he was the head of the family business, Greenlane Nurseries, and the owner of the family's manor. He had responsibilities he'd never wanted but had assumed anyway. And sitting in the dark, damp cave, all of his doubts about his abilities were magnified. He wasn't doing any of it as well as he should be.

He looked at the spot where he had found Gil's crumpled body. After all that violence, the grimoire hadn't even been there. And if it wasn't for Avery taking Caspian unawares, there might have been more deaths, too. He rubbed his face with his hands, trying to be rational and reminding himself that Caspian had apologised, that he had been under as much pressure from his father as they had been to find their grimoires. But he couldn't subdue the sharp spike of anger that was always so close to the surface. Yes, he tried very hard to bury it, and most of the time he did, but now wasn't one of those stronger moments.

Bollocks. He was being morbid. He needed to get out of here. This wasn't the way to remember Gil's life. He was also being unnecessarily negative. The business was fine, and he had El, who despite everything had stuck with him. What was bothering him more than anything was his magic. Hundreds of years of the Jacksons' magical legacy was swirling within him, and he wasn't doing it justice. Rather than go to work that day, he'd popped in for a couple of hours and then left, heading straight home, where he'd immersed himself in both grimoires, familiarising himself with the magic that resided in their pages. El had been right; he was improving, and had pulled off a couple of great spells when pushed, but he generally lacked discipline...for magic, at least. He had plenty of discipline for surfing.

The cool stone against his back was soothing, calming his thoughts as he regarded the jumble of old crates and barrels. Another of his ancestors' secrets was smuggling. Maybe his subconscious had known what he needed after all. He remembered the coins that had been thrown at Avery on Sunday, and the death of the man on the beach. Were those events really related to smuggling?

Reuben stood and headed to the old wooden crates, lifting the lids on a few to find nothing but dust and sand. These would have been here since the late 1700s or early 1800s. His family must have been heavily involved in the local smuggling industry; after all, the access to this cave was under the glasshouse. They'd joked about it last year, and then he hadn't really given it a second thought. But now he wondered who was involved? It would be easy enough to find out. Anne Somersby had done the family trees of all the witches. He could match up the dates to known names.

Seized by a sudden urge to look at the sea, he left the cavern and trudged up the narrow passage to the smaller cave. No one had been down here since the events last year, and he could still see the jumble of footprints in places in the earth. He quickly found the mechanism that released the door into the next cave and pushed it open, stepping onto soft sand. A strip of daylight pierced through the gap in the wall opposite him. The sound of crashing waves reverberated in the bare space, and he inhaled the strong smell of the sea, smiling as it lifted his spirits. He felt his magic respond to the water, his natural element, and was about to walk to the beach beyond, when he felt *something*.

Reuben paused, feeling as if someone was watching him. He pressed his back to the rock wall behind him, scanning the space, but there was no place to hide here.

His peripheral vision picked up a flicker of light to his right, and he whirled around, seeing the faintest outline of a lantern containing a warm, yellow flame before something struck his chest. His head cracked off the wall and he fell, winded, to his knees. A strong, weather-beaten hand materialised in front of him, grabbing his t-shirt at the throat and lifting him up so that Reuben's feet were swinging off the ground. Bad breath hit him like a punch, and without waiting to see what happened next, Reuben lashed out with his magic, sending a blast of pure energy at his unseen attacker.

It retreated, and Reuben fell awkwardly. Remembering one of the basic banishing spells Alex had taught them, he cast it at the shadow that hovered on the far side of the cave.

Unfortunately, the spell wasn't strong enough, and the spirit hadn't finished with him yet. It swelled, broad-shouldered and malevolent, and from the middle of its bulk, Reuben saw a flash of steel as a weapon came whirring across the cave.

Reuben rolled and tried to cast a circle of protection around him, but he wasn't quick enough. The dagger embedded in his shoulder, skewering a tattered, ragged piece of paper. The blade burned like fire, and gritting his teeth, Reuben wrenched it out of his flesh to use in defence.

But before the shadowy figure could advance any further, another figure manifested between them, a shape so familiar to him that Reuben froze in shock.

Gil.

He swiftly advanced on Reuben's unknown attacker with a whirl of darkness and magic. They clashed, melding into one, the fury of their encounter reverberating around the cavern. Stunned, Reuben struggled to identify who was winning before they suddenly vanished, leaving only a scattering of gold coins behind in the sand.

Reuben just sat there, wincing with pain and breathing heavily, adrenalin keeping him poised to attack, but only the sound of the distant surf broke the silence. Blood poured from his wound, but he ignored it. The pain in his chest was far worse as the tightness of grief took over, so powerful he suddenly couldn't breathe. When he did finally inhale, it was a shuddering, ragged effort that shook his entire body.

For what seemed like endless minutes, he just sat there, shaking. Gil had saved his life. And he couldn't even thank him. As he wrested control of his body, Reuben took deep breaths to steady his nausea, and then leaned forward to pick up the paper that had fallen next to him. A wave of dizziness dulled his vision, but he staggered to the far exit that was bathed in daylight. Inhaling the fresh sea air, he looked at the blood-stained paper in his fingers.

Written in an ornate script were the words: *Blood will be my vengeance.*

★ ⚙ ⬧ ✦ ⚙ ⬧ ✦ ⚙ ⬧ ✦ ⚙

Newton shone his torch along the dark tunnel and frowned.

"Inez, I'm not sure we should go on. The walls are crumbling quite badly here."

She paused next to him, her own torch flashing around the roof and along the ground. "But look, footprints. This is the way they came."

He turned to look at her determined face. "That doesn't mean it's safe. They were after treasure. We aren't. I quite like being alive."

They had been walking through the uneven, musty passage for about five minutes, moving steadily inland from what Newton could tell. The tunnel turned in places, disorientating him, so he wasn't completely sure, but the slope was ascending, hopefully towards a near exit.

"But Newton, it can't be much further," Inez argued. "This could give us a real clue as to who broke into these chests."

"Could it? Or will their transport and any sign of them be long gone?"

"Yes, that's likely, but they might have left evidence at the other end. We might even get a clear footprint! Not like these sludgy ones that we can see here. They're so trampled, they're unusable."

Inez slipped past him, taking the lead, and although Newton felt he should order her back, he was also torn. He liked Inez's enthusiasm. She was very different to Moore's calm and even-tempered approach.

In places there were trickles of water down the tunnel walls, and the air was damp and stale. Newton couldn't help but wonder how often this place had been used in the past. At intervals he paused to examine the thick, wooden beams overhead, and the sturdy supports along the side. This passage had obviously been shored up at least once. But, he also thought that it had started out as a natural rock passage that had been enhanced over time.

The sound of Inez's footfalls vanished, and he shouted, "Inez, wait!" He hurried to catch up, noting the passageway had turned up ahead. He couldn't even see Inez's torchlight.

A scream broke the silence and Newton ran, forgetting any pretence of being careful. He rounded the corner, but the passageway snaked onwards, and over the sound of his pounding feet he heard an ominous thump and the slither of falling rock.

Shit. Had she triggered a landslide? Had the tunnel collapsed? Suddenly wary of being buried alive, he slowed, rounding the bend ahead cautiously, and then blinked with shock.

The passage had widened, and outlined in the bright beam of light from Inez's fallen torch, something small dashed across his path, rasping and wheezing in a distinctly non-human way. He whipped around, trying to see the figure. It leapt at him and he instinctively swung his torch, his only weapon, connecting with something hard. He heard a solid crack and the impact shuddered up his arm. An anguished grunt and hiss made his skin crawl, and then the figure skittered away. Without stopping to think of what he'd just encountered, Newton dashed forward, seeing Inez's body lying on the ground beyond her torch.

He crouched over her, shouting her name. But as her head flopped heavily towards him, he saw that her skull was crushed and her eyes were lifeless.

Inez was dead.

Eleven

A lex searched the first floor of Caspian's house, hoping he would find something to indicate who had attacked Caspian while Avery was gone.

However, so far he'd found nothing, and his attention wandered as he searched. The last time he'd been in this house was when Sebastian, Caspian's father, had still been alive. They'd broken in to get Reuben's grimoire and Sebastian had died at Helena's hands. It was hard to believe that was almost a year ago. So much had changed since then. For a start, Caspian had been their enemy, and now he was a friend...of sorts. Alex doubted he would ever really consider him one, especially since he'd made it pretty clear he wanted Avery. Alex was a confident man, always had been, within reason. But there was no doubt that Avery was flattered by Caspian's attention. She was far from shallow, but the big house and impressive bank account was something he couldn't compete with. Caspian was also a powerful witch, and clearly charming enough when he wanted to be. Bastard.

Alex tried to subdue his worry. He loved Avery, adored her, and he knew she loved him. He hoped that would be enough.

Her voice startled him as she called from the hallway. "Alex, where are you?"

"In here—one of the bedrooms," he shouted, heading to the door.

But in seconds she'd entered the room, looking at him with concern. *Avery was truly beautiful*, he reflected. Her pale skin and red hair were stunning, and she had the sweetest, gentlest smile—plus a wicked temper, on occasions. She was also clever and sharp-witted. He liked that. He didn't want a simpering girlfriend, he never had.

"How's Caspian?" he asked her.

"I didn't linger. I waited until Eli arrived to help Briar and then left them to it, but he didn't look good." She grabbed his hand. "I didn't wait because I was worried about leaving you alone here."

He brought her hand to his lips and kissed it. "I'm fine.

"No more spirits?"

"None."

"Have you found anything?"

He shook his head. "No, not really. Any protection spells Caspian had on this place have vanished."

"Maybe they were overloaded? Or another witch destroyed them?"

He grimaced. "Maybe. It's weird. I can't even find a trace of them."

Avery wrinkled her nose. "I can smell brine! And I see there's sand down the hallway." She tried to laugh. "At least Helena is not this messy."

Alex noticed a mark on Avery's neck, and pushed her hair back. "There are finger marks on your throat! What happened?"

"While you were being tackled, I was attacked from behind." Her hands touched the marks and she shuddered. "Horrible, cold hands. Helena can't touch me! How are these spirits so strong?"

"Good question," he said. "And one I have no answer to—yet. I presume that witch is making them stronger than normal, and is potentially behind this." He'd been pondering that ever since Avery had left. Of all the witches, he was the most skilled at banishing ghosts and negotiating the spirit world, but right now, he felt inadequate.

Avery glanced around the richly appointed room, looking uneasy. "We should leave. I feel like we're snooping, and if we can't find anything…"

"You're right," he agreed. "But before we go, follow me. It's a good job you came to look for Caspian when you did." He walked across the room, down the hall, and back into Caspian's room, Avery trailing behind him. He pointed at the jeans and t-shirt on the bed. "He was wearing his gym gear, wasn't he? I reckon he'd gone running or something, and he'd been attacked after that. Maybe just before lunch."

"That makes sense," Avery said thoughtfully. "But who would attack him? And why?"

"Something else I have no answer to," he told her. "Is the council meeting tonight? You said you'd spoken to Genevieve, right?"

"Yes, of course!" Avery looked surprised. "I'd almost forgotten that. We'll meet at Crag's End as usual. Bloody hell, Sally and Dan will have no idea where I am!" She checked her phone for the time. "It's after four. I'll ring them in a minute, but I'll take you to the pub first?"

"Please," Alex nodded. He took her hand, realising he'd been very abrupt with her on the phone. "I'm sorry if I shouted earlier. I was worried that you'd get hurt coming here alone. And," he voiced what he really thought, "I hate you being alone with Caspian. But you know that."

"I know you do. Don't you trust me?" Her eyes narrowed with a spark of anger, and disappointment too, he realised.

"Of course I do!" He didn't know how to describe what he felt. And then it struck him and his anger boiled to the surface. "I just hate the way he flirts with you all the time. It pisses me off! It shows an utter disrespect for *me*. He's point-scoring, and he uses you to do it. I hate that, too."

Avery nodded, and her expression softened. "You're right, he does. Sorry. I won't let him do that again. But he is still our friend, and right now he's in a bad way at Briar's. With luck, Eli will have found a way to contact Estelle, and we need to go. Ready?"

He pulled her close and kissed her, leaving her breathless, and then he grinned, happy to know he could still bring a flush to her cheeks. "Yes. Let's get out of here."

Within seconds they were back in Alex's flat, and he fell to his knees as the expected nausea and dizziness hit him. At least it lasted only mere seconds now. Her hand appeared in front of his face. He grabbed it, and she hauled him back to his feet, saying, "Come on, cowboy. We must be due a glass of something after that."

"All right. I'll stand you a glass of wine."

Before the words had even left his mouth, Alex felt his phone buzz in his pocket and then it started to ring, and at the same time so did Avery's. He frowned and headed across the room to answer, telling Avery, "It's Newton."

"I've got El," she said, answering quickly as she turned away, too.

"Hey Newton," Alex said, looking out at the sea from the kitchen window. "How's it going?"

"Badly. Very badly."

Newton sounded grimmer and angrier than he'd ever heard him—in recent months, at least. He'd yelled at Alex often enough when they first met. Alex's stomach twisted and he glanced at Avery, hoping his friends were okay, but she was still talking too, her brow furrowed.

"What's happened?"

"Inez Walker is dead."

"*What?* How?" An image of Inez flashed into Alex's mind, replacing the view in front of him, and he leaned against the counter behind him in shock.

"Something jumped us in the tunnel; she was alone and *I wasn't there.* Fuck it! Fuck, fuck, *fuck*!" Newton sounded on the edge, as if his voice was about to break.

Alex overcame his momentary shock. "I'm so sorry, Newton. What can I do?"

"You can find what the fuck this damn creature is that crushed her skull!" he shouted.

"Of course! But I meant, what I can do for you? Where are you?" Alex was more worried about the living than the dead at this moment.

Newton took a deep breath and exhaled heavily. "I'm with Moore, at the station, but I've only just arrived here. I've been at the bloody site all afternoon."

"What site?"

"The place where the sinkhole collapsed into the cave. Looe."

"Come to the pub when you're done. We can talk. Pints are on me."

"I don't think I'll be good company."

Alex knew Newton wouldn't have called if he wanted to be alone. "You can stare into your pint all night if you want. Just come. I have news for you, too."

"What is it?" Newton asked, his voice suddenly sharp.

"Not now. Later." If anything, he knew that would make Newton come round. "You've got enough to worry about now. And look, I really am sorry. She seemed a nice woman."

"She was, and she didn't deserve that. I'll see you later."

Alex ended the call, but he barely had time to get over his shock when Avery shouted to him across the room. "Alex!"

He turned. "What else has happened?"

"Reuben has been stabbed by a ghost! Just like Caspian."

"*What*? Is he okay?" Reuben was his best mate. The knot in his stomach tightened.

"Yes, he's with Briar now. Want to come with me? It's just a shoulder wound," she added, "so he's okay-ish." Avery crossed the room to him, frowning. "What did Newton want?"

That needed to wait. "Let's get to Briar's shop first."

And in seconds, his guts were in his boots as they used witch-flight once again.

★ ✦ ◦ ✧ ★ ✦ ◦ ✦ ✳ ✦ ◦ ✧ ★ ✦

Avery took in Briar's herb room, sighing with relief when she saw Reuben sitting on a chair, shirtless. El was next to him, pale and distracted, pressing a dressing into his right shoulder. Briar and Eli were working at the counter.

"Reuben! Are you okay?"

He smiled ruefully. "Not too bad, considering I've been stabbed." He nodded at Alex behind her, and then to Caspian lying prone on the couch. "I think I'm doing better than those two."

"Cheeky sod," Alex said, bent almost double as he inhaled deeply. "I bloody hate witch-flight. Who did you piss off?"

"Some hulking bloody spirit on Gull Island." He started to shrug and then winced. "*Ow*. Bastard threw a knife at me and I wasn't quick enough to block it." He looked across at Caspian again. "At least I fared better than him."

Briar had been measuring out dried herbs, but she paused and glared at him. "You've still been stabbed!" She nodded at Eli. "It's a good thing we closed the shop. We've turned into a hospital."

Eli laughed grimly, but concentrated on whatever he was making in a bowl, his hands grinding something with a pestle.

"It wasn't all that happened, though, was it, Reuben?" El said, her eyes serious as she watched him. "Gil appeared."

Reuben stiffened, his gaze falling to the floor, and when he spoke, his voice was thick with emotion. "He saved my life."

"Gil?" Avery's voice sounded shrill with surprise, and she made an effort to calm herself. "He actually appeared?"

"Sort of." Reuben looked broken, although he was trying his best to hide it. "He was a barely-there shape, to be honest, but I recognised him straight away. He tackled the other spirit and then they just disappeared. I couldn't even thank him."

Avery struggled to find the right words, but Alex said, "I'm so sorry, mate. But at least he's looking out for you."

"Yeah, I guess so. I shouldn't need him to save me though, should I?"

"He's your big brother, that's what he does."

"But why now?" Reuben asked, genuinely confused. "I haven't seen him all year!"

Alex leaned against the counter. "I don't know either, but there's obviously a disturbance in the spirit world, enough to shake up lots of things. I'm glad we have him on our side."

"But I don't want him battling other spirits!" Reuben said, annoyed. "I want him resting in the afterlife...whatever that may be!"

Briar lifted her head from her task and watched Reuben. "I think Gil's doing what he needs to do right now. Hopefully when this is over, we won't hear from him again."

Reuben just nodded, his eyes firmly on the floor again.

El's hand was resting on his arm, to comfort both of them, Avery thought, and she squeezed it gently. She was trying to be calm, but Avery could see she was struggling. "What were you doing on Gull Island? If you'd been seriously injured, we would never have found you!"

He looked sheepish. "Reminiscing about Gil, actually. Hearing about him yesterday made me want to see the cave again, so I went." He glanced at Caspian. "I got a bit angry, and then I started thinking about smuggling, and who exactly would have been involved in our family. Anyway, I headed to the cave by the beach. Remember it, Avery?" he said looking at her.

She nodded. "Of course. It had the hidden catch in the stone door." She remembered how Reuben had found the mechanism, allowing them to enter the cave beyond that led to the rocky beach.

"That's where I was jumped." His eyes took on a far away expression. "I saw a lantern—a ghost lantern. Who knew there could be such a thing? And then I was hit in the chest and lifted clean off my feet. That's never happened before!"

Avery imagined not. Reuben was a big guy.

"And then," he continued, "a knife came out of nowhere—with this." He reached into his pocket with his left hand and pulled out a blood stained note. "It says, 'Blood will be my vengeance.'" Avery was relieved to see his humour finally return as he attempted a smile. "Ominous, isn't it? And it left a handful of these." He reached into his pocket again and produced a couple of gold coins, which he handed to El. He added, "I'll give you the knife later."

Alex strode forward, taking the note and scanning the message. "Vengeance? For what?"

Reuben shrugged and winced again. "I have no idea."

Alex looked from the note to Caspian, who appeared far better than he had earlier, even though he was still unconscious, and frowned. "Why were you two stabbed?"

"I don't know," Reuben said. "You're the one with the crystal ball."

Alex looked at him impatiently. "Thanks!" He started to pace. "If restless spirits want vengeance on you, then it suggests that your families must have pissed them off in the past."

Reuben looked at Caspian suspiciously. "I hardly think we'd have worked together."

"You might have," Avery said. "Remember all that stuff I found out about Helena? Our families were all merchants in the sixteenth century, and potentially yours were still in the eighteenth. You could have been affected by smuggling and decided to combat it together."

Reuben shook his head, his face wrinkling with disdain. "But *we* were involved in the smuggling business, from what I can tell. That doesn't make sense!"

"Intriguing," El said, "and worrying. You could be attacked again."

Eli stopped grinding herbs and leaned on the counter to look at them all, arms crossed over his broad chest. "Potentially, you could have been more badly injured than you were, if not for Gil. The spirit certainly could attack you again. Caspian, too. It's odd that he could have been killed, but wasn't. Sounds like the spirit is biding his time...or *their* time. This could be just the start."

Avery saw Alex flinch. "I have some bad news too, I'm afraid. Inez

Walker was killed today."

Everyone gasped, and Avery asked, "How?"

"Her skull was crushed by some kind of creature. She was with Newton in the tunnel that led off that cave collapse in Looe." He held his hands up. "That's as much as I know."

Briar's voice was sharp. "And Newton?"

"He's uninjured—I think—but upset. Angry, actually. I told him to come to the pub later."

Avery's legs suddenly felt weak, and she needed to sit down. She sank onto a stool and used the table to prop herself up. "I had a weird conversation this morning in the shop, after we came back from the museum, El."

"Of course. I'd forgotten to ask about that," Briar said, pouring hot water onto the herbs they'd prepared, and releasing their pungent scent into the room. She dropped the cotton cloths into it, keeping busy as she tried to hide how upset she was. "Did you find anything useful?"

"A few interesting things, but my customers mentioned a smuggler that I read about at the museum—Cruel Coppinger."

El nodded. "I remember that name."

"According to them, he was very active in White Haven, maybe Harecombe too. I think we should focus on him. I'll ask Dan to help."

"And Oswald had news," El reminded her before addressing the group. "They found the victim's car, the one in Fowey. It was on the National Trust car park, out of town."

"That's not close to the beach!" Alex said.

"Exactly," El said darkly. "What does that mean?"

Just then Caspian stirred and groaned, sending Briar hurrying to his side, and Eli picked up the dressing and started to treat Reuben's wound. At the same time, a loud banging sound came from the front of the shop.

"That's probably Estelle," Eli said. "Gabe managed to tell her about Caspian."

"I'll get her," Alex said, already leaving the room.

Within seconds Avery heard raised voices and Estelle appeared in the doorway, dressed in a smart skirt and silk blouse, her long hair brushed back from her shoulders. She looked coolly professional, but her eyes blazed with a mixture of fury and worry. "Where is he?"

"I'm here," Caspian said weakly, as he struggled to sit up. A ray of afternoon sunshine illuminated his pale face, showing dark shadows beneath his eyes.

Briar laid her hand on his shoulder, pushing him back down. "Don't move. You've been stabbed."

Confusion clouded Caspian's face, and he glanced around the room, trying to orientate himself. He finally saw Avery, but he looked quickly away to Estelle, who was now at his side.

In typical Estelle manner she hadn't bothered to greet anyone, instead striding across the room as if they didn't exist. She dropped to her knees next to Caspian, examining his injuries. He was bare-chested, partially covered by the blanket that had slipped as he struggled to sit. His bruises looked worse now, and a large one bloomed across his cheek.

"What the hell happened?" Estelle asked, her voice sharp as she looked first at Briar, and then the rest of them suspiciously.

"He was attacked by ghosts," Briar told her calmly. "Avery and Alex found him, and they brought him to me."

Estelle's eyes narrowed and her voice dripped with disdain. "Spirits? A likely story. Did one of *you* do this?"

Avery was so astonished at the accusation that she couldn't speak, but Briar's voice was hard and her dark eyes sparkled with an emerald light as the Green Man rose in her. "How dare you! I have spent hours tending to him. We've saved his life, you ungrateful bitch!"

Estelle recoiled in surprise, and then she stood, clenching her fists as magic sparked around her. Briar stood too, the scent of earth and old magic pouring off her. Estelle took a quick step back.

Before either could say or do anything else, Eli intervened, stepping between them, his bulk shielding Briar. "You should be more grateful, Estelle. I suggest you apologise."

Estelle squared her shoulders and looked up at Eli as if about to speak, but Caspian interrupted. "Estelle, please stop. I feel like death, and can do without you fighting the people who helped me."

Estelle stared at Eli for a moment longer and then turned to Caspian. "You remember what happened?"

"Vaguely. Will you please sit down?" Despite his obvious pain, his voice was firm.

Estelle glared at them all once more, and then her shoulders dropped. "Go on."

The tension in the room eased, and Eli returned to finish Reuben's dressing, as Avery exchanged a worried glance with El. Briar perched on the sofa next to Caspian, as if to protect him from Estelle, her hand resting on his. Her voice was gentle as she said, "Don't overdo it."

He smiled at her, albeit weakly. "I couldn't if I tried. Everything aches." He pressed his hand to his side. "And this feels like a red hot poker has been stuck in my side."

"That's where you were stabbed."

"What happened?" Estelle repeated sharply.

"I'd just been for a run around the grounds and was heading to the shower, when my protection spells on the house suddenly collapsed and I was struck from behind. The next thing I know, I was fighting for my life against some surprisingly strong ghosts." He rubbed his face and then winced with pain. "It's a bit of a blur, actually. Something struck my head, and I don't remember anything else. I certainly don't remember being stabbed." He looked confused. "I don't understand how I'm here now."

"Genevieve couldn't get hold of you," Avery explained. "She asked me to call you to tell you about tonight's council meeting. When you didn't answer me, and your office said you were at home, I headed to your house. I knew something was wrong when I realised your spells were gone. I called

Alex for backup."

Alex was standing next to Avery now, his warm hand on her shoulder, and he gave it a reassuring squeeze as he answered. "It's a good job she did, too. You still had two spirits in your house. They're both gone now. We found you in your bedroom, unconscious and bleeding."

Caspian looked shocked, and so did Estelle. "What could do this?" he asked, struggling to sit up again. "And why?" He tried to laugh. "I know I piss people off, but not usually the dead."

"I was attacked, too," Reuben told him, as Eli finished bandaging him up. "More spirits. I think we're being targeted." He passed the bloodied message to them and Estelle frowned at it, pinching the paper between the end of her finger and thumb like it carried a disease. "'Blood will be my vengeance?' Is this a joke?"

Reuben shook his head. "Nope."

Estelle looked between him and Caspian. "You two? Why?"

Reuben gave her his most charming smile. "I have no idea, but I aim to find out. And if I were you, Estelle, I'd watch my back. Because if our families are being targeted, that means you might be next."

Twelve

A very examined the grim faces of the members of the Witches Council who sat around the long, wooden table at Crag's End.

Not all of the members were present. Claudia had sent her apologies, as had Charlie from Polzeath, Hemani from Launceston, and Gray from Bude. Estelle was there in place of Caspian, her eyes narrowed with annoyance. The windows were open, allowing a warm breeze to circulate around the room, and it carried the scent of roses and lavender from the garden.

Avery had just related the events of the afternoon, and every single member was looking at her, most exhibiting worry, but Mariah and Zane clearly showed dislike. She shifted in her seat, uncomfortable with the level of attention she was getting.

Genevieve spoke after her, swinging her gaze to Estelle. "How is Caspian now?"

"Better," she conceded, "but still weak. I've settled him at home, and renewed all of the protection spells—for whatever good they may be worth. My uncle is with him."

"I'm glad to hear it." Genevieve looked back at Avery. "It's good you checked on him when you did. He might have died."

"It's lucky you asked me to," she answered. "He was very weak. But it *is* odd. The spirits could have killed him at any time, and yet they didn't. I don't understand what's happening."

"Of course," Zane said sharply, "there is only *your* word to go by on this."

Avery was too tired to argue and just glared at him. "Oh, shut up, you idiot."

Her disdain was more shocking than if she'd argued, and Zane's mouth fell open in surprise.

Rasmus's gravelly voice broke the stunned silence. "Well said. We trust each other in this group, and Avery has more than proven her worth here, as have the other White Haven witches, which is more than can be said for you, Zane." Ignoring Zane's furious face, Rasmus turned to Oswald, who was trying to conceal his amusement. "Oswald, I understand you have been looking into the death in Fowey?"

Oswald nodded. "The victim, a young man called Miles Anderson, was found on the beach, with pretty much every bone in his body crushed. His car was parked out of town, not too far from the coastal path."

"Someone could have picked a fight with him and then pushed him over the cliff," Eve suggested.

"But," Avery said, "Newton thinks the fall wasn't enough to have broken so many bones. And there was no sign of a struggle at the top. They searched quite a large area, I gather."

Oswald continued. "The locals also report an increase in supernatural activity. Nothing concrete, of course, and certainly no ghosts looking like sailors! Just rumours about piskies. But they did say that the young man had been seen about town recently, and hanging around the castle ruins."

"He could have been looking for something," Rasmus suggested thoughtfully. "But it really doesn't give us much to go on."

Eve was sitting opposite Avery, and she looked at her sadly. "I'm really sorry to hear about the policewoman. That's awful."

Avery had updated them on all of the recent news, and she smiled at Eve. "Thanks. I hardly knew her, but it is terrible, and it sounded as if Newton was upset. I'm hoping he's at the pub now, speaking to Alex."

"There are several things worrying me," Genevieve said. "Obviously, these unnaturally strong spirits, and what could be a very destructive supernatural creature. They both seem to have appeared very recently. Simultaneously." Her arms were resting on the table in front of her, and she leaned on them, staring at Avery. "Tell me what Newton saw, again."

"Well, I only know what I heard via Alex, but he said that something scuttled down the tunnel, something small. He hit it with his torch, but didn't get a clear picture of it because it was too dark. But if he hit it, then it's not a spirit."

"But you said you felt the spirit's hands around your throat earlier," Zane said, "and that one picked Reuben up. Therefore, it must have some physical presence. It could have been a ghost that Newton encountered!"

Avery looked at Zane's accusatory glare and nodded. "It's possible. But Newton is a policeman, which makes him very observant, and he reacts well under stress. If he thinks it wasn't a spirit—and he's seen enough of them—then I trust him."

Jasper intervened. "We can't forget that these events are linked to treasure. Guineas were thrown at Avery, there were some at Caspian's house, a few were left when Reuben was attacked, and one was placed in Miles Anderson's mouth. It's seems pretty obvious to me that someone has found buried treasure and disturbed some spirits...and they are seeking revenge."

"Miles?" Genevieve asked. "Or someone else?"

"It could have been Miles," Oswald said. "Potentially he, and maybe someone else, found the buried treasure, and that's why he was killed. This has to be about smugglers! We all know there were a lot of them in Cornwall."

"Absolutely," Genevieve agreed, nodding.

Oswald looked puzzled. "I'm confused that there are both doubloons and guineas, but there must be a connection."

"What about witches?" Rasmus looked at Estelle. "Why was Caspian targeted? Did your family clash with smugglers in the past?"

Estelle rolled her eyes. "I have no idea, Rasmus! You're talking about a few hundred years ago. It's possible, I suppose."

"You were, and are, shipping merchants," Avery told her. "I think it's very likely you would have clashed about shipments." She turned to the rest of the table. "Reuben has caves under his grounds, and a long passage leading to Gull Island. We know his family was involved in smuggling. But, we don't know if they clashed with a particular group. Reuben has already started to look into it."

Rasmus grunted. "I think you should do the same, Estelle. Your life may depend on it."

She nodded, stiffly. "I will, but I'd be very surprised if we worked with the Jacksons."

"So would Reuben," Avery said, dryly. She caught Eve's eye and suppressed a grin.

"Mariah," Genevieve said abruptly. "What do you know about the cave collapse in Looe?"

Mariah looked surprised at being addressed. She normally remained as quiet as possible. "Only what has appeared on the news. The locks on the wooden chests found in the bottom of the cave were recently smashed, and there were the remains of three bodies found—very old ones, obviously. Looe, like everywhere else, has an extensive smuggling history. One of our most notorious smugglers was Cruel Coppinger."

Avery watched her while she talked, not wanting to reveal that she'd seen her photo at Jamaica Inn's Smuggling Museum. She also hadn't told the group about a witch walking the spirit world. If it was someone around this table, she certainly didn't want to alert them to the fact that she knew, or that Alex had walked there, too. She glanced around the rest of the table, but no one looked guilty or worried at all.

Mariah was warming to her subject as she continued to address the group. "He didn't earn the name 'Cruel' for no reason. He and his posse beheaded a revenue officer. He was considered almost supernatural. His gang was called the Cruel Gang, too. They controlled much of this part of the coast."

Avery recalled her earlier conversation with her regulars at the shop. "Including White Haven and Harecombe."

"Yes," Mariah confirmed.

"Why was he considered supernatural?" Eve asked.

"He arrived in the middle of a storm, his ship breaking up on the shore. The locals had come to watch the wreck, as they often did, hoping for bounty, and he strode out of the waves, leapt up behind a local woman on her horse, and absconded with her. This was on the north coast, not the south. She became his wife—somewhat unwillingly, I gather," she said, eyebrows raised. "Anyway, he was huge, Danish—a Viking striding out of the past. Some called him a demon."

"You seem to know a lot about him," Oswald said. "Do I recall correctly that you gave something to the Smuggling Museum once?"

She nodded, unconcerned. "One of Zephaniah Job's ledgers. He was the smuggler's banker, and very good at it apparently. My grandfather was fascinated with smuggling, and an old friend left him all his papers when he died. He found the ledger in the collection and was determined to donate it. Most of them had been destroyed in a fire after Job died, probably deliberately. I just organised it. He told me all sorts of tales as a child. And of course, Cruel Coppinger is well known in Looe. We have a pub named after him." Mariah smiled, looking at everyone's expectant faces. "And what's more intriguing is the manner of his end. He just disappeared into the sea one night, and was never seen again."

"Drowned?" Eve asked.

Mariah shrugged. "A ship was seen anchored offshore, and he rowed out to it on a small boat."

Avery leaned back in her chair. "That's intriguing. So he has no grave here?"

"No. But plenty of his gang would have had burials here. I'm just not sure where they would be."

"This could be related to him, even with that enigmatic exit," Genevieve said. "I'm just wondering what could have set this whole thing off. Something must have happened recently."

Avery said, "White Haven Museum is putting together a new exhibition about smuggling. It's not open to the public yet, so I have no idea what they're planning to show, but maybe that has something to do with it."

"Very possible," Genevieve said, nodding. "Perhaps a researcher discovered something they shouldn't have." She looked around the table. "We need to work together on this. Anything that we can find out could be valuable. Reuben and you, Estelle, should check your family histories carefully."

Estelle didn't look impressed at being given instructions by Genevieve, and she gave an abrupt nod of acknowledgement.

Genevieve's gaze swept around the table. "Is there anything else before we go?"

The council members shook their heads, and Avery noticed many of them appeared worried by the turn of events.

"All right," she said with a sigh. "In the meantime, I suggest we all watch our backs, and enhance our protection spells until we know what we're up against."

★ ❂ ⬦ ✶ ❂ ⬦ ✻ ❂ ⬦ ✶ ❂

Alex poured Newton another pint and set it in front of him, concerned about his friend. Concerned about both of his friends, actually.

Reuben sat on the barstool next to Newton, nursing his own pint. He was stoic regarding his injury, but every now and again he winced, and he used his left arm to pick up his pint, not his right. El sat next to him, casting him surreptitious, worried glances. Briar was next to Newton, her dark eyes that were now ringed with emerald fire, were full of concern.

On Tuesday nights the pub was usually half-empty, and tonight was no different. They had the freedom to talk easily without being overheard by anyone other than Zee, and Alex didn't mind him listening. Newton had arrived an hour ago, looking more depressed than Alex had ever seen him, and he leaned on the bar, struggling to maintain his composure. Since he'd arrived, he'd run through a range of emotions, from fury, sadness, and frustration, to feeling like a failure, and now he'd settled into a brooding determination to avenge Inez's death.

"And worst of all," Newton said, talking to his pint rather than meeting their eyes, "we didn't even find one scrap of evidence to indicate who might have broken into those old chests. It was all a fucking waste of time."

Briar squeezed Newton's arm. "It feels like that now, but we will find out what did this."

Newton turned his troubled grey eyes on her. "We better. I feel sick."

Alex glanced up as he saw Avery arrive, her face pensive but also determined, and he relaxed at the sight of her. He turned automatically to grab a wine glass and pour her favourite red wine, and by the time she'd drawn up her stool, he slid it in front of her. She smiled at him and murmured her thanks before turning to Newton. "Newton, I am so sorry about Inez."

He brushed it off. "Thanks, but I won't rest until I've caught who did this." He shook his head. "She was starting a new life, post-divorce. She should have been safe here."

Avery nodded. "Yes, she should have been. I have a feeling though that this could escalate even further."

"Why? What happened at the meeting?" El asked, alarmed.

"Nothing there, particularly," Avery confessed. "It's just this general feeling I have. However, Oswald told everyone about the supernatural events around Fowey."

"What events?" Newton asked straight away.

"Just local accounts of the feeling that spirits are in the area, and the idea that piskies are stirring up trouble. Oswald did say that most people thought it was just Cornish stuff and that it wasn't anything to worry about, but..." She shrugged. "He did say there was a lot of speculation about the Spanish raids in the sixteenth century. Not surprising, really, after the doubloon."

"But they were much further down the coast," Alex said.

"Doesn't stop them from talking!"

"Any issues anywhere else?" Alex asked, sensing that Avery had other news.

She smiled at him, a gleam in her eye. "No one else has noticed anything unusual in their area. But Mariah told us about Cruel Coppinger."

El nodded. "The smuggler we read about this morning?"

"The very same. He was a violent man with a violent gang, and she agreed with what a couple of my customers told me earlier. He *was* particularly active around here. He also had supernatural associations." Her eyes widened with intrigue. "He arrived in a storm, a hulking Viking striding out of the waves, and left by the sea too, never to be seen again!"

"Viking?" Briar asked, confused.

"He was Danish, and also reputed to be demonic," Avery added for good measure. "Although, that may have been to do with his size. He was massive, apparently."

"Maybe 'demonic' is more to do with his cruelty," Reuben suggested. "Either way, it's interesting. It gives me something to look into in my own history."

"*Interesting* is not the word I would use," Newton said crossly. "Sounds like a bloody nightmare! Three people are now dead."

The witches all fell silent, chastened, and Alex calmly said, "We haven't forgotten that, Newton. But it is important that we have something to work on. We are as keen to avenge Inez's death as you are."

Newton nodded, briefly meeting his eyes, before staring into his pint.

"There's something else," Avery said quickly. "Oswald asked Mariah about the donation to the museum. She says her grandfather found the ledger, and she didn't seem the slightest bit concerned at the question. In fact, apart from Zane being his usual grumpy self, no one looked remotely guilty or shifty."

"You were thinking about the witch walking the spirit realm," Alex said.

Avery nodded, slumping over the bar with her chin in her hands, and Alex realised what a long, busy day it had been. "I was," she admitted. "But everyone looked normal!"

Newton drained his pint. "I can't do this right now. I'm beyond tired and I need to sleep." He stood, his stool scraping across the floor. "I also need to work out what was in that tunnel."

"I hope you're not planning to go back out there alone?" Briar asked him, suddenly alarmed.

"No. I'm going to bed. Aren't you listening?"

"I mean tomorrow. Or the day after?" she said, trying to keep the impatience from her voice. "Whatever it was could still be there!"

"The whole place is lit up like a sodding Christmas tree now," he said impatiently. "A police officer died! SOCO have been tramping around there. It's been searched from top to bottom, and there's nothing there. *Nothing!*" Newton was almost shouting, and Alex shot him a warning look. Suddenly aware of his surroundings, Newton lowered his voice again. "If you want to help me, find out what that creature was and how to kill it."

Without waiting for a response, Newton left, and Briar made as if to move. "I should go after him."

Alex leaned forward, placing a hand on her arm. "He needs to be alone. He knows we care."

"Does he?" she asked, looking upset. "He didn't look like it."

"Of course he does," Alex said softly. "Men deal with things differently. We rage and stomp about, but he knows. He just needs some time."

"So, what are we going to do?" El asked. "I certainly don't want to wait around and let Reuben get attacked again. I've finally persuaded him to stay at my flat!" She shot him an annoyed glance.

"For tonight only," he told her. "I need to look at my family history, and I can't do that at your place."

"You could bring your books!" El said, continuing what was obviously an earlier argument.

"It's not just my grimoires. It's a whole load of books. I have a library, you know!"

"Do you?" Avery asked, looking surprised.

"Yes. I barely go in it," he conceded, "but I figure there must be something useful in there."

Alex couldn't help but laugh. "Only someone who doesn't like reading could look so underwhelmed at having his own library."

He shrugged. "Sorry. I don't even know what's on the shelves."

Avery's mouth hung open, emitting a strangled cry. "*What?*"

"Wow. You've just committed the cardinal sin in Avery's eyes," Alex told him. He rubbed Avery's shoulder. "It's okay, babe. Don't have a stroke."

Avery looked at Reuben, horrified. "But Reuben, you could have first editions in there, and leather-bound masterpieces..."

"I could. I admit it, I'm a heathen. Feel free to check it out sometime." He smiled at Avery, an attempt to appease her.

"This isn't helping," El said, narrowing her eyes at Reuben. "We need a plan! How do we find out what's happening?"

"Well," Alex said decisively, "I think this new exhibition in White Haven Museum is worth looking into. Let's see if we can find out more about it; the theme, who's organising it, etcetera. I know it's not open yet, but we could visit the museum anyway, look around the other exhibits, and ask a few questions. I can go tomorrow morning."

"Good idea," El said. "I'll come with you, while Reuben here fulfils his family history obligations."

Alex was aware of Zee's looming presence next to him, as he sidled closer. "May I make a suggestion?" he asked.

"Sure," Alex said.

"You mentioned supernatural creatures. Why don't you talk to Shadow? She's kicking her heels around now, and driving us all mad," he said, rolling his eyes. "She sees piskies on the moors. Perhaps she sees other things."

"Piskies!" Briar said, amazed. "She's never told us."

Zee shrugged. "She doesn't like to advertise it—and may not thank me for mentioning it—but it sounds like you need help."

Briar nodded. "Thanks, Zee. I'll call her first thing tomorrow."

"In that case," Avery said to Reuben brightly, "guess who's helping you tomorrow?"

Reuben groaned. "You're going to be such a task master!"

"Yes I am! It's your own fault," she admonished him, and Alex tried to suppress a smirk at her peremptory tone. "You should never have mentioned your library!"

Thirteen

C aspian reclined on the cushioned sofa in the informal lounge that overlooked the back of his house, watching Estelle pace back and forth in front of the unlit fireplace.

The patio doors to the garden were open, and the night sounds carried inside—the hoot of an owl, the tinkle of the fountain, and soft sough of the warm summer breeze through the leaves. Caspian had been waiting anxiously for his sister to return from the Witches' Council meeting, and he'd been forced to listen to his uncle moaning about their obligations. He'd been too tired to object, and could only hope that Estelle hadn't alienated everyone. He'd worked hard to make connections over the last year, separate from those of his father. He wanted friendships that were on a more equal footing.

However, Caspian also knew that his Uncle, Maximilian Faversham, resented Caspian's approach, and so did Estelle. He didn't care. They could complain all they wanted. He was the head of the family and the business, and he called the shots. Even now, while recovering from his attack.

"Estelle," he said, more aggressive than he should have been, "you're making my neck ache. Will you please sit down and tell us what happened?"

Estelle shot him a look of pure loathing. "I don't know how you stand that group! We don't need them, we never have! Listening to them planning and plotting all night was excruciating. What do we care about the other covens, or bloody smuggling?"

Caspian couldn't believe her short-term memory; he was still bloodied and bruised in front of her. "Have you forgotten already, Estelle, that I was half-dead when Avery and Alex found me earlier? If it weren't for them, there'd be no *half* about it! And," he continued when she fixed her steely glare on him, "Avery only came looking for me because of Genevieve!"

Max looked sheepish. "That's true, Estelle. They do have some uses." Max was his father's younger brother, shorter in stature, with a thinning head of dark grey hair. Like his father, he had a mean streak in him, but he was also cautious. Years of doing business had taught him that. He headed up their overseas branch, and spent half of his time in France. Like all of them, though, he was a skilled witch, and his strongest element was fire.

"I should have known you'd take his side," she said scathingly, before stalking to the drinks cabinet and pouring a stiff gin and tonic. *That was a joke in itself,* Caspian thought, catching his uncle's eye. He almost never took Caspian's side. They both still seemed to blame him for his father's death.

When Estelle finally turned around, she looked more composed, and she sat down in a deep armchair, opposite their uncle and next to Caspian. "There seems to be some consensus that Cruel Coppinger could be behind this—or should I say, his spirit."

"The notorious smuggler?" Max asked.

"Yes. It seems he had control of this area, although I can't see what that has to do with us!"

Caspian gestured to their old family grimoire on the side table next to him, which he shared with Estelle. "I've had a cursory look in that, in case there's any reference to smuggling, but found nothing so far."

His uncle snorted. "It's a grimoire! Did you really expect to?"

"It's possible," Caspian reasoned. "Spells are annotated in there, suggestions squiggled in corners. There may have been a reference to a useful spell, but," he fell silent as he considered the vast number of spells in there, and the almost indecipherable writing in places, "I admit it's a long shot. Tomorrow, when I have more energy, I'll look in the study. There are some local histories in there that might be of use." He appealed to both of them. "If our business was threatened, we would have retaliated. I take it, Uncle, that you don't remember any family stories about smuggling?"

Max shook his head. "None. But you're right. We would have hit back if our livelihood was threatened."

"But," Estelle countered, "we would also have *led* any smuggling enterprises in this area if there was profit in it. Maybe Coppinger wanted a cut? Or wanted to take over our area?"

Caspian tried not to roll his eyes, and failed. "We were—are—legitimate business men. We couldn't have been thought to be smuggling! We were rich. We had a position in society to maintain."

"So how do you explain the Jacksons' involvement? Avery mentioned that cave today, the one where you killed Gil. They were clearly involved in it!"

Caspian winced, and not from the pain of his stab wound and all of his bruises. "His death was an accident. I didn't mean to kill Gil!"

"Whether you meant it or not doesn't matter. The fact is, you did kill him!" Estelle looked at him almost triumphantly, rubbing his nose in something he so deeply regretted. Something he would never forgive himself for.

"You shouldn't look so pleased about it. I hate that I did—and you should, too."

"If I was in your position I'd have done the same thing, and been proud of it," she sneered.

"Don't be ridiculous!" Caspian struggled to sit up and wished he hadn't as a searing pain pierced his side, and he broke out in a cold sweat. "You have no idea how it feels. I wouldn't wish that on anyone!"

"Maybe Avery can come over and comfort you," Estelle said, uncaring as to the pain she was causing him, physically and emotionally. "Although, she actually can't. She loves Alex, not you. Thank the Gods."

Fury flashed out of Caspian, rising up like a cobra, and before he could even think, he had willed her mute. He watched as Estelle struggled to speak, her hand at her throat, and her lips pressed closely together as if stitched by an unseen hand. Her eyes flashed as she tried to hurl a spell back at him. But he was ready for her; his protection spells were strong after what had happened that afternoon, and more than ready for her magic. Estelle moaned, her face contorting as she stood, and her fists clenched.

Max leapt to his feet. "Caspian, stop that now!"

He ignored him and glared at Estelle. "I've had enough of your vicious tongue. Say one more word against Avery and I'll rip it out!" Caspian blinked at the force of his own anger, but he wasn't about to back down now. Although he couldn't stand up, power radiated from him, and he noted both Estelle and his uncle took a step back. "You have never known love, Estelle, but one day you will. Then you'll understand. You'll know how it feels to have your heart ripped out when you're rejected because you're such a miserable, spiteful bitch. I wonder if that will be Barak." He smirked, even though what he said gave him no pleasure. "I've seen him watch you, and you watch him. But he's far nobler than you can ever be. I hope I'm there to see him break your heart. Now, get out. When I hear your car leave the drive, I'll release the spell."

For a moment, Estelle didn't move, looking at him wide-eyed with utter shock, and then those eyes narrowed with a calculating look that promised revenge. She turned, grabbed her bag, and stalked out. His uncle stood, uncertain.

"You'd better go, too," Caspian said. "Talk her down from taking her revenge on some poor, unsuspecting bugger. I'll be fine."

"I know she can be difficult, but she is your sister. And you're injured."

"Go," Caspian insisted, suddenly eager to see the back of both of them, and realising he could always call Gabe for help. "I need to be alone."

His uncle gave him a long look, as if about to say more, and then he shook his head, put his glass down, and left. Caspian waited, tense, listening to the sound of slamming doors and the whine of retreating engines as they drove down the drive. When silence finally fell, Caspian dropped back against the pillows behind him, releasing the spell on Estelle.

What had he done? He'd crossed a line, and he doubted that Estelle would ever forgive him. He recalled the fury in her eyes. *Would he have to protect himself from her now?*

And all because she'd taunted him about Avery.

He thought he was over her. That he'd buried his feelings too deep for them to hurt him again. But he was a fool. Love didn't work like that. And it was love, as much as he hated admitting that to himself. He had never said the word aloud, especially not to Avery, but she knew. She had to. He'd hidden it for months behind flirting and sarcasm, but the night of the Crossroads Circus, it had broken free, and he couldn't help himself. He looked out at the dark garden, but he saw only Avery, swirling in the centre of the crossroads, majestic with power. And he saw her pity when she looked at him. No, not pity. *Sorrow.* She loved Alex; that was obvious. There was no place for him in her life. Another time, another place, maybe.

What burned more than that, though, was the fact that Estelle knew of his feelings! And Alex knew, too. Alex looked at him with wariness and resentment, maybe fear too, at the possibility of losing Avery. He shouldn't, he was sure of that. But at least he didn't crow about his victory. Alex was too classy for that.

And that meant that probably everyone knew how he felt. Caspian hated that. He felt exposed, raw. And the only way he could deal with it was to embrace the pain of his rejection. At least he knew he was alive.

He shook his head and sipped his whiskey, feeling its warmth softening his despair. At least he had something to distract him now. He wanted to solve the mystery of why his family had earned the enmity of unknown spirits, and how they were strong enough to have breached his very strong protection spells.

With the help of his uncle, Caspian had layered them again on his return, making them stronger than before, and adding in specific protection against ghosts. But he should do the smart thing and call Gabe. Extra help wouldn't go amiss, and maybe he should add additional security to the warehouse, too. It was a huge place, stocked with all manner of shipments and equipment—and his staff. If he'd been targeted here, they could be, too. He reached for his phone.

★ ⚘ ⬧ ✴ ⚘ ⬧ ✳ ⚘ ⬧ ✴ ⚘

"Sorry about yesterday," Avery said to Sally. "Everything went a bit mad after I called Genevieve."

They were in the kitchen of Happenstance Books, making their first coffee of the day, and as Sally pulled the mugs from the cupboard, her face was etched with worry.

"I'm just glad that you're okay," Sally said. "But I'm sorry to hear about Reuben. It sounds like he had a lucky escape."

"Very! Caspian wasn't so lucky."

Sally's face tightened with disapproval. "Well, as you know, I'm not a fan of Caspian, but I am sorry he was injured. But," she reached for the milk, "I'm so sad to hear about Inez Walker. Poor Newton. Is he okay?"

Avery sat in a chair at the table, recalling his anger the night before. "Not really. He blames himself, which is ridiculous, but also understandable. I would, too."

Sally finished their drinks, and bringing the cups to the table, sat down next to her. "You really have no idea what could have attacked her?"

"I keep coming back to spriggans—you know, the ghosts of giants I talked about with Dan. But, it's just a theory. Did you know," she leaned closer, "that Shadow sees piskies on the moors?"

"No!" Sally's eyes widened. "Really? That's amazing. Then the stories are true!"

Avery grinned, pleased to see her friend seemed to have forgiven her for the flash of magic that had scared her the other night. "I know. Briar is going to call her to see if she's seen any other faerie creatures. She could help us find out what Newton's mysterious attacker was."

"Good." Sally blew on her coffee, sending an eddy of steam up, and then sipped it, closing her eyes briefly. "Oh, that's lovely. Just what I needed. I must admit, I didn't sleep too well last night. Events seem to have escalated very quickly."

"They have," Avery admitted. "Three attacks in one day, three deaths, and other than vague guesswork, we're still in the dark about why. And of course, Helena is still missing, imprisoned somewhere in the spirit world." She rubbed her face, overwhelmed by the sum of it all. "I didn't even know that was a thing!"

"I'm not magical, Avery, so it has me worried, for me and my family, and Dan. If Reuben and Caspian were attacked, despite their magic, we would have no chance."

Avery reached forward and grabbed Sally's free hand. "I genuinely don't think you need to worry. The spirits seem to be targeting specific people, for now."

"What about the man walking his dog?" Sally reminded her. "He was just going about his business, and now he's dead."

"Wrong place, wrong time."

Sally shook her head, releasing her hand from Avery's hold. "And that could happen to any of us, too."

There was no denying that. Sally had an excellent point. "You're right. He didn't stand a chance. But we're working hard on this."

"Do you think it's Cruel Coppinger, like Mary and Fred said yesterday?"

"It's certainly possible, but still just a theory. I'm going to help Reuben search his library today. I may know more then." She smiled at Sally with what she hoped was a reassuring expression. "I'll go mid-morning, if that's okay."

"That's fine," Sally said, rising to her feet. "I'll go and open the shop up, and hopefully Dan will be here soon. As far as I'm concerned, Avery, you take as much time as you need, because I think this violence is only the start."

★ ⦿ ◈ ★ ⦿ ◈ ✲ ⦿ ◈ ★ ⦿

El stood in front of a glass cabinet, looking at the objects displayed within it: evidence of White Haven's rich history.

Strictly speaking, White Haven Museum was more than just educational. It was situated in a Georgian building on the hill looking over the town, and in addition to displaying White Haven's history, it housed an art gallery, a gift shop, and a very busy café. The artwork they displayed was a mixture of paintings, watercolour and oil, charcoal and pencil drawings, and prints, all depicting the surrounding countryside and Cornwall in general, and mostly created by local artists.

The room El was currently in was an exhibition about the local industries. It featured archaic farming implements found in the soil in the hills around the town, old fishing equipment, and black and white photos of the farming and fishing communities. White Haven had always been a fishing village, and of course a trading one. Compared to some of the other museums in Cornwall, this one was small, but its displays were impressive, and it was a popular attraction.

The room was bathed in morning sunlight, and as it warmed her, El took a deep breath, feeling the heat ease the knots in her shoulders. The knots of anxiety that had accumulated by worrying about Reuben. She wasn't just worrying about his stab wound; she was also anxious about his lack of confidence in his magic, and the nearing anniversary of Gil's death. Reuben, despite his confident swagger about many things, was deeply unsure of his magical abilities, and although he'd made great headway over the past year, was still nowhere near as proficient as he wanted to be. Or *should* be, considering his family. A couple of months ago she thought that was all in the past, but it seemed not.

El shook herself out of her worry, and looked around the room once more. It was pointless being in here, interesting though it was. It shed no light on smuggling, or anything pertaining to their current problem.

She decided to find Alex. They had arrived together about half an hour ago, but had split up to search the exhibits. She headed through the stately rooms converted to exhibition halls, finally arriving in the art gallery, and found Alex looking at a large painting of a stormy sea, on which a rigged ship with tattered sails floundered. Huge waves crashed on a rocky beach, and men clustered on the sand, watching and waiting. *Smugglers, waiting to plunder the wreck.*

Alex looked lost in thought, and she gently nudged him. "It's impressive, isn't it?"

He looked at her and grinned, looking slightly piratical himself with his long hair and swashbuckling goatee that he was currently sporting. "It is. Very atmospheric." He turned back to it. "It depicts smugglers, though. I'm wondering why it's here, if they're setting up a smuggling exhibit."

"Maybe they plan to move it?" El stepped away from him, idly looking at the other artwork. She stopped to admire a watercolour of White Haven in bold purple, black, and grey, thinking how good it would look on her wall. "Did you see the entrance to the new bit?" She jerked her head towards the other rooms. "It will be in the room at the back of the building."

He nodded, and pushed his hair away from his face, wrinkling his nose with annoyance. "I did. It doesn't give much away, does it?"

"No. But we could ask someone."

"Before we do, come and see this."

Alex led the way across the gallery to the image of a man with a scowling face, a heavy beard, red-rimmed eyes, and dressed in old-fashioned sailor's clothing. His hair was as black as night, and he stood on the deck of the ship, staring, it seemed, right at El.

She shivered. "He's unpleasant looking."

Alex raised an eyebrow. "I'm not surprised. It's Cruel Coppinger. Or an artist's representation of him, at least." He pointed to the small printed card on the wall.

"Wow." El looked at the image with new appreciation. "So that's the demon pirate. I feel he's looking right through me."

"Maybe we should talk to the local artist. It's the same one who's done many of the seascapes, including the one I was just looking at."

El looked at him, perplexed. "I suppose we could, but why?"

"They might have done some research that could help. Could save us some time."

El shrugged. Avery and Alex loved their research, but she was a bit more like Reuben. She found it time consuming and annoying. But, Alex was normally right about these things. "I guess we could try," she conceded.

She saw movement in the corner of her eye and turned, momentarily alarmed, to find it was an older woman in a museum shirt. She smiled at them. "I notice you're interested in our painting of Cruel Coppinger. It's brooding, isn't it?"

Alex stepped back to allow her room. "It is. We were just admiring the artist's other work—like the seascape over there."

The gallery assistant nodded. "Anthony Carter. He lives quite close to here. He's kindly agreed that we can display these in our new exhibition that opens next week."

"We were wondering about that. Will Cruel Coppinger be part of that exhibit?"

The woman smiled, excited. "Oh, yes. The curator has been doing some wonderful work!" She bounced on her soles, a curiously childish gesture, El thought, for a mature woman. "We actually had a remarkable find a few months ago when we cleared out some of our basement areas. I'm sure you know that many museums have so much stock that they can't possibly display it all?" They nodded, wondering where she was going, but she ploughed on. "We found more documents about Zephaniah Job working with Coppinger, which was amazing, because it was presumed that it had all been lost, as well as some other items I'm not familiar with! We can't wait for it to open. This painting will move at the end of the week."

"Wow," Alex said, eyes wide as he glanced at El, and she knew he was trying as hard as she was to hide his excitement. "So you actually found new material?"

"Yes! Such good fortune, and we were so lucky that Ethan was released to help us!"

"Ethan James?" El asked, recalling his name from the photo she'd seen the day before. "Did he assist with Jamaica Inn's Smuggling Museum, too?"

The woman looked surprised. "Yes, he did. He's well known for his expertise on the subject, so it was natural to ask him to help us. He's actually based at Helston's Shipwreck Treasure Museum, so he's here only for a short time, you understand. It means he could incorporate some items that haven't made it into the other museums, too."

El nodded at Cruel Coppinger. "So, he's a big figure in our local history, then?"

"Absolutely! He caused so many problems for everyone. Incredibly headstrong, by all accounts." Her eyes darkened as she looked at him. "And cruel, of course. That's why he got his name. There was a bounty on his head, but of course, everyone was terrified of betraying him."

"I'm not surprised," El said.

The assistant continued, unabashed. "Actually, the anniversary of his disappearance, as near as we can work out, is this weekend, so we timed the opening to coincide with it. Anyway, I'll leave you to it, but there are some leaflets about the new exhibit in the gift shop and by the entrance, so feel free to pick them up before you leave. I'm sure you'll love it."

El watched her walk across the gallery and then looked at Alex. "New material? That can't be a coincidence."

"Perhaps not. Coupled with the anniversary of his death, it all sounds ominous to me." Alex checked his watch. "Coffee time. I'll treat you to cake in the café, and we can chat then."

"You're on. And I'll get a leaflet to look at."

Fourteen

Briar watched Shadow prowl around her herb room as if she expected to find something dodgy, energy rolling off her. Briar was exhausted just watching her.

"What are you looking for, Shadow?"

"Nothing!" Shadow turned to her, her violet eyes wide with surprise. "Why?"

"You look like you think I might have hidden a body in here!"

Shadow laughed. "I wouldn't tell, even if you had!" She sobered immediately. "Have you? Have you mashed their bones into a paste, saved their blood, and put their hair in a spell?"

Briar tried to laugh, but it came out as a strangled cry. "Of course not, you daft idiot! What kind of witch do you think I am?"

Shadow just winked. "Never mind."

Briar stopped chopping the geranium leaves she was preparing and dropped them into hot water, inhaling the scent with pleasure, and then readied the next herbs, eyeing Shadow while she worked. "Are you bored?"

Shadow wagged her head. "Maybe. But I am intrigued by your random spirit attack. And of course Caspian was attacked, too."

"You heard about that?"

"Caspian phoned Gabe last night. He wanted additional protection for his house and the warehouse."

"For his house?" Briar asked, surprised. "I can see his reasoning, but still, I'm surprised."

A mischievous grin spread across her face. "He argued with Estelle."

"Did he? Over what?"

"Her being a bitch! What else?"

That was far too simple an explanation. "She's always been one of those. Something must have happened."

"He didn't go into details." Shadow looked disappointed. "But he sent his uncle away, too. Although he renewed his protection spell, I guess the attack has shaken him up."

Briar had planned to check Caspian's wound later that day, so maybe she could find out then. She changed tack. "Was the warehouse attacked?"

"No. It was as quiet as the grave. Anyway," she said, pulling herself up onto the counter and leaning her arms on her knees, "I'm guessing you called me for a reason, so how can I help?"

"Well," Briar paused, looking forward to Shadow's reaction, "I hear that you see piskies!"

She sat up abruptly, looking shocked. "Who told you that? It was that bloody womaniser, wasn't it?"

Briar laughed. "No, it wasn't Eli. It was Zee."

"Gossipmonger! You just wait 'til I see him later."

"Why didn't you tell us? It doesn't need to be a secret, does it?"

"I guess not. I suppose I wasn't sure what you'd think about another bit of the Otherworld in this one."

"I think it's great!" Briar said, and then she frowned. "Well, if they're harmless. I guess that brings us to why I wanted to speak to you. You've heard about Inez Walker, I presume?"

Shadow nodded, suddenly serious. "Yes. I met her brother-in-law. He was the one who took my statement. "

"Well, Newton was with her when she died, and he said that there was something supernatural in the tunnel—something small and fast. Inez was hit hard, her skull crushed, and Newton was almost attacked too, until he whacked whatever it was with his torch. But, there's no evidence of what it could be. And combined with the man who was found crushed in Fowey..." She trailed off.

"You think it's something supernatural that I might be able to see?"

"Yes. Some kind of Otherworldly something."

Shadow frowned. "I'm certainly willing to try, but I've really only seen piskies so far. Well, I call them *pixies*, actually." She smiled. "They're sort of an unexpected present. They pop up when I least expect them to."

"What do you mean by 'pop up?'"

Shadow spread her hands wide. "I can't predict it. They are there one minute and gone the next."

"Where do they go?" Briar asked, confused.

"Good question. I think it's sort of like what I can do when I'm in the woods. I blend into the landscape. I don't think they actually pass between worlds. In fact," she paused, thoughtful. "I'm sure of it."

Briar nodded. "Have you heard of spriggans?"

"I don't think so, but you may have a different name for them here. What are they?"

"According to folklore, they are small, wizened men, incredibly strong, that possess—sort of—the ghosts of giants."

"Giants? Wow."

"They also guard buried treasure."

"Hence the connection to the current events," Shadow said, thoughtfully. She stared at Briar. "There were giants here, once?"

"According to our myths, yes. Cornwall is renowned for them. Were they in the Otherworld?"

"Yes, but there aren't many now, and they keep themselves isolated. I don't know about spriggans though, or if we have an equivalent." Her face brightened, and she jumped off the countertop and walked to the door. "Okay, I'll do some investigating."

"Well, be careful," Briar called after her. "They're violent!"

"Don't worry. So am I," Shadow said, before she shut the door behind her.

★·⊕·◌·★·⊕·◌·✳·⊕·◌·★·⊕

Reuben groaned and looked up from the old book open in front of him, the words swimming before his eyes.

He was reclining in a deep armchair in front of a large stone fireplace, currently unlit due to the summer heat. "This is so tedious," he said to Avery.

She was sitting at a table under the long windows that overlooked the gardens at the side of the house, and her red hair glowed in the sunlight that streamed in. She looked up at him, vague for a moment before she focussed. "It's great! You have an awesome library."

He looked around at the oak shelves stacked with books from floor to ceiling, the only wall not to be affected the one with the windows. The shelves were filled with paperbacks, hardbacks, and classics with leather covers and gilded titles, as well as very old books worn by many hands over time.

"I suppose it is impressive," he admitted. "Not that I've really been in here for years."

"I can tell. It has an unloved feeling. At least it's clean."

"That's what cleaners are for."

"You should get this catalogued! You could have all sorts of hidden gems tucked away in here."

"You could do it."

Avery shook her head. "I'm not a rare book dealer. I wouldn't know what I'm looking at. You need a professional."

"You sell books!"

"*Regular* books! Two completely different things."

It sounded like a lot of hard work to him, but he wanted to keep Avery happy. "Maybe I should...one day. Have you found anything, anyway?"

When Avery had arrived a couple of hours before, they searched the library and found that the shelves had been organised into categories. They had discovered a section full of books about Cornwall that encompassed a mix of history, myths, and folklore, but nothing that was particularly relevant to Reuben's family history. Nevertheless, they had pulled a few pertinent titles and started to read them.

"Not really," she said, disappointed. "Just information that we already knew about spriggans, Púcas, and piskies. What about you?"

"Only some generic smuggling stuff. Nothing about the Jacksons specifically. This book talks about Coppinger, and he really does sound like he was an evil bastard. He extorted, smuggled, tortured and murdered people, and generally terrorised the neighbourhood. North Cornwall, in particular. I can't imagine we would have worked with him. But then again, our families did some questionable stuff in the past."

"They did," Avery admitted, "but they also did good things. Maybe your family fought with him for the rights to smuggle here. You know, force him back to the north."

"It's possible." He leaned back and looked thoughtfully at the shelves again. "If we *had* been involved with Coppinger, we wouldn't be likely to leave evidence just lying around, would we?" A recollection of old boxes filled with papers in the attic made him sit upright suddenly, jerking his injured shoulder, and he winced. "Ow. I've just had a thought."

"Did that hurt your head?" Avery said, teasing him.

"Funny. There are some boxes of letters in the attic—the regular side, not the spell room. I remember seeing them when we moved some old furniture up there a few years ago. I wonder if there's something in those."

"Letters! Reuben, they sound fascinating!"

What was it with Avery and the written word? "They could be full of boring crap!"

"And they could be full of Jackson secrets!" She was already standing, her face flushed with excitement. "Come on. Let's check."

☆·◉·◌·☆·◉·◌·✻·◉·◌·☆·◉

Alex watched El over the rim of his coffee cup, worried about her. She looked distracted, and although her makeup had been applied with her usual skill, she lacked her typical energetic glow. He knew she was worried about Reuben, just like him, but he also didn't want to pry and upset her.

They were seated under the window on the second floor of the museum, looking out to the street below, a glimpse of the sea visible through the gaps between buildings on the opposite side of the road.

He decided to talk about one of her favourite subjects instead—weapons. "Have you had a chance to inspect those daggers yet?"

"I have!" She dunked her marshmallow in her mocha latte and popped it in her mouth, eyes widening with pleasure. "This is *so* good! I was so hungry, I thought I might die!"

"It's a marshmallow! How can it possibility fill you up?"

"That's what the cake is for, idiot," she said, gesturing to the large slice of lemon drizzle cake beside her cup. "This is an *amuse-bouche*."

"I have honestly never thought of a marshmallow as one of those before."

She gave him a wicked grin. "It's the sweet version."

He laughed. "You've got a hell of a sweet tooth, El. You're as bad as Reuben is with curry. Well, just about anything, really. So, what have you found?"

"Well, I popped in to see Dante earlier, and he agrees that they are late-eighteenth century. The one that was thrown at you has a double-edged blade, which is typical, and a bone hilt. Once I cleaned it up I found tiny initials on it—CG."

"Cruel Gang?"

"Could be," she said, forking a mouthful of cake up. "Or they are the initials of the owner's name."

"And the other one?" Alex prompted.

"It's far more ornate, a walnut hilt, with some lovely engraving on it. But no initials on that one."

Alex was disappointed. "Damn it. I'd hope we'd get some clues from them."

El shrugged, unperturbed. "It was always a long shot. Hopefully Reuben will find something today, with Avery. She has a nose for finding things."

"She certainly does." Alex hesitated a moment, and then took the plunge. "Is Reuben okay? I feel horrible about Gil, and I know I upset him the other night."

El swallowed a bite of her cake, and grimaced. "Hold on. This needs to be warmer!" Glancing around to make sure she wasn't being watched, she held her hands above her cake and Alex felt her magic flare as she warmed it up. She took another bite and smiled. "That's better. I can concentrate now. So, Reuben. Yeah. I think the initial shock has worn off, but it's the other stuff that it has set off that worries me."

Alex gripped his coffee cup. "Like what?"

El stared at her fork, as if she wasn't sure how much to say, and then she met Alex's eyes, resigned. "He's doubting his magical abilities again, and is consequently disappointed with himself. He feels he's failed Gil and isn't living up to his family legacy."

"That's rubbish," Alex said, angrily. "His magic is strong. He just needs to use it more!"

"I know! And I've told him that, but it's almost like he shies away from it sometimes." El rested her fork on the table, her cake half-finished. "It's like he's in denial."

"But he's done some fantastic spells! The fog he conjured at the circus, the spell to find the mermaids... And he never turns away from a fight. He tackled the vampires head-on!"

El laughed, despite her worry. "Yes, he did, with that ridiculous water gun."

"He's inventive! And I never doubt that I can rely on him."

"But it's not courage that he lacks," El pointed out. "He's strong and quick, and very loyal to us. It's his magical self-confidence that is troubling him."

"And he'll only get that by using it more." Alex groaned. "I wish I knew how to help him. He did fight off a spirit the other day, though," he said brightly. "That must have boosted his confidence."

"True." El picked her fork up and speared another piece of cake. "But I think it's more deep-seated than that."

"I doubt it helps being in that big house all by himself."

"Oh, he loves that! He doesn't use half the rooms, but he really enjoys being there." El looked at him speculatively while she chewed her cake, and when she swallowed, she said, "Do you like living with Avery?"

"I love it." He didn't hesitate. "It's the best thing I've ever done, and I'm relieved she puts up with me. I just wish Caspian would back off."

El froze. "What's he done?"

Alex almost choked on his coffee. "You haven't noticed?"

"I've noticed that he flirts with her. But that's okay. You flirt."

His anger rushed back and he wished he could control it more, but Caspian annoyed the crap out of him. "It's more than flirting. He's made it very clear that if I wasn't around..." He trailed off, his meaning clear.

El reached across the table and squeezed his hand. "It doesn't matter. Is Avery flattered? Sure. Who wouldn't be? He's rich and good looking, and is less of a dick than we first thought. But he isn't meant for Avery. You are. And she knows that. You two are adorable together."

"Adorable?" Alex winced. "I sound like a teddy bear."

"You are. In the best possible way," she teased. "Seriously though, I get that it's irritating, but that's Caspian's way." She studied him. "Don't you start doubting yourself, too. Or Avery. I've got enough to worry about with Reuben."

He smiled, properly reassured, and saluted her. "Yes ma'am."

Fifteen

Dust clouds rose around Avery as she lifted the lid on a wooden chest and peered inside.

"Bloody hell, Reuben. I take it your cleaner doesn't come up here."

"Of course not. It's the attic."

Avery coughed, summoned air, and sent it spinning around them both in a gently revolving circle, carrying the dust away. "That's better."

"You're very practical with your magic," Reuben observed. He was a short distance away, opening up more boxes.

"It's meant to be practical. I use mine everyday for all sorts of things." She lifted a bundle of papers out of the box, setting them on the floor, and then sat cross-legged on an old, dusty rug that was probably worth a small fortune, and proceeded to sort through them, talking as she did so. "I use it for protection. I have a spell on my shop to help customers find their perfect book. I warm my tea with it when it gets cold. I use it to prepare herbal drinks depending on my mood. It helps to bolster my garden. I use it to gather herb bundles, pick my plants at the optimum times, and loads of other things." She shrugged. "I can't imagine *not* using it daily, and it certainly doesn't need to be showy." She looked up at him, and found that he was watching her, frowning. "It's like breathing to me."

Reuben shuffled to the floor and started emptying another box. "Maybe that's where I'm going wrong. I don't use it like that."

"What about in the nursery? You said you'd spelled the hanging baskets for Beltane."

"Yeah, I did that. And I head to the greenhouses on occasions at night to spell the plants, so I don't freak out the employees. Gil had a timetable. I just follow that."

Avery smiled. "Well, there you go then." She knew he wasn't as comfortable with his magic as she was, and didn't want to make a big deal out of it. "Try doing the same things around the house. Little things. Spells in your cooking, enhancing your space, that kind of thing."

"Not showy, you say?" He looked puzzled.

"No. Magic is sometimes the gentlest of things. Like when El weaves her magic into her jewellery, or Briar sprinkles it into her candles and lotions. They are both subtle, like a caress." If Reuben was puzzled, Avery was doubly so. Surely Reuben knew that. She tried to explain it better, leaving the papers she'd found resting in her lap. "The big spells we do—throwing fire and energy balls, me commanding air and making mini tornados, huge protection spells, the cleansing of White Haven—they're unusual. Until this last year, when we've been practically forced to because of everything that's happened, I hardly ever did those showy things. Personally, I feel that magic is more effective when it's subtle." She tried to make him laugh. "Sneaky, I know. And also far more dangerous, potentially, because you can do things to people and they have no idea. Which is why we don't, obviously. Blessed be, and harm none."

Reuben's expression seemed to clear, and he smiled. "I haven't thought about magic like that for a long time, but you're right. That's exactly how it should be. It's become this big thing in my head, and I don't think it needs to be."

"No, it shouldn't. But having said that, we also shouldn't forget how lucky we are. We're gifted, and we shouldn't squander that, or neglect it. Anyway," she said, not wanting to lecture him, "you have a huge collection of private papers here." She gestured to the boxes and wooden chests littered around them. The attic was huge, running the length of the main area of the house, with a proper set of stairs leading up to it. The far end had been opened up to reveal Reuben and Gil's previously hidden spell room. The rafters were high, with narrow windows set under the eaves, and lots of old heavy furniture was stored there. The place was an antique dealer's dream. "It's a good job it's so dry up here."

"Yes, it is. It's odd that these papers aren't in the library."

"Maybe they were deemed *too* personal." She winked. "I guess we'll soon find out."

An hour of searching had gone by when Avery finally found a name she wasn't expecting. Both she and Reuben were now surrounded with bundles of letters, old diaries, estate accounts, invoices going back decades, and more personal things, like party invitations. It was a fascinating insight into life at Greenlane Manor. They had called back and forth, shouting out what they'd found, and Avery was itching to start cataloguing it, wishing she had family archives this extensive.

The years were completely jumbled up, letters from the nineteenth century mixed up with those from the eighteenth, and before. Some family members seemed to have saved lots of things, and yet there were big gaps in time periods, too. But now, she suspected she'd found something useful.

"Reuben, this letter is from a Serephina Faversham."

He looked up, startled, a smear of dust across his cheek. "*What*? Are you kidding?"

"No. It's to someone called Virginia."

"Serephina?" He looked horrified. "What kind of a bloody name is that?"

"The posh kind. Any idea who Virginia is?"

"Hold on." He dug into his jeans pocket with his left hand, his right he was still hardly using, and extracted a crumpled piece of paper. "I noted down a few names from my grimoire and family tree."

"Blimey," Avery said, surprised. "That's organised of you."

"How dare you! I do take *some* things seriously. Like getting stabbed." He scanned the paper. "Yes! I have a Virginia listed, as well as Jerome, Adele,

Talwyn, and Lowen. They are names across about a 70-year period—just in case. Virginia, Talwyn, and Lowen are also in my grimoire."

"Super cool names," Avery observed. "Well, this is just one letter. Hopefully there are more in this bundle."

The paper was creased and brittle, and before she handled it any further, Avery said a quick spell to preserve the paper, satisfied when she felt its effects.

"What's it say?" Reuben asked impatiently.

Avery frowned as she read the contents, and then looked up at Reuben triumphantly. "Essentially, after much polite dithering, Serephina has asked for help dealing with the troublesome *Dane* and she suggests a meeting. 'Despite our differences, we have much to gain.'" She picked up a couple of letters from the same bundle and passed them to Reuben. "I think it's pretty clear who the Dane is. Check these out. I think we're on to something."

★❀❖❂★❀❖★❀❖★❀

It was a triumphant group that met that night in The Wayward Son, and Reuben settled back in his chair, comforted by the reassuring presence of his friends after what had been a stressful day.

All five witches and Newton were seated around a table in the back room, empty plates pushed aside and drinks topped up, as they continued to share their news. Briar had told them about Shadow's plan to investigate spriggans, and Alex and El had updated them about their museum visit.

El placed a couple of leaflets on the table. "Unfortunately, these don't tell us much. They've kept the contents of the exhibition very vague."

Reuben watched as Avery picked one up. He'd read it earlier. It was a single-page flyer, basically saying the exhibition would highlight the complicated smuggling history in the region, and focus on some colourful characters.

"You're right," she said as she scanned it. "I doubt it can differ that much from the one we saw in Bodmin."

"I think it will be smaller," El told her. "But it will be more localised, too. They might mention the local beaches and caves that would have been used, that sort of thing."

Reuben laughed. "Maybe my family's smuggling history will be revealed. Although, I would have thought I'd be contacted if that was their plan." It wasn't something he was worried about, but he was curious to know if the tunnel to Gull Island was recorded elsewhere. "I think what's more interesting is the stuff they found in the museum basement."

"Absolutely," Briar said, agreeing with him. "Perhaps Ethan found directions that led to buried treasure...potentially *Coppinger's* treasure. Perhaps he's aiming to keep it for himself."

Avery looked sceptical. "A highly respected museum curator? I doubt it!"

"I guess we'll just have to do more digging," El said.

"I'll look into him," Newton said. He'd recovered his composure from the previous night, although a grim determination had settled over his hard features. He'd listened more than chatted, so far. "You'd be surprised what disgruntled employees can get up to."

"You two are looking very smug," Alex told Reuben and Avery. "Like you've found something exciting."

Reuben grinned. "We have. My stash of paperwork in the attic revealed that Virginia Jackson was approached by Serephina Faversham to help tackle 'the Dane.'" He said it ominously, like it was a pantomime.

"Really?" Newton asked. "Did she say yes?"

"It seems Virginia agreed, because the next letter detailed a time to meet—neutral ground in West Haven, the coastal path—and there was one more letter after that. Serephina thanked Virginia for her ideas, and suggested another meeting." Reuben sipped his beer. "That was it. No details."

"Sensible, really," Newton said. "Anything that is written can be incriminating."

Alex tapped his glass, impatient. "So, there's no suggestion of what they actually did?"

"No," Avery answered. "We searched lots of other letters, but nothing gave us any clues. And essentially, we have no idea if they were successful or not."

"Did you tell Caspian?" Briar asked.

Reuben shook his head. "Not yet. We thought we'd tell him tomorrow. I've decided to go to his place."

"Are you sure that's wise?" El asked. She was sitting next to him, and she nudged him gently, her gaze searching his face.

He knew why she was worried. He'd been furious about Caspian when he reflected on Gil's death, but he'd since pushed it aside—with difficulty. "Our families are linked together with this. We were then, and we are now. I'll show him the letters. Hopefully, he'll have family records, too."

Newton nodded. "Let's hope he has. Your old families and massive attics have probably got all sorts of secrets stored in them."

"I haven't found any others," Reuben protested. "Although, I must admit that I haven't searched all that stuff up there. I will keep looking."

El nodded, but she still looked concerned. "Do you have any idea about Virginia's magic?"

"No. Her name is in my grimoire, but I can't identify any spells that are written by her; I'll keep looking." As much as Reuben was struggling with Gil's death, he had to admit that this mystery was giving him something positive to focus on.

"Well," Newton said, clearing his throat. "I have heard from Cassie. They've started investigating Fowey and Looe, but I've told them to be very careful. I can't have another death on my conscience."

"You shouldn't even have one on it," Briar said firmly. "Inez's death is not your fault."

He shrugged, but it was pretty clear Newton wasn't letting go of his guilt that easily. Reuben also thought that Cassie, Ben, and Dylan would keep digging, regardless of Newton's advice.

"Have they found anything supernatural yet?" Alex asked.

"A few heightened readings, but nothing conclusive."

El said, "We found a local artist who painted smuggling scenes." She turned to Alex. "Do you still think it's worthwhile contacting him?"

"Yes, actually. I've looked him up. He has a small studio on the road to West Haven. It's open tomorrow, so we could go if you want to. I'll go alone, if not?"

"The shop is covered, so I can manage it." El looked at Reuben. "If you're happy to see Caspian without me?"

"I'll be fine," he assured her. And besides, it would be good to be alone for a while. He'd have time to think over the recent events. Right now, he needed space from everyone's worry. He could see it in their eyes. Not that he really wanted them to know that. He smiled and drained his pint. "I'll get another round."

★·❂·◈·✦·❂·◈·✼·❂·◈·✦·❂

Newton sighed as he looked at the body at his feet, her eyes glassy as she stared up at the cloudy night sky above. He crouched next to her and gently shut her eyes.

It was a little past three in the morning when he had been summoned from his bed, and it was now just after four. Dawn was close. He could feel the subtle change in the air, and that intense silence that seemed to fall just before the sky started to lighten.

He looked at Moore, who crouched next to him. "Tell me again who found her."

"A guy walking home from his girlfriend's place." Moore stood and pointed. Newton followed suit, staring in the direction of Moore's outstretched arm. "His girlfriend works in the caravan park, staying on site, and he lives," Moore swung around, pointing to the outskirts of Perranporth, "over there. He's a baker and has an early start. He decided to walk across the sand. It's the easiest route. Not that he'll get there on time now, poor bugger."

They were standing on the edge of Perranporth Beach, close to the Rock Bridge. The girl's crumpled figure was almost lost in the darkness at the base of the cliff face, not far from the path that led to the town. That was the only reason the man had seen her.

"Her face is completely battered," Moore observed, shaking his head. "It's almost impossible to make out her features. Who would do this?"

"Or *what*? And her body is battered, too. It's like she's been put through a mangle," Newton added. "Where's the bloke?"

"At the top, giving his statement. He's pretty shaken up. He thought he'd be accused."

Newton stared at the cliff face towering over them, and the holes scattered across the surface; adits. *Relics from the mining industry.* "Bollocks," he said, as recognition dawned. "They'll lead away from the mines, won't they?"

Moore turned to see what Newton was talking about, and then nodded. "Yeah. The tin mining was extensive here. There'll be miles of tunnels."

Newton flashed his torch across the ground, and spotted some crumpled metal. He carefully made his way towards it, and realised it was the remnants of a grill. "Moore! This has come from one of those adits. She must have come through one of them!" He groaned and rubbed his face, horribly weary.

Moore looked horrified. "Why would a young woman be poking about in those mines? They'd be dangerous, especially if you didn't know your way. I bloody wouldn't risk it!"

A thought struck Newton, and he marched back to the victim again, crouching next to her. "That reminds me," he said, pulling some gloves on and gently opening the victim's mouth. His torch picked out a dull gleam. "Well, this confirms it." He extracted a gold coin and stood up. "Another one."

"She *is* linked to the other deaths!"

"The lure of bloody treasure!" Newton said, infuriated at what people did for greed.

Moore watched him slip the coin into an evidence bag. "Is this her retribution for discovering gold? And is she part of a larger group?"

"Fuck knows," Newton said angrily.

"Someone has found some kind of map," Moore said. "That's the only conclusion!"

"Unless there's a serial killer around here with a gold coin fixation."

"I think we both know this is something else! Your supernatural encounter still hasn't been explained. And something forced that grill and this victim out of the adit!" Moore's head jerked upwards. "Someone has been in the mines, looking for smuggler's treasure—and maybe found it. They must have disturbed something."

"*More* treasure, you mean."

"We've only found a few coins so far, and some empty wooden chests," Moore pointed out. "That doesn't really tell us anything."

Newton handed Moore the evidence bag, frustrated with the amount they still didn't know. "Make sure that gets to the lab early. We're presuming this is a supernatural death, but what if she stumbled across the thieves and was killed? Are there more dead bodies in the mine?"

"Why highlight that her death has to do with gold at all? Wouldn't it be better to keep that a secret?"

Newton groaned. "None of this makes sense!"

Movement up above caught Newton's eye, and he realised the coroner had arrived. He watched him descend the steps, a precise but slightly shabby man, called Arthur Davidson.

He nodded at Newton and Moore. "Morning, gentlemen." He didn't waste time with pleasantries, immediately crouching to examine the girl. He swore under his breath. "She looks like she's been through a mangle."

"I know, and I can't explain why," Newton said, frowning at the horribly unnatural angles the girl's body was in.

Davidson spent a few moments examining her, and then straightened. "Hard to say right now, but the broken neck was most likely the cause of death, though obviously she's suffered severe trauma. She's covered in scratches and contusions, too. I can tell you more later, of course. What was she doing here at such an early hour?" He looked at the cliff top. "A fall, I suppose."

"Maybe," Newton said, uncertainly. "We think she came through an adit."

"Really?" Davidson looked alarmed. "She was in the mine?"

"Just a theory, so far."

"Any ID?"

"None."

"Well, I need to remove the body now," Davidson said, all business. He frowned and then added, "I'm sorry about your colleague. I'll be doing her PM today. I presume you'll be there?"

Newton closed his eyes briefly, wishing he could turn back the clock. "Yes. I'll be there."

"In the meantime, Guv," Moore said, checking his watch. "Let's grab an early coffee while SOCO does their thing." He gestured across the sand to where a café was already opening, ready to serve the surfers who were arriving in the dawn light.

Newton had forgotten this was a surfing beach. He nodded, knowing he needed something to fortify him for the day ahead. "Sounds good."

Ten minutes later, Newton had a steaming hot coffee and a bacon and egg sandwich in front of him. A green wash of colour lined the horizon, of which they had a perfect view. He and Moore sat in a window seat in the nearly deserted café, watching the surfers prepare themselves. Although clouds were rolling in, and the warm weather of the previous few days was cooling, it wouldn't stop them from surfing.

Newton took a bite of his sandwich and tried to organise his jumbled thoughts, but it was Moore who started the conversation.

"We need to find the connection between these deaths. A firm one. Not vague conjecture about *something* supernatural."

"But I did see *something supernatural* in that tunnel."

"I know, and I don't doubt you. But other than gold coins, empty wooden chests, and old bones, we have nothing that *really* indicates buried treasure, and nothing that suggests a supernatural creature killed the other three victims."

"What about the mangled mess of the first guy, Miles Anderson?" Newton asked through a mouthful of food.

"But the second? Although he looked horrified, it wasn't a particularly supernatural death."

"Maybe not, but Inez's was, and this could be." Newton frowned at the rock face, the early morning light illuminating the adits. "What the hell happened in there? Bloody hell. We're going to have to go in."

Moore paused, his bacon butty halfway to his mouth. "Can't we just investigate the adits from this side?"

"We will, but that won't tell us what happened inside." He could see Moore's reluctance. "Sorry. I don't want to go in either, but we need to know where she died. There'll be more evidence in there, even though we risk a supernatural attack."

Moore nodded. "I know. What are your friends suggesting it could be?"

"Spriggans. They're very strong, ghosts of giants that guard buried treasure. And perhaps some very agitated spirits. My friends have been attacked and injured by ghosts. I suppose they could be responsible for these deaths, too." He frowned as another thought struck him. "That girl was young.

Mid-twenties, I reckon. You?"

"Agreed."

"I know her features are badly smashed, but she's dark-haired, like Miles Anderson's girlfriend." They had been looking for her for the last few days, and she had remained stubbornly elusive. "Let's check—just in case."

Sixteen

Reuben looked at Caspian's shocked face and laughed, despite the situation. "I know it's unlikely, but see for yourself."

He handed him the three letters they had found, and while Caspian read them, he watched him out of the corner of his eye, while pretending to look at Caspian's study. Caspian looked better than he had two days before, but he was still pale, and he leaned back in the big leather office chair, his hand resting on his wound. There was a tightness to his lips that Reuben thought was more to do with the pain of his injuries than the letters. He had a sleek computer on his desk, and it seemed that although he was injured, he was determined to work.

It was just after nine on Thursday morning, and Reuben had set out early, wanting to find out as much as he could before the day advanced. On the way into the grounds, Reuben had seen Barak patrolling the perimeter, and he'd waved, the big man waving back before he continued his rounds. He'd thought that interesting. Caspian clearly wasn't taking any chances.

Caspian put the letters down and looked at Reuben. "Interesting. You say you found them in your attic?"

Reuben nodded. "Have you any family letters anywhere?"

Caspian's gaze drifted around the room and then finally back to Reuben. "Maybe. Not in here, certainly. We could look in the attic." He attempted a smile. "I guess, like you, we have all sorts of skeletons up there."

"Metaphorically only, I hope." He nodded to the window and the gardens beyond. Barak was now making his way towards the house, an easy stealth to his movements, despite his size. "What's with Barak? Don't you trust your defences?"

Caspian winced as he sat up straighter. "I have strengthened them considerably, but seeing as I'm moving like an old man right now, I thought it would be wise."

"Yeah, my shoulder aches. It was lucky the blade missed my lung. I probably shouldn't have driven here," he confessed. "Briar will kill me."

Caspian's hands grasped the edge of the desk, his knuckles whitening as he stood. "Needs must. I'll show you the attic." His face tightened as he tried to walk, and Reuben stopped him.

"No. Stay here." A rush of guilt flooded him. *Caspian looked like shit.* "You shouldn't be working. You should be in bed. How did you even get dressed?"

Caspian sank back into his chair, sweat beading his brow. "With difficulty. And painkillers. And witch-flight to get here, obviously. It's odd, though. My powers seem to have weakened, too. I'm not going to risk it again."

That was something to confess, Reuben thought, surprised. It was unlike Caspian to admit any weakness. He was seeing an unexpectedly human side to him, shorn of his smugness. "Where's Estelle? I would have thought she'd be helping you."

"Did you? Have you met my sister?"

Reuben had stood ready to leave, but now he sat again. "But you're injured. What about your cousins, or your uncle?"

"I sent my uncle and my sister away a couple of nights ago. I decided I'd rather be alone." Caspian's eyes were wary, and Reuben guessed that was as much information as he would get.

"Is Briar coming to see you?"

His face softened. "She's already called. Yes, she'll be here this afternoon. I'm surprised you didn't come here together."

"I wanted to come first thing," Reuben said, lying. As gentle as Briar was, he didn't want her company, either. "Why don't I search the attic? Unless, of course, you're worried about family secrets."

Caspian shook his head. "Right now, I don't give a crap. Second floor, at the end of the hall. There's a narrow door in the panelling. I'm sure yours must be similar. Greenlane Manor is about the same era as this, isn't it?"

"It is. Nice to be a pillar of society, right?" Reuben said sarcastically as he stood again. "I'll see you in a few hours. Take it easy."

★·◉·◌·★·◉·◌·✶·◉·◌·★·◉

Avery finished her call with Newton and returned to the shop, trying to work out what was going on.

It was nearly ten o'clock on Thursday morning, and the week seemed to be passing in a blur of death and injuries. She sat on the stool behind the counter, barely focussing on the shop around her. It was quiet, fortunately, and both Dan and Sally were stocking shelves with new books and other goods.

She was worried about Caspian and Reuben, and the safety of the rest of her friends. *Especially Newton*. He had just told her about the death of the woman on Perranporth beach, although she had also heard about it on the morning news. Newton had managed a lucky escape when he was with Inez. If anything supernatural was still hanging around the murder scenes, Newton could be at risk. She hoped Cassie, Ben, and Dylan would be able to detect something useful.

But what could *she* do? She stared absently out of the windows, considering her options. Helena was trapped in the spirit realm, Gil had promised to help, and Alex couldn't risk going again. She wouldn't let him try, even if he wanted to. Someone was searching for buried treasure—and maybe finding it—and had unleashed terrible violence along with it. And then there was Cruel Coppinger. Were he and his gang the vengeful spirits they were dealing with? And if Reuben's ancestor had colluded with Caspian's, what kind of spell had they used? And more importantly, what spell could they use to stop all of this?

A sudden thought struck her. If someone was on the trail of buried treasure, finding caches hidden across Cornwall, then potentially they had some kind of protection; something to guard them against a supernatural attack. *Magical protection.* It brought her back to the witch Gil had seen walking the spirit world. *Was a witch helping them, and stirring up spirits? Perhaps the spirits were meant to be a distraction?*

The bell at the shop entrance rang and she looked up, surprised to see Alex entering with four coffees and a bag with *Sea Spray Café* on it. She smiled. "What are you doing here? I thought you were with El."

He handed her a cup. "She bailed. She's needed at the shop after all. Do you want to come?"

"Yes!" She sighed with relief. "I'd love to see what we can find out."

She searched for Sally, but both she and Dan were already heading to the counter, Dan eyeing the bag. "Anything good in there, Alex?"

"Of course," Alex said, laughing. He put the bag on the counter and opened it. "I'm actually buttering you up. I need to borrow Avery."

"Ah, your penance," Sally said, slapping Dan's hand and beating him to a muffin. "We'll let you, as long as you two promise to be careful."

"Of course we will," Avery remonstrated. "We're just going to a gallery."

Dan had already taken a large bite of an éclair, and he wiped the cream off his lip. "To see what?"

"Anthony Carter's paintings at his studio in West Haven," Alex told him.

Sally rounded the counter to sit next to Avery. "I've heard of him." She looked warily between Alex and Avery. "Has he got something to do with these deaths?"

"I hope not," Avery said, shocked. "But according to Alex, he paints smuggling seascapes."

Alex nodded. "I was admiring his painting of Cruel Coppinger in the museum the other day. I thought perhaps he might know some snippets of useful information."

"I've been doing some reading on Coppinger," Dan said. "Did you know he had a son? He was born mute and deaf, and was a sociopath by all accounts. He liked torturing animals. And he was thought to have pushed another kid over a cliff."

"Really? That's horrible." Avery shuddered. "What happened to him?"

"No idea, and I've read a few accounts now. He's not mentioned. He certainly wasn't rumoured to have disappeared with his father. He might not have survived childhood, or he could have gone on to have kids."

"So there might be Coppingers in Cornwall, even now?" Sally asked, alarmed.

"Maybe it's his ancestors who are searching for the gold?" He scowled at Sally, and in an exaggerated Cornish accent cried, "Pieces of eight, Capt.!" Dan was clearly joking, but as soon as he finished the sentence, he seemed to realise what he'd suggested. "Oh, wow. That could be a thing."

Avery looked at Alex. "Yes, it really could be! What if someone discovered their deep, dark family history, and clues to his hidden gold?"

"Personally, I think it's more likely someone found something in the museum archives." He turned back to Dan. "Did he actually make any money?"

"Lots. In fact, in later years he would pay in cash for lots of things, a mixture of all sorts of currency—doubloons, dollars, and ducats, as well as guineas. And pistols. He paid his lawyer that way when he purchased a farm."

Alex almost spit his coffee out. "The doubloon found in the first victim's mouth. That would explain the link."

Avery was about to have another bite of her pastry, and it hovered inches from her mouth, forgotten. "Who did he marry? Can you remember?"

"Somebody Hamlyn." Dan's face wrinkled with concentration. "I'll have to check. But, from what I can tell—and these accounts are fantastical—no one disliked his wife. They felt sorry for her. She was a victim, too."

"Okay," Alex said, frowning. "Coppinger's body was never found, right?"

"No. He supposedly rowed out to a ship in a storm and was never seen again. His own ship was called Black Prince. I don't know what happened to that, either—or if that was the one he sailed away on."

Avery nodded. "Mariah told us that. Weird, isn't it, that he arrived and left in a storm? It sort of adds to the myth around him."

"I wonder how his disappearance ties to Reuben and Caspian's family," Alex mused.

Sally was brushing crumbs off the counter, and generally tidying the area ready for customers, but she paused, looking between Alex and Avery. "What are you talking about?"

Avery quickly filled her in on what they'd found the day before. "Reuben is going to see Caspian today, and find out if he has any letters in his family archives."

"Wow." Dan looked puzzled, and then suspicious. "The Jacksons and the Favershams working together. Wonders will never cease. Unless, of course, it was a double-cross."

"*What*?" For the second time that day, Avery looked at Dan, astounded. "I didn't even think of that!"

"You're too nice, Avery, that's why. But you should know better. The Favershams are slippery characters, even now, if you ask me. Maybe you shouldn't assume the best of them just yet."

"But Caspian was attacked—almost killed!" she reminded him.

"But he wasn't, was he?" Sally said softly. "The ghosts prowled around, waiting for you to arrive. Was it a set-up?"

Avery's thoughts whirled. She did not believe that Caspian had allowed himself to be so badly injured as a ruse. He was half-dead when they found him. It didn't make sense.

But Alex was already interrupting her thoughts. "Shit, Avery. Reuben is going there alone, this morning! He could be there now!"

He was already reaching for his phone, and he punched a number in and put it to his ear, frowning. For anxious seconds they watched him, and he eventually hung up. "No answer."

★🌑🌑✳🌑🌑✱🌑🌑✳🌑

Reuben looked up from the paperwork scattered around him, and rubbed his neck wearily.

He'd spent one hour up there, and he was already over it. He rolled his shoulders and winced, wishing he hadn't. His injured shoulder still ached, and he sighed as he looked around. *Different house, same attic...almost.* It was a large room with a long, low-raftered roof and dusty gabled windows that stretched across a good portion of the house, crammed with old furniture. *He and Caspian should open an antique shop together.* He laughed at the thought. *Talk about an odd couple.*

Grey light filtered in, the sun banished by the clouds, and he looked around, wondering if there was somewhere else he should look. He was currently wading through love letters and business letters, and it was all so tedious, though intriguing. Most of the business stuff seemed to be above board, and the love letters revealed hidden passions he wouldn't have expected from Caspian's rather staid and seemingly uptight family. He put them aside quickly, feeling like a voyeur despite the fact the subjects were long dead.

He hauled himself to his feet and started to meander to the far end of the attic, hidden in shadows, noting the antique tables, chairs, and old bedsteads, all heavy oak furniture that was solid but dark, and crates of plates and glasses. Nothing looked particularly expensive; he imagined

Caspian's family would be keeping the best objects on display, or had sold them.

He spied a couple of wooden chests behind a stack of rugs and old sheets, and some large objects swathed in blankets. Threading his way through, he ended up dislodging the stack of moth-eaten sheets. They slid to the floor, dragging the blankets with them, and a cloud of dust enveloped him. Remembering Avery's advice, he used his magic to clear the air, and saw that he'd uncovered several bookshelves groaning with paperwork.

Deciding that spending his whole day up here was not an attractive idea, he elected to try using magic again—a simple finding spell, using a piece of Serephina's letter and a pinprick of his blood, for the connection to Virginia. They were related, so it should work. He dropped his blood into a small silver bowl he took from his backpack, added a portion of the letter, and uttered the spell. At first it didn't seem to work, and then as the smoke eddied towards the shelves, he saw a stack of paperwork start to wobble and then slide haphazardly towards the floor. A package of letters teetered out and smacked him in the chest before landing on the floor.

For a second, Reuben could only stare at his feet, shocked. He actually hadn't expected that to work. He crouched and scanned them, ignoring the dust, and realised he'd found Virginia's responses. These letters were all business. There was no chit-chat or social niceties, and they gave no clue to either of the women's personalities, but it was clear that they were determined. Virginia confirmed her interest in meeting, but again there were no details. The next letter from Virginia said she had considered the plan they had discussed and agreed with it in principle, but suggested a different time of execution. But there was no hint of what that plan was. Damn it, these women were sneaky.

But before Reuben could do anything else, he smelt the strong scent of seaweed behind him, and he flattened and rolled, sending a searing pain through his shoulder. A shadowy figure lunged out of the gloom, pinning him to the floor with surprising strength, and strong hands wrapped around his neck.

★.✹.◊.✦.✹.◊.✲.✹.◊.✦.✹

Once again Alex stood next to Avery on the grounds of Harecombe Manor, quickly subduing his dry retch, as Avery hammered on the front door.

They had debated trying to use witch-flight to get inside, but neither wanted to surprise Caspian, or risk injury from his protection spell. They both had a shock when Barak answered the door, and Alex noticed the Empusa's blade was in a scabbard, strapped to his side.

His bulk blocked most of the hall behind him, and he peered down at them, his frown quickly turning to smile. "Hey, guys! Come to join Reuben?"

"Is he okay?" Avery asked, quickly shoving past him and entering the house.

Barak looked at them, puzzled. "Yes, he's fine. Why wouldn't he be?"

Avery's eyes were darting everywhere, her fists clenched, and Alex could feel her power growing as she asked, "Where is he?"

"In the attic." Apparently, Barak could feel her power building, too. "What are you doing, Avery? You look ready to fight."

Alex didn't want to accuse Caspian of deception. After all, they might be wrong. "I think we're both a bit jumpy after the events over recent days. We decided he shouldn't be alone," he hedged.

A whirling blackness manifested in the corner, and all three of them jumped, but it was just Caspian, looking sallow-skinned and clutching his side. "What's going on?" He looked between them all, and then especially at Avery. "Why are you glaring at me?"

She stuttered, and then said, "I read the cards and saw that Reuben was in danger. Where is he?"

"In the attic. He offered to search alone." He grimaced. "I'm not that steady on my feet right now."

Alex studied him. This was no ruse. Caspian looked awful. And to be honest, Alex knew deep down that Caspian had too much regard for Avery to hurt one of her best friends. If he thought he'd stand any chance with her, he wouldn't risk that.

Avery started to speak. "Maybe we should check on him, just—"

"Something's up there!" Barak interrupted her, his head jerking upwards to stare up the stairs.

In seconds he'd shed his t-shirt, revealing his muscled chest, and his wings appeared. They were enormous, the feathers so inky-black they had a blue sheen to them. He soared up through the huge stairwell to the upper floor, and in a flash Avery had vanished, too.

Alex couldn't believe she had abandoned him. Then again, he was still feeling sick from the first trip. He ran for the stairs, yelling, "Avery! Wait for me!"

Even as he was saying it, he knew it was pointless; she'd already gone. Caspian was curiously silent, and Alex glanced down at him as he rounded the landing and then skidded to a halt. Caspian was backing away from a shimmering figure that was coalescing in his hall. A spirit.

Caspian was in no position to fight. In fact, from this angle he looked horrified, scuttling backwards as quickly as his injury allowed. Alex wondered why he wasn't using witch-flight, but maybe he was too weak.

Alex was torn.

His girlfriend and best mate were above somewhere, and who knows what they were facing. But Caspian was here, unarmed and clearly too weak to fight back. Caspian didn't even look up at him. He either thought he'd already gone or was buying him time, because the spirit that was slowly taking shape, solidifying into the lean, weather-beaten figure of a smuggler, replete with old-fashioned clothes and a wickedly sharp dagger, hadn't seen him. The spirit scowled, showing blackened teeth, and Alex caught a glimpse of a long scar that ran down the side of his face, puckering his lip.

Alex uttered the words to the modified, rune-binding spell he'd been researching only the night before, and a flurry of runes dazzled in the gloom of the hall, wrapping themselves around the spirit. The blade flashed, tearing through them, and he stopped his advance, turning to leer up at Alex.

But Alex was already on to his next spell as he ran back downstairs, and runes again filled the air, this time composed of fire. He started to banish the spirit, but it ran towards him heedlessly, his all too real blade flashing in the light. Then the runes wrapped once more about the now snarling ghost. As quickly as his blade flashed, destroying the runes, more appeared until he became overwhelmed, and Alex advanced with his hands outstretched, a wall of power building as he pushed the spirit back, cornering it in the hall.

The spirit was thrashing now, and a low, unearthly moan seemed to come from his core, setting Alex's teeth on edge. With the final word of his spell, he thrust the heel of his hand outward, and the runes started to eat into the spirit's shimmering form. His mouth opened wide in a soundless scream as it vanished.

Alex whirled around, defences raised, wary of another attack, but the hall felt eerily empty. Caspian had collapsed on the floor.

★·❂·◔·✳·❂·◔·✱·❂·◔·✳·❂

Reuben's vision started to blacken, but he was damned if he was going to be killed by a ghost.

The spirit now felt so unnervingly solid that Reuben brought his leg up beneath him, and kneed the spirit in the groin. He wasn't above playing dirty. Besides, did spirits even have genitals?

It appeared they did. It grunted, emitting a powerful blast of stale breath in Reuben's face, and before the spirit could respond, Reuben punched it with his left fist that was loaded with magical energy. His attacker flew backwards, landing in the pile of blankets.

Reuben tried to grab his backpack. He'd brought the shotgun with him, loaded with salt shells, but his hand scrabbled and grabbed only air. The spirit lunged at him, but Reuben rolled to the side, vaulted to his feet, and threw a ball of pure fire, catching it squarely in the chest. It flew across the attic, its clothes smouldering on its withered frame.

But it didn't stop.

Instead it disappeared, reappearing seconds later mere inches from him. It picked Reuben up and threw him against the bookshelves. Reuben grunted, winded, and felt the bookshelves start to wobble behind him. Rolling again, he narrowly missed being hit by the falling bookcase.

But the thud as it hit the floor masked another noise. The door at the far end of the attic flew open, smashing back against the wall. Barak strode in, bare-chested and grinning with malevolence, Avery hot on his heels. The Empusa's sword slashed before him, whirling so quickly Reuben blinked with surprise. Barak didn't give the spirit a second to respond. He released the sword and it flew through the air, taking the spirit's head clean off. It rolled to Reuben's feet before both body and head vanished.

For a second, Reuben couldn't speak. He was staring at Barak, astonished, and the big man grinned. "You okay?"

"Er, I think so."

Avery ran towards him, streaking past Barak who was already checking his surroundings, and she landed next to him with a thump. "Reuben! I was worried sick." Her eyes travelled across him, checking for injuries, before finally staring at his wounded shoulder. "You're bleeding again."

"Not surprising. It hurts like a bastard." He leaned back against the wall, wincing as the pain burned through his adrenalin.

She sat next to him, taking deep breaths. "I thought we'd be too late."

"For what? Why are you even here?"

She paused, frozen, words stuck in her mouth before she finally said, "I thought it was a trap."

He considered her words, and nodded. "I think it was."

Her eyes widened, and he could see the disappointment there, before a steely resolve settled. "Caspian?"

"*No*! Have you seen him? He looks like death. No, this was something else. Help me to my feet, and let's head downstairs."

Seventeen

Newton was beyond tired. His head pounded from his interrupted sleep, and it wasn't helped by the pressure coming from his DCI, demanding results. And burning beneath that was the fury of Inez's death.

He was seated at his desk, which was situated at the police station in Truro in an unobtrusive corner of the building. The best place for the small but increasingly busy paranormal division, apparently. That was fine with him. The less people he saw right now, the better. But he did need to recruit a new officer to replace Inez. He shook his head. *That could wait.* What was important right now was finding who was behind this spate of deaths, and if there was a connection between the victims.

Newton started sifting through the files again, lost in the details of Miles Anderson's life, jerking his head up with surprise when Moore knocked and walked in.

"Success with the ID." Moore leaned against the frame, a triumphant smile on his face. "She's Jasmine Connelly, twenty-six years old, from Carlyon Bay."

"Miles's elusive girlfriend! That's brilliant." Newton realised that sounded awful. "Well, not really, but you know what I mean." He stood up and started to pace his office. "Where had she been for the last few days?"

"Bunked up with their accomplices, I guess."

"If there were any. It might have been just those two. But," Newton sighed, "there'll be more. I know it." He circled back to her file, glancing through it before looking at Moore again. "Let's call her mother and arrange a visit. We need to organise a formal ID, but I want to know a lot more about Jasmine. She's our key, I feel it."

✦·✪·◌·✹·✪·◌·✻·✪·◌·✹·✪

"By the great Goddess!" Briar said, glaring at Reuben. "Why don't you ever listen to me?"

"I listen!" he said crossly. "How was I to know that I was going to get attacked at Caspian's? Can you feel the protection on this place? How did they get in?"

Briar was too furious to answer, although she had to admit he was right. Caspian's house vibrated with magical protection. Briar, Alex, Avery, Barak, Reuben, and Caspian were gathered in Caspian's living room that was next to the hall, the closest and easiest place to get Caspian to. He was lying on a sofa, clearly exhausted. Reuben was pacing, holding his shoulder awkwardly, while Barak, Alex, and Avery conferred in the corner.

Briar turned her attention to Caspian, kneeling next to him. His face was covered with sweat, and he was watching her; he was scared and her fury vanished as worry took over. "You should have stayed in bed."

"I'd probably be dead by now."

"Maybe not," she said softly, sensing his frustration. "It was a good idea to get Barak here."

Caspian glanced over at Alex. "It was Alex who saved my life." His eyes looked haunted. "My magic is so weak."

"It is odd," she confessed. "I know you're physically weak, but your magic should be unaffected."

"Maybe I'm cursed."

"I don't think so. Hush a moment."

She hunched over Caspian, her hands once again on his wound, and she sent her healing powers down through his skin and muscle. She could almost feel the damage, the torn flesh that struggled to heal. Briar closed her eyes, and reaching deep into herself, accessed the Green Man. His wild, earthy energy filled her senses and bolstered her magic, and a gentle heat radiated from her palms. She started to knit the wound together, calming the inflammation. When she was satisfied that was done, she ran her hands over the rest of him, a few inches above his body, feeling his energy. She frowned, sensing it had changed.

When she opened her eyes again, Caspian was staring at her. "You found something."

"Your energy feels off. I don't know why, *yet*. But you can't stay here. You can move in with me."

"This is my home."

"I don't care. Unless Estelle will help you."

Caspian's eyes shuttered. "No."

Reuben's voice startled them both. "Your house is the size of a tea cup, Briar. Caspian can stay with me."

Caspian twisted his head to look up at him. "You want *me* to live with you?"

"Well, not forever. I'm not asking for your hand in marriage."

Despite his pain, Caspian laughed out loud. "Thank the Gods for that. I'd have had to disappoint you."

Briar smiled up at Reuben, her heart swelling with pride. *How unbelievably generous he could be. And to Caspian, of all people.* "I think that's a fantastic idea. Thanks, Reuben." Briar realised Caspian still looked doubtful, and she needed to convince him. "Reuben's place is close to all of us, if there are problems. Better than here. And I can come and see you together. Please say yes."

For a moment he didn't answer, clearly not comfortable with the idea, but eventually he nodded. "All right. If you're sure, Reuben."

"I'm sure."

"But," Briar pointed at both of them sternly, "you are not to overdo it!

I'll ask El to watch over you."

Reuben moved to the end of the sofa so that Caspian could see him better. "We need to work together to find out what spell our ancestors used. With us both under one roof, we can work quicker, and protect ourselves better, too."

Barak must have overheard them, because he headed to his side. "And we can defend your place, too."

Reuben nodded. "Cheers, I think we'll need it." He looked back at Caspian thoughtfully. "I think I know why they didn't kill you the first time. The spirits hoped to get to me, through you."

"That sounds far too organised and sentient to me," Caspian protested. "Spirits don't plan, surely?"

"But they got past your defences, again," Briar pointed out.

"No, they didn't," Avery said, as she and Alex finally finished their quiet chat and came to join them. "They never left. Caspian's enhanced protection spells just sealed them in."

"*What*?" Caspian struggled to sit up, and Briar helped him, putting cushions behind him. "You mean they've been here since I was first attacked?"

"We think so." Avery glanced at Alex and said, "Alex banished one, but the one that attacked me disappeared, and we, stupidly, assumed it had gone. The one that attacked you, Reuben, looked like the one that attacked me. The other one must have been here all along, too."

"I didn't suspect a thing!" Caspian looked horrified.

"Neither did we," Avery admitted. "These spirits are getting assistance from a witch. Gil told us as much. We have to find who, and stop them."

"The good thing," Alex added, "is that the defences you've got now are solid, and we can do the same at Reuben's. Specific spells to block spirits and ward the property." He looked thoughtful. "We can cleanse your house, just to make sure, and then do the same at Greenlane Manor. I think we should all work together to protect your place, Reu. We can go over there later, get El too, and our combined powers will do it."

"Sort of like what we did on Samhain," Reuben said. "Good idea. You agree then, Caspian? You can bring anything you need, but I'd like a few papers from the attic, too."

Caspian looked surprised. "You've found the letters, then?"

"Just before I got slugged by the ghost." He pulled them out of his jeans pocket. "But I want to make sure there's nothing I've missed."

"I'll come up there with you," Barak said, already moving to the doorway, the Empusa's sword in his hand.

"And I can pack some stuff for you, Caspian," Alex offered.

"Thanks, yes please, and," Caspian looked slightly uncomfortable, "thanks for your help earlier. It would have killed me if you hadn't stopped it."

"I'm sure you'd have done the same for me," Alex answered, brushing it off. "But now, it's payback time. I'm sick of being on the defence. We need to fight back."

★ ⑨ ⑥ ✳ ⑨ ⑥ ✸ ⑨ ⑥ ✳ ⑨

Avery assessed the front of West Haven Gallery as Alex parked the car.

It was situated on a side street that led to the beach, just off the main road between White Haven and Harecombe. It was technically part of West Haven village, even though the majority of the settlement was on the other side of the main road, where Rupert lived in the House of Spirits. In this part there was a small community of modern houses, many large, and a smattering of boutique shops, cafés, and the gallery. There were quite a few cars parked, and Avery could see the start of the boardwalk that led through the dunes to the beach. It was a beautiful spot, and she started to relax.

As soon as they were satisfied that Reuben and Caspian were okay, they left Barak and Briar to oversee Caspian's move, and Avery had flown her and Alex back to Happenstance Books. Alex had used his car to drive them to the gallery. Now, as she leaned back in the passenger seat, she sighed.

"What was that for?" Alex asked as he turned off the engine.

His dark eyes were watchful, and the wind caught his hair, so that it whipped across his face. They had driven with the top down, but the increasingly heavy clouds threatened rain.

She twisted in her seat to look at him. "I think my adrenalin has finally worn off. I feel horribly guilty. We should have made sure those spirits had gone!"

"We thought we had!"

"They could have died."

"At least we know Caspian didn't set a trap," Alex said. "What do you think happened between him and Estelle?"

"What do you mean?"

"He was abrupt when Briar asked him about her staying. I know she's difficult, but I get the feeling there's more going on."

He was right; Caspian had seemed cagey. "Maybe they argued about the business. Or, more likely, about us. She was so prickly during the meeting the other night. So superior!"

"Well, with luck, she'll never have to go again." He nodded towards the gallery. "We better go in. Let's hope the artist is there!"

They exited the car and entered the gallery, and Avery paused to take in the clean, white walls lined with artwork, as well as the prints, cards, sculptures, and local pottery on display. They meandered around the space, stopping and starting, idly picking up prints and cards, before coming to a section filled with smuggling seascapes. A large, stormy image caught Avery's eye. It was moody, showing a wrecked galleon half swallowed by the waves, its cargo of casks and crates strewn across the beach as figures scurried around.

Alex was at her shoulder, and he asked, "Can you imagine living in those times?"

"It sounds quite lawless, but I guess it's something you learnt to live with. But these paintings really draw you in." She moved on to the next. "They were doing the locals a favour, though. Import taxes were huge. No wonder they turned to illegal activities." For a moment, with gulls calling outside the shop, and the breeze carrying the scent of the sea and sand in through the open doors, Avery could almost imagine herself on the cobbled quays and the rough beaches as a storm rolled in. "It almost seems romantic!"

Alex laughed. "You would think that! I saw *Jamaica Inn* on the sofa last night!"

He was referring to the book by Daphne Du Maurier, and Avery looked at him sheepishly. "I must admit that the visit to Bodmin put it in my head, so I snagged a copy from the shop. If anything, that book certainly dispels the romance. It was brutal."

"I spy an artist," Alex said, nodding to a large archway and a light-filled room beyond. A grey-haired man with a large beard was seated in front of an easel, painting, oblivious to the few customers who were watching him.

They headed to his side and watched him quietly for a moment, before Alex said, "Excuse me, are you Anthony Carter?"

For a moment he didn't respond as he finished his brushstrokes, and then he looked around, startled. "Sorry, did you speak?"

"Yes, sorry," Alex said, "I didn't mean to disturb you."

He repeated his question, and the man smiled. "I am. Sorry, I get very focussed when I paint."

Avery smiled, amused at all the sorries. It was so English. She wondered how Anthony could possibly concentrate with people watching him, and asked, "Do you do all of your work here?"

"Heavens, no! I spend a couple of mornings here a week, just to be visible really, but I work mainly in my studio. I live close by."

He looked as if he really wanted to get back to painting, so Alex spoke quickly. "You have a lot of smuggling themes. Just wondered if you were an expert on the subject?"

"Not at all," he said, topping his palette up with paint. "I have a keen interest, of course, but I think the images of wrecked ships are quite evocative, and so do my buyers. They're my most popular paintings, so I keep doing them."

"I saw your painting of Cruel Coppinger," Alex told him, "in the White Haven Museum Gallery. That's what drew me here, really. Do you know much about him?"

Anthony laughed. "Oh, that old devil. I know just the folklore around him. He had quite a reputation. Obviously I have no idea whether he really looks like that, but he was supposedly a giant of a man, demonesque, with a fearsome reputation." He tapped his head. "That's how I see him."

"I gather he was active in this area," Avery said.

He nodded. "I believe so. He was expanding his territory from the north, but ran into some trouble here. I think some locals worked against him."

"Really?" Avery asked, glancing at Alex. "Any idea who?"

"No idea, but I believe they were successful—eventually. It wasn't long after that when he disappeared, swallowed up by the sea that brought him! Marvellous story, isn't it? Suitably dramatic!" He smiled at them dismissively, and turned back to his painting. "Anyway, I must get on."

"Of course," Alex said, looking disappointed. "Thanks, anyway."

They walked away, and Avery headed to the postcards and prints. "I'm going to buy a few. I think they're lovely."

"I was hoping he'd know more," Alex said, hands in his pockets. He glanced around the gallery while Avery searched. "It's frustrating. It seems like Coppinger's story is all folklore and no facts!"

She looked at him and winked. "But there's a kernel of truth in there. This was a long shot, anyway. Treat me to coffee?"

"I raise you to a pub lunch!"

She made her final selections and grinned. "Deal!"

El tried to subdue a smirk as she watched Newton stare between Caspian and Reuben, exclaiming, "Seriously, Caspian's staying *here*?"

It was just before seven in the evening, and they were in Reuben's cosy living area that was situated off the kitchen, commonly called the snug. Caspian, looking the part of the invalid, was set up in the corner of the sofa, his feet up on a Turkish-style ottoman. The other witches and Ash, the Nephilim, were seated around the room, and various drinks and snacks were placed on the central coffee table. Newton had just arrived, helping himself to a beer, and he perched on the end of an armchair, confused.

"Yes," Briar said abruptly, trying to head off an uncomfortable conversation. "It's best they're both here, and Caspian can't stay on his own."

Newton frowned. "So there was another attack today?"

El reached for the bowl of chips and grabbed a handful. "I'm afraid so. I must admit. I've been worried sick all afternoon. I couldn't get away from the shop."

"We've been fine," Reuben reassured her.

"You were beaten up by a ghost!"

"All in a day's work," he said, shrugging nonchalantly, despite the pain the movement was clearly causing him.

Idiot. El knew he was making light of it, to reassure her more than anything, but it wasn't working. Reuben was being stalked. A sudden thought struck her. "You know, both of you being here could be a bad idea. You're both being targeted, and now you're conveniently here together!"

"But it's double the magic! Triple, with you here," he said, smiling roguishly.

"Except my magic is not what it was," Caspian reminded them.

"It will be," Briar said. "I think you have residual bad energy left from the spirits, and I'm going to purge that soon." She gestured to the kit at her feet. "I have everything I need."

"And I will be here all night, patrolling," Ash told them. He was currently at the window, surveying the grounds. "With the sword, of course. But your protection feels strong."

"We'll add to it anyway," Alex said.

"How was the gallery?" El asked, disappointed she couldn't go. Zoe hadn't been able to work that day and she'd had to go in.

Alex wrinkled his lip, looking unimpressed. "It was a nice gallery, but not that useful as far as information went. Anthony did say that some locals banded together to get rid of Coppinger, and that they were eventually successful. I'm not sure what that means." He shrugged. "Anyway, the result was that Coppinger disappeared, getting on board a ship in the middle of a storm, never to be seen again. But we already knew that."

"What year was that?" Caspian asked.

"I was talking to Dan about it," Avery answered. "It was sometime in 1805."

"And he arrived when?" Newton asked.

"1792. Dan told us something else very useful, too. Coppinger was so wealthy by the end that he paid in cash using all sorts of currency, including doubloons!"

Newton nodded. "That helps explain a few things. I have news, too!" He had an air of excitement about him, which was unusual.

"Go on, then!" Reuben said, clearly impatient.

"The dead girl is called Jasmine Connelly, and she was Miles Anderson's girlfriend."

A ripple of intrigue ran around the room, and Avery asked, "The first victim?"

Newton nodded. "She's been missing for days. Well, avoiding us, at least. There was a gold guinea in her mouth, too. And SOCO confirmed that she came out through one of the adits—one of the bigger ones."

El frowned. "I thought they were all closed off?"

"They are. She was pushed through one, at speed, I would say, forcing the metal grill out. She looked like she'd been in a tumble dryer. Every bone broken, all scratched and bruised." Newton was pretty hardened to death, but even he looked disturbed. "The force used to get her through there must have been major."

"Not water?" Caspian asked. Adits were used to drain excess water from the tin mines.

"It's been too dry, and so was she." Newton took a deep breath. "And there's more. We investigated her background today—looked at family, friends, etcetera. It turns out that she works at Charlestown's Shipwreck Treasure Museum. Her cousin also works there, and just happens to be the curator of the White Haven Museum exhibition. Ethan James."

"Seriously?" El asked, surprised. She glanced at Alex. "We heard about him when we visited yesterday, but never met him. Interesting connection!"

"It is." Newton looked relieved to have a lead. "I'll be going to talk to him tomorrow."

"Why not right now?" Avery asked, looking annoyed.

"Because there's nothing to link him to her death—other than his job."

"But someone is obviously searching for lost treasure, and White Haven Museum did find previously lost papers on smuggling which he now has access to," Caspian pointed out.

"But there's nothing to suggest that *he* found a treasure map! It could be just Miles and Jasmine. And if I can remind you, I'm a detective. I need evidence!" Newton said crossly. And then he sighed and adopted a conciliatory expression. "However, it *is* suspicious. My angle is the coins. I'll be asking for his expert opinion on them, and questioning if his cousin might have uncovered something. And obviously I'll be watching him closely to see how uncomfortable he looks...or how guilty. I'm sure there's more to this."

"Of course there is," Alex agreed. "There's the violent, probably supernatural manner of their deaths, the supernatural something that you saw, Newton, evidence of the old chests—"

"Dated to the late 1700s or early 1800s. We had the ones found in Looe appraised," Newton interrupted him.

Alex nodded. "There are the other paranormal activities in Fowey, too. And the unnaturally strong ghosts."

"Plus," Reuben added, "evidence that our ancestors colluded to stop a smuggler, *the Dane*, who *must* have been Cruel Coppinger."

"What are the dates on your letters?" Ash asked.

Reuben frowned and swiped the letters from the table where he'd placed them. He grinned. "1805. Same year as when Coppinger disappeared." He turned to Newton. "Is there anything fishy about Ethan?"

"Not that I can tell. We ran a quick background check on him late this afternoon. He's worked in Charlestown at the Shipwreck Treasure Museum for years. No police record. Liaises with Jamaica Inn's Museum, too. He's obviously well respected."

"Don't forget he knows Mariah, the witch from Looe," Avery reminded them.

"Only through a donation," Newton said warily. "I doubt he knows she's a witch!"

"And," Avery persisted, "Gil told us a witch has walked the spirit world! Caspian," she said abruptly, "what sort of powers does Mariah have?"

"Water. And," he sighed, raising his eyebrow, "spirits. Her water strengths make her emotional connections strong, and combined with her psychic abilities, it makes her powerful in that area."

"See! Mariah could be involved!" Avery said, appealing to them all. "She could be the witch who's stirring up the spirits."

"I know you don't like her," Newton said, "but that is pure speculation."

"And so is us thinking that this is about treasure. All we have are tantalising crumbs so far. It doesn't mean we're wrong!"

El recognised that gleam in Avery's eye. It meant that she had the bit between her teeth and she wasn't about to back down. Everyone else knew it, too.

"Where does Ethan live?" Alex asked, looking suspiciously innocent.

"Carlyon Bay, why?" Newton asked.

Alex looked dumbstruck. "The same place as Miles and Jasmine?"

"The very same," Newton admitted, but he held his hand up in a stop sign. "But I am not leaping to conclusions!"

"I am!" Alex said. "I think we should watch him tonight—very carefully, of course."

Newton sipped his beer, considering his suggestion. Finally, he said, "If you know you won't be spotted, then I think that would be an excellent idea."

Alex looked at Avery. "What do you think?"

"I like it, a lot!" She checked the time on her phone. "We could give it another couple of hours until it gets dark, and start then."

"Great," he agreed.

Caspian shuffled in his seat, looking much brighter than he had only an hour or two before, and said, "I'm worried about where the girl was found. Have you investigated the mines close by?"

There were tin mines all across Cornwall, and a warren of them in Perranporth.

Newton shook his head. "Not yet, but we will, tomorrow. Those mines have been shut down for years, and we're worried about safety, but we have a local expert who knows the mines well, identifying where we should look. A small team will go with him." He looked grim. "We have to do this, but I'm worried what we'll find—especially if there's something supernatural there."

Newton looked wracked with guilt, and El knew he was dreading a repeat of what had happened to Inez. "I'll go, too. If the team meet something odd, they'll be sitting ducks."

"El!" Rueben looked at her, incredulous. "That's a ridiculous idea. You could get hurt!"

"And so could they. I have magic on my side. The team going down there won't." The more she thought about it, the more she realised she had to go; her conscience wouldn't allow her not to. "In fact, I insist I go."

"But you might give yourself away. You know, your magic," Newton said. He looked worried, but was clearly interested in her suggestion.

"Who's going?"

"I will, obviously, plus the local mine expert, Moore, and another couple of officers assigned to my team."

"You *are* the paranormal division," El reminded him. *If there were consequences, she'd just have to manage them.* "And you told us that they know you have help, and Moore knows all about us. I'm prepared to do it."

"I'm not," Reuben said, protesting. "Unless I come, too."

Reuben's normally teasing blue eyes were fired up with a mixture of anger and worry, but El wasn't put off. "No way. You're injured, and you have stuff to do here. Where you're protected," she reminded him forcefully.

Reuben tried to keep his anger bottled. "Someone should go with you."

Before anyone could volunteer, she said, "I'll be fine! I know what to expect, which means I'll be prepared."

Alex looked unconvinced. "Are you sure you don't want one of us to come? Or ask a witch from Perranporth? I bet they're wondering what's going on right now!"

"You and Avery could be up all night! Briar is busy healing this pair of miscreants, and I don't want another coven involved. This is the best option."

Newton turned to El. "Are you sure, considering what happened to Inez?"

"I'm especially sure because of that. I'm a witch, none of you are."

"Thanks." Newton smiled. "Actually there's something else we should check out. Miles's car was parked at the National Trust car park by the Fowey Estuary, close to St Catherine's Castle. We haven't found a thing, but Ben said they'd picked up odd readings there. Maybe," he looked at Alex and Avery hopefully, "you could check it out tonight, while you're up that way."

"Sounds like a plan," Alex said, looking at Avery for her approval and getting it. "I think you're right, El. This could be a long night for both of us."

Eighteen

A very and Alex pulled to a halt on a quiet street in a housing estate in Carlyon Bay, just to the north of Charlestown.

It had been years since Avery had visited Charlestown, and she had forgotten what a charming place it was. They had driven through it before heading to Ethan James's house, passing the Shipwreck Treasure Museum. It was obviously closed, but it was a large place, very well maintained, and it also had a clay mines exhibit, too.

"Maybe we should visit the museum tomorrow," she suggested as she settled herself in the passenger seat of her van, ready to watch James's house. Alex had offered to drive, and she was pleased to not have to concentrate on the drive.

He shook his head. "I'm giving up on museum visits. Whatever's going on now certainly won't be advertised in there."

"I guess you're right," Avery admitted, feeling like they were still clueless. "I think this might be useless, too. What if he sits inside all night? We'll learn nothing."

"If nothing happens tonight, we come back tomorrow." He turned to her, and she saw his frown in the light from the street lamp. "Jasmine was his cousin. It's too much of a coincidence. Potentially, if he's involved, he'll be laying low tonight."

"Do you think he was there when she died?"

"Perhaps. If he was, he might be terrified. It could spell the end of whatever's going on."

Avery stared down the street, not really focussing on the houses in front of her, instead imagining the mangled body of Jasmine. "So far, all of this is happening on the south coast. I'm a bit baffled as to why Perranporth is involved."

"It's an almost straight run across the country. Maybe whoever hid this treasure wanted to spread it around in an effort to confuse anyone who might search for it. Well, other than those who were meant to find it."

"So, you think Ethan has stumbled upon a map or clues or something?"

"He must have!" Alex barked a laugh. "This is so suburban, though. It's hard to think there's skulduggery among the hedgerows!"

"I guess his house is at least a bit more secluded," Avery noted. "But you're right. A nosey neighbour would spot something."

"I've already noted twitching curtains," Alex confessed. "Let's throw a veil of illusion over the van, before somcone calls the police on us."

They combined their magic, and with a whoosh, a shadow swept over them, and by mutual agreement they fell into silence to watch the house. Unfortunately, an hour later, nothing had happened, except someone had walked past with their dog.

"I can't even see a light on in the house," Avery said, feeling restless and stretching the kinks out of her shoulders.

"Maybe he's out."

"Or we're too early for him to be going out, and he's lurking in a back room." Avery glanced at her watch. "It's close to half past eleven. Maybe we should head to Fowey and come back here later."

"Agreed," Alex said. He turned the engine on and pulled out, and Avery quickly dropped the spell.

Avery studied the isolated spot as Alex parked. The National Trust car park in Fowey was situated down a country lane, offering access to the woods, walks, and the coastal path. It was pitch black outside, and they were completely alone. When they stepped out of the van, Alex flashed his torch around. A light breeze blew off the sea, and the land seemed hushed around them.

He lowered his voice, seemingly hesitant to disturb the silence. "This will be a tricky walk in the dark to the castle."

"I could fly us there."

Alex's tone dripped with sarcasm. "Fantastic. I'm so glad you learned to fly."

She poked him in the ribs. "I'm very useful, you know that!"

"That's the only reason I keep hold of you," he teased her, kissing the top of her head affectionately. "And maybe a few other things."

"You're so cheeky, Mr Bonneville!"

"I know. Isn't that why you love me?"

"Most of the time. Your cooking helps."

He laughed at that, but a wild cry disturbed the night, and Avery whirled around.

"It's just a fox," Alex reassured her, "from over the fields."

"Of course," she said, feeling like a fool. "Sorry, I'm jumpy!"

They walked to the start of the track that led to the cliff top, and the moon edged from behind a cloud, lighting the landscape.

Alex gave a small cheer, and she could hear the relief in his voice. "We can see enough in this light. I think we should walk some of it, or at least head into the woods first. Miles was here for a reason. We need to find it."

"Agreed," Avery said, "but I also know you're avoiding witch-flight."

"So would you if it made you sick."

She laughed, and pointed in the direction of Coombe Farm Bed and Breakfast. "Let's head that way. The path will lead us through the woods to the coastal path and the castle."

Alex turned his torch off, and once beneath the trees, the night sounds erupted around them. They both draped themselves in shadows and progressed quietly, Avery raising her awareness as she searched for any sign of magic. They had been walking for several minutes when she detected a strange energy.

She placed her hand on Alex's arm. "Do you feel that?"

"I think so," he said cautiously.

She grabbed his hand. "Come on."

Their progress slowed as the path began to get harder to find in the dark, but she followed what increasingly felt like wild magic, finally plunging into the undergrowth.

"This way."

"We're going off the path!"

"The magic is getting stronger! I have to follow it," she whispered back, afraid to break the spell that seemed to have fallen around them.

Without another word she forged onwards, fighting past branches and tripping over tree roots until they came to a clearing that led to the sea. She could see the moonlight on the waves and hear the crash of the surf, and still following the wild magic, headed closer to the coast before veering back into a dense patch of trees. She finally halted in front of a jumble of huge boulders.

"What's going on?" Alex asked, turning on his torch again.

"Can't you feel it? We're surrounded by old magic—ancient magic! It's at its most powerful here!"

"I don't know how you do that," Alex confessed. "I don't feel it as strongly as you." He played his torch across the area before them. "You know, this looks like a collapsed tower to me, or a folly?"

Avery squinted at the jumble of stones. "You might be right!"

"Okay. You focus on the magic, I'll hunt around."

Avery quieted her mind, wishing Briar were with them, as she was more attuned to the earth. She slipped her boots off, wriggled her toes into the loam, and then lifted her arms to call the air, her most powerful element.

For a moment, she tuned out the soft scurrying of night creatures, the barks of the foxes, and even the sounds of the surf, and enveloped herself within the two elements. The earth warmed her feet and the air caressed her cheek, carrying the promise of secrets about to be uncovered. And then she felt a current of damp, stale air trickling somewhere ahead of her, and something hollow beneath her feet.

Terrified she would lose the sensations if she moved too quickly, she waited, slowing her breathing and letting her awareness strengthen, like a signal. The scent of musty air escaping from somewhere beneath the earth grew stronger and Avery walked, almost in a dream state towards it. She ignored the sharp stones beneath her feet, winding around the rocks until she came to the far side. Again, she felt the wild magic swell around her.

Alex had completed his search and followed her cautiously, and now he stopped too, flashing his torch around. "What have you found?"

She pointed a couple of feet away to the base of a block of stone. "I feel something hollow beneath us, and I think the entrance is there. It must be a tunnel!"

The scent of things long buried was stronger now.

Avery went to advance, but Alex's arm flew out to stop her. "Wait." He trod forward, carefully testing the ground with his weight, and examining the earth underfoot before he nodded. "Okay, it feels fine."

"Stand back. I'm going to use air to move that. I'm sure there's an entrance beneath it."

"It's huge! Are you sure you can?"

She nodded, excitement stirring her blood. "I'm sure."

They scooted back several feet, and then Avery gathered wind around her, directing it forward and shaping it like a giant lever. She had never used her magic quite like this before, but her intent was clear. Slowly, the stone trembled and moved as the edge lifted slightly. As the balance started to change, she levered more forcefully until it tipped and rolled, revealing a narrow rift in the ground ahead.

★·✹·◌·✦·✹·◌·✱·✹·◌·✱·✹

Caspian stirred in bed, wondering for a second where he was. The bed felt different, as did the space around him, and he experienced a moment of confusion before remembering he was at Reuben's place.

Ugh. Briar's potion was strong! But, to be fair, it was just what he needed. He hadn't slept well for days, and he needed deep, healing sleep. But, it was certainly too early to get up now. It was still dark outside. He squinted at the clock next to him. 1:00am. Crap. Why the hell was he awake now? He flopped back down on the pillow, relieved that the pain from his stab wound was now a dull ache rather than something sharp, and he felt stronger. Whatever residual effects the fight had caused, Briar had cleared them out. She really was an excellent healer.

Caspian squeezed his eyes shut in an effort to block out thoughts of the last few days, causing stars to speckle his vision. He couldn't believe he was sleeping in Reuben's home, or that he hadn't heard from Estelle yet. Although, he shouldn't really be surprised. He had let his temper get the best of him. He was used to her digs and scathing mockery. Nothing ever pleased her. But the comment about Avery was simply one too many.

Avery.

It didn't matter what he did, his thoughts always circled back to her. He saw her in his mind's eye. Her pale, freckle-dusted skin, red hair, and laughing green eyes. She was strong, yet so kind, and he saw a determination within her not to give up on their friendship, despite his feelings. A dull ache returned in his heart. That kind of thinking would do no good.

A strange noise disturbed his thoughts, and suddenly awake, he sat up in bed. But the room was silent, and he felt the weight of the protection spell wrapping around the house like a warm blanket. Earlier that evening, they had combined their magic, adding another layer of protection that repelled ghosts. Nothing was entering Reuben's house uninvited.

He heard the noise again, but it was coming from the garden. He got out of bed and padded to the window, pulling back the heavy curtains to look over the long lawns at the back of the house. The noise was louder there, a kind a whispering or shushing that had nothing to do with the surf crashing on the cliffs at the garden's edge. Something shimmered to his right, and he focussed on the glasshouse, dappled in moonlight. A spectral body emerged from the shadows, accompanied by a dull clinking. It seemed to limp, or rather, lurch across the garden. And then there was another, and another. They were half-formed ghosts that seemed to hover between worlds. One of them looked up and Caspian stepped back, alarmed, but it was too late. It had seen him, and it fixed him with a malignant grin as a shaft of moonlight fell on it fully.

It was the ghost of a smuggler, dressed in nineteenth-century clothes, the glint of metal in his hands, and fire in his eyes. Next to him, his fellow looters lined up, half a dozen in all, looking up at his window. Then they separated as they made their way towards the house.

Caspian's mouth went dry. They were planning to attack.

Nineteen

Alex insisted on leading the way down the steep stairway that led into blackness. A witch-light bobbed ahead of him, revealing rough-hewn walls and stone steps worn smooth from the passage of many feet.

They had blanketed the tunnel entrance with a protection spell, although they hoped that in the woods in the middle of the night, no one would find it. Fire was balled in Alex's hands and he cautiously advanced, Avery on his heels. The air was stale, but every now and again he smelled the sea.

Avery whispered, "This must go down to the beach!"

"It also must have blocked access through, or everyone would know about this."

The lights caused their shadows to flicker wildly, and Alex proceeded slowly, wary of attack by a supernatural creature. But so far, nothing stirred. Eventually they reached a short passage, and there they had to make a decision. Steps headed downwards again, but another passageway branched to the left.

"Shit. Which way?" he said to Avery.

She threw a witch-light down the passage, watching as it illuminated around a bend.

Her eyes gleamed. "That could lead to St Catherine's Castle. It's the right direction—I think. If I'm not utterly disorientated."

He nodded. "I think you're right."

"But I suggest down first. Then, depending what we find, we go there next."

Alex was already pointing his torch down the steps, sending another witch-light ahead. It revealed more uneven rock walls and smooth steps, and also something else. He frowned. The darkness stirred below.

"Avery," he whispered, retreating into her, "I think there's something down there."

"There's something the other way, too. I can feel it."

"What? Where?"

Hardly daring to turn away from whatever was below him, he followed Avery's stare. Alarmed, Alex saw the witch-light still visible at the bend, and in its pale illumination, a shadow stretched and changed, becoming outlandishly large in the tight space. He glanced down the stairs, horrified to see something approaching from down there, too.

"Shit, Avery, we need to back up—"

Before he could even finish his sentence, the unknown attacker was streaking up the stairs, and without hesitation, Alex hurled a fireball.

In seconds, chaos erupted as they fought off their attackers.

A small but surprisingly strong creature had smacked into Alex's chest, throwing him to the ground. The ugliest, wizened little creature was furiously grappling with him, and wild eyes stared into his. It grabbed Alex's head between its strong hands and squeezed. Terrified his brains were about to be turned to mush, Alex thrust a powerful surge of magic under the creature, and threw it against the rocky ceiling, pinning it there while it writhed with frustration, snapping and snarling like a rapid dog.

"You didn't expect *that*, did you?" Alex yelled.

Avery was engaged in her own battle next to him, rolling down the tunnel in a blur of limbs. But he couldn't help her, not yet.

From out of nowhere, the spriggan—because that's what Alex was sure it was—produced a giant club and swung it wildly, narrowly missing Alex's head. Its shadow stretched and elongated, and its shadow-arms reached for

Alex's throat. With horror, Alex realised he could feel the cold, clammy fingers on his skin, and he grasped one of the shadow-limbs with his free hand, trying to loosen its steely grip.

What the hell kind of power did this creature have?

Alex quickly decided that guile was needed, not strength. Mentally rifling through his store of spells, he uttered one to send the spriggan to sleep. At first it didn't seem to work, but he repeated it, full of intent and conviction, and with a snap, the creature fell unconscious and Alex let it drop to the floor. He turned to see if he could help Avery, but she had finally succeeded in wrapping her attacker in a twisting mini-tornado, and it whirled in place, a bundle of limbs and shrieks as it tried to break free. Alex levelled his spell at it, and within seconds it too fell unconscious, and Avery lowered the creature to the ground.

Avery was lying on the floor, covered in dirt. "Bloody hell! They are strong! They look like Gollum in *Lord of the Rings*!"

Alex laughed and pulled her to her feet. "Did it whisper '*my precious*' to you?"

"Fortunately not, but it was a vicious little thing." She dusted herself down, and eyed their slumped bodies suspiciously. "What did you do to them?"

"Put them to sleep. I couldn't bring myself to kill them." He walked over to one and crouched to examine it. "It really does look like a little old man, except for the weirdly large baby head. They have to be spriggans!"

Avery joined him, tentatively turning it over with her foot. "I agree. Look at its scrawny little limbs. How can it be so strong?"

"Maybe they really are the ghosts of giants in some strange, miniature form? That one produced a club from nowhere and tried to smash my head with it. And its shadow could grab me, too!"

"And they can manipulate their shadows to grow. It's no wonder Inez and the other victims didn't stand a chance, if that's what they faced!" She frowned at Alex. "How long will your spell hold?"

"A couple of hours I hope, but let's bind them with magic, too."

"I hate to say this, but they're too dangerous to keep alive."

"They've lived down here long enough without causing harm. It's only because we've disturbed them."

"True." But Avery still looked worried. "Let's bind them for now, and see what's down here. If *they're* still here, then maybe there's treasure. Potentially, we could use another type of binding spell to restrict their strength long term."

They worked quickly, binding both spriggans with strong webs of magic, and hoping there were no more waiting for them, headed down the steps.

★ ⑨ ⬦ ✳ ⑨ ⬦ ✶ ⑨ ⬦ ✳ ⑨

El stood next to Briar, Reuben, Caspian and Ash, staring through the patio doors in the snug, out to the back garden. Briar had opted to stay over that night, weary after her healing spells.

"I can't see a thing," Reuben confessed.

"Trust me. There were at least half a dozen," Caspian said.

They had all thrown on jeans and t-shirts, and El and Ash clasped the Empusa's swords.

"I can't see them, even with my sword," El said. She stepped closer to the window, trying to see down the side of the house. "The good thing is, our protection feels strong. They won't get in."

Ash shook his head. "I still don't like it. They're planning something."

"They can plan all they want." Reuben looked coolly confident. "What are they going to do? Attack my roses?"

"They could attack the greenhouses and the nursery," Ash said, looking at him thoughtfully. "That's your livelihood, and you employ a lot of people—including me! Or, they could creep into the town."

Caspian's arms were folded across his chest as he stared at the garden. "It's interesting that they seemed to come from your glasshouse, and that there are so many of them. Maybe our ancestors wrecked the ship that supposedly carried Coppinger away and killed all of the pirates, not just him. Perhaps the wreck is close by?"

"Good suggestions," Reuben said nodding. "But, it still doesn't answer why they're active now."

El looked between them, still unable to believe that Reuben had extended his hospitality to Caspian and that they were both under the same roof. Reaching a truce was one thing, but this was something else entirely. And Caspian was different too, in a way that she couldn't quite put her finger on. But there would be time enough for speculation afterwards.

El pulled a hair tie out of her jeans pocket and quickly wrapped her hair into a high ponytail. "I don't feel comfortable knowing that they're out there and we're doing nothing. Why don't we head out, Ash, and get rid of them?" She raised her sword and grinned.

Ash smiled, lighting up his handsome Greek face. "I think that's an excellent suggestion." He looked pointedly at Caspian and Reuben. "You two must stay here. Briar can guard you."

"I don't like that suggestion at all! I'm not a bloody invalid!" Reuben said, outraged.

"Actually, that's exactly what you are," Briar pointed out, hands on her hips.

Reuben looked as if he wanted to say something very rude to Briar, but he turned and glowered at El again. "What's with you? Have you got some sort of death wish?"

She knew he felt useless because of his shoulder, and tried not to snap. "Of course not. I have magic and the Empusa's sword. We'll be able to see them! Don't you trust my abilities?" She cocked her head to the side, amused.

Reuben tried to speak, but got all tongue-tied. He glared at her, eventually admitting, "Of course I do."

"There we go, then. And besides, if they try to get in by breaching one point, you three need to stop them. This is our safe retreat!"

"Don't worry, we can handle it," Briar said, not giving Reuben a chance to respond.

Ash and Caspian watched the exchange with amusement, and Ash said, "Great. It's settled, then. Allow me."

He unlocked the door and exited. El followed, blowing a kiss at Reuben as she did. He gave her one last, furious glare before locking the door behind them.

✦·◈·◇·✦·◈·◇·✱·◈·◇·✦·◈

Avery studied the small cave at the bottom of the steps, disappointed.

"No treasure!"

"But there are bones!" Alex pointed to a corner of the cave where a jumble of bones and a skull rested, rotten clothing still visible.

"Wow!" Avery hurried over, hoping a spirit wasn't about to emerge and attack them. "His weapons are still here!"

Next to the bones were a rusting dagger and flintlock, lying on the sand.

Alex grinned at her. "Brilliant! An actual pirate's body!" He surveyed the space and gestured to a wall of rock through which they could hear the crash of the waves. "There's no access to the sea."

"Yes, there is. Look, a pool of water at the base of the rock." It was almost imperceptible in the darkness, and they hurried over to investigate. Avery shone her torch into the water. "I bet this feeds into a sheltered cove, right under the cliff face, and I would also bet it's only a short passage. This is so cool!"

"We should come in the daylight sometime. Maybe use Ulysses or Nils to bring us here. But for now, let's go up the other passage."

After a quick sweep of the cave to ensure they hadn't missed anything, they hurried along the next tunnel, passing the unconscious and bound spriggans, soon arriving at the base of more steps leading upwards. Before Alex had time to push ahead in his protective way, Avery headed upwards, eager to see what was at the top. After a steep rise, she came to a small square landing and a heavy wooden door.

"This is old!" Alex observed. "Maybe as old as the castle. Which was what? Fifteenth century?"

"Sixteenth," Avery told him, examining the thick iron bands that bound the wood. "Dan said it was built in Henry VIII's time, like a lot of the castles in Cornwall, once we'd left the Catholic Church."

Although St Catherine's Castle was smaller than many, more of a keep really, it had served to protect the Fowey estuary and was perched on the rocky promontory, affording good views of the town and sea. It had also been used in the Second World War. While they talked they tried to open the door, but it was shut tight.

"Is there any suggestion of dungeons or cellars below the castle?" Alex asked.

"I don't think so."

"Maybe we're under another building? Or it's just a cave?"

"I think it's time to use a little magic to find out."

Avery laid her hand over the ornate keyhole and used a spell to unlock it. Then, running her hands around the edges, she loosened the swollen and buckled wood and together they pushed the heavy door open. A wave of musty, damp air hit them.

The witch-light glided ahead, revealing a cavernous space, on the far side of which were three heavy wooden chests, all bound with iron. Next to them were casks of varying sizes, and bundles of rotting cloth.

Alex couldn't keep the glee out of his voice. "Herne's bloody horns! Pirate treasure."

Twenty

El and Ash crept to the left, along the side of the house, pausing to peer cautiously around the corner.

"I can't see them," Ash confessed, pulling his t-shirt off as he spoke.

For a moment, El couldn't work out what he was doing, and quite frankly was trying not to be distracted by his muscled chest. She kept her eyes fixed firmly on his face, reflecting that actually Reuben's physique was more than a match, which made her feel a little smug.

"What are you doing?" she asked him.

"Flying, of course."

In a flash, enormous wings erupted from his shoulders, and El blinked with shock. While she knew the Nephilim had wings, and had seen them from a distance, she had never been so close before.

"Holy crap. They're impressive." Ash's wings were a beautiful golden brown, or at least they appeared to be in the moonlight.

"Thanks," he said, with a knowing smile. "I'm sure I'll spot them from up there. I'll keep an eye on you, too."

"You won't need to," she said, raising an eyebrow. "But thanks, and good luck."

She watched Ash soar upwards, and then kept heading left towards the far corner of the house. Greenlane Manor has been added to over the years, so that although the main building was medieval, there were other, more modern additions, and by that she meant Elizabethan and Victorian, giving the building odd angles and a quirky layout.

For a few minutes, she couldn't see a single ghost, not even in the distance, and was beginning to think they were either at the nursery, or that the sword wasn't working. And then up ahead, in a small courtyard edged with service rooms, she spied a couple of ghosts looking as real as she did. Well, sort of. They were blinking in and out like a weak signal, and El realised they were trying to pass through the walls of the house, but were being blocked by the protection spell. The section of wall shimmered with each attempted breach, and she grinned. Their spells had worked.

Without hesitating, she ran, sword raised. Before they were aware of her presence, she attacked from behind, slashing across the back of one, and then as he turned, fury etched onto his ravaged face, she slashed across his belly too, before plunging the blade in. With an unearthly shriek, the spirit completely vanished. But before she could attack the second, it charged her, tackling her to the ground and raising its knife. El punched out with a ball of fire and air, knocking it backwards, and then while it was spread-eagled against the wall behind, plunged the sword into his stomach.

A whirl of activity in her peripheral vision caught her attention, and she spun around in time to see another spirit run at her from the old stables. He was short but stocky, with a full, dirty beard and ragged clothing. He hurled a knife at her and she swatted it away with magic, and then he pulled a nasty-looking sword from its scabbard. With a leering grin he rasped at her, his strong, Cornish accent and old dialect making him almost impossible to understand.

"So, young maid, ye seek to fight old Tom Trenary? I'll give ye a fight ye won't forget." He swished the blade in front of him, daring her.

For a moment, El was tempted to blast him away with magic like she had the other two.

But this could be fun.

She returned his grin and raised her sword. "All right, old man. Let's see what you've got."

★·❂·◌·✯·❂·◌·✼·❂·◌·✯·❂

Alex gazed at the hoard of gold, coins, and jewellery in the chests they had broken apart, and couldn't stop his mouth from falling open. He couldn't believe that after all their speculation they had actually found treasure.

"By the Gods! This is worth a small fortune!"

Avery dipped her hands into one of them, like a cup, and lifted out a pile of golden guineas, her eyes wide with excitement. "Wow. Actual pirate treasure!"

They had thrown several witch-lights up, and the gold and jewels glittered in their light.

"We have to declare this."

"Not yet, we don't. Not until we've solved this." She dropped the coins back in the chest. "This is what Miles was searching for."

"And was killed for—by the spriggans guarding it."

"So, why is this still here?"

"Miles was looking on his own," Alex said. "That's the only reasonable explanation."

Avery shook her head, looking perplexed. "Maybe whoever is involved is planning to come back for it. After all, they took the treasure from Looe, despite the fact that there's a spriggan there."

"Maybe. I still think we're missing something." Alex walked over to the casks, pulled a bung out and sniffed, before recoiling. "Christ. That smells rancid. I presume it was brandy."

"And these," Avery said, crouching by the rotten bundles of cloth, "would have been silks and fine linens." She lifted a few pieces, but they disintegrated quickly. She stood, wiping her hands on her jeans. "What a waste."

Alex started pacing. "Originally, these must have been hidden with the plan to come back to claim them later, and something stopped them. Either they were caught, or killed."

"Maybe they were caught by Reuben and Caspian's ancestors' spell."

Alex nodded, his thoughts racing with scenarios. "We're getting closer to working this out, I'm sure, but I don't think we should leave these here."

"Agreed." Avery looked thoughtfully around the space. "Why did Miles get attacked? The fact that he was killed by the spriggans suggests that he must have been either in here or close by. But the entrance above was sealed. He could not have got in here that way. The stone is far too heavy for him to have shifted alone, and it looked undisturbed."

Alex nodded. "He could have come in through the pool below, but he wasn't wet, either."

In their excitement at seeing the chests and casks, they hadn't explored the rest of the place, and now Alex's gaze swept around the room. It was definitely manmade, constructed from huge stone blocks, with a low, beamed ceiling, and the floor was beaten earth. It definitely felt like a cellar. The far side of the place was still in shadows, and sending a witch-light ahead of him, Alex walked over, flashing his torch across the walls, and finding a narrow doorway.

He called over his shoulder, "Avery, there's another room."

Alex proceeded cautiously. Beyond was a series of small, connected rooms, mostly empty except for some disintegrating wood. They were swathed in cobwebs, and as he walked, dust kicked up around them. When he finally reached the end, he found a narrow stone staircase leading to a hatch in the ceiling.

He turned to Avery, who had followed him. "There's the way out." He ascended the stairs and pushed the hatch upwards, but it didn't budge. "It's sealed."

"We could try to move it with magic," she suggested. "But, if it's covered with earth or rock, or even another building—"

Alex sighed. "We'd be crushed. Damn it." He studied it for a few more moments before heading to Avery's side. "I guess we'll just have to accept that it's sealed. It's certainly been undisturbed for years. The dust hasn't moved, and the cobwebs are thick. There's no way Miles came in this way."

"Come on." Avery grabbed his hand and pulled him back to the main room. "I'll use witch-flight to get these chests to my van, and then we'll seal the entrance again."

"And then I suppose we should release the spriggans," Alex said. "Let's hope they don't decide to follow us outside, or that will be a whole other level of crap to deal with."

★·۰·ة·★·۰·۰· ✳·۰·ة·★·۰

El was working up a sweat. Tom Trenary may be old, and a ghost, but he was reasonably adept with the sword. Fortunately, El had youth on her side. Tom, however, was mean. And their fight was drawing attention.

While they circled, parried, and attacked, the clash of their swords drew two more ghosts, and El had the feeling they were waiting to swoop in if Tom lost, ready to end her. She was surprised they hadn't already. As if he'd read her mind, Tom leered at her and gave an almost imperceptible nod to their observers. He unleashed a furious attack designed to absorb all her attention, and the other two swept in on either side.

If Tom was willing to play dirty, so was she. Still fighting, El released a wave of power and it pulsed out around her, sweeping back all three ghosts and sending them crashing against the surrounding walls. Then more ghosts arrived, fire and malevolence burning deep within their empty eye sockets, and she realised she was hemmed in.

Fortunately, within seconds Ash landed next to her, and without hesitating they tackled them all in a messy, brutal fight. Ash used his wings to sweep the spirits either out of the way or to herd them into tight spots, and then finished them off with the sword, while El used magic to compliment her blade. The spirits, however, flashed in and out, disappearing and reappearing seconds later in concerted attacks. For a few minutes it felt as if they might be overwhelmed, but the combination of wings, magic, and the swords gave them the upper hand. Eventually it was over, and the ghosts were despatched by the Empusa's swords to whatever grim fate befell them.

Ash turned to her, breathless. "Sorry. I didn't mean to interfere, but it looked too much fun not to."

She laughed. "Apology accepted. I'm just glad I managed to wipe the smile off Tom Trenary's face. And besides, taking on so many all on my own was probably a bit much."

"Oh, I don't know," he said, taking her in from head to toe. "You seemed to be doing just fine."

She returned his scrutiny, determined not to be outdone by a Nephilim. "You, too! I guess we better make sure there are no others lurking around here."

Ash folded his wings behind his back and led the way out of the courtyard and further around the house. "There was no activity by the nursery, and besides, simple damage seems pointless, especially when you consider that both Caspian and Reuben are rich."

"But why the concerted attack?" El asked, confused. "Is it really just about revenge?"

"Revenge is always a powerful motive."

A loud explosion broke the silence of the night. They both froze, looking at each other in shock, and then El ran towards the noise, and Ash flew. As El rounded the corner at the far end of the house, she saw a plume of smoke and flames.

What the hell?

The explosion had blown a huge hole in the wall, and another half a dozen ghosts were swarming inside. Ash was already swooping down, and he grabbed one, while striking down another. El charged in, killing the one at the rear, before being caught in a powerful blast of magic that came from inside the house, propelling them all backwards. At the same time, roots exploded out of the ground like writhing limbs.

El flew through the air, landing in a heap on the ground, heavily winded, and the Empusa's sword fell from her hand. She dragged herself to her feet, panic stricken. The spirits had faded to shimmering, barely-there shapes. She lunged at the sword, getting a hand on it just as a spirit rushed at her. As soon as her hand touched the hilt she could see it clearly again, and she angled the sword upwards, impaling the ghost as it leapt. It slid down the blade, pinning her in place until it vanished with an anguished scream.

The roots snaked through the air, trying to pin the spirits in place, but it was difficult. They moved constantly, manifesting elsewhere in the blink of an eye, trying to avoid the thrashing roots that managed to spear a couple of them, shattering bones like glass. Ash and El waded among them, ducking and dodging, finally finishing them off with the swords.

When the last one vanished, Ash and El waited, swords readied, El not quite believing that it was over. She looked at the destruction all around them. The earth was a churned-up mess of roots and fallen masonry, and a ten-foot hole had been blown in the house.

Reuben.

Her heart in her mouth, El was about to run inside when he appeared in the gap, flanked by Caspian and Briar. His hands were on his hips as he surveyed the mess, and he pursed his lips at El and Ash. "That's the last time I let you two out to safeguard the house."

★ ❂ ◌ ✩ ❂ ◌ ✳ ❂ ◌ ✩ ❂

Avery and Alex sat in the Bedford van, down the street from Ethan James's house, and Avery yawned, struggling to keep her eyes open.

"I'm knackered now."

"Let's just give it another half an hour," Alex said, checking his watch.

"But I doubt we'll see much tonight."

Avery leaned back in her seat and chewed her lip, mulling over the recent events. "Ethan *must* have found a map in the White Haven Museum papers. That's the only explanation."

"We don't even know if it is Ethan yet." Alex shuffled to get himself more comfortable. "Or if it is, who else is involved. Or the identity of the witch who must be helping them."

"I'd love to know where the museum papers came from."

"Does it matter?"

"I guess not," she admitted with a sigh.

"They were probably donated years ago, which is why they've been gathering dust. But you'd think people check what they donate!"

"We get donated items, remember?" Avery said, shaking her head. "Or I buy books from house clearances. People don't look at what's in there. Not really. What's puzzling me, if it is him, is why would a very respectable museum curator turn into a thief?"

"Turn to the dark side, you mean?"

She giggled. "Yes. Surely cataloguing all of that stuff and having it in your museum would be huge!"

"Selling it on the black market would be bigger."

"Only if you have connections. I wouldn't know where to start."

"I reckon museum curators would know all about it. Even from the position of trying to stop it. He'd know more than we think."

The sound of a door shutting stopped their conversation, and they both froze, watching the end of the drive ahead. Avery used the binoculars, watching a slight figure wearing jeans and a hoodie emerge on to the road, the hood pulled over their head. They crossed the road, heading to a car parked on the opposite side, facing them, and Avery and Alex slid down in their seats, Avery grateful they had used their shadow spell again.

The figure looked furtively to either side. It wasn't until they passed under a streetlight that Avery got a glimpse of their face, and she groaned as their suspicions were confirmed.

It was Mariah, the head of the Looe Coven.

Twenty-One

Reuben studied the hole in the wall of his billiards room and mourned one of his favourite spaces, a place where he and Gil had spent many happy hours.

"Well, what a bloody mess. I suppose I should be grateful that they didn't blow the whole bloody house up."

The dust had finally settled, but bricks were strewn inside and out, and the billiard table was upended, as were other items and furniture. Caspian, El, Ash, and Briar were with him, inspecting the mess.

Caspian's eyes narrowed as he inhaled deeply. "Gunpowder. It's very distinctive. I guess it's something they'd be familiar with." He turned to look at Reuben. "Intriguing."

"That's one word for it." Reuben looked up at the cracks in the ceiling. "For spirits, they're remarkably destructive."

"And remarkably solid!" El added. "I know I was carrying the Empusa's sword, but they had a real physical substance!"

Ash nodded. "I agree." His wings had now disappeared and he was wearing his t-shirt again. "They are certainly bridging two worlds now, and that's ominous."

El righted one of the upended chairs and leaned against it, thoughtful. "It reminds me of when we encountered the ghosts at White Haven Castle last year. They had a strong physical presence too, and we thought that was because of our magic."

"Good point," Briar agreed, "which lends weight to our beliefs that the spirits are being strengthened by a witch." She looked a little sheepish. "Sorry about your garden, Reuben. I'll fix that in the morning."

"No need to apologise," he said breezily. "You helped get rid of them. Thank you." Reuben was always amazed by how much power Briar wielded in such a small frame.

"The important thing," El said, moving next to him and sliding her arm around his waist, "was that they didn't get to either of you. But wow, your families must have really pissed them off!"

Caspian scratched his head. "That's something I know we've been good at for a long time. And this, to me, has the feel of a curse. We were good at those, too."

Just then, a door banged at the front of the house, and Avery shouted, "Hello?"

"Down here," Reuben shouted back.

He had called Alex after the attack, taking a chance that they'd still be up, and wanting to make sure he and Avery were okay. Alex leapt at the chance to come over, telling him they had news. In a few minutes, Alex and Avery stood next to them, mouths hanging open.

"Bloody hell," Alex said. "I thought we'd had a crap night. What happened here?"

"Ghosts," Ash said dryly.

Alex looked sceptical. "With *explosives*? Or was that one of you?"

Reuben laughed. Well, he tried to; it got stuck in his throat. "Nope. That was them." He finally turned away from the hole in his wall and had a good look at the new arrivals. They were both dishevelled, their clothes rumpled and their faces smeared with dirt. "You're filthy. What have you been up to?"

"Spriggans and buried treasure," Avery said, unable to suppress a grin.

Everyone's attention now left the smoking ruins and switched to Avery. Briar almost stuttered. "You've found treasure?"

Alex and Avery were both grinning insufferably, but at least it was taking

Reuben's mind off repair bills and feeling like he had a death warrant on his head.

Alex preened. "Yes, and if you fix us a drink, we'll bring it in."

Five minutes later, they were assembled in the snug, after plugging the hole with yet more protection spells. Ash had volunteered to keep watch, anyway. Three wooden chests were in the middle of the room, their lids open, revealing the collection of gold coins and jewels within.

Reuben stood transfixed, arms folded across his chest. "Herne's magnificent hairy balls! You actually found treasure."

In fact they were all mesmerised, standing in a circle, just staring.

"Where did you find this, again?" Briar asked.

"We think we were beneath St Catherine's Castle," Avery said, going on to explain the hidden tunnels. "I'd like to go back in the day, actually, just to check the grounds, but I doubt we'll find a thing."

"That place is a complete ruin," Caspian agreed. "If there's an entrance, it's been long buried by earth and rubble."

"How much do you reckon that's worth now?" El asked.

"Hundreds of thousands of pounds, probably," Alex estimated. He stepped forward, picking up a few coins to examine. "A few guineas, doubloons, and..." He frowned. "Something else I don't recognise."

It was as if he'd broken a spell, and they all started to pull coins and jewels out, a palpable excitement filling the room.

"But," Alex continued, "we think this is part of a larger hoard. It has to be, or why does there seem to be a few sites involved?"

Reuben looked at his old friend and nodded. "Something like this must have been in the chests in Looe. Maybe they carried it out in bags instead."

Caspian had retreated to the sofa again, the night beginning to take its toll. "Bags would certainly look less conspicuous." His hand rested gently on the site of his stab wound, and Briar immediately headed to his side to offer another healing spell.

"You should go to bed and sleep," she advised him.

Caspian shook his head. "I'm not missing out on this! Besides, I need more whiskey to get me to sleep after all this excitement."

"I know exactly what you mean," Reuben said, heading to the cupboard where he kept a bottle and glasses. His head was buzzing with the events of the night, and after passing round drinks to those who wanted one, he sat down. "Tell us about Mariah again."

Avery looked bleak with disappointment. She always thought the best of people, and no doubt Mariah's betrayal was a shock. Actually, to be fair, it was to Reuben, too. He just happened to be more cynical than Avery.

"There's not much to tell," she said, easing into the armchair. "She snuck out of Ethan's home looking very shifty. She has to be involved, and not in a good way." She looked at Caspian. "You know her better than any of us. What do you think?"

He met her eyes briefly, before glancing at the rest of them. "I'm afraid that since I have become friends with you, she and Zane are ignoring me. They feel I've betrayed them." He gave a dry laugh. "They were big fans of my father, and our families go back many years. But, Zane and Mariah are both vindictive, narrow-minded, and spiteful. I'm honestly not surprised she's involved. She probably knows a lot more about that cave in Looe than she's letting on. What was she like at the council meeting?"

Avery shrugged. "Her normal self, really. If anything, I found her more animated than normal, but maybe that's because she was being questioned about smuggling in Looe. She certainly didn't seem awkward or guilty."

Briar's hand flew to her chest. "I hope she wasn't behind Inez's death. Or the man on the cliff top."

Alex shook his head. "I think that's the spriggans. But she must be responsible for the super-powered ghosts."

"Wow," Briar said, flabbergasted. "Should we tell Genevieve yet?"

Avery answered immediately. "No. We're sure she didn't see us, and what if other witches are involved?"

"But Genevieve wouldn't be. We can trust her," El said.

Reuben looked at his friend's pensive faces. "I think Avery is right. Let's keep this between us. Whatever her reasons are, she's involved. Maybe she's connected to pirates in some way, or maybe she's a close friend of Ethan's and is getting a cut of the treasure. I don't actually care. The important thing is working out how to stop her."

"Agreed," Avery said decisively. "And El, you should tell Newton in the morning, before he sees Ethan."

"Well," Reuben said, sipping his whiskey to fortify himself, "I guess me and Caspian must persist in finding out what our families did. Although, they seem to have covered their trail very well."

"If you struggle, I could try to summon one of their spirits," Alex suggested warily.

Avery rounded on him. "You are not going into the spirit world again!"

"I'm not suggesting I do," he said patiently. "I'll call them to me. In a full circle of protection, too. They might even have a way to help Helena."

"Okay." Reuben nodded. "We'll keep that option in mind. And now, before I collapse and my adrenalin wears off completely, tell us about these spriggans."

★ ⚬ ⸱ ⚬ ⸱ ★ ⚬ ⸱ ⚬ ✳ ⚬ ⸱ ⚬ ⸱ ★ ⚬

Avery looked at Dan and Sally's shocked faces and laughed. "It's incredible, isn't it?"

They exchanged bewildered glances, and Sally said, "I guess that's one word for it." She lowered her voice and looked around the shop, making sure it was still empty. "Where is it now?"

"At Reuben's. Neither he nor Caspian are leaving the house, and it's fully protected, so that seemed like the best place." She grimaced. "I mean, there is the slight issue of the hole in the wall in Reuben's billiards room, but I think they're trying to fix that with magic today."

They were behind the counter at Happenstance Books at just after nine the next morning, discussing the treasure. Despite the fact that Avery had slept for only a few hours, she had awoken refreshed and energised, fuelled by their success the night before.

Sally's eyes narrowed with suspicion. "I am still shocked that Caspian has moved into Reuben's place. Are you sure Reuben will be safe?"

Avery tried to reassure her. "I'm certain. He was seriously injured. They're both being targeted, and they're helping each other."

"So you're sure now it wasn't a set-up to get Reuben?" Dan asked, referring back to their conversation of the previous day.

"Positive. I told you, if we hadn't arrived there yesterday, Caspian might be dead."

"All right, I'm convinced." Dan turned to Sally. "She *is* a good judge of character."

Sally still looked doubtful. "If a little too willing to see peoples' good sides sometimes."

Avery was annoyed. "Sally!"

Sally looked contrite and hugged her. "I'm sorry. I just worry about you. Honestly, the things you get up to lately. And I'm still freaked out by your flying thing."

Avery felt terrible and hugged her back. "I'm so sorry about that. It was instinctive. I didn't mean to scare you." She held Sally's hands and looked at her worried expression. If she'd been in Sally's shoes, she'd be worried too. Avery's life was odd, and she was lucky that Sally and Dan accepted it so well. "In fact, I apologise to both of you. I take you for granted and I shouldn't."

Sally smiled softly. "No, you don't."

Dan pretended to vomit. "Ugh. Pack it in you two soppy idiots."

"Piss off, Dan," Avery joked as she hugged Sally again.

"I'm just looking forward to gossiping about you again," Dan teased. "We'll do it over elevenses, when you've buggered off on some mad pursuit.

I presume you have one today?"

Avery tried to look affronted, and then had to concede he was right. "I'm going to have a look at St Catherine's Castle in the daylight, just in case I can see where the entrance to the cellar might be."

Dan frowned. "I've never heard talk about deep, dark cellars, but maybe they were blocked up years ago, and all reference has been lost."

"Or, the entrance is in the grounds," Sally suggested, "and the cellar isn't attached to the house, but is something completely separate."

"That's actually a good suggestion, Sally," Avery admitted.

Sally looked smug. "Thank you."

"Oh, you two! Blah, blah, blah," Dan said, waving his hand airily. "Back to the pirate treasure. What's in it?"

Now they both glared at Dan, before Avery said, "Lots of gold coins, some jewellery, and some gems. I'm no expert, though. The boys will get Newton round later today to look at them."

"Can we see them?"

"I guess so. But you both have to keep this very quiet! Like *top secret* quiet."

"Witches' honour," Dan said, saluting. "Now, what about the sprig-gans?"

"Oh, good. I'm glad you've brought that up. They were crazy strong! They had massive shadows that could actually touch us, but they looked like funny little wizened men."

Dan's eyes lit up. "Fantastic to know that these folklore creatures really exist! I wish I could see one."

"No, you don't," Avery told him. "They are vicious and deadly. I'm convinced now that one of them killed Inez and the other two victims. We had to bind them and spell them to sleep."

"I'm glad you didn't kill them," Dan said, relieved. "And it means the lore is right. They do guard treasure. Fascinating."

"Let's just hope Shadow can communicate with them in some way. It would be nice to have them on our side," Avery mused.

"Talk of the devil," Sally said, nodding to where Shadow was striding past the window. "Here she is."

The bell jingled as Shadow strode in, and her eyes lit up as she joined them. "I have news!"

"Spriggan news?" Avery asked, feeling hopeful.

"Absolutely!" She looked around, frowning. "No customers yet?"

"No, so get on with it," Dan said impatiently.

Shadow huffed. "It's a good thing I like you. Anyway, after I spoke to Briar, I had a think about what they may be and whether they had a link to my world, but I honestly couldn't think of anything similar. I decided I had to see one first hand, so I headed to Looe last night with Gabe, and ventured down to the tunnel where Inez died." She smiled at them triumphantly. "And I found one!"

"Strange you should say that," Avery confessed. "So did we. Two of them actually, in Fowey."

Shadow's shoulders dropped and her smile faded. "Oh! Did you talk to them?"

"Talk? Ha!" Avery snorted. "They tried to kill us. We had to bind them with magic and put a sleeping spell on them."

Shadow relaxed and smiled again. "That's okay, then."

Avery wasn't entirely sure what was *okay* about her and Alex nearly being killed, but she presumed Shadow hadn't wanted her to steal her thunder.

"Did they speak English?" Dan asked, intrigued.

"A mix of English and old fey, actually."

"Hold on," Avery said, "why didn't it attack you?"

Shadow leaned her hip on the counter. "It did, initially. We went in fully armed, but Gabe was more than a match for its strength and managed to pin it against the wall so I could speak to it. It also helped that I bribed it with fey metal."

"What kind of metal?" Sally asked.

"I offered it one of my fey-made armguards from my armour in exchange for information, and its little eyes gleamed!" She laughed. "And it was that easy!" Shadow's version of easy was very different to Avery's. "It seems that it kills on instinct. It doesn't really plan its attack. It's quite a simple creature, really. Inez and Newton disturbed it, and it lashed out. They love precious metals—it sort of calls to them, and the reason it's still hanging around that passage is because it still scents gold. " She shrugged nonchalantly.

Sally crossed her arms and huffed. "You shouldn't look so pleased about it. Inez is dead!"

"I'm not pleased about *that*!" Shadow shot back. "I'm pleased I could speak to it." She tried to make her tone more conciliatory, and clearly struggled with it. "It *is* part giant, too. That piece of folklore is correct. I could sense the spirit of one contained within it."

Dan shook his head, confused. "But how does that even work?"

"I don't know...and as I said, it's a simple creature. It is what it is, so it couldn't tell me. But it's ancient, I could tell that, too. They have probably been part of the landscape here for millennia, hidden underground, guarding ancient hoards, or even base metals in the ground."

"I felt it, actually," Avery said, recalling the ancient magic she had sensed the night before. "Old, powerful magic, and you're right. It's completely rooted in the earth. Did it know anything about the pirate treasure?" she asked. "Or had it been motivated by someone in some way?"

Shadow shook her head. "It didn't know anything. From my admittedly limited interaction with it, it's like a bloodhound. Or should I say dragon?" She nodded to herself, as if confirming her own idea. "Yes, that's exactly it. Dragons love gold, too. It calls to them, and they sniff it out and sit on it. Spriggans are the same."

"So it couldn't tell you where other treasure might be, or whether more spriggans are there?" Avery persisted.

"No. But at least we know a way to stop them from being violent."

"Have you spoken to El about this yet?" Avery asked. "She's going to Perranporth to investigate the tin mine this morning. This will be really important for her to know!"

"No. But in that case, I'll go to see her now." Shadow pulled her phone out of her pocket and quickly texted her, and then patted the messenger bag she carried. "I've got a few trinkets in here for all of you—just in case."

Dan's eyes widened. "Fey metals?"

Shadow grinned as she pulled out another armguard and some fey coins and placed them on the counter.

"By the Gods," Dan said, examining the armour. "This is amazing workmanship."

He was right. The engraving was intricate and breathtaking, but the metal was light, too.

"Not '*by the gods*', but fey masters," Shadow said, her eyes taking on a faraway look. "Such skill."

Sally looked at her, concerned. "Are you certain you want to give these away, Shadow? Surely they're precious to you?"

"They are, but I've kept the bigger pieces. And besides," she addressed the counter rather than them, "my friends' safety is more important."

Avery, Dan, and Sally shared astonished glances before Shadow looked up at them again, her violet eyes bright, and Avery once more reflected on what a contrary creature she could be. She smiled at her. "Thank you. We appreciate it."

"My pleasure," Shadow said, dropping her gaze shyly. "Anyway, I'll leave these with you, and go see El." She shouldered her bag, and then paused. "Oh, I knew there was something else. Have you seen the news this morning?"

They all shook their heads, and Avery said, "No, why?"

"That blonde reporter was on, doing a piece about White Haven Museum. She was interviewing Ethan James. It turns out that part of the stuff they found were Zephaniah Job's old ledgers. They contain a mine of information about smuggling connections and money across Cornwall, apparently."

Avery nearly spat her coffee out. "Seriously? Wow."

"Does that help you?"

Avery's mind raced with possibilities. "Yes, I think it might."

"Great! Call me if you need me!"

They watched her go, and then Dan slid her gifts under the counter as they watched a couple of customers enter before turning to Avery. "So, Zephaniah Job. His ledgers weren't destroyed after all. He could have all sorts of secrets in them!"

"I agree. Now I'm convinced that Ethan found a bloody treasure map!"

Twenty-Two

Caspian walked around Reuben's kitchen while he spoke to Gabe on the phone, moving gingerly so as not to aggravate his injury. "Are you sure there's no damage?"

"None at all," he reassured him. Gabe had phoned him to explain that the large warehouse in Harecombe was attacked by ghosts during the night, but the protection spells had held. "Barak and Niel said they could just about see them, and it was a half-hearted attempt only. I'm hoping they won't bother again."

"I think there must have been a dozen here last night, as well as the ones at my place earlier. How the hell many are there?"

Gabe grunted in his usual, non-committal way. "Hard to say. Depends what your ancestors got up to, doesn't it?"

"Yes, it does," Caspian conceded. "No injuries, then?"

"None. They sent the regular staff inside, so all good there." Gabe fell silent a moment, and then asked, "Is there anything we should know about Estelle?"

"No, why?" Caspian answered quickly. *What had she said now?*

"Nothing, she's just a bit, er, *crankier* than usual."

"Well, that's Estelle for you." He refused to elaborate. He couldn't, anyway. *Who the hell knew what she was thinking right now?*

Caspian heard Reuben enter the room, and he turned to see him head for the fridge, nodding at him in greeting. Caspian nodded back. Gabe continued to update him, telling him how he and Shadow had found a spriggan, as well. Caspian paused in front of the patio doors, not really noticing the fine drizzle starting to fall as he absorbed the news, and then they chatted about the business for a few more minutes before hanging up.

Reuben looked none the worse for his late night, and was busying himself getting bacon and eggs from the fridge. He glanced up at Caspian. "Breakfast?"

Caspian didn't normally have breakfast, preferring only coffee before heading to the office, but this morning it appealed to him. Perhaps it was the overcast weather, or the odd, bunkered-down mood he found himself in, sharing Reuben's house. He nodded. "Yes, please. Sounds great, actually."

"Bacon and eggs always does. Did I hear you mention spriggans?"

He nodded and updated him on Shadow's success with fey treasure.

Reuben paused, about to put the bacon in the frying pan. "Is she telling El?"

"Apparently, although she headed to Avery's first."

It was strange; he found himself reluctant to say Avery's name, as if he might give his feelings away, but Reuben was too worried about El. And besides, he didn't strike Caspian as the type to discuss love lives—or the lack of them. He doubted Reuben had ever had a lack of love life, ever. He watched his easy, laidback attitude, and noted he was like that with everyone, a subtle but supreme confidence in himself. Caspian exuded confidence too, and a tinge of arrogance—he'd been accused of it often enough—but he also knew that he didn't always feel that way, and he doubted Reuben did, too.

Reuben just nodded and continued to cook. "Good. I'm worried about El, but she's headstrong, and magically strong, so I have to trust her."

"Have to?"

Reuben laughed. "Yes. But I do, anyway. Those bloody mines are dark and damp and treacherous though, so I'm glad Shadow can help."

"I take it El and Briar are already at work?"

"Yeah." Reuben sighed and met Caspian's eyes, looking grim. "We have to find out what our ancestors did!"

Caspian refreshed his coffee cup and sat down at the wooden table in the corner of the room. "But what if we can't? Does it matter?"

Reuben turned around, half an eye on the bacon, and slung a tea towel over his shoulder. "I suppose it depends on what we want to do, or can do." He shifted his weight, leaning against the counter and waving the spatula as he spoke. "Virginia and Serephina cast a spell together to stop the Dane—we know that much. We assume that it was either to protect their businesses, the towns, or both."

"Or could it be revenge for something? Someone who was hurt, or a business that was damaged?"

Reuben nodded. "Maybe, but whatever the motive, they acted together, in an unusual show of trust."

"Unless, of course, at that point in our history, they actually were friends," Caspian countered, amused by the thought.

Reuben gave a wry smile. "It's possible." And then his expression sobered. "But why not go to the Witch Council? That would be their obvious support, right?"

"Actually, I don't think the council existed then. And remember, it was harder to communicate between towns far away. Penzance would have meant hours of travel, unless they went by boat. The roads were probably awful. Closer would have been better." He tried to recall what his father had told him. "I don't think the council existed until later on in the 1900s...not like it is now, anyway."

"I guess it doesn't matter," Reuben reasoned. "But I do think the spell is important. It was designed to get rid of Coppinger, and it worked. He disappeared, and it looks like his men went with him. Piecing it together, they must have wrecked the ship he was trying to escape in. Some of his men would have been on that, but others would have been here, surely, continuing the business."

Caspian nodded. "That would make sense. He had a big operation, was ruthless, and surely energetic, when you consider he was moving down from the north of Cornwall."

Reuben turned to flip the bacon. "But Bodmin was the central hub. A network carried smuggled goods there from all over Cornwall, and then on to the rest of England. They would have all known each other—or of each other, at least."

"And would have probably divided Cornwall between them."

Reuben laughed. "But there's clearly no honour among thieves, is there, if Coppinger was moving into other areas."

"I would imagine he was universally disliked. Actually, *hated* is more likely. He terrified people." Caspian had also been reading the books about smuggling that El and Avery had bought in Bodmin.

"You happy to have your bacon and eggs in a sandwich?" Reuben asked, already slicing crusty bread.

"Absolutely."

Reuben plated their breakfast up and carried them to the table, where he took a seat, too. He had a large bite, sighing with satisfaction as he swallowed. "Awesome. So, I suggest we head up to my attic where my spell books are, take yours there too, and search them thoroughly. I honestly think the key to understanding what's happening now is to understand what happened then."

Caspian wiped crumbs from his mouth. "I'm not so sure it will help, but what else are we going to do, locked up in here all day?"

Reuben looked at him, surprised. "I really want to know what we did that was so bad we're being targeted all these years later. It must have been the mother of all spells! Big juju! And frankly, I don't want to be stuck in here for months."

"Don't worry, I'm in. Your hospitality is great, but I prefer my own bed."

"Then let's do this, Caspian. Come on, before we even go up there, in an exercise in narrowing down our search, if you were to stop a murderous madman who was terrorising the country and risking your business right now, what would you do?"

"What would *you* do?" Caspian asked, slightly affronted. "I'm not the only one with magic."

"But I'm charming and guileless," Reuben said, his blue eyes wide and a huge smirk on his face. "I haven't got a mean bone in my body. You're the sneaky shit here, with the family history of making curses and holding momentous grudges."

Okay, so they were at this stage in their strange truce.

"Fair point," he grudgingly conceded. He took another bite of his sandwich and leaned back in his chair, running through his options while he chewed. The word *truce* resonated, and an idea struck him. "Okay, I'm a rich businessman who needs to bring my shipments in, but the damn pirates are trying to scuttle my ships and steal my goods. The man at the root of all my troubles is also threatening the locals, forcing them to work for him, and generally making the place hell. So, rather than plan an outright attack, because he has a *lot* of men, I decide to make a truce. In exchange for a cut of my profits, he allows my ships free passage. But," Caspian gave a victorious smile, "I double-cross him. But not just him...his gang, too. I invite him and his men to a neutral venue, and spring the trap—with your help."

"Why not just kill him, or curse him from a distance?"

"Because I want to do this in one big hit," Caspian countered. "And I want to know that it worked. I want to *see* it!"

Reuben nodded. "I like it. It's logical. But what do you do to trap them?"

"I use a cave, a smuggling cave, or a storage place somewhere. It has to be close—for both of us. When they're trapped, I either kill them immediately, or leave them to a horrible, slow death. As you observed," Caspian said, cutting his eyes at Reuben, "I'm a vindictive bastard, so it will be some kind of curse-inflicted agony."

"That would be far more likely," Reuben agreed. "You are mean."

"Well, you helped me! You have a lot to lose too, remember. White Haven is overrun with smugglers, and you're losing money!"

"But the stories say that Coppinger was seen rowing out to sea in a storm. No, hold on, rowing out from *an island* in a storm, to his big ship, where he was never seen again."

Caspian nodded. "True, but it could just be a fanciful story."

"Or—" Reuben leapt to his feet and started pacing, and Caspian almost spilled his coffee in surprise. "That's exactly what happened! Why come to Harecombe, across country? I'd bring my ship, Black Prince, and weigh anchor off the coast, bringing some of my men ashore. But not all of them, because, frankly, rumours have reached me that you are a sneaky, not-to-be-trusted-businessman. That's kind of why I like you—we're the same."

"Thanks, I think."

"*Or*, maybe I think this is a sign of weakness, and I decide to pounce." He rounded on Caspian and pointed at him. "You are offering a truce, but I want it all. I am Cruel Coppinger, the demon smuggler, used to having my own way. I decide to attack *you*!"

Caspian had to admit he was enjoying this ridiculous role play. It was fun, and actually productive. Clearly Reuben thought so too, as he strode about his kitchen, swishing his spatula like a sword. Caspian pointed back to Reuben. "But you, Cruel Coppinger, don't know that I've enlisted the support of my neighbours, the do-gooding, simpering, too-terrified-to-say-boo, Jacksons."

"Ha! You may think that's an insult, but it's to my advantage! I lure people in with charm, and then, *a-ha*, I attack like a ninja assassin! I flank the Cruel Gang, and add to your curse to overcome them."

"I thought *you* were Cruel Coppinger?"

Reuben looked startled. "Oh yes, I am. Okay." He paced again. "I come ashore to meet at the agreed *rendezvous* point, but some of my men have arrived before me and are laying in wait to attack you and your family...or whoever you bring with you. When you arrive, we go through the motions, until I feel the time is right, and then attack."

"But I'm prepared, and at a given signal, the Jacksons attack, too."

"Furious, and knowing I'm out-manoeuvred—but not out-gunned, because I have backup—I abandon my men, because I care more about me than them, and retreat."

Caspian continued, "I go after you, but am delayed because of your men. We manage to kill or curse some of them, and then as soon as I can, I pursue you!"

"But I'm way ahead by now, though I daren't take my boat...I'm a sitting duck, it's too obvious. So, I flee into the tunnels." Reuben looked at Caspian. "So this is where it gets murky."

Caspian roared with laughter. "*This* is where it gets murky? I think the whole thing is bloody murky!"

"Oh, ye of little faith!" Reuben strode across the kitchen again. "I head down the nearest tunnels, because I know them all by now. I am a cunning pirate, the biggest badass of the sea, and I flee to where I don't think anyone can find me...right under the sneaky Jacksons' nose! Their own tunnels!"

Reuben stopped dramatising and turned to Caspian. "We *were* smugglers—in some way. I'm not sure why or how. I mean, you're right...we were in trade. Maybe we thought we'd get better profits. Maybe we were coerced by Coppinger."

Caspian shook his head. "You're witches. You wouldn't have been coerced. You might have thought it was a good deal—at first—and then realised that you got in bed with the devil."

"No. That doesn't work. We'd have still done something about it."

Caspian looked at him thoughtfully. "You had your own smuggling business. Just some local-level stuff. You're the lord of the manor, the simpering, do-gooding, look-after-your-own, look-after-the-village kind of family. Maybe Coppinger was moving in on you. Maybe he had something on you. And remember, you don't do curses. You're trying to manage it. You want my help."

"You know, I think we're close with this. Our reasoning is good."

"I agree. And it could be that he fled to Gull Island. The stories talk about Gull Rock, but it might not be."

"But we've both seen the caves on Gull Island," Reuben said. "There are no rotting bones there, or treasure."

Caspian met Reuben's gaze, knowing they were both thinking of the fateful night of Gil's death. "No, there weren't. But there were a lot of old chests and crates in there. What if there's a hidden tunnel under all that? Did you ever check?"

Reuben sat down as if all his energy had left him. "No. I only went back for the first time the other day." Caspian felt as if the whole room had closed down around them and his heart raced as Reuben continued. "I still didn't search it. I was there for some space, actually, after I learned that Alex had spoken to Gil in the spirit world."

Caspian was suddenly unsure of what to say. He'd apologised before, but it had been short, in passing, something he was embarrassed to talk about. He was also scared of breaking whatever strange accommodation they had arrived at between them. And then he frowned. "Was that where you were attacked?"

"Yes, in the cave leading to the beach."

"I didn't see that one."

"It's just beyond the big one."

Reuben's face was carefully schooled, but Caspian was sure there was a lot going on beyond that calm exterior. He had another thought. "Where else has a lot of tunnels and is neutral ground?"

Reuben looked puzzled, and then said, "West Haven."

"We didn't explore all of those tunnels."

"But the police did."

"Did they? What if there was another disguised doorway, or access to another section. What if there's another tunnel that leads to Gull island? Another cave?"

"Lupescu's cave wasn't it, that's for sure," Reuben pointed out.

Caspian remembered the attack from the night before. "I saw those spirits emerging from your glasshouse last night. What if the place where Cruel Coppinger was finally defeated was on Gull Island all along?"

They both looked out of the window to the small isle that lay draped in mist and drizzle.

Reuben spoke first. "Another cave." He nodded and sighed. "We know goods were smuggled ashore there. The big cliff on the far side shelters the beach from the mainland. It's possible."

Caspian turned away from the view and focussed on Reuben again. "I would chase him down and finish him straight away. I wouldn't allow him to regroup and strike back. And when I was done, I would hunt down his remaining men. Or just extend the curse to the rest of them."

"And I'd be with you. Once we'd started this thing, there would be no going back. We had effectively started a war."

"And if I couldn't track down all of his men, which would be tricky," Caspian admitted, "even with magic, I would curse his treasure, ensuring that anyone who tried to move it would die. Or something of the sort."

"If we cursed the treasure, wouldn't that mean it would *still* be cursed?" Reuben asked, looking through the door and into the snug where the old chests still sat.

Caspian eyed them warily too, and unable to detect anything remotely like magic coming from them said, "Maybe not the treasure, then. Just the men."

"What about the ship? Did it get away, or did we sink it? Or did the storm do it?"

"Or did we summon the storm, and bring the ship down?" Caspian asked.

Reuben huffed out a deep breath and leaned back in his chair. "Wow.

Double-crossing him and cursing his gang would be a very good reason to come after us now."

"But don't forget they've been enhanced somehow, probably by Mariah, who has to be the witch Gil detected walking in the spirit world. Maybe her family was involved all those years ago, and this is her chance to have her revenge on us?"

"Or maybe this is just opportunistic. They found out the connection to us, and decided to have fun." Reuben sighed. "Whatever. We need to stop them—for good. They're strong, in the spirit world, too. They've captured Helena."

Caspian nodded. "So I gather, and set Gil in action. Of course, the other option is that the curse tied them to the treasure, or their bones, meaning they couldn't rest." He frowned. "Seems short-sighted though. You'd want them gone forever." He stood and carried his plate to the sink. "Come on, Reuben. Enough maybes. Let's find this damn spell and work out what they did. You're right, it's the key. Then, I think we need to head out there."

His gaze lingered on the island in the mist, sure that somewhere under it lay the answers to Coppinger's doom.

Twenty-Three

After thirty minutes of slow progress through narrow tunnels, El wondered again why she'd volunteered to come with Newton.

Wheal Droskyn, which was the name of the tin mine at Droskyn Point in Perranporth, was one of the oldest in Cornwall, parts of it estimated to be 2,000 years old. Fortunately, the oldest workings were shallow, but that didn't make the experience any better. The newer parts went much deeper, with shafts that dropped deep into the earth, one leading into a cave that was known to have been used for smuggling in the past.

El was dressed in jeans and boots, complete with a hard hat, for which she was very grateful. The tunnel was low in places, and they had to duck and squirm through tight passages, watching their every step. In the end only the four of them had gone in, and Newton had left two constables outside the entrance to stop anyone from following. Jethro Carter, their guide through the mines, was at the front, followed by Newton, and Moore was behind her.

El's headlamp illuminated the stonework, some of which was stained blue from thin seams of copper deposits, although this was mined predominantly for tin. She wished she could use a witch-light, but Jethro's presence made it impossible. Jethro had expressed disbelief that anything was hidden in here, explaining that because the oldest mines were easily accessed by the narrow path along the cliffs, many people had explored here over the years. The newer, deeper sections were sealed off on the whole. Although, he did say there were a couple of access points through narrow shafts. All of the mine workings above ground had long since been pulled down, and major shafts had been capped for safety.

They reached an intersection of tunnels and Jethro paused to pull out his map, addressing them as he did so. "The way to the left is where our particular adit accesses, but as I said, I doubt you'll find anything there. This area has been explored countless times, and there are certainly no remnants of treasure." He frowned at them. "I've been down here, admittedly years ago now, and I never saw anything, either. Unless, of course, someone hid something more recently."

Newton shook his head. "No, I doubt that. But whether anything's there or not, I do want to try and find where the girl could have been."

Before they entered the mine, Newton had told Jethro some very basic information, but the lack of clarity was obviously very frustrating for him. While they talked, El extended her magic, trying to sense a supernatural presence, but so far all she could feel was cold, damp air, and the metals that were layered through the earth. In the pockets of her coat were a piece of Shadow's fey armour and a few fey coins, for bribery purposes, but she hoped she wouldn't have to use them. It struck her that mines would be a natural place for spriggans to be, considering the metals that were all around them.

Moore was silent, as usual, just staring around the space suspiciously. He looked as tired as Newton. Both of them had thick stubble and shadows under their eyes as if they hadn't slept for days, and El was sure that Moore had been as affected by Inez's death as Newton.

"Keep going left," Newton said, finally ending their discussion, and Jethro turned and led the way again.

They passed dark entrances—crawl spaces, really, that El peered down nervously—but Jethro ignored them, leading them deeper and deeper as he explained that they had reached a newer section of the mine. The tunnels were shored up in places with huge wooden beams, but they bulged alarmingly at some points, while other areas dripped with moisture.

"You're lucky," he said to them as they walked. "Many newer areas are inaccessible, unless you have climbing equipment. These hills are riddled with shafts." They entered a large cave, the deeper parts running to their right, and he took out a flare and lit it, hurling it into the darkness where it illuminated a pool of water and a dark exit at the end. "Through there are shafts filled with water. It's treacherous. The part we're heading to is dry." He looked at all three of them. "Are you sure you want to go on?"

"A woman has died," Newton said abruptly. "Yes, I do."

They eventually reached a big, barred gate that lead to another area of the mine, and Jethro swore.

"Someone has broken the padlock."

"*What*?" Newton pushed him aside.

The gate was rudimentary, set into the rock wall to block the narrow tunnel that led deeper into the earth. A chain and padlock had secured it, but it now hung loose, the chain cut cleanly through.

Newton turned to El, his expression saying everything before he nodded at Jethro. "It means we're on the right track, then. Go on, but slowly!"

Jethro was a man in his fifties, with grey hair, a grizzled beard, and a gruff manner. He wielded a heavy, handheld torch as well as his headlamp, and he hefted the former like a weapon before heading down the passage. El glanced at Moore, but as usual he looked inscrutable and just waved El ahead of him.

"Do you want me to go first, Newton?" she asked him.

He shook his head. "No, but stay sharp."

They progressed deeper, passing other passageways, and El quickly lost her way. This was terrifying. If something happened to Jethro, who was clearly very comfortable with finding his way down here, they could be lost forever.

Eventually, he called over his shoulder, "We're nearly there. The adit runs off this tunnel."

The tunnel widened and the roof lifted, finally bringing them to a larger area. However, when they reached it, Jethro swore again. "What the bloody hell?" He trailed off, looking dumbstruck at a hole in the rock face. "That's new."

"It is?" Newton asked, excited.

"Absolutely. I haven't seen it before. Look at the edges where the stone has been broken, and the new rock fall."

He was right. Although rocks of various sizes were strewn across the ground, some of them had edges that weren't discoloured by age, and the border of the new hole in the wall looked fresh, too.

Jethro pointed to the dark, low tunnel to the side and crouched, shining his torch down it. "You can see daylight down there. That's the beach. It carries water out of here. As you can see from the damp ground, it can get very wet in here. We're lucky it's only drizzling."

El crouched, spying a tiny pinprick of light at the far end. *This is where it happened. Jasmine was killed here.*

She stood quickly, extending her magic perception, again searching for something supernatural, or the ancient magic that Avery said she'd felt, but nothing seemed out of place, and she shook her head at Newton, who watched her carefully. He nodded, directing Jethro to keep to the side, and after flashing his torch light across the ground, stuck his head through the newly-made hole. El stood next to him. Their torchlight illuminated another cave beyond, and at the far side, on a rudimentary rock shelf, were the remnants of old, wooden chests.

"Bingo," Newton said softly.

Jethro squeezed next to them, looking in too. "Incredible. Are you telling me that those have been in there all this time?" He stepped back and examined the rock face. "I have *never* noticed anything abnormal about this wall."

Newton was already clambering over the lip and stepping into the cave. El followed, her power pulsing at her fingertips, and as soon as she entered the cave, she felt it. An ancient presence that watched them. She threw out her arm to block Newton, but before she could assess what was going on, a creature exploded out of the darkness, throwing Newton against the wall and sending her rolling across the floor before *something* landed on her chest.

★ ● ◌ ✶ ● ◌ ✷ ● ◌ ✦ ●

Alex groaned as he exited the kitchen of The Wayward Son, hearing Jago laughing loudly at the terrible joke he'd just told him. The other kitchen staff groaned as well, but Jago didn't care; the worse the joke, the more he laughed. As the door swung shut behind him, Jago's laughter was replaced by the chatter and music in the pub.

Friday lunchtime was often busy in the pub. Everyone was winding down for the weekend, and despite the grey drizzle and mist that had set in outside, everyone seemed determined to have fun. A few lights were on to alleviate the gloom, and the low music added to the atmosphere. Alex served a few customers and took some food orders, and then noting Zee was restocking the glasses, headed to his side to help.

"I hear you had an interesting night," Zee said, absently polishing a glass.

"That's one word for it. I take it Ash updated you?"

He nodded. "Did you know Caspian's warehouse was attacked, too?"

"No!" Alex said, alarmed. "Anyone hurt?"

"Fortunately not. Caspian's protection spell held." Zee looked worried. "They seem to be scaling up their activities."

"I agree. I just wonder what set them off in the first place. It has to be the fact that their treasure has been disturbed."

"Seems logical," Zee agreed. He looked across the pub. "Your ghost hunters are here."

Alex turned to see Cassie, Ben, and Dylan take seats at the corner of the bar, and he hurried over to them. "Is everything okay?" He looked them up and down, but they didn't seem to be injured.

"We're fine," Cassie assured him. "Why so worried? You've got a line between your eyes."

His hand flew to his forehead. "Have I?"

She sniggered. "Don't worry. I'm sure it's not permanent."

"I bet it will be," he grumbled. "We're having a nightmare at the moment."

"So I gather," Dylan said. He was distracted, eyeing the menu in his hand. "Let's get a pint and some food and then we'll tell you what we've found."

Alex nodded, quickly sorting their drinks and taking their order, and then Ben lowered his voice and leaned forward. "We decided to take some general readings in the areas that have been affected by current events."

"Newton told us."

"Fowey, Looe, here, and Perranporth," Dylan explained. "And we noticed something odd."

"Odder than spirit activity?"

"Yes," Cassie answered, sipping her cider. "We've calibrated our instruments, based on what we've learned over the last year, so that we're more specific in our searches."

Alex was confused. "Isn't that counterintuitive? Won't you fail to pick up on stuff?"

Ben shook his head, impatient. "No. We search wide and then narrow it down. And we position ourselves above towns too, which is pretty easy in a lot of Cornish coastal towns. We can set ourselves up on the hill, and take readings for the whole place."

"Especially at night," Dylan added, "using the thermal imaging camera."

All three of them were looking very excited as they started explaining, and Alex was intrigued.

"We've been taking base readings over the last year," Ben said, "as a matter of course, and knowing how interesting Cornwall can be, and we've definitely found changes."

"Hold on!" Alex looked at them, amazed. "You took readings across Cornwall? Wasn't that a huge amount of work?"

They all shrugged, and Cassie, said, "Sure it was. But we did it over months, more as data-gathering, really, for our website."

Dylan's eyes widened. "You'd be amazed at the sort of supernatural energy that's out there. We're going to study some of the old sites next—you know, dolmens, stone circles, remains of old forts—and put all that on our website, too." He grinned. "We're kind of making a map of the spookiest places in Cornwall!"

"Wow." Alex was impressed. "That's great advertising for you. And very useful for us!"

"Exactly," Ben said. "So all of this work is valuable all around. Anyway, considering the recent events, we went back to the places where the deaths occurred and noticed another type of energy. *Your* type."

"What do you mean, my type?" Alex asked, confused.

"Witch-type!"

"You can differentiate?"

"Sure," Cassie nodded. "We took your readings, remember? Your energy signature is different. Well, when you do magic."

"I guess that confirms what we suspected, especially after last night," he told them, and quickly updated them on spotting Mariah leaving Ethan's house.

Dylan looked pleased. "Great, so that corroborates us too, not that we really doubted that."

"So where is *our* type of energy?" Alex asked.

"Well, we see it in the centres where you witches are based. The coven members, I mean," Ben said. "Obviously there was a big cloud of magic over White Haven, but that's gone now. Looe and Fowey are hotspots, and that's to be expected. But," he faltered, glancing at the others, "there's some over Gull Island, too."

Alex gripped the counter in alarm, and then tried to calm himself. "I guess that sort of makes sense. Reuben's house was attacked last night, too. And he was attacked in the caves there."

"It's big, Alex," Cassie said, eyeing him nervously. "The energy pouring off that place is very strong."

Alex started to feel very uneasy. It may be an island, but there was a path running from it to Reuben's house. *Was last night's attack the start of something bigger?* He should phone Reuben, just to check on him. And then he thought of El and Newton heading down Wheal Droskyn. Unpleasant images of them lying dead and broken in a mineshaft filled his head.

"Did you see anything over Perranporth? El and Newton are there today."

"Oh, yeah," Dylan said, huffing. "We've saved the best 'til last. We saw a really old energy signature there! We even went on to the beach to check. Not too close, because of that girl's death, but close enough. It's enormous. Giant-sized."

★ ❂ ⬩ ✳ ❂ ⬩ ✱ ❂ ⬩ ✳ ❂

El slammed her power against the creature on her chest, sending it flying, and then lashed at it with a wave of fire, throwing it back against the rock face. She dropped the fire, but used air like a battering ram to hold it in position, and staggered to her feet. She could feel seams of metal behind the spriggan, and decided she could use it.

Her magic was particularly attuned to metals, especially after years of working them, and she reached for them now. Tendrils of tin emerged from the earth, and she fashioned them quickly into a cage, securing the spriggan in place and enhancing its prison with magic.

Out of the corner of her eye, she saw Moore wrestle with Jethro, trying to keep him from entering the cave. Moore couldn't see Newton, and El heard the panic in his voice as he shouted his name. Wow. He actually spoke.

"I'm okay," Newton shouted back. Well, groaned would be the better word. "Stay back."

He dragged himself to his feet, and checking that El was okay, they both advanced on the furious spriggan.

"Nice reflexes," he said to El admiringly, but without taking his eyes off the creature.

"I should have been quicker." She was annoyed with herself. She had known they would likely be attacked, and had still ended up on her back.

Newton was pre-occupied with their prisoner. "That's an ugly little thing. Like some bloody deformed baby." He grimaced. "So this is a spriggan!"

"It seems so," El murmured, taking in its odd appearance.

She pulled the fey metal out of her pocket, waving it in front of the spriggan's eyes. It immediately watched it with ill-concealed greed.

"This is yours, little man," she said, "if you promise to behave."

It shot her a calculating look as it grasped the bars of its cage.

"Understand me?" she asked, studying it. "Or I can do worse than pin you to the wall." She hated to threaten it. It was like Shadow had said. It acted on instinct, but that's what made it even more dangerous.

"Wait," Newton said. "Do you think it can answer questions?"

"You can try."

She continued to hold the fey armour in front of it as a reward, as Newton said, "This is yours if you tell me who came here."

It hissed, looking at Newton malevolently, and for a second El didn't think it either could or would answer, and then with a horribly grating voice it said, "Four humans came, three left. One death for one death."

El and Newton glanced at each other, puzzled.

"What do you mean?" Newton asked.

It snarled and then pointed to the far end of the cave, lost in darkness. Newton flashed his torch that way, lighting up the tiny, lifeless form of another spriggan.

El felt rage build within her. Someone had killed it! Logically she knew that spriggans were violent, but still, it was sad, and it had obviously retaliated, killing Jasmine.

Newton pressed on. "Men or women?"

"Two men, two women." It flicked its angry, beady eyes at El. "Hair like that one."

"Blonde?" Newton asked.

"Like silver. Much power."

"What did they take?"

"All the gold, all the gold, all the gold." It kept repeating it over and over again in its rasping little voice, making El's skin crawl. "Give me the fey treasure!" Its hands flexed with greed.

Newton looked balefully at El. "I doubt it can tell me anything else."

"I have a question." She turned to the creature. "Why are you still here?"

"More gold. More gold. More gold."

Again it glanced nervously to the side, and in the light of Newton's torch, they saw a few spilled coins.

"Okay," Newton said. "We're going to give you this, and then you leave, for good. More men are coming, and I don't want to hurt you. And you need to take your friend."

It looked as if it was about to argue, but it clearly understood what Newton was saying, because it nodded. El released her magic, dismantled the cage, and handed it the armour. In seconds it scampered across the ground, grabbed the other body, and disappeared through a barely there crack in the wall.

El kept her magic readied, just in case. "What now?"

"Now I get a team in here to examine every inch of this place, to see if we can find some evidence of who was here." He shook his head, frustrated, as he looked around. "They must have found an old map with this hidden cave, and worked out how to get to it. They're determined, I'll give them that."

"It has to be Mariah!"

"I agree. And I think it must be Ethan, too. Like you guys, I don't believe in coincidences, and there are too many connections."

"And there's someone else. Another man."

"He has a brother. It could be him, or maybe a colleague." He patted El's shoulder and gave her a weak smile. "Thank you for coming."

"My pleasure." She hesitated, and then said, "Well done for not wanting to kill it—even after what one of them did to Inez."

"Yeah, well, like you said, it acts on instinct. I'll save my revenge for those who started this whole thing."

El smiled. "Fair enough, but I'll hang around here, just in case." Despite the fact that the spriggan had vanished, she didn't want to take any chances. "If you can explain me being here."

"The team were okay in Looe. I think the crowds put it off attacking again."

She shrugged. "I'm here now. Let me be useful."

"All right. I'll think of something."

"When are you going to interview Ethan?"

"This afternoon. I'll leave SOCO to it here, if you're okay with that?"

"Absolutely. Catch us up with a pint later? My treat."

"You're on." He nodded to Jethro, where he stood looking at both of them wide-eyed with shock. "And you might want to glamour that one. Make it good."

★ ⑨ ◌ ★ ⑨ ◌ ✳ ⑨ ◌ ★ ⑨

Alex stared at the three investigators. "When you say *giant*, do you mean just a big wave of energy?"

"No." Dylan looked excited, the complete opposite of Alex's feelings. "We mean an energy field in the shape of a giant was visible on the cliff top. Just briefly, and then it vanished."

"A giant? An actual giant!"

"Yes," Ben nodded, also grinning. "That piece of footage may actually get us on the news. It must have something to do with those spriggan-creatures you mentioned."

"Fuck it! El and Newton are there today." Alex tried to be logical. They knew this might happen, but at least Alex had faced a spriggan with another witch. Alex reached for his phone, anxiously watched by his three friends who no longer looked so excited, and called El and then Newton. Neither of them answered. "Crap."

"But they're down a mine, right?" Dylan pointed out. "They wouldn't get the call, anyway."

At that point, Avery walked in and sat on a stool, her broad smile disappearing as she looked at their expressions. "What's going on?"

Alex quickly updated her, half expecting to see Avery race out of there, but she nodded calmly instead.

"She'll be okay," she reassured him. "Shadow popped into the shop this morning with a tip and a present—fey metal and coins. She gave them to El. They worked well as bribery, apparently, when she and Gabe found the one at Looe."

"Yeah, but you have to get it to stop bashing your brains in first!" Alex reminded her. "You're very blasé about this. Inez died because of one of those!"

"I haven't forgotten that," she said, infuriatingly calm. "But El is forewarned, and we weren't. She'll be okay. Can I have a wine, please?"

He shot her an annoyed look and then grabbed a glass, wishing he could have a pint, too. "When did you get so Zen all of a sudden?" he asked as he poured her drink. "That's normally my job."

"Of course I'm worried, but I trust El. She's a strong witch."

"Agreed," Cassie chimed in. "Sorry we alarmed you, Alex." She told Avery what they'd seen on the Perranporth cliff top, stunning her into momentary silence.

Avery took a large sip of wine as if to fortify herself, and when she finally spoke, she said, "Proof of giants! That's amazing. Actual Cornish giants! Just that one, or are there more?"

"Isn't one enough?" Alex asked. What was the matter with them all?

"Only one so far," Ben answered. "But now that we've seen one, I think we should check other areas that folklore tell us had giants. Their spirits could still be there, striding the landscape."

Alex groaned. "They could be, but I really hope you don't find any more, and that this little spate of attacks has been stirred up by these events." He studied Ben, Cassie, and Dylan's faces, each one pleased with their success, and felt bad that he couldn't be more enthusiastic. He knew they were upset about the recent deaths, they weren't monsters, but he also understood how important this was to them. "You didn't see one in Fowey or Looe?"

"No, just Perranporth," Dylan said. "But, like we said, it vanished in seconds. We could have missed the others."

Cassie looked apologetic. "Sorry, but just because we've seen it won't make things worse."

"Of course it won't, and it is amazing," Avery said, shooting Alex a warning look that told him to be nicer. "I can't wait to tell Dan and Sally. In fact, you must bring your footage to show us. We really should all see it, too!"

"That's partly why we're here," Ben said. "To see if we can arrange a time."

Avery nodded. "I think we're heading to Reuben's tonight. I'll check. You should come if you're free. Just be aware that they're under a lockdown up there, all sealed up with protection spells."

All three nodded immediately.

"Just check with Reuben, and we'll be there," Ben agreed.

"So, Avery," Alex said, "did you have success this morning?"

Her face fell. "No. A complete bust at St Catherine's Castle, as expected. But the good news is that everything seemed settled up there. No weird findings or magical happenings. I thought I'd pop in, have some lunch, and then head back to the shop. But I have another suggestion for tonight. I think you should scry to watch Mariah. We're on the back foot on all this, and I'm sick of it. We need to get ahead."

Alex nodded. "All right. That's probably a good idea."

He paused when Anna approached carrying a couple of bowls of fries, and she placed them on the counter with a cheery, "Here you go, guys," before heading back to the kitchen.

Dylan reached for a chip. "I've just thought of something else we should do, too. Set the camera up to point at Gull Island again. That could prove very interesting!"

"Excellent," Avery said, reaching for her phone. "I'll ring Reuben and organise it all."

Twenty-Four

R euben ended the call with Avery and said to Caspian, "Well, that's sorted, then. Everyone's coming around tonight."

Caspian looked up from his grimoire. "Who's everyone?"

"The witches, plus Ben, Dylan, and Cassie. They have thermal imaging footage they want to show us."

Caspian studied him for a moment, an almost unreadable expression on his face, and then he asked, "Do you all do this a lot?"

"Catch up for drinks and watch weird thermal imaging footage? Yes to the first, not really to the second," he answered, sitting again at the old wooden table in the attic spell room. "Why?"

Caspian had a sort of lost look on his face, which was a weird word to use, but it suddenly made Reuben feel very sorry for him. "No reason," he answered. "It just seems you have a busy social life. You're very close, your coven."

"We are. We get together in each other's houses, and in Alex's pub. It's what friends do, right?" Even as he was saying it, Reuben got the distinct impression it wasn't what Caspian did. Before he could consider whether it was an okay question to ask, he said, "You must catch up with your friends a lot. Or your family, at least. They're your coven, aren't they?"

Caspian gave a dry laugh. "No, we do not. We discuss business, mainly."

"But you have non-business friends?" he asked, starting to turn the pages of his grimoire in an effort to keep the conversation light. For some reason, he felt he was on unstable ground.

"My business friends are my friends," Caspian said, "and we socialise in fancy restaurants or over boardroom tables."

Caspian's voice had taken on an edge, and Reuben risked a glance at him, but Caspian was studying his grimoire, too.

Regret. That's what Reuben heard in his voice and saw on his face.

"And Estelle? She must be a riot at Christmas!" Reuben's tone was cheeky, hoping to get something positive from Caspian.

Caspian looked him straight in the eye. "Now I know you're taking the piss."

Reuben leaned back, all pretence at reading his grimoire gone. "I'm not taking the piss. She is your sister, and for all you bicker, I'm sure you must get on, really."

"We tolerate each other, and I think that might have just run its course, too." He shrugged. "So be it. I'm sure we'll muddle together for the business." He nodded over at Reuben's end of the table, and the grimoires open in front of him. "Anyway, have you found anything useful?"

"No. But I'm sure I will. You?"

"No, and it's beginning to piss me off."

"Me too."

Once he and Caspian finished their breakfast, Reuben had taken him up to what had once been the hidden attic. Since Gil and Alicia died, Reuben had decided to take out the brick wall that divided his spell room from the main attic, and now it could be accessed without having to use the hidden passageway in the walls. He'd debated whether it was wise to take Caspian there, and then laughed at his paranoia. Caspian knew he was a witch. He wouldn't give a crap where his spell room was, and no casual visitor would ever see the attic. And if he ever split up with El, there was no way he would become involved with someone who didn't know he was a witch. Life was far too complicated for that. For the last few hours they had once again examined the grimoires for potential spells used on Coppinger, but all Reuben had achieved was a headache. They even used witch-light to reveal invisible spells, and had then tried finding spells, but still hadn't discovered anything their ancestors may have used. They'd debated a couple that might be plausible, and then dismissed them just as quickly.

Reuben pointed to the stack of papers he had found in Caspian's attic, just before he'd been attacked. "What about those?"

He shrugged. "Interesting letters, but nothing that suggests what the spell could be, or where it was finally executed."

Reuben looked around the attic, distracted. "I guess any of these spells that we've found could be adapted, but I just have a feeling I'm missing something. I think Virginia would have been keen to hide any evidence...like in their letters, really. The contents were kept deliberately vague. I suspect the spell is either right under our noses and we've missed it, or it's hidden in this house somewhere—or at yours. I know there are hidden passages all around this place."

Caspian laughed. "I once found an entire secret room in Harecombe Manor."

"A torture chamber?"

"No! I don't think we were that bad, thanks Reuben."

"Just kidding." He sighed. "Virginia wouldn't have been proud of cursing a load of men, even if it saved the town. She'd have hidden the spell really well."

Caspian shook his head. "We're thinking about this all wrong. This was Serephina's suggestion. It's our family's spell, not yours. It has to be in my grimoire. And although I'm sure Serephina wouldn't give a crap about cursing a whole load of smugglers, I doubt she'd have wanted to shout about it, either." He smiled. "You said the spell would be under our noses."

"Yes, but how does that help?"

"There's a spell on it, something to hide it."

"But we've already used witch-lights and finding spells! I don't get it."

"I think the entire page has been hidden, and that requires a different spell to find it."

Reuben was still confused. How many layers of subterfuge could you use to hide a spell? But Caspian started to look very excited and grabbed the letters, making a pile of them on the table.

"Have you got a silver bowl, Reuben?"

"Sure." He stood to take one off the shelf. "Are you doing another finding spell?"

"No, an unveiling spell. Where are your letters?"

Reuben picked them up from the corner of the table, and watched Caspian add them to his own stack and place them all in the bowl. "I hope you're not attached to them, because I need to burn them."

"Wait. Let's take photos of them first, just in case." If Reuben had learnt anything from the other witches, it was to take notes and have backup plans.

"While you do that, I'll get the herbs I need—if you don't mind."

He looked at Reuben uncertainly, and Reuben wished he'd stop standing on ceremony. "Stop asking, Caspian. Assume it's yours."

Caspian gave a small smile and started to prepare his ingredients while Reuben took photos of all the letters with his phone.

Five minutes later, they were both seated opposite each other, with one solitary candle in front of them, the bowl of letters mixed with herbs, and Caspian's grimoire. Reuben eyed it warily. Caspian's grimoire had a very different feel than his own. Some spells exuded an undercurrent of menace, and while there were some spells in his that gave a prickle of unease because of the power and intent within them, the spells within Caspian's gave him the shivers. Pushing his misgivings aside, he clasped Caspian's outstretched hands, struck by how odd this unlikely pairing was.

"My reasoning," Caspian explained, "as I said, is that you're right. This spell is in here, and we can't see it because it has been thoroughly hidden. I have a few unveiling spells I've used before, but this one should be the best for this purpose. I'm trusting our bloodlines and magical heritage will help."

"Do I need to do anything?"

"Just lend your energy to mine."

Silence fell as Caspian took several deep breaths, and then he intoned the spell. The letters in the bowl burst into flames, and the smoke wafted over the table. A light breeze sprang up, and the candle flickered as Reuben felt Caspian's power extend. Reuben offered up his own, and Caspian weaved them together, and then directed the smoke over the grimoire. It wrapped sinuously around it, teasing the pages apart. For a moment, the smoke hesitated as if meeting resistance, but Caspian raised his voice, and with it his magic, and the spell strengthened.

Suddenly pages flickered violently, from one end of the book to the other, so quickly it seemed the book might tear apart. Then a wave of power blasted from it, throwing Reuben out of his chair and against the wall as raucous cries filled the room.

Everything went black.

★·❂·◌·✳·❂·◌·✴·❂·◌·✳·❂

As Briar exited her old Mini on Reuben's drive, an explosion resounded from above, glass showering around her as a wave of magic sent her crashing to the ground.

Flat on her back, she stared horrified at the upper level of Reuben's house, seeing an oily, green vapour pouring from the attic windows. Even from down here she could feel the power of the spell; it reeked of lost souls.

Scrambling to her feet, she raced to the front door, spelled it open, and ran up the broad flight of stairs. The spell was stronger inside, and she could hear screams from above that made her skin crawl. Shit. Was that Reuben or Caspian?

Horrified, she ran even faster, her heart slamming in her chest, trying to reason through what she could feel. Desperately trying to contain her panic, she shouted, "Reuben! Caspian!"

There was no response.

The first and second floor were being pounded with waves of magic, and the thick green vapour that had poured from the upper windows eddied around her, filling her lungs and seeping into her hair and her clothes. She summoned the Green Man from deep within her, then blasted rich, earthy magic around her like a shield, filling her instead with a clean spring power. But her heart was in her mouth as she reached the door to the attic. It had blown off its hinges and was lying on the floor.

Briar slowed, her hand on the doorframe as she peered up the narrow stairs into the gloom, wary of being attacked by spirits. Nothing moved, and the cries were ebbing away.

Throwing caution aside, she ran up and immediately felt as if she'd been plunged underwater. The attic was bathed in a murky green light that rippled across the walls and old, disused furniture, and everything seemed muffled. She heard the faint crash of the surf upon a distant shore, and inhaled the strong smell of the sea.

The green light was denser at the far end where Reuben's spell room was. Cautiously, she walked across the room, feeling the damp air swirl around her and settle on her skin, and desperate to dispel the strange sensation, forced the murk out of the broken windows, leaving the smell of blossoms in its place.

She finally halted on the spell room's threshold, unable to see anything in the gloom. The watery quality was thickest there, and a murmur of voices twisted around her; she felt anger, and the thick stench of vengeance. She tried to enter, but the magic pushed her back.

What had they done?

Briar was terrified now, and called out, "Reuben! Caspian!"

There was no answer. Screw this. She had to get in there. She focussed, trying to work out what magic she could feel and how to dispel it. She slowed her breathing, easing her panic. The voices were distracting, but she ignored them, concentrating only on the magic. Elemental water was strong here, entwined within the binding curse, and it was old, made with strangely familiar magic.

Briar pulled her earth magic from deep within her, feeling the Green Man rise again. "I need your help," she muttered to him, pleased when she felt his power ripple through her veins. She slipped her shoes off, feeling the wooden floor beneath her bare feet, warm and grounding, and forcing through the resistance, started to absorb the water into her earth magic like a sponge.

Briar resisted the urge to run in, knowing she had to contain the curse first. She would be useless to them if she got caught up in it, too. She caught a glimpse of Reuben and Caspian, each on either side of the room, their chairs upended, and the more she saw, the more horrified she became. This part of the attic was a wreck—shelves blasted off the walls, magical paraphernalia strewn across the room, and Reuben's grimoires in a heap in the corner. But Caspian's grimoire was in the centre of the wooden table, green light radiating from its open pages, words writhing in the air above it.

They must have found the curse used to bind Coppinger and his men, and what an ugly curse it was. Briar had no idea what exactly it contained, but she could feel its malevolence, and she had no doubt that the voices that still murmured in her ears were the souls of smugglers. She used a protection spell to contain Caspian's grimoire and the curse pouring from its pages, and then ran to Reuben's side.

Reuben was unconscious and partially upright, his shoulders and head propped against the wall. His breath was shallow and uneven, and he was horribly pale, but at least he was alive. Briar turned her attention to Caspian, and to her relief found he was alive too, but also unconscious, lying in a twisted heap under collapsed shelving. She rolled him gently over, checking his stab wound. Blood was trickling from it once more, but there were no new visible injuries, other than head wounds from where they had both struck the wall.

Briar shook Caspian gently, but although his eyes flickered beneath their lids, he didn't stir. She ran her hands inches above his body, familiar now with his energy, but something was horribly wrong. His life signs were low, and his magic a shadow of what it had once been. She reached for the nearest rug, wrapping it around him, and then returned to Reuben.

Briar had never felt so overwhelmed as she gazed at her friend. Reuben was vibrant, full of life and boundless energy, but now he was like a rag doll. Forcing herself to examine him dispassionately, she came to the same conclusion she had with Caspian. She rocked back on her heels, staring between them both. Whatever had happened had taken them both unawares, and had occurred within seconds of her arrival.

She needed to call the others.

Twenty-Five

A very stood next to Alex, gazing in horror at their friends' motionless bodies, and then at the malevolent curse that struggled to free itself from the pages of the grimoire, as if it was alive.

Briar had waited for them on the threshold of Reuben's spell room, but she had been busy. She had already set her bag up that contained all of her herbs and gems for healing spells, and was going through it methodically, muttering to herself as she worked on the most appropriate spell to help.

"I think we should take them downstairs," she suggested, breaking in on Avery's thoughts. "Either a bedroom or the snug, where I can keep a close eye on them. Can you use witch-flight to take them?"

"I'm not sure that will be a good idea," she said. "They're unconscious, their magic is subdued, and I don't know how the flight might affect them. It probably won't, but I'm terrified of making things worse."

"That's fine," Alex reassured her. "Use air to cushion them, and we'll float them down the stairs." He turned to Briar. "I think you're right. The snug is the best bet, rather than us all being spread out across this huge house."

He'd barely finished his sentence when El raced through the attic door, smeared with dirt and looking exhausted. She paused at the sight before her, and then tried to push past Alex, but he held her back.

"Just wait, El. The curse is still in that room, and we don't really know what it's done. We don't want you affected, too."

She glared at him. "Alex! That's Reuben lying there! I need to get to him."

"And you will. Let's just think this through, first."

Briar squeezed El's arm, trying to calm her down. "He's right. I've been in there and put a rudimentary protection around that grimoire, but the room feels weird, and so do they."

"Well, leaving them in there isn't going to do them any good!" El shot back, her blue eyes like ice.

"We're not going to," Avery said quickly. "But we need to be logical. We have no idea what's going on, and frankly, if Briar had arrived only five minutes earlier, she might have been caught up in this, too."

El took a deep breath, rubbing her hands over her face and smearing more dirt across her cheeks. "Sorry, you're right. I'm just worried. Look at him! Look at them both. They look so helpless. Is this what I looked like when I was cursed?"

Alex nodded. "I'm afraid so. But I don't think they *are* cursed. I think they've just been caught in the remnants of it!"

Avery summoned air, needing to do something, and she whisked it around the main attic, dispelling the rest of the green, watery quality that still lingered in the corners, and then directed the wind to Reuben. It wasn't easy to lift and cushion a body, even as skilled as she now was with air, but she worked slowly and patiently, and when Reuben was lifted sufficiently high enough, she brought him out of the room.

As soon as he was next to her, El took his hands. "He's so cold!"

"His spirit is buried deep within him," Briar explained. "So is Caspian's, and their energy is low. I'm planning a healing spell that should stabilise them."

Avery could tell Briar was very worried, and had a feeling things were worse than she was saying, but she concentrated on taking Reuben downstairs. "El, run ahead please. Grab blankets and sheets, and we'll make them comfortable on either the floor or the sofas."

El nodded, looking relieved at having something useful to do, and leaving Briar and Alex to talk about their options, left them to it.

It was fifteen minutes later when they all met again in the snug, with Caspian and Reuben laid next to each other in the corner of the room. El and Avery had made them as comfortable as possible, and Briar set up her herbs and potions.

"Can we help?" Alex asked her, watching anxiously.

"No," Briar said, shaking her head. "I'm going to stabilise their energies first. They're all over the place, and their magic is ebbing and flowing like the tide. It's so weird." She was on the floor, resting back on her heels, perplexed. "When I first arrived, I heard shouts...screams, really. I think I was hearing the smugglers' last moments." She shuddered, her dark hair tumbling around her face. "Now that I've had a chance to think about this, I believe the spell blasted out from the book, catching them completely unawares. Not only were they knocked unconscious, but the curse buried their spirits. It sounds weird, I know, but I think that's what I sense. I'm sure I can draw them back."

Alex studied them, arms across his chest. "That makes sense." He glanced at Avery. "Come on. Let's head up there and try to work out what happened."

"Let's also cleanse the house while we're at it," she said. "Have you got any sage, Briar?"

"Sure." She rummaged in her bag and thrust a bundle of dried herbs at Avery. "It's my own blend, similar to what we used at Beltane."

Avery lit the smudge stick with a spark of magic, and as she and Alex made their way back to the attic, they worked a cleansing spell, flushing the remaining toxic energies away, and saving the last of it to purify Reuben's attic. They eyed Caspian's grimoire warily, edging as close as they could around the protection spell.

"I have never seen a spell like that before," Alex said, half admiringly, half fearful.

"It reminds me a bit of your rune spell," Avery admitted, thinking of how the runes lit up the air and wrapped around their victim.

The words were whirling above the pages, the lines of text writhing around each other and showing no signs of slowing down.

"True." He leaned closer, squinting at the spell.

"Can you make out any words?" she asked Alex.

"It's old, I know that. The English is old-fashioned from the odd word I can make out, but the page itself is blank—as if the words have lifted clean off it. And I think I can see water swirling around, too. Briar was telling me the whole attic felt like it was underwater when she arrived."

Avery stared into the words, mesmerised, seeing dark blues mixed in with the green at its heart, the spell pulsing and throwing off sparks. "It's like the *spell* is underwater."

Alex met her eyes briefly. "I think you're right. I'm going to see if I can make out a few lines," he said, settling himself onto a chair.

Avery examined the room while Alex studied the spell, looking for clues among the mess on the floor. She crouched next to a silver bowl, the remnants of ashes in it. She sniffed it carefully, smelling paper and the faint whiff of burnt herbs. "I think they were doing some kind of revealing spell, Alex." She frowned. "Where are the letters?"

Alex only grunted, so she searched on her own, righting objects as she went and restoring order to the room, but the letters had gone. They must have used them to find the spell; it was logical, after all.

She told Alex what she'd found and he grunted absently again, finally saying, "So, not only did their ancestors veil their intent in cryptic letters, but they hid the spell, too. It was either because they were ashamed of it, or it was too powerful to share." He leaned even closer, the green light illuminating his face.

"Or," Avery added, "they knew it had a tendency to backfire."

Alex shook his head. "No, I don't think that's it. Maybe they hid it as a means of stopping someone from reversing it?" He frowned, rubbing his stubble as he stared at the grimoire. "None of this makes sense!"

"What if their spirits are so low that Briar can't get them? Would you have to?"

"I don't want to, but if that's our only option, of course I will."

"I think we should summon Gil, instead. Tonight."

"We said we'd never do that."

"But there's still no sign of Helena! And," she added, "tomorrow is the anniversary of Coppinger's disappearance. Anything could happen!"

"All right, I'll think on it. But now, I just want to study this. And perhaps we should call Estelle."

"I suppose we should." She could already hear Estelle's sharp, accusatory tone, and knew the reality would be so much worse.

"She's Caspian's sister, and will be well-versed with curse spells," Alex pointed out, but then he hesitated, too. "Let's see how far I get with this on my own."

"You're not studying it alone! I'll help, as soon as I've sealed the windows in some way," she said, moving to his side and squeezing his hand. "Two witches are better than one."

"That's what Serephina and Virginia thought, and look what they did!"

"They rid the world of Coppinger and his Cruel Gang! That's a plus, right?"

"*Was*," he said, turning back to the book. "Until now."

★ ☀ ◈ ✦ ☀ ◈ ✳ ◉ ◈ ✦ ☀

Newton studied Ethan James, and although they had barely started the interview, Newton was already annoyed with him. Moore stood at his side watching dispassionately, but he knew he was taking everything in.

They were in the corner of the large exhibition room at White Haven Museum, where half a dozen staff were putting the finishing touches on the displays. There was an atmosphere of controlled panic mixed with the buzz of anticipation and excitement. Newton had to admit that the exhibit looked impressive. Spotless glass cabinets displayed smuggling curios, and there were interactive displays too. There was a loud discussion at the far end of the room about what should be displayed more prominently. It seemed a little late for such discussions, but what did he know about how museums worked?

He tried to block the noise out as he again addressed Ethan. "As I said, Mr James, we do need your advice on the gold coins found at the scene of all three crimes. I'd also like to ask your opinion on the wooden chests that were found in Looe, and the human remains that were next to them. We feel you can offer us great insight, considering your speciality."

Ethan was a slim man in his forties, dressed in jeans and a shirt, attempting to look casually trendy. He was well-groomed and clean-shaven, and Newton was disappointed. He'd half expected him to look like Indiana Jones.

Ethan's lips narrowed. "This is a terrible time, I'm afraid. I am far too busy. As you can see, the exhibition opens tomorrow. I can recommend a couple of colleagues who can help."

"But I don't want to speak to your colleagues. I want to speak to *you*. You see, there's also the matter of your cousin, Jasmine, who was found in a mangled heap on Perranporth Beach."

Ethan blinked and swallowed. "Ah, yes. That was quite awful."

"Yes, it was. Were you close?"

He shook his head quickly. "No, not at all. I barely saw her."

"Oh, really? Even though she works at Charlestown with you? Her mother said that Jasmine had seen you recently, and seemed excited about something," Newton told him, an image of the crying, distraught woman filling his mind. "Any idea what that was?"

Ethan kept his expression carefully neutral. "No idea. I've been spending my time here, rather than Charlestown. I'd run into her briefly in Carlyon Bay, but that was all. It was so quick, I'd forgotten about it."

"She obviously had a passion for smuggling, like you."

Ethan was looking pale, but he was trying his best to bluster on. "Many of us do. That's not a crime. Er," he glanced around at his colleagues, who despite their busyness were watching them surreptitiously. "Should we go into my office?"

Now, he wanted his office! "Certainly. Lead the way."

He led them down a narrow set of stairs into the basement and opened the door to a windowless office, crammed with furniture and files, and by the time he sat behind his desk, gesturing Moore and Newton to sit too, he seemed to have composed himself.

"Right, you were saying?"

Newton threw the coins wrapped in evidence bags onto the desk. "These were found in the victims' mouths. What can you tell me about them?"

He looked reluctant to pick them up, but when he did, he examined them carefully. "Well, this one is a Spanish Doubloon, seventeenth century, and the other two are English Guineas. One is eighteenth and one nineteenth century." He put them back on the desk quickly, as if they might burn his fingers. "Not terribly uncommon, or particularly valuable."

"But if they were part of a hoard they would be, surely?"

"Well, that depends on how big the hoard was. It would be more valuable for historical purposes."

"It would also make an amazing display."

"Fascinating!" Ethan agreed. "But the chance of finding a hoard is incredibly low."

"I guess so." Newton studied him. Ethan looked uncomfortable now, his eyes darting around the room, and Newton said, "However, we believe the broken chests found in the cave in Looe contained treasure that was stolen recently, and we found evidence of more today in Wheal Droskyn. A few coins were left behind. We believe the thieves fled in panic. It was where Jasmine died."

"Wheal Droskyn?" Ethan's eyes were wide now, although he was desperately trying to maintain a calm façade. He started to stutter. "Er, what led you there?"

"The adit that Jasmine's body was forced through. She had a horrible death. Violent. Painful." Newton leaned forward, arms resting on the desk. "Are you okay, Mr James? You look unwell. Would you like some water?"

"No! I'm okay. Obviously, I'm upset at the manner of my cousin's death. Any idea who did this?"

"We have our suspicions." Newton decided to push him further. He'd put money on Ethan being involved. He was pale and sweating now, shuffling uncomfortably in his seat. "And we also believe that Jasmine's deceased boyfriend, Miles, was involved, too. I suspect they were behind the theft in Looe. This is what she must have been so excited about. And we believe there are accomplices."

Ethan pulled himself together. "Why on Earth would you think that?"

"Well, there's no evidence of the treasure in the house they shared together. No maps or papers that indicate how they knew where to go. And of course, the treasure in Wheal Droskyn is gone. If Jasmine was on her own, the treasure would still be there, surely."

"I suppose that's logical. But," he laughed incredulously, "I think your imagination is running away with you. I doubt they found a hoard of any kind. There would have been remnants only, the rest stolen long ago."

"The broken locks happened very recently. And the cave in the mine was also a recent find. Was Jasmine involved in this exhibit? Could she have found an old map in the new material that was discovered here?"

Ethan laughed, but there was a calculating expression behind his eyes. "Treasure maps! Please, Detective, I think that's a little far-fetched. No, she wasn't involved here, and everything we've found is upstairs, on display." He stood abruptly, his chair scraping against the floor. "Now, if you'll excuse me, I have an exhibition to finish. We open tomorrow, and I'm anxious that it should be perfect."

Newton and Moore stood too, and as Ethan came around the desk, they shook hands. "Thank you for your time, Mr James, but if you do think of anything else, please let us know."

"Of course!" He hustled them out of the door and up the stairs, and Newton watched him enter the exhibition, amused.

He turned to Moore. "Verdict?"

"Guilty. He's in it up to his neck."

"Let's have him watched tonight. I bet he'll be scurrying off somewhere as soon as he's able to."

Twenty-Six

Caspian was lost in a sea of green-blue mist.

He was formless, unable to discern arms from legs, or fingers from toes. He couldn't even feel any sensations, and for the first time in days, was free from the pain of his stab wound and bruises. With growing horror, he realised his spirit had left his body.

But he wasn't spirit-walking. There was no silver cord tying him to his body. He was somewhere else, and he had a horrible feeling he was in the spirit world. If the spirits of the smugglers found him, they would surely kill him, severing his spirit forever from his body, trapping him here.

Unless he was already dead.

He tried not to panic and concentrated on his surroundings, finally hearing distant voices. They were familiar. *Were they voices of the dead? No.* It was Briar, and then Avery and Alex, but he couldn't make out what they said.

That meant he couldn't be dead. He was hovering somewhere in between.

What the hell had happened? Trying to think was hard. He couldn't focus, and his thoughts drifted randomly. He'd been working a spell, but something else had happened.

Reuben! He'd been working with Reuben, and something had exploded from the pages of the grimoire. The voices of his friends were reassuring, grounding him, but he needed to know if Reuben was here. *But was this really the spirit world, or something different? Why did he feel as if he was drifting on a tide?* Drawing on the voices from above like an anchor, he cast around for Reuben's magical signature, and finally felt it. Relieved, he drifted towards it like a leaf on a current, shocked to hear Reuben's voice in his head.

"Caspian?"

"Reuben! Are you okay?"

"I'm great, except for the fact that I can't feel my body."

Great? Great was odd...

Caspian continued, regardless. "*We've left them behind. That bloody spell.*" Now that he was talking to Reuben, he had a sense of his shape and being, which helped ground him even further as he found his footing in this strange place. "*We need to get back to our bodies before we're discovered.*"

"By who?"

"The smugglers' ghosts, you idiot! We're in their world—I think."

Even in the spirit world, he could discern Reuben's dry scepticism. "*Pull the other one, Caspian.*"

"Look around! Where the hell else do you think we are?"

"I'm on a beach."

"What?" *Caspian looked around him, confused.* "No, you're not. We're in the middle of nothingness!"

"No, I'm on a tropical beach. It's so warm! I'm watching the sea right now."

"I thought you said you couldn't feel your body?"

"I can't, but I know I'm on a beach."

"That doesn't make sense."

"Neither do you."

Of all the people to be stuck in some sodding limbo-land with, he was with Reuben-bloody-surf-mad-Jackson! "*Reuben! Focus! How can you be on a beach when we were in your attic only minutes ago?*"

"You were in my attic? Weird."

"We were looking for the curse that killed Coppinger!"

Silence fell, and then he said, "*Oh yeah, I thought that was a dream.*"

"No! That is reality. Your beach is a dream. "

"Come and look at it, then you'll see. "

Reuben's voice seemed to be drifting away from him, and Caspian realised that Reuben could be dying. Or was he already dead? Was that why he was on a beach and Caspian wasn't?

Perhaps, Caspian reflected, he should be grateful for the weird, green mist rather than being in his happy place. Where would that even be? Avery's arms, that's whe*re*. He could feel her now, her softness, her slim body within his hold, her lips that tasted like honey. He'd drown in her, and he'd die happy.

★·☀·◌·✳·☀·◌·✲·☀·◌·✳·☀

Alex's eyes burned with fatigue, and he sat back in his chair, frustrated.

"I can make out a couple of lines of this spell, at best!"

"More than I can," Avery confessed, leaning back in the chair and stretching. "I think we have to admit that we can't do this."

"I hate being defeated by a spell."

"We're not good at curses, and there's a lot of elemental water in this. That's one of my weakest elements."

Alex exhaled heavily. "Mine, too. At least we've got a feel for the shape of it, even if we don't know the details."

"Come on," Avery said, rising to her feet. "I'm starving, and I want a glass of wine. No, *need* a glass of wine. And we should update the others on our lack of progress."

Alex glanced at his watch, groaning when he saw the time. "Shit, it's after seven. No wonder we're knackered and starving. Let's go downstairs and see who else has arrived." He looked around at the attic, properly focussing on it for the first time in the last couple of hours, and realised the malevolence and despair he'd felt earlier had vanished. "You did a good job of cleansing this, Avery."

"I had to. It felt toxic."

So many things here reminded him of Gil. "This must be weird for Reuben, being surrounded by Gil's stuff."

"*Their* stuff."

"Yeah, but still." He looked at Avery's tired and frustrated expression, her wild red hair soft on her shoulders. "I'm not sure I could stand to see all your stuff around me if anything happened to you. I think the memories would be too painful."

She stepped forward into his arms, snuggling against his chest. "I know what you mean, but I'd find it comforting, too."

He inhaled her fresh scent of musk and roses, and nuzzled her neck. "You make all this worthwhile."

She leaned back to look up at him, puzzled. "What do you mean?"

"Magic is great, but it's nothing without someone to share it with." His fingers trailed across her cheek. "I'm lucky. Seeing Gil's spirit again reminded me of him and Alicia, and it still burns me how awful that was—her deception. Their lies to each other."

"I agree. But we won't do that."

She sounded so certain, and yet she had kissed Caspian and kept that from him. His doubt must have showed, because she tightened her grip around him.

"Caspian kissed *me*," she reminded him forcefully, "just in case that's going through your head, and I told you about it! And I guarantee it won't happen again!"

"I know. I trust you, but it still niggles me. Especially since I've come to realise that Caspian isn't going anywhere. He's one of us now, in some weird annoying way." He wanted to say he was like a bad rash, but he decided Avery wouldn't appreciate that.

"And we're stronger for having him as a friend."

"As long as we don't have to put up with Estelle, too."

"Oh, she hates us, so we won't." She stretched up to kiss him. "Come on, mister. Food time."

When they reached the bottom of the stairs, El was just closing the front door, and white plastic bags were on the floor around her, filled with cartons.

"El! You bloody superstar. I smell curry!" Alex hurried forward and picked up a couple of bags as she turned to smile at him. She looked tired, but seemed a little less bleak than she had earlier. And cleaner. "You've showered!"

"I had to. I stank of Wheal Droskyn," she said, picking up two bags and handing them to Avery, and then another two for herself before walking down the hall. "Have you had success?"

Avery shook her head. "No, other than identifying a couple of lines. We'll update you when we're all together." She gestured to the bags. "Why have we got so much food?"

"Because *everyone* is here! Ash is down in the billiard room, so I'll take some down to him."

They stopped in the kitchen, finding beer for Alex and wine for Avery, and when they entered the snug, they found that Ben, Cassie, and Dylan had just arrived, the room full of chatter. Alex glanced at Reuben and Caspian, but they were still lying unconscious under the blankets.

He greeted the others, and then said to Briar, "No luck, then?"

"Not yet." She gestured to the gemstones she'd used on various points of their bodies, and the herbs burning steadily in bowls around them, their fragrance scenting the room. "I'm drawing out their spirit, and stabilising their energies, but they're slow to respond. Did you have luck with the spell?"

Alex rolled his eyes. "No. But from the couple of lines I could read, it's a doozy. Let's hope Caspian can decipher it. Before we get into it, let's eat."

After a flurry of activity they all settled themselves into the snug, plates perched on laps, with the various naan breads and accompaniments spread across the coffee table. A low fire was burning in the grate, and Alex looked outside for the first time in hours, seeing that rain was falling heavily now, and a sea mist had rolled in, obscuring the grounds from view.

He settled in his chair and started to eat, listening to El update them on her day.

Ben groaned. "I can't believe we missed another spriggan!"

"But it sounds like you've recorded the essence of one," Briar pointed out. She was still seated next to the two unconscious witches, keeping a close eye on them while she ate what seemed to Alex like a tiny portion of food. "I can't wait to see the footage."

Dylan mumbled through a mouthful of curry, "I'll put it on in a minute."

Alex turned to El. "Did SOCO find anything while you were there?"

She frowned and shrugged as she tore a piece of naan. "They certainly searched the place thoroughly, and they took my footprints and finger-prints to rule me out, but I don't know. I certainly couldn't see anything obvious."

"Did you pick up any magic signatures you might recognise again?" Avery asked.

"No. The place felt swept clean. It was only the news from the spriggan himself that told us anything."

Cassie put her empty plate on the table, and said, "So there were two men and two women, one of whom was Jasmine—who is now dead."

El nodded. "Yep, and we have no idea who the others are, except for the fact that the woman was blonde. Silver-haired as the spriggan said." She shrugged again. "I'm presuming Mariah, but I hate to jump to conclusions. Newton hopes to come by later, so we'll see if he has any updates. He was going to interview Ethan. Now your turn," she said to Alex and Avery.

Alex said, "The spell is complex, heavily rooted in elemental water that harnesses the power of the sea, and it's definitely a curse. I can understand why Serephina needed help to execute it."

"But why has it affected Caspian and Reuben?" El asked.

"They hid the curse with the aid of another spell—obviously a strong one. We think," he glanced at Avery, "that they did a kind of unveiling spell, and when that lifted, it knocked them out." A thought struck him. "Maybe they had to veil the spell because it was so strong, rather than hide it just for the sake of it. It's struggling to get off the page now, like it's alive."

He wasn't sure he'd explained it very well, but the others nodded anyway, and Cassie asked, "Is that common, for a spell to try to escape like a living thing?"

"Bloody hell, no!" Avery exclaimed, horrified. "I can't imagine anything worse. I can only think that it was a regular spell that they embellished, and it just became too much to control. Hence, the spell to contain it." She sipped her wine, looking thoughtful. "I couldn't make out any of the text, but Alex could—just a couple of lines. Enough so that we know it's a very ugly curse." She referred to the notes that she pulled from her jeans pocket. "It's quite chilling. It says, 'As your spirit leaves your body, it will be forever bound to the object of your desire.' We're presuming their desire is gold."

"Seriously?" Cassie exclaimed. "Chilling doesn't cover it *at all*!"

"I guess that explains why the spirits want vengeance," El pointed out. She had settled into an armchair next to the fire, and was sipping her beer, all the while keeping an eye on Reuben. "I would, after that!"

Briar leaned forward, her elbows on her knees. "Was it directed at Coppinger and all his men?"

"Hard to say. The only other line I could make out was, 'To all who have lost and failed to grow old, thou shall know their pain a thousand fold.'"

"A thousand fold?" Cassie repeated. "If that's all you can read, what else is in that horrible spell?"

A silence fell on the room as they absorbed the enormity of the curse, and Ben nodded slowly. "So what now?"

"Great question," Alex admitted. "We know there's a curse, we assume it involves Coppinger, and we know it's horrible, which helps us understand some of what's happening. Potentially, when they found the first of Coppinger's treasure in Looe, they disturbed the spriggan, and maybe the spirits of the three dead men. This could have been the trigger event for the other spirits to rise, maybe accidentally at first—"

"And then Mariah decided to strengthen the ghosts," Avery cut in. She shook her head. "I still don't understand how she knew this was related to Reuben and Caspian. I mean, did she decide that making the ghosts stronger would be fun, just for the sake of it? Or was it a calculated move to have her revenge on us? She's never liked us, and feels Caspian has let her down."

"Like Caspian said," Alex reminded her, "she's like me. She can commune with spirits. She must have talked to Coppinger...or his men. They would have told her what happened."

"Which means they would have known who cursed them," Briar said. "It must have happened up close and personal. But there's still much we don't know."

"Like what Mariah did to make the ghosts stronger," Alex admitted. "I'm not sure how she's done that." Alex glanced across to Reuben and Caspian. "What's worrying me most is that we haven't encountered Coppinger's spirit yet. He could be stronger than all the others. And the anniversary of his death is tomorrow. But this doesn't answer your question, Ben." He turned to face him. "Now, we need to stop the spirits and send them back to where they belong. And that means dealing with Mariah."

Dylan stirred. "Time for some light relief, I think." He plugged his USB into the TV and in a few seconds had found the file. "I haven't brought it all. I'm sure seeing big, magical clouds above certain places doesn't interest you much, but this is Perranporth earlier this week."

The film was shot on the beach, looking up towards the cliff top. Initially all it showed was a hazy blue glow along the cliffs, brighter at certain points. Then a flare of light flashed across the screen, leaving the image of a giant on the cliff top, two arms and two legs clearly visible. It seemed to watch the sea, and then as it turned they saw that it carried what appeared to be a club in its hands. It strode inland, taking gigantic strides, and then vanished into nothing again.

Alex could scarcely believe his eyes. "Holy shit."

Dylan was grinning from ear to ear. "Impressive, right? You wait until we put this up on the website!"

Avery was still looking at the screen. "By the Gods! Are you telling me that *thing* is contained within that little spriggan that attacked us?"

"And me!" El said, half horrified, half impressed. "Amazing." And then she stopped laughing and said, "The enemy of my enemy is my friend...right?"

"It's too late to be philosophical," Ben groaned.

"No, it's not. The spriggans killed Jasmine because another spriggan died. It loathed 'the silver one,' which I took to mean that Mariah killed the spriggan. Maybe we could use its anger to help us?"

"I'm not sure," Alex said warily. "The ones we met didn't seem that bright or willing to listen to reason."

"I'd forgotten you encountered *two*!" El said. "Maybe they were mated? To lose your mate, or even a friend, is good motivation." Her face fell. "Mind you, I wouldn't—no, *couldn't*—go back down that mine again. It was a maze! A bloody death trap."

"You might not need to," Dylan suggested. "The creature clearly comes to the surface sometimes. Something to think about, I guess."

"I thought you were going to film Gull Island again?" Alex asked.

Dylan looked doubtful. "I will, but it's cold and wet out there now, and I'm not sure if we'll pick up anything."

A groan disturbed their conversation, and they all turned to look anxiously at Reuben and Caspian. Both of them now displayed a sheen of sweat on their pale faces, and Briar dropped to her knees next to them, running her hands above their bodies.

"We're losing them, I can feel it. It's like their spirits are sinking. We need to help them."

"How?" Alex asked, already moving to her side.

"We lend them our strength." She glanced around the room. "Quick! Circle, everyone. Now!"

★ ⦿ ⬦ ✕ ⦿ ⬦ ✳ ⦿ ⬦ ✕ ⦿

Caspian's thoughts were suddenly pierced by Briar's sharp voice, and the notion of Avery's body disappeared. Briar was calling to him, and he could feel his body again, sort of.

Part of him hated it. He'd never felt so happy, so content or complete. He tried to dive back into his dream state again, but Briar's voice became louder, more insistent, and he felt a tug on his body as his aches and pains started to return.

As quickly as Avery disappeared, he thought of Reuben and shouted his name, hearing a faint cry in return. He had the feeling that if he followed Briar's voice right now, he'd be back in his body, but then he'd lose Reuben, and he didn't know if he could hear her, too.

Deciding to ignore her voice, he focussed on Reuben, and as if he was washed up by an incoming tide, he found himself on Reuben's beach, blinking in the sun.

Reuben was standing on golden sand, surveying the sea, and he grinned at Caspian. "*You made it!*"

"We have to leav*e!*"

"Caspian, you're such a killjoy. Let me teach you to surf."

"I don't want to learn to fucking surf! You're dying!"

Caspian's exasperation fuelled him. He was losing Reuben; *El* would lose Reuben. He was not going to be responsible for another Jackson's death. Rage filled him, and without knowing quite how he did it, he tackled

Reuben, knocking him to the sand, instantly feeling his own body become more real as he sat on Reuben's chest and stared down at his shocked face.

"Dude?"

"Reuben, listen to Briar!"

"You're hallucinating!"

And then Briar's voice broke through to them both, clear and commanding, and Reuben looked around, shocked.

"How did you do that?"

"I didn't!"

Caspian knew he was in danger of slipping from the beach again, while Reuben just lay there, like a grinning idiot. He needed to anger him into action.

"You know why I killed your brother? Because he was weak! And you are weak! Your whole family is weak, just like your friends."

Reuben suddenly focussed. "*What did you say?*"

"I said, I killed Gil deliberately, and would do it again in a heartbeat."

Caspian was still kneeling on Reuben, but now Reuben reared up beneath him, throwing him to the side, and then punched him, again and again. "*You bastard.*"

Inexplicably, Caspian felt his lip split and his head thud against the sand, but he sneered at Reuben. "*You bet I am!*" And for good measure, he punched him back.

The beach vanished instantly, and so did Reuben.

"Reuben! Where are you?"

"Where are you, you shit?"

"Right here! Can't you find me, you idiot?"

Caspian could feel Reuben's rage, and also confusion, but before he could say anything else, Briar's voice resounded around them as she summoned them. Voices cradled him, and then Caspian was sharply aware of feeling his aching wound, the warmth of indoors, and a hard surface beneath him.

His eyes flew open, and he took a sharp breath in, shooting upright. "Reuben!"

For a moment, Caspian couldn't focus, and then he became aware of a circle of people around him. But it wasn't them he was looking for. He twisted in panic, and then saw Reuben lying next to him, still out cold. *Pain*. That was what Reuben needed.

Without thinking, he punched Reuben's wounded shoulder, and heard a gasp run around the watching circle. But he ignored them, holding his breath until Reuben's eyes flew open and he shouted out, "That fucking hurt!"

Caspian started laughing hysterically, and fell back on the floor. *Job done.*

Twenty-Seven

Reuben looked at Briar, and then at the drink in her hand. "I said I want a bloody whiskey, not some hideous herbal tea!"

She looked outraged. "I've just saved your bloody life, you ungrateful shit. You need tea to strengthen you!"

He took a deep breath. "I'm not ungrateful, but I am in shock, and whiskey helps shock. And for the Gods' sake, give Caspian some, too. Look at his face. He couldn't look more disgusted with that horrific concoction."

They were in the snug, and he and Caspian were sitting in the big, comfy armchairs on either side of the blazing fire, while their friends sat around them watching the exchange. Outside, rain was pouring down, and night had fallen.

Caspian cradled his cup, the steam rising around his face, but he was openly laughing at Reuben. "Maybe you should listen to Briar. This tea is actually quite good."

"Thank you, Caspian," Briar said, throwing him a beaming smile, before glaring at Reuben. "You were nearly dead! This tea that I have so lovingly made for you is restorative."

"But whiskey would be better."

"If you drink the tea, I will get you a whiskey."

"Blackmail?"

"You bet. And you won't get curry, either, until it's gone."

He looked across the room, seeing everyone looking amused. "You all think this is so funny, don't you?"

"No, actually," El said, the smile slipping from her face. "You scared the crap out of us. Drink the tea, and I will bring you whiskey. And curry."

He grunted with annoyance and stuck his hand out. "All right. Give me the cup, and while I make my eyes bleed with this stuff, you can tell us what the hell's going on."

Cassie was tittering. "You're so funny."

"Don't encourage him," El told her crossly, before turning back to him. "Listen closely while we explain."

Ten minutes later, Reuben's confusion had vanished, and with a whiskey in hand he felt more like his normal self, although his shoulder really ached. He remembered the lead up to the spell, although that was more like a dream now.

"Elemental water, you say? That might explain why I was on a beach."

"And why I felt underwater," Caspian added. "It was so odd, like I was floating in some vast ocean. And you're a water witch, Reuben. You probably felt comfortable in it, in some weird way—hence, the beach."

"Your energies were ebbing and flowing," Briar told them, "just like a tide. You definitely were caught in the edges of that curse."

Reuben looked at Caspian, who now had his own whiskey, and was staring into the fire. "Sorry I hit you on the beach."

He lifted his gaze and shrugged. "Sorry I provoked you. It seemed my only option. I'm sorry I punched your shoulder, too."

Reuben grimaced as he gingerly felt his wound. "It really aches. But I guess it worked." He winced as he realised his head ached too, and he patted it, feeling for a wound. "Why does my head hurt?"

"You whacked the wall," Alex said. "We found you in a crumpled heap in the attic."

"Oh, that explains it." He sighed heavily. "At least we succeeded. We found the curse. So, what now?"

"Well," Avery said, "we need to decide on our next plan. Tomorrow is the anniversary of the curse. The spirits are getting stronger. We've been discussing the options, and essentially we'll have to send the spirits back to where they belong. Which could mean facing Mariah."

"And where do we do that?" Reuben asked.

"Well," Alex said, "it seems like there's a lot of activity on Gull Island. I think that's where we need to go." He nodded towards the three parapsychologists. "They've picked up a lot of energy over there."

"Reuben and I have already discussed this," Caspian said, "and I think there could well be another passageway leading from the main cave, under the crates. And last night, the spirits came from the glasshouse."

Reuben nodded. "He's right. We never fully explored under there. Unless, of course, there's a whole separate cave and entrance, which is possible, but unlikely."

"Why unlikely?" El asked. "There could have been a rock fall over the years, which would have disguised any cave entrance, or filled a previously useable cove. And they could have been linked, regardless. This whole country is riddled with caves and tunnels for smuggling—the islands, more so! They were perfect pirate hangouts."

"We should go and check," Dylan suggested, clearly getting excited. "We could end this tonight!"

"We?" Caspian asked. "How are you going to help?"

Dylan folded his arms across his chest as he looked belligerently at Caspian. "I may not have magic, but I can help!"

"Whoa!" Alex said. "Of course you can, but slow down. We're not just marching down there until we have a plan. We need to banish the spirits, and try to stop Ethan and Mariah. Ethan should be easy, but Mariah? That's a different matter."

"And of course, if there's more treasure, spriggans may be there, too," Briar reminded them.

"This morning," Reuben told his friends, "we walked through the possibilities, and think that when Coppinger tried to escape from what he realised was a trap, the spell extended to his ship." He nodded towards the window and the darkness outside. "They could have run the ship aground on Gull Island."

"Surely the wreckage and their bodies would have been found," El said.

"Depends how big the storm was, and if no one went there for days... Well, the remains could have been swept out to sea."

Briar was kneeling on the floor in front of the fire, and she said, "So any treasure that's there now would have been there before the night they cast the curse?"

"Why not?" Reuben said. "Coppinger was clearly in the habit of stashing his treasure in out of the way places, as security."

"But Gull Island? That seems crazy," Dylan pointed out. "Your family or smugglers working with you could have found it."

"I don't know." He rubbed his face, suddenly weary. "It seems deviously genius to me. You hide it right under your enemies' noses. And it's accessible for an easy getaway when you have your own ship—Black Prince."

Avery grimaced. "I've got a headache, and I'm tired, but I feel we should be doing *something*!"

Ben asked, "Can't you just do a spell now to end it all?"

Avery looked nervous. "It's possible, but that would entail doing something big—like the curse, but not a curse—and I'm not sure it would work."

"Why not?" Dylan asked.

Alex answered. "There are many components. The spirits, the spriggans, Mariah... And we still don't really know how the curse works. A couple of lines isn't enough to understand it."

A knock at the door interrupted them, and El hurried to answer, quickly returning with Newton, who looked surprisingly cheerful.

"Good news?" Briar asked him, as he found a seat on the sofa.

"Very. Ethan is shifty as hell, and we're following him." He grinned broadly. "He's just turned up at Mariah's place in Looe. I think they'll be on the move again soon."

"What makes you say that?" Alex asked.

"Because in our interview today, I told him we suspected Jasmine and Miles were involved in stealing treasure and had accomplices, and I think he won't wait. If there's more to find, he'll go after it tonight. Or try to hide what they have. My officers will call if they stir. In the meantime," he sniffed, "can I smell curry?"

★ ● ● ★ ● ● ✱ ● ● ★ ●

Avery paced the attic room, watching Alex attempt to see Mariah using his scrying bowl. He'd been trying for well over fifteen minutes, and he hadn't moved a muscle.

She shivered inside Reuben's borrowed sweatshirt. It was cool in the attic, the sound of the rain loud on the roof and through the windows that had no glass in them. She had sealed them with a protection spell, but it wasn't really designed to insulate against weather.

At the other end of the attic, Dylan had set up his thermal imaging camera, focussing on Gull Island. He too was locked in his own world, and she was grateful for it. It was dark and quiet up here, and it gave her time to think. All the others were still downstairs, no doubt discussing their options. She eyed Caspian's grimoire warily. The book lay open, the curse still circling above the page in its ghoulish green light, and again she tried to work out why.

They'd discussed many possibilities, so many that her head hurt. But the only one that really made sense, to her at least, was that the curse was still active, and although it didn't seem tied to the treasure they had already found, she had a feeling it was still affecting Gull Island in some way. She was also convinced that Mariah had made the smugglers' ghosts stronger, and that Helena had become aware of that and in her effort to intervene had been captured.

But what were they doing now?

She walked to the window and looked towards Gull Island in the distance. The mist had cleared a little, and the dark bulk of the island could just be seen through the drizzle. It looked so innocuous, and she hoped that whatever Dylan had seen before had gone. She glanced across to him, but he was transfixed with the image, a pair of headphones clamped to his ears, oblivious to her presence.

A groan drew her attention to Alex and she turned to him, seeing him flex his shoulders, finally looking up with a sigh. "Nothing."

She headed to his side. "Nothing at all?"

He rubbed his forehead and leaned back in the chair, his expression hard to read in the subdued light. "Nope. I searched over Looe looking for magical signatures, but there's nothing, and I was focussing on the area she lives, too. She has a veil of protection over her, much like us. Either that or they've already left, but I'm sure Newton would have been told."

"Okay. So we don't know what they might be planning, but I guess that shouldn't stop us. Dylan is right. We have to go to Gull Island, tonight."

"I agree. If Coppinger's power is growing and he's planning on attacking Reuben and Caspian again—and maybe the town—I'd rather stop it now."

"Even if we find nothing, at least we'll have ruled it out," Avery reasoned.

"I'll eat my shorts if you find nothing!" Dylan appeared next to her, as silent as a cat, and Avery jumped.

"Bloody hell! What are you, some kind of ninja?"

Dylan slid his hand around her arm and tugged her. "Come and see this. You too, Alex." He led them back across the attic and showed them the screen attached to his camera. "Look at that! That's even bigger than it was last night!"

Avery stared at the image, trying to understand what she was looking at. "What's that thing that looks like a thundercloud?"

"A build-up of psychic energy, and it's over the entire island." He pointed at the screen. "Look. It doesn't bleed over the sea, so I know it's not to do with the weather. The sea itself is cold, that's why it's blue."

"Crap," Alex said. "You say it's getting bigger?"

"Yep, and denser. But don't ask me what that means. Nothing good, I'm sure." He frowned. "If I was to hazard a guess, I'd say it meant the presence of many spirits, but I'll check with Ben."

Alarmed, Avery asked, "Alex, is there any way to banish these ghosts from here?"

"Nope. I have to be there."

Avery looked at the curse spell again, pulsing at the far end of the room. "That thing is still going, and I think while it did its job well back then, I don't think it's helping us now. It's keeping the spirits active, somehow."

"Ably assisted by Mariah," Alex said. "She's obviously reached some kind of compromise with them."

"Yeah, she's promised them Reuben and Caspian," Avery huffed.

"Oh, crap! Look," Dylan said, pointing at the screen again. He directed their attention to a point on the right of the island where a shape was coming into view. "If I'm not mistaken, that looks like the bow of a ship."

He was right. The image was blurry, but it did look like a ship, and within a few seconds, they could see a sail too, as the whole thing slid into view.

"Please tell me that's a regular ship just cruising past," Alex said, his voice strained.

Avery blinked as if to clear her vision, and looked from the camera out of the window and back again. "Er, I don't think it is, Alex."

His voice rose with alarm. "Are you saying that's a ghost pirate ship?"

Dylan tried to sound horrified, but he wasn't really. He could barely disguise his glee. "Yes, yes it really is!"

★·🌑·◐·☆·🌑·◐·✦·◐·◑·☆·🌑

Caspian stood in the attic with everyone else, including Ash, and like the others, was watching the screen with a mixture of amazement and horror.

"Well, that settles it," Briar said, determination radiating from her small frame. "We have to go there now."

"And do what, exactly?" Newton asked.

"Get rid of them!"

"Armed with cutlasses and your own bloody pirate ship? This isn't the Pirates of the bloody Caribbean!"

"Not even the *Pirates of Penzance*?" Dylan asked cheekily.

"No!" he shot back.

Briar glared at Newton. "I know that! I don't mean I'm going to get on the phantasm ghost ship. I mean the island. We have the Empusa's swords, one Nephilim, a witch who's good at banishing spells, and the rest of us who wield elemental magic!" She rolled her shoulders and jutted her chin out. "We are more than a match for Mariah!"

"Actually," Caspian said, hating to admit it, "I can't fight with my wound. It's much better than it was, thanks to you, but I'm not at full strength. I think I should tackle that thing." He nodded to his grimoire.

"I'm not sure that's a good idea. Finding it nearly killed you!"

He smiled at her affectionately. He had started to think of Briar as a little sister, a much more pleasant version than his real one. "I'm good at curses, remember? I'll be fine."

"What are you planning to do?" Avery asked him, turning her back on the window.

"Like you said, it's active, and still has something to do with what's going on now. If I can break it, or reverse it, then it will help you banish them." He directed this at Alex, and then looked at Ash and El. "I know you have the swords, but you can't dispatch them all."

Ash stirred, his hand on the Empusa's hilt. "I'd ask my brothers to come, but Shadow, Gabe, Nahum, and Niel are in London. They left today. Barak and Eli are at the warehouse, and Zee is in the pub."

"And that's where I want him to stay," Alex said, eyeing the ship across the bay. So far it seemed anchored in deep water, but they had wondered if it might attack White Haven. "Having a Nephilim in town might be useful."

"We'll obviously come with you," Ben said, his tone brooking no argument. "You taught us simple banishing spells, and we have some of your other portable spells with us in the van."

"You carry them with you?" Reuben asked.

"Of course. We never know when we might need them."

"While I don't want to leave you alone," Reuben said to Caspian, "I'm not staying here! My shoulder is fine!" he said to Briar, before she could complain.

"Actually, Reuben," Caspian said, "I think I'll need you."

His eyes flashed belligerently. "Why?"

"Because our ancestors fashioned this curse together. There's a lot of elemental water in it, and you're the water witch. I think if they cast it together, we need to break it together."

Reuben fell silent, his mouth working, before he finally said, "But you're the curse expert."

It seemed to Caspian that Reuben looked suddenly uncertain, some of his natural confidence shaken and a wariness behind his eyes, but Caspian pressed on. "Yes, but I'm an air witch and one of my weakest elements is water. I need you." He nodded at the others. "They need you. Here."

Reuben glanced at El, and she nodded encouragingly. "I think he's right. Besides, one bad fall on your dodgy shoulder could mean you're vulnerable. And Caspian shouldn't be alone here."

Reuben swung his gaze back to Caspian, resentment oozing from him. "Okay. If I have to."

Caspian thought they had achieved a new level of friendship today, but now he doubted that. However, this wasn't the time to be second-guessing. "Thank you." He addressed the others. "What will you do if Mariah and Ethan turn up? Potentially, there's more treasure there that they have probably left until last because of the curse. Like you said, Newton, you've forced their hand. If they don't get it now, they might lose out."

Avery didn't hesitate. "We'll deal with them, too."

Twenty-Eight

A very stood in the large cave under Gull Island, currently illuminated by a dozen witch-lights, and wondered if they'd got it wrong.

She was there with El, Briar, Alex, Newton, Ash, and the three investigators, all armed to varying degrees. Newton and Ben held shotguns, El and Ash had the Empusa's swords, and Dylan carried the bag of portable spells that she and the other witches had made. They had proceeded cautiously down the tunnel, Ash leading the way, all of them wary of meeting vengeful ghosts, but so far everything was quiet.

Too quiet.

"If we can't find this mysterious passage that we think exists but have no proof of, then we're stuck!" Newton said, annoyed.

They had already pulled a large portion of the old wooden boxes out of the way, and so far the ground underneath was solid earth.

Alex looked up from the area he'd been searching. "Can you save the frustration until we've finished, Newton?"

"We're losing time! Ethan could be up to anything right now, and I'd never know because there's no bloody coverage in this godforsaken pit!"

Newton's team hadn't seen any movement before they entered the tunnels, and everyone knew he was frustrated.

"Have you got any better leads?"

Newton scowled. "No."

"So stop whining, and help us search!"

Avery suppressed a grin and also returned to moving the boxes out of the way, directing them over the heads of the searchers using a current of air and on to the area that they'd already searched. The magical energy was strong in here, building in pressure around them, so despite Newton's complaints and Avery's own doubts, they were in the right place...or thereabouts.

"Maybe we need to get on the beach," El suggested, her hands on her back as she arched backwards to ease the kinks.

"Good idea," Avery agreed. "We might be able to detect a kind of magical path to the centre of the energy."

Alex straightened up, looking doubtful. "I'm not sure we should split up."

"We'd save time," Ben said.

Briar marched decisively to the middle of the cave, closed her eyes, and wiggled her bare feet into the ground. "I'm going to feel for changes in the earth, to see if I can detect another tunnel or something. Just ignore me while I work."

"And I," El said, ignoring Alex's doubts, "am going to head to the beach."

Avery nodded and headed to her side. "Great. I'll come with you."

"Wait," Dylan called over. "I'll come, too. We can use my thermal camera again. It's picking up nothing significant here."

Avery could hear Alex muttering under his breath about headstrong women as she left with El, and a few minutes later they were in the smaller cave where Reuben had been attacked. The sounds of the rain and the sea crashing on the beach were loud as they edged through the scrubby bushes that veiled the cave. As soon as they were in the open, the wind hit them, as did spray from the thundering surf and the heavy rain. They were drenched in seconds.

"Shit!" El exclaimed, raising her voice to be heard. She looked at Dylan. "It's wild out here. Can you use that thing in the wet?"

"Not this bloody wet," he said, rain dripping off the end of his nose. "I'll head to the entrance, in the shelter."

"Wait!" Avery pulled a current of air around them, using it like a shield, and combined it with a protection spell, remembering that Eve had used something similar when she was conjuring the storm. All of a sudden, they were in a protected bubble, while the elements raged around them.

Dylan looked around, startled. "Wow! That's super cool!"

Avery smiled, feeling incredibly smug. "Yes, it is. I have actually never tried that before!"

"In that case, super brain," El said, "Is there some kind of spell we can use that can show us magic in a thermal way like Dylan can do?"

"You're the fire witch, you tell me!"

"Fair point," she said, slicking her wet hair away from her face, and issuing a little warmth from her palm to take the worst of the water out of it. "Challenge accepted. Just let me think a moment."

Giving El a few minutes of silence, Avery moved to Dylan's side. He was panning the camera over the rocks and beach to either side, and then he swept it up to the cliffs behind them.

"Bloody hell, you can see it more clearly from here," he said, pointing up and to the right. "The epicentre appears to be over there."

Avery nodded. "Further inland. Have you checked the sea for the ship?"

"Ooh, no." He turned around, panning across the ocean, and within seconds they could see it. Avery's heart faltered.

The ship had two long masts and was fully rigged with sails, and its long, spar-like bow protruded from the front of the ship. It sat steadily in the sea, unmoved by the strong winds and the high waves.

"Shit! That's big!" Avery squeaked out.

"Very. I believe that's a sloop." He squinted at the image. "I wonder if that's Black Prince."

"I don't care what it is, as long as it stays there."

"You know, I think I can see figures on it."

"Please don't say that." Avery squinted into the spray. "What do you think it might do?"

"I don't know. But it's a ghost ship. Surely it can't do much!"

"Did you see the hole in Reuben's wall? Does it have cannons?"

"They modified them for all sorts of things," Dylan told her. "They would originally have been merchant ships that were stolen and refitted for smuggling purposes."

Avery huffed. "Okay, there's nothing we can do about that right now, and it doesn't look like there's a way to the centre of the energy from here. The cliffs are too steep. I think we should head inside, see if they've found a tunnel."

Dylan folded his camera away. "It was worth a shot. El? Any luck?"

El was staring at the cliffs in fierce concentration, saying what Avery presumed to be a spell. Before she could answer, a boom sounded above the noise of the storm and a cloud of dust and debris carried on a wave of magical energy blew through the opening of the rock and billowed around them, held at bay by the protection spell. The ground rocked beneath their feet and Avery staggered, almost falling, until Dylan pulled her upright.

Avery didn't hesitate. She ran back to the cave entrance, getting pelted by rain again, but she could barely get in. The cave had completely collapsed.

★ ❂ ⬧ ✷ ❂ ⬧ ✢ ❂ ⬧ ✷ ❂

Reuben watched Caspian working, utterly frustrated. He should be with his friends, not here, trying to undo some complicated, knotty spell that was completely beyond his abilities.

"Reuben," Caspian said, not taking his eyes from the spell. "I can feel your annoyance. Help me!"

"I don't know how!"

"That's because you're not focussing!"

"Because I'm worried about my girlfriend and our friends out there!"

Caspian lifted his head and stared at him, and Reuben felt pinned beneath the intensity of his gaze. "*Water.* I want you to focus on water!"

Reuben clenched his fists and with a deep breath, counted to five and released them again. "Okay. I'll level with you. I don't do this type of thing. I don't know how to unpick a spell."

"But you know how to make one?"

"Er, yes, I guess so."

"What do you mean, guess? You have a grimoire full of spells, a good chunk of which are based around elemental water, and I've seen you work water magic, so what is wrong?"

Reuben wrestled with how much to say. He hated to confess he was useless, but Caspian should know he couldn't rely on him. "I'm not that good a witch, Caspian. I use my magic more instinctively, and sporadically. The others, and you, seem to use it all the time. I don't. Sorry. You've got the dud one."

Caspian had been leaning on the table, but now he straightened. "That's bullshit."

"No, it's not. It's the truth." He stared back at Caspian, unflinching, and waited to see the disappointment and derision he was due.

"I get it. You were late to the party. You ignored your magic, pretended it didn't exist, and now you're still doing it."

"I'm not ignoring it. It's just not there."

"Of course it's bloody there. I've seen you use it, and I can feel it now! You used it on us in my home last year! And on those bloody vampires. And at the Crossroads Circus," he said, reminding him of what El had pointed out.

"It was a fluke."

Caspian looked up at the ceiling. "The Goddess give me strength." He levelled his gaze at Reuben again. "Water elemental magic is malleable, moody. It flows, seeping through cracks and finding ways through all sorts of things, much like water itself does. It wears things down over time. And, in large quantities, like the sea or raging rivers or masses of rain," he threw his arms out, indicating the rain they could hear falling on the roof, "it is immensely powerful! But it is also intuitive, like you."

"I'm not intuitive."

"Yes, you are. You are one of the most intuitive witches I know. You feel every one of your friends, I can tell. You tune into them, their moods, their doubts, their happiness. That's why you're the joker. You like to put them at their ease, massaging the mood of the group, picking them up when they're down, celebrating with them when they're happy. You do it so instinctively you don't even know you're doing it."

Reuben fell silent, debating whether Caspian was taking the piss, and then cast his mind back to when he was with them. Did he do that?

Caspian continued, "They like spending time with you, everyone does. You're popular because you flow with people. You roll with your moods—or rather, *their* moods. Water is the most emotional element, more so than the psyche. We're made of water. Water is life-giving, which means you have some healing abilities, too. And bodies of water—rivers, springs, lakes—are considered sacred spaces. And of course, you surf. You'll use your magic then too, as I'm sure you know, but again because it's so instinctive, you don't even question it. Am I right?"

"You might be right about the surfing," he grudgingly admitted.

Caspian smirked. "I'm right about it all. And that elemental magic is deep within you, like a well at your centre, and you have barely begun to tap it."

Shadow had said a similar thing when he'd first met her, so had Oswald once, but this was the first time anyone had picked up on some of the things he did and hadn't even noticed. He began to feel just the slightest bit more positive. "Perhaps."

"The trouble with elemental water is that it is so malleable, so…well, watery. You think you've got it, and then it's gone again, but you have to remember it's still always there, and it flows through your veins, rich and full of life."

"And how is that going to help me now?"

"I need you to be at your most instinctive. Let your emotional awareness flow around this spell. Water is a big part of it." Caspian stared into the spinning words. "I think they used it because this is about cursing pirates, who are at their most comfortable at sea. And like I said, water in a mass is incredibly destructive. It sweeps away everything before it. But," Caspian studied the spell from different angles, "this is structured differently to any spell I've seen before. The words are tangled together, like a knot, and we need to find the end of it to untangle it and read it fully. That's what we're looking for."

"The end of the thread." Reuben looked at the spell again, trying to let his instincts take over. He took a deep breath, and then addressing the spell rather than Caspian, said, "Thanks."

"I didn't do anything."

"Yes, you did."

"Thank me when we've cracked this thing. And by the way, don't do anything too dramatic. We don't want to end up unconscious again."

★·✦·✧·★·✦·✧·✸·✦·✧·★·✦

Briar was covered in a layer of sand and earth, the ground hard beneath her, a dull ringing in her ears.

For a moment she was stunned, and then as reality filtered in, she leapt to her feet, brushing earth from her eyes and blinking rapidly to clear her vision. She was on the far side of the cave and the air was filled with dust, clogging her nose and throat. She reached for her t-shirt, pulling the hem over her nose and mouth as she tried to see the others.

Ash was circling overhead, the beat of his huge wings helping to clear the air. Around her, the others staggered to their feet, Ben pulling Cassie free from a mound of earth, and Newton cocking his shotgun.

But where was Alex, and what had happened?

"Alex!" she shouted, running to where she had last seen him.

He had been searching the final area they had uncovered. She scrambled over the debris, horrible memories of Gil's death flooding back. They had found him behind the boxes, his neck broken, his eyes vacant.

For a second, grief overcame her and she couldn't breathe. If Alex was dead...

In seconds, Newton had ran past her, throwing the remnants of boxes out of the way with surprising strength. He was quickly followed by Ben and Cassie, while she just stood there, unable to move.

What was the matter with her? She needed to focus. She needed to find Alex.

A blur of wings above her made her look up, and Ash streaked to where the mound of rubble and earth was biggest, grabbed something that was sticking out of the surface, and hauled a limp body out.

Briar collapsed, her eyes filling with tears. No. No.

★ ◉ ⬧ ✦ ◉ ⬧ ✳ ◉ ⬧ ✦ ◉

Avery stared at the wall of rock, desperately trying to move it with her magic, but it stayed firmly put, and she could feel tears threatening to fall. She blinked them back, furious with herself.

"There's no way past that," Dylan said to Avery, his hand on her shoulder. "And if you succeed in some way, you might bring more down in the process." He nodded up to where a huge crack ran across the rocky roof of the cave, and pulled her back with him so they were well away from the cave entrance and any potential rock fall.

"I have to get through." Water streamed down her face as the raging weather buffeted them, and she shook his hand off. "Our friends are through there."

"We need to find another way," he said calmly, holding her gaze with his own.

She took a deep breath. He was right. She had to focus. But all she could think of was Alex. "What if they're injured, or..." She couldn't bring herself to say the word.

"And what if they're not? What if this debris has just fallen between us, not in the main cave? Come on; let's get back to shelter and El."

He pulled her across the stony beach and into the bubble of protection, where El was still focussing on the cliffs. As they entered she started to smile, and then she saw their faces. "What's wrong?"

"A rock fall has blocked the cave," Dylan said quickly, shooting a nervous glance at Avery. "We have no idea how big it is, but we can't get through."

El was stunned into silence, her shoulders sagging, and she looked towards the entrance. "How bad?"

"Very," Avery said, finding her voice. "I couldn't move it with magic."

A portion of rock suddenly sheared off with a rumble, completely occluding the entrance, and Avery was suddenly grateful for Dylan's calm advice.

"Thanks," she said to him. "I wasn't thinking straight."

"You're worried about Alex, it's understandable. El, any luck?"

"Yes. I've been focussing on energy and heat signatures, and I can see a section up there that's emitting an energy similar to what's above us." She pointed halfway up the cliff face over on the right. "I think it's the entrance to a passage, or another cave."

Dylan grabbed his camera and focussed on the area, magnifying the image, and Avery saw that El was right. It was like a flame, flickering within the cliff.

Pushing her fear about Alex aside, Avery took a deep breath. "I can fly up there. Give me a moment, and I'll check it out. If it's clear, I'll come back for both of you."

And before any of them could complain, she summoned air and vanished.

★·◉·◈·✶·◉·◈·✳·◉·◈·✶·◉

As Reuben teased the last of the elemental water away, the words of the spell floated free, lining up into orderly sentences, still hovering over the page.

"Well done," Caspian muttered. "Let's see what this says."

Reuben had been working on the opposite side of the table, but now he moved around and sat next to Caspian, studying the words with him. It had taken a good hour to unravel the spell, and the start had been the hardest. Essentially, the tendril of elemental water was as sinuous and undulating as a stream, and grasping it was like trying to pick up water between your finger and thumb. But as he'd relaxed into it, he'd finally made the connection.

As he worked on his part, Caspian untangled the other. It felt like they were performing surgery together, and was certainly weird, but oddly satisfying. And Caspian, surprisingly, had been incredibly patient and utterly focussed.

As he studied the words, Reuben realised it wasn't just an incantation; it listed the ingredients, too. Salt water, dried and ground kelp, sea holly, thrift, and sea kale, as well as dragon's blood, cinnamon, camomile, and sandalwood. Right at the beginning was Coppinger's name.

"Bloody hell, Reuben, this is a horrible spell," Caspian said, raising an eyebrow in masterful understatement. "The strength of it lies in the fact that it directs the evil of Coppinger and his gang back at them." He pointed to a line of script. "'And by your hand, all that walk with you shall suffer your fate. By wealth, by stealth, each raid by blade, to all who have lost and failed to grow old, thou shall know their pain a thousand fold.'"

"It does extend to his men, then."

"Absolutely. The spell turns the offenders' ill deeds back on them 'a thousand fold.' Then it uses their greed to bind them to the treasure, ensuring it acts as a poison, rendering a slow and painful death. Their spirits are then denied rest. It says, 'As your spirit leaves your body it will be forever bound to the object of your desire, and ye shall never rest. Not by night, by day, by dark or full of moon, by sunshine, rain, or snow. Thou shall always be a slave to that which wrought your doom.'"

"The ingredients are water-based plants or seaside plants, too," Reuben noted. "I guess that explains why the water element is so strong. How do we break it?"

"Good question."

While Caspian stared at the words, Reuben stood and stretched his legs, heading over to the thermal imaging camera still trained on the island. He frowned and squinted at the image. "Er, Caspian. There's been a development."

"What?" He was at his side in seconds.

"The ship. It's heading back to Gull Island, and there seems to be some big plume of energy rising even higher. Like an explosion."

The ship had almost disappeared again, only the stern visible.

They stared at each other bleakly, and without another word, returned to the spell.

Twenty-Nine

Alex heard voices shouting his name, and felt someone gripping his shoulders, shaking him. His eyes jolted open. "Herne's horns! What the hell's going on?" he groaned.

"You scared the shit out of us, that's what!" Newton said, looming over him.

"I did? What did I do?" He struggled to sit up, and Newton extended a hand, helping to pull him upright.

Alex's head pounded, and he rubbed his face, feeling it covered with dust and grit. He blinked, the black spots in his vision finally clearing, and he saw Briar sitting next to him, pale and silent. "Briar, are you okay?"

"I am now! For one horrible moment..."

Memories of the explosion flooded back, and he suddenly remembered finding a trapdoor covered by layers of earth, alerted to its presence by the seal of magic.

"I think I found the passage!" He looked around him, realising he was sitting on a mound of dirt a short distance from where he'd originally been. Ash, Cassie, and Ben were there now, peering into a hole in the ground and talking quietly.

"I remember now. I released the door, and felt a surge of power. I tried to deflect it." He looked behind him. "That way."

Newton nodded. "You successfully deflected it, but you've also brought the next cave's roof down."

"*Shit*! Avery!" He'd reacted so instinctively that he'd had no time to think about where to direct the blast. "What if they were in there?"

Briar regarded him steadily. "Hopefully they've thrown up a protective shield, or were on the beach, but it would be good to know for sure. Any chance you could try to connect to them? I mean," she glanced to where the hole in the floor beckoned, "we need to go, but it would be good to see if they're okay first."

"Sure." He nodded wishing the ringing in his ears would stop.

Newton stood up. "I'm going to join the others. Make it quick, Alex. We need to get moving."

As he trudged over to the others, Briar said, "Are you sure you're okay?"

"I'm fine. Sorry I gave you a shock." He knew exactly what she'd been fearing...and remembering.

"I'll forgive you." She stood, too. "I'll give you some privacy and see you over there."

Alex took a few deep breaths and then reached out his awareness, feeling for Avery with his subconscious. He'd done this before, and because of their strong connection he could normally find her quickly, but now...nothing. Frustrated, he kept trying, but it was as if something was blocking him, and he realised it was probably the strong magic that was pouring through the trap door. He rose to his feet and joined the others, staring at the steps leading downwards.

"Any luck?" Briar asked.

"Nope. Too much energy buzzing around." He tried to sound more confident than he felt. "I'm sure they're fine."

"I agree," Ash said, turning to him. The Nephilim looked as dusty as the rest of them, but his eyes burned with intrigue. "Glad to see you're back on your feet." He gestured to the passage. "Quick question before we head down there. You say this was sealed?"

Alex nodded. "Yeah, with magic. Nothing complex. I didn't expect that surge of power to come out of it."

"Well," Briar said, "unpleasant though that was, I think it confirms we're heading in the right direction. The centre of Virginia and Serephina's spell is through there."

Ben's EMF meter was issuing a high-pitched, steady whine, and he said, "There's some serious psychic energy in there—*lots*! I think this is spirit central."

"Why do I have the feeling we're entering a crypt?" Cassie asked.

Ash swept the Empusa's sword from its scabbard. "Unfortunately, I think that's exactly what this is. Ready?"

"Ready," Alex answered, already taking the first step downwards. "Let's finish this."

★·◉·◌·★·◉·◌·✳·◉·◌·★·◉

Avery led Dylan and El down the tunnel that cut into the cliff, a witch-light bobbing ahead of them.

When she'd used witch-flight to fly to the tunnel's entrance, she found a series of shallow steps carved into the rock, leading up to the headland above, and she'd wondered if it was an escape route. Confirming the tunnel was clear, she'd fetched the others, and they'd now been walking inland for several minutes, on a steady downward trajectory. She quickened as she heard the boom of surf, and seeing a glow of green light ahead, extinguished the witch-light. Feeling the light was ominously familiar, she cautiously edged forward before coming to a sudden stop, the others clustering around her.

"What's going on?" El asked.

"Herne's bollocks," Dylan muttered as they took in the space in front of them. "It's a bloody pirate lair!"

They were at the side of a large cavern that glowed with a green and blue light. It emanated from a spectral, blazing fire on a beach edging a deep-water cove. The light made it seem as if the whole place was underwater, just like Reuben's attic. The bay was cut off from the sea by a massive wall of fractured rock that had sheered a ship in the bay in half. The rotten timbers wallowed in the deep water, leaving only the bowsprit, masts, and tattered sails visible.

Tiers of rock led up from the beach, filled with wooden barrels bound with iron, old wooden boxes, and chests. Rough tables and chairs, mostly decomposing, were grouped on the far side, behind which was a dark archway that Avery presumed led to another cave or tunnel. The upper levels of the cave were cloaked in shadow.

Even more chilling were the bones of dozens of men spread across the levels.

This was definitely the centre of the curse. Avery could feel it drenching the air around them.

Before Avery could even begin to work out what to do, there was a slow handclap from the top tier, and a glowering figure materialised out of the shadows, fire gleaming where there should be eyes. It was a broad shouldered, powerfully built man, wearing old-fashioned clothing and knee-length boots. He laughed, the sound booming out around them.

In seconds, dozens of other figures appeared, and Avery froze as a blade was pressed to her throat, a weather-beaten, ghoulish face leering into her own.

★·۰·◌·★·۰·◌·✦·۰·◌·★·۰

Alex heard shots, shouts, and the sounds of clashing metal. He ran, heedless of the uneven floor and poor light, until he saw a whirling blade slicing through the air.

He batted it away, and yelled, "Something's coming!"

A spectral hand grabbed his shirt beneath his throat and lifted him up, smashing him against the roof. Alex twisted, narrowly avoiding smacking his head, and punched out a blast of pure energy on instinct.

The ghost vanished, and Alex crashed to the floor, but another spectre emerged as Alex struggled to his feet, furious at having been caught out. The gathering energy was completely throwing him, leaving him unable to detect anything remotely magical or supernatural around him.

But Ash was already thundering past him, the Empusa's sword swinging to dispatch the spirit, and then he charged onwards. Newton hauled Alex to his feet and they raced after him, finally emerging onto a narrow shelf of rock at the back of a large cave.

For a bewildering moment, Alex thought he was underwater, as green light rippled around him, and then he saw Avery, El, and Dylan below, furiously fighting a dozen spirits that surrounded them. Magic flashed, swords clashed, and Dylan blasted his shotgun.

Alex had a moment of pure relief at seeing them alive, and then horror at their predicament. But Ash, wings outstretched, was already soaring down to assist them. Alex felt a sharp sting across his ear and the shattering of stone as a bullet ricocheted past. A spirit sneered at him, only feet away, with an old-fashioned musket in his hand. Before he could fire again, Alex uttered a banishing spell, satisfied as the spirit vanished with a howl.

His relief was short-lived, however, as other spirits manifested around them. Before he could attack again, he was aware of Cassie, Ben, Briar, and Newton lining up next to him, advancing as one.

The next few minutes were bewildering.

Alex hesitated to think of their attackers as ghosts. They may have an Otherworldly shimmer to them, and could pop in and out of vision, but they had a startlingly strong physical form, capable of touch. He and his friends were weaving in and out, ducking, diving, throwing spells and desperately trying to avoid the quick stab of blades. He was vaguely aware of Ben pulling bottled spells out of his pocket, and felt a blast of fire race past him as Cassie hurled a globe at the nearest spirit.

"Whoa!" he shouted, rolling to avoid the blast. "Careful where you throw that!"

"Sorry!" she yelled, breathless, and then out of nowhere, a spirit appeared and threw her down the tiers of rock like a rag doll. Fortunately, she rolled athletically, leaping to her feet again.

Alex turned away, a flash of movement distracting him.

A giant man grabbed Alex around the throat and pinned him to the wall. His breath was rancid, and Alex recoiled. Fire burned where his eyes should be, and he rasped in his face. "You made a mistake today, boy! You'll all die. No outsider breaches my cave and lives."

Boy?

"Screw you!" Alex yelled, convinced he was now fighting Coppinger.

He pressed his palm to Coppinger's face, scorching him with elemental fire, and his clammy skin started to slip from his features, revealing the bone beneath. But Coppinger tightened his grip around Alex's throat. He was horribly strong, fuelled by rage and hate, and his spirit was powerful.

A resounding blast caused Coppinger to drop him and vanish, and Newton appeared to his right, already reloading his shotgun. "You okay?"

"Not really," Alex said, bewildered and breathless. "I think they're toying with us."

"And someone else has just turned up," Newton said with a scowl, and he pointed to a flurry of activity below.

Ethan had just entered the cave from another entrance below, closely followed by Mariah and Zane. As Alex stared down at them, Mariah lifted her gaze and smiled at him triumphantly.

★ ◑ ◔ ★ ◑ ◔ ✱ ◑ ◔ ★ ◑

Caspian took a deep breath and looked up at Reuben's anxious face, willing himself to be patient. "Have you got a way to break this?"

"No. We're taking too long," Reuben said to him.

284

"Shut up and keep trying."

But he was right, Caspian reflected. They had untangled the spell a good half an hour ago, and he was still no closer to working out how to break it. He'd glared at it, and paced around it, but it refused to give up its inner workings. He'd had one interesting idea, but was worried about the repercussions on his friends.

That word brought him up short. *Friends*. He'd never viewed the White Haven witches as that before. Well, Briar maybe, and certainly Avery. But Alex, El, Reuben, or Newton? Never. He blinked and rubbed his brow. He was getting soft in his old age.

Or maybe loneliness was driving him to it.

He'd never thought of himself as lonely, ever. But being around Reuben these last few days had made him realise how few true friendships he really had. *How sad did that make him? Could he even count Gabe as a friend? Or Shadow? He employed them, so maybe not.*

Annoyed with his sentimental internal waffling, he focussed on the spell, starting to talk it through.

"Focus, Reuben. This is a big spell, encompassing all of Coppinger's men, his treasure, his ship, and the deep ocean. Elemental power at its strongest. It uses their greed against them. It has tied their spirits to the treasure, making them forever restless, and Mariah has used that, fuelling their spirits somehow."

"Are the spriggans a side effect?" Reuben asked, leaning back in his chair, his hands behind his head. "Or are they part of this spell?"

"They're not mentioned, so they are not part of the spell, no. They're drawn to the treasure, and as natural Otherworldly creatures, they are unaffected by the curse. Anyway, forget the spriggans." He stared at the spell again, the words shimmering in the air before him. "Curses are hard to break. It took all of us to lift the spell from El. If you remember, that was an earth-based spell."

Reuben nodded. "Yes. It suffocated her spirit, burying her alive."

"This one uses water in a similar way. It's like the curse is *suspended* in deep water. I can sense its weight. You untangled a stream of it from the words, but water is still an integral part of it. I'm wondering, if we can get rid of the water, will the curse crack?"

Reuben sat forward, leaning his arms on the table. "You're saying the water is protecting the curse, like a bubble. Which is why my attic felt like it was underwater earlier."

"Yes."

"But what about the words of the spell? Won't Coppinger's spirit still be bound to his treasure?"

"I don't think so. Once the water's gone, so are they! In theory, at least." Caspian struggled to find the right words. "It's like letting the bathwater down a plug hole. It will take the cursed spirits with it."

"So we need to create a plug hole?" He looked alarmed, his voice rising. "Like a bloody great whirlpool? That's insane!"

"I know." He worried his lips with his fingers, staring into Reuben's wide blue eyes. "Where would we siphon it to?"

Reuben was silent for a moment, his gaze drifting to the spell again. "I've got a better idea! We freeze and shatter it."

Caspian blinked with surprise. "I like that idea better. Although, we run the risk of freezing everyone to death."

"I think that option is better than sucking them into some great whirlpool of doom."

"Of course, we could also superheat the water, turning it into steam and evaporate it."

"And boil them to death instead?"

Caspian grimaced. "Let's go with the ice thing. I think it's the lesser of the three evils."

"Ya think?" Reuben said sarcastically. He flexed his fingers and glared at the spell. "Let's get this shit-show on the road."

Thirty

Newton scrambled down the rocks towards Ethan, but Ethan had cast him one long, hard look and then ignored him, racing with the witches to the treasure chests stacked at the side of the beach.

A ghost manifested directly in front of Newton and he shot it, satisfied to see it explode and vanish. He marched through it, firing at another one that appeared right behind it.

Mariah was focussing on bagging up the treasure with Ethan, but Zane, the weasly-faced witch who Newton had a vague recollection of from All Hallows' Eve, had paused and faced them. Even from a distance, Newton could see his mouth moving.

Briar was next to Newton, and she threw a blazing fireball at Zane, but he deflected it and threw one back, causing them both to dive to the floor.

Then something very peculiar started to happen. The skeletons lying across the cave began to twitch, and as Newton regained his feet, so did they. Every single one of them. And they weren't animated by the spirits, who, although dwindling in number, were still fighting furiously. Newton could barely keep track of his friends, lost in the melee.

"What the actual—"

"Holy shit!" Briar exclaimed. "He's animated the skeletons."

"I can see that!" Newton said, reloading quickly. "How?"

"Let's worry about that later."

Briar stamped her foot, and a ragged crack split the ground from her feet to Zane's. Zane was holding another ball of fire in his hands, ready to hurl it, but Briar's magic caught him off guard. He staggered backwards and the fireball shot into the roof, sending shards of rock flying like shrapnel.

Distracted, Newton didn't see the charging skeleton coming at him until it was too late, and the next thing he knew, he was flat on his back.

★.❀:◌:✳:❀:◌:✱:❀:◌:✳:❀

El fought her way free of the immediate group of spirits that had ambushed them and stood next to the water's edge, buying herself a few moments to assess what was happening and where she should go next.

Ash was still fighting his own battle, his huge wings sweeping back and forth as he laid waste to the spirits and skeletons that were clambering from the wreck. He balanced on the bowsprit, incredibly agile, and El was lost for a moment as she admired his skill. A shout distracted her, and she turned to see Avery struggle under another onslaught, Dylan right next to her. El was about to abandon her position to help them, when a familiar figure appeared out of nowhere with a whirl of magic that scattered the spirits.

Helena.

El grinned. She had escaped and now wanted revenge.

Did that mean...

El scanned the cave, hoping to see Gil, and to her relief saw him helping Alex fight the hulking spirit of Coppinger on the upper level. A few tiers down Cassie and Ben fought back to back, and on the far side of the cave Briar was hauling Newton to his feet as she threw a skeleton against the wall. Despite the madness of the situation, El felt herself relax slightly.

The very fact that the spirits had so much physical substance was helping them. Everyone seemed to see them, and although they vanished and reappeared bewilderingly quickly, her friends seemed to be keeping one step ahead. But Alex clearly had no time to banish them, and that was a major problem—especially now that the skeletons were on the move.

Zane and Mariah's arrival had further complicated things, and El wondered how best to thwart them. Mariah was gathering the gold coins with Ethan, Zane protecting them more than attacking anyone, and for a fleeting moment, El wondered what they thought they would do with it. They couldn't possibly think they could get away with it? There were too many people here, witnessing their actions.

And then she realised there was only one reason for their confidence. *They were planning to kill them all.* They either thought the spirits would do it, or they had another plan.

A spriggan suddenly exploded out of one of the chests, showering gold everywhere, and Mariah shrieked as it sent her sprawling. In a split-second its shadow grew, swelling until it was towering above them. It swung its enormous club, catching Ethan in the chest and throwing him into the rotting ship, where he landed with a splintering crash.

Everyone froze—including the spirits.

The spriggan didn't, however, and as the club swung towards her, El ran.

★ ● ◌ ★ ● ◌ � ● ◌ ★ ●

Avery grabbed Dylan, and without warning used witch-flight to take him to the edge of the cave and the entrance to the tunnel they had entered in.

He collapsed on hands and knees, retching. "Herne's balls, Avery! That's bloody horrible!"

"Would you rather your brains be bashed in?"

"Er, no." He staggered to his feet and then stopped, transfixed as he watched the spriggan sweep his enormous club back and forth.

Their friends were running and ducking as old barrels and boxes went flying, and Ash flew around the spriggan, trying to distract it. Sensibly, everyone else was scurrying to the edges of the cave, and El appeared next to Avery, breathless from her scramble.

But something else was distracting Avery.

It was starting to feel very cold. She could see her breath in front of her, and the green, underwater quality of the cave was turning a glacial blue. Alarmed, she looked at the water, and saw ice forming where it met the beach. In mere seconds it spread across the bay and towards the wrecked ship.

"Guys, I think Caspian and Reuben are doing something. It's freezing in here."

Looking back to the cave, she saw fingers of ice clawing up the rock walls, across the ground, and over the barrels and splintered wood.

They needed to leave, quickly. Avery turned to Dylan. "You stay here and guard this exit. This is our only way out. Have you got any salt shells left?"

He patted his pocket, and immediately reloaded. "Yep. No problem."

"Good." She turned to El. "We need to get everyone out of here—right now!"

El didn't wait, and ran towards Briar and Newton, shouting loudly.

Avery manifested next to Ben and Cassie, halfway up the tiers of rock that were now sheer ice, appearing in front of them so unexpectedly that Cassie yelled in shock. Avery pointed to where Dylan stood at the side of the natural amphitheatre. "Join Dylan, and make your way to the end of the tunnel. There's a set of steps cut into the cliff face. It leads upwards to safety."

"But—" Ben started to object.

"Look around, Ben! This place is turning into one giant ice cube." As if to punctuate her point, snow started to fall, and an icy stalactite crashed to the floor next to them, along with Ash.

"She's right," Ash said, and without waiting for Cassie's permission, he wrapped his arms around her and soared across the cave.

"You too, Ben!" Avery shouted. "*Go!*"

She watched him scramble away, and then looked up to where Alex and

Gil were still fighting Coppinger. She grabbed the icy stalactite and flew to Alex's side, catching all of them unawares, especially Coppinger. She hefted her weapon like a spear, plunging it straight through his chest, and he flew backwards.

"Alex! Time to leave!"

He looked at her with a mixture of relief and bewilderment on his face. "But I haven't banished them yet!"

"I don't think you'll need to. Look around! We'll end up an ice exhibit if we don't move."

Snow was falling thicker now, stinging their skin as it hardened into hail. But it seemed Coppinger had no intention of letting them leave. He charged them like an enraged bull, and just as Avery was about to respond, Helena joined Gil and they both shielded Alex and Avery as they faced down Coppinger together.

Helena extended her arms and flames flickered along her entire body, thick black smoke pouring from her, creating a barrier that Coppinger couldn't pass.

Gil turned to them. "We've got this. Helena has a lot of anger to burn off."

Avery stepped towards him, wishing she could hug him. "Gil! I wish we had more time. Will we ever see you again?"

He gave her a weak smile. "I'm aiming to retire after this, so I hope not."

"But you can't stay! You'll be caught up in whatever's happening here!"

He winked as Helena screamed like a banshee and launched herself at Coppinger. "We'll be just fine."

He ran to join Helena, and all three of them vanished from sight in the thickening blizzard.

Alex's hands were already around her waist, and without waiting another second Avery transported them to the tunnel's entrance.

Only El was waiting there, and she sighed with relief at their arrival. "Come on, everyone else is out."

"Ethan?" Avery said, catching sight of his twisted body now partially consumed by ice.

"Already dead."

The ice was already spreading down the tunnel, so with one final look at the icy maelstrom, they raced to join the others.

★·۞·۵·★·۞·۵·✕·۞·۵·★·۞

Reuben stared into the heart of the block of ice, continuing to lower the temperature.

The pool of elemental water that he'd connected to deep within him was powerful, and he closed it like a fist around the spell, his hands on either side of it as it turned slowly above the pages.

Little by little he'd lowered the temperature, seeing the ice form first around the outside and then thicken, moving ever towards the centre, where the words of the spell were now trapped. Caspian had offered him some power, but he found that he didn't need it. Once he'd tapped into his own, it was like he'd released a dam. It was actually a struggle to slow it down.

He glanced up at Caspian, who was unmoving, opposite him. "One more push and it will be frozen solid. What do you think?"

"It's been a good fifteen minutes already. That should have given them plenty of warning. Hold on." Caspian ran back to the thermal imaging camera, and then returned within seconds. "It's an icy blue over the island now, but I can see odd heat spots right on the top of the cliff. I'm no expert on thermal imaging, but I think they're human signals. Go for it."

Reuben lowered the temperature again, watching the ice become cloudy and more dense, the words within it disappearing entirely. Reuben knew it was now solid all the way through. Minute crystals formed over the surface, building up and creating starburst patterns, and Reuben accelerated the growth, until the cube was contained within a giant, beautiful snowflake.

Reuben smiled at his handiwork. "Call me Picasso. I could make money out of this."

Caspian's lips twitched. "Maybe in another life."

"What now?"

"Now, we break it. May I?"

"Be my guest."

"You might want to lean back," he warned.

Caspian uttered a short phrase that Reuben couldn't quite catch. Instantly fractures ripped through the ice, the cube exploding outwards with such force that Reuben shielded his eyes. The words of the curse flew up and out, letters tumbling over each other, throwing Caspian and Reuben off their chairs with a resounding crash. Reuben lay on his back and stared up at the ceiling, seeing letters still whirling before they dissolved into nothing.

Winded, he shouted, "Caspian? Are you still alive?"

He groaned. "Yes. But I'll have a serious headache."

"When you tell me to lean back, you may want to specify an area next time."

"Sure, Reuben. The next time we crack an evil curse, I'll bear that in mind."

★·✹·◌·✦·✹·◌·✳·✹·◌·✦·✹

The second Avery reached the cliff face, she realised just how precarious the steps were, and it didn't help that the rain was steadily falling, making them treacherously slippery.

But Ash was hovering in the air in front of them, his enormous wings protecting them from falling, and although Avery wasn't worried for her own safety, she was relieved for everyone else. She could have used witch-flight, but she wanted to be with her friends, escaping together, and as soon as she reached the grassy cliff top, she saw them clustered a short distance from the edge.

"Is that everyone?" she asked, quickly scanning the group.

They were a bedraggled bunch, shivering and soaked from the rain, and Newton hustled them into action, shouting to be heard above the wind. "That's it, we're all here. Head down the slope to the beach. The police launch is on the way."

They raced across the grassy headland, and then down the long slope to the shore that faced White Haven, slipping and sliding on the slick grass, and it was only when they reached the beach that they stopped and caught their breath. The rain finally fizzled out, but a damp wind buffeted them, catching their hair and ruffling their clothes. Across the waves the town glittered, its warm yellow lights clustered around the harbour and scattered across the hills like stars. A lone engine broke the silence of the night, and they saw a boat streaking towards the shore.

"That must be Mariah and Zane," Briar speculated. "I saw them race out of the cave, but there was no way I could follow them."

Newton was watching them with narrowed eyes, his lips tight. "I've called Moore and told him to back off in case they get violent. The police will have no defence against their magic, and right now, I'm not sure what they're capable of."

"I agree," El said. "I honestly think they were planning to kill all of us in there. Otherwise, why be so brazen?"

That was a horrible thought, but El was right, and Newton nodded. "We'll catch up with them eventually."

"That reminds me," El said, reaching for her phone, but it rang before she could dial and she smiled as she answered. "Reuben!"

Even from a distance, Avery could hear his voice and El drifted away to talk to him in private, reassuring him of their wellbeing.

Ben, Dylan, and Cassie had caught their breath and were grinning from ear to ear, Ben asking, "Did you see that bloody spriggan? Even the spirits were scared of it!"

"I'm not surprised!" Cassie said. "We just came face to face with the ghost of a Cornish giant!" Her eyes took on a faraway glaze.

Dylan snorted. "And the ghosts of many, many murderous pirates!"

"Like I'd forget that! It will give me nightmares!"

"At least," Alex said, brushing his hair away from his face, "you weren't face to face with Coppinger. He was determined to kill me."

Avery slid her arm around his waist. "But he failed. Are you okay?" she asked, drawing him away from the others as they continued their excited chat.

"I'm fine. A bit shocked from seeing Gil, but it was good, too."

"At least we know Helena is free!"

Alex stared down at her. "Remind me not to piss her off. She's mean."

"But she helped us!"

"I'm just glad she's on our side."

Newton joined in again. "I'm going to have to come back here tomorrow, to see if we can get any evidence." He looked inland uneasily, as if he was staring through the ground and into the cave. "I'm giving it overnight in the hope that it will be safe tomorrow."

"We should come with you," Alex immediately said. "Just in case. Will you have a drink with us tonight? We're heading to Reuben's."

"Unfortunately not. I have many things to do, including contacting Ethan's relatives."

Avery's good mood immediately vanished. "You saw his body, then?"

"Flying across the cave like a broken doll? Yes, I saw it. We'll collect that, too." He hesitated a moment. "Do you think the treasure will still be there now that the curse has been broken?"

"Probably," Alex said cautiously. "Why?"

"I was just thinking that it would be an excellent addition to the White Haven exhibition. It would be nice to salvage *something* from this bloody mess."

Thirty-One

A very leaned back in her chair and sipped her tea, listening to the chatter in Reuben's snug.

They had all arrived about an hour ago, and had finally dried out. El was looking proudly at Reuben, who was sitting in front of the fire on the rug, and she said to him and Caspian, "You two are so clever! What an ingenious way to break the spell!"

"It was all Reuben, not me," Caspian said softly. He was sitting in an armchair, and he raised his glass in a silent salute.

"Yeah," Reuben said, shaking his head. "He had some crazy whirlpool idea that would have seen you all sucked into oblivion. And let's not forget the steam!"

Caspian just smiled at him. "Yes, so don't give me your bullshit stories again."

Avery frowned, and then realised what Caspian must be referring to. *Reuben's self doubt.* It seemed they weren't the only ones to share interesting experiences that night.

"Hold on a minute," Alex said, leaning forward from his spot on the sofa. "Are you telling me that I didn't need to banish hordes of angry spirits, and we could have sat by the fire all night while you two worked upstairs?"

Reuben laughed and looked slightly sheepish. "Ah, my friend! That might be the case, but wouldn't you have regretted missing all that fun?"

"No. Coppinger tried to kill me, on multiple occasions!"

"I would have missed it!" Ben cut in. "That was amazing. I just wish we could have recorded some of it."

Dylan gave an abrupt laugh. "Ha! I was too busy fending off spirits to film it! At least we have the other footage. I'll start editing it tomorrow."

"You guys showed some impressive fighting skills today," El told them.

Cassie smiled at her. "Thanks. We've been practising, although with our exams and everything we've been neglecting it lately. No excuses anymore."

"Have you got a team name yet?" Reuben asked.

"Yes, we have!" Dylan said, excited. "After much argument," he shot Ben an annoyed look, "we are called Ghost OPS, which stands for Objective Paranormal Studies."

"I like it," Reuben said, nodding his approval. He gave a sly grin. "I can call you GOPS, as in '*help, help, call the GOPS, I'm being attacked!*'"

"If you have to," Ben said, groaning, as they all laughed. He turned to El, probably just to shut Reuben up. "Hey El, your sword fighting looked pretty good tonight."

"Well, that's thanks to Shadow. She's been giving me private lessons."

"Has she?" Ash said, surprised. He was sitting on the floor too, leaning back against the sofa and sipping a beer. "She kept that quiet, and that's unusual, because she loves to brag!"

"Interesting housemate?" Alex asked, laughing.

"You could say that."

"Why have they gone to London?" Avery asked him, remembering what he'd said earlier.

He shrugged. "No idea, yet. I'll call Gabe later."

Avery wondered how true that was, and what they were now involved with, but she didn't say anything else. With luck, Shadow would update them eventually.

"I have a question," Ben said, looking at Reuben and Caspian. "Did your ancestors seal that cave? Because Alex had to use magic to open it, and when he did, energy exploded out of it."

"I believe so," Caspian said, but he looked uncertain. "The details of what they did remain murky, and even though we deciphered the whole spell, we can only conjecture how it really happened. I suspect it didn't play out quite as they planned, but once they had Coppinger cornered with most of his men, they used the curse. From what you've said, there were multiple entrances into the cave, and I guess they must have sealed them all."

"They sheered the cliff face off too, crushing the ship and splitting it in half," Avery said. "The bay looked to be a natural deep water harbour that allowed the ship to enter the cave. Amazing, really. It was a proper pirate hangout!"

Briar had been sipping her tea as she listened, but now she roused. "I think that's why Mariah left that place until last. They knew it was cursed, and knew it would be the trickiest to access, despite their magic and her compromise with the spirits. I wonder what she'll do now?"

"She and Zane will have to hide, surely?" Reuben said. "They attacked me and Caspian, stole treasure, and although they're not responsible for the deaths, they were very much involved."

Caspian's eyes hardened as he looked at Reuben. "I agree, but it will be hard for the police. I wonder what Genevieve will say."

"And what about their other coven members?" Alex asked. "Are they involved?"

"I guess we'll soon find out," he answered ominously.

★·✦·◆·★·✦·◆·✳·✦·◆·★·✦

Caspian stood on Reuben's porch the next morning, looking across the gravelled drive to Briar's Mini. She had turned it around, and was now waiting for him with the engine running.

He shook Reuben's hand. "Thanks for your hospitality. It's been...interesting."

Reuben laughed. "That's one word for it. You could stay another day or two, until your wound is healed."

"I'm fine now—well, apart from the odd twinge. And I don't have to fear attack by ghosts again."

"What about Mariah or Zane?"

"I think they'll leave well enough alone. And my protection spells will be strong. Make sure yours are, too." He stepped onto the drive, and Reuben followed him as Caspian looked up at the attic's shattered windows. "Are you sure you don't want help with those?"

"I'm going to do it the old-fashioned way and get glaziers in, and hire a builder for the wall." Reuben hesitated, and then said, "Thanks for all your help, with everything." He shuffled, looking suddenly uncomfortable. "I know I struggled a bit."

"You did just fine. Better than fine." Caspian was feeling unexpectedly sad to be leaving. He'd found that he was very comfortable around Reuben and the rest of the White Haven Coven, and it was a strange feeling, one that had been growing for a while. It was a feeling he'd buried, but couldn't anymore, and didn't actually want to. He debated just turning away and getting in Briar's car, but there was one more thing he needed to say. He looked Reuben directly in the eye. "I really am sorry about Gil. I'm responsible. I caused it, even though it wasn't my intention. You have been incredibly forgiving, and I don't know if I could have done the same in your shoes."

Reuben's gaze dropped to the ground, and Caspian hoped he hadn't said the wrong thing, but then he looked up again, as if he'd mastered his emotions. "It's been hard, I won't lie, but thank you. I appreciate it. And now you need to move on, and so do I...from all sorts of things." Caspian heard Avery and Alex's voices coming down the hall, and Reuben spoke quickly. "And you need to move on from her, too."

"Easier said than done," he confessed, and having said it, he already felt lighter.

Reuben just nodded, and then Avery and Alex were with them, Avery saying, "There you are! I thought I'd missed you." She stepped forward, enveloping him in a hug. "Thanks so much for your help, again. It's becoming a habit. You're on team White Haven now!" She stepped back and smiled at him, leaving him feeling bereft, but once again grateful for her kindness.

Caspian laughed. "Don't let Estelle hear you say that." *Something else he needed to deal with.* He quickly reached forward and shook Alex's hand, aware of his cool glance that said everything. "Alex. I'll see you soon."

And not wanting to linger, he headed quickly to Briar's car.

★·●·◦·★·●·◦·✳·●·◦·★·●

Reuben stood next to Newton and Alex, watching Moore and another couple of officers examine the cave.

They had set up huge lights and a generator, after accessing the cave via the tunnel from Reuben's glasshouse, and Reuben tried to imagine how it would have looked the previous evening in the watery green light.

"Wow," he said, spotting the splintered remnants of the ship. "That's incredible. It's all incredible!"

Alex grunted. "It looks a damn sight better today than when it was full of bloody ghosts and animated skeletons. Although the pressure of the ice has crushed all the wood."

"Yes!" Newton exclaimed, hurrying across to the ruined chests and piles of gold. "The treasure is still here!"

"Slow down." Alex said, rushing to follow him. "The spriggan might still be here, too!"

"Oh come on," Newton scoffed. "This place turned into solid ice. It would have surely killed it! We're probably surrounded by tiny little pieces of it."

Reuben listened to their banter as he followed them with his easy stride, taking in the abandoned weapons, the skeletal remains, and the piles of shattered wood. It was cold and damp, with water dripping down the walls and forming pools across the tiers. It was hard to believe his magic had filled this place with ice. There was certainly no curse remaining, or any palpable psychic energy. It just felt very empty. He could hear the surf pounding outside, but the only evidence of it inside were the gentle waves that splashed on the now inland beach.

Ethan's body was still lying twisted on the spar, and once Newton was happy that the place was safe, the coroner would be called in, as would SOCO. Reuben wondered what the ice had done to his body, and shuddered. Turned his innards to mush, probably.

Newton's shout broke through his thoughts. "Hey Reuben, do you mind if the police set up on your grounds by the glasshouse? It could take days to process in here."

He walked over to join them. "It's fine, as long as they don't mind me being incredibly nosey!"

"It will be out of bounds until they've finished, you pillock."

"Thanks, Newton. You're always so nice." In the harsh white lights that illuminated the cave, Newton looked very tired, and he thought he'd trade an insult. "Are you sure you slept last night? You look like shit."

"Barely." He watched Moore and the other two officers exploring the tiers of rock. "I called Maggie Milne this morning. I thought I should let her know about Mariah and Zane. We had officers watching their houses, but there's been no movement, and their cars are gone." He turned to Alex and Reuben. "I've never had to chase witches before, so I'm not exactly sure what I should do next in regard to safety and magic."

"What did she say?" Alex asked.

"To tread carefully, and involve other witches." He gave them a long, questioning look.

Reuben tried to laugh and failed. "Are you saying you need *us* to find them?"

"You're the only ones I trust."

Reuben looked at Alex's bleak expression, and knew he was thinking the same as him. He didn't want to fight other witches, or hunt them down, but if they were a danger—and they probably were—they'd have no choice.

★·◉·◑·★·◉·◑·✳·◉·◑·★·◉

Avery ended her call with Genevieve and walked back to the counter to join Dan and Sally.

It was late morning in Happenstance Books, and because it was a Saturday, the place was busy. All three were capitalising on a lull and taking a quick coffee break. Sally had opened a packet of chocolate digestives, and she dunked one in her coffee as Avery leaned on the counter.

"What's the verdict?" Dan asked. He'd decided to celebrate the museum's smuggling exhibition that—despite Ethan's death—was still opening that day, by wearing a t-shirt that said, *All the best pirates smuggle books.*

Avery had already updated them on the events of the night before, and there had been a mixture of emotions from them both—excitement, horror, wonder, amazement, and now worry at the thought of Zane and Mariah's disappearance.

"Genevieve is furious, but she doesn't want to jump to any conclusions or make rash decisions. And I agree. We have time."

"But won't that give *them* time?" Sally asked. "They could be planning anything!"

"They're not bloody Voldemort activating his dark mark," Dan said. "And I'm pretty sure Genevieve won't need to unleash any Dementors, either."

Avery giggled, but Sally glared at him. "I know that! But they've been very underhanded, and were behind Reuben's attack. He could have been killed! Caspian, too. All of you, really," she added, turning her attention to Avery. "And Zane has never liked you, Avery. He could blame you for needing to flee!"

Avery sobered. "I know, and we're not taking this lightly, but we need a plan. It's Litha next week, and we'll all be gathering to celebrate at Rasmus's place, so that's when we'll decide on a plan, too." She sipped her drink, thinking about her conversation. "Genevieve is going to visit the Looe and Bodmin Coven members if they're around, and also let the other covens know today, just in case Zane or Mariah contact someone for help. Personally, I think they're a long way from here by now."

"Good." Sally took another biscuit. "Well, I'm just glad you're safe, and despite everything, I will still be going to that exhibition. Do you think they'll add the treasure, too?"

"Maybe. Surely at least some of it, once they've assessed it."

"And what about the chests you found and took to Reuben's?" Dan asked.

"I took those back to the big cave first thing this morning, once I knew it was safe." She had risen early and flown there with Alex. "It'll be easier to pretend it was part of that treasure than tell anyone about the room beneath St Catherine's Castle. It also means we can leave those spriggans well alone."

Dan looked confused. "Why was Miles killed if he didn't even get in there? You said there was no way he could have entered the place."

"I've been thinking on that, and I can only presume he got too close and triggered them somehow. It's odd, though. It's close to a popular walking spot, and I imagine lots of people are around there all the time. They haven't attacked any of them."

"Unless, of course," Dan suggested, slightly tentatively, "Mariah orchestrated it to get him out of the way. And then let them attack Jasmine. You mentioned that you and Alex had managed to control them, and El also did, and I know you said they were strong, but why couldn't Zane and

Mariah stop them?"

A chill rushed through Avery as she considered Dan's words, and realised that actually made a lot of sense. Her legs went weak, and she sagged against the counter. "Shit. You might be right."

He stared back at her, Sally watching them wide-eyed. "Maybe," he said, "they intended for Ethan to never leave there, either."

"And the man walking his dog!" Sally added. "Maybe he saw something, because he was nowhere near the cave in Looe, either!"

Avery staggered to the stool behind the counter. All the odd things that had happened made a lot of sense if Dan was right, which meant Mariah and Zane were far more dangerous than they thought. She took a deep breath, deciding to think on it and discuss it with the others later.

"Thanks, guys. I have a horrible feeling you might be right, Dan. Now, let's do something positive, because this is depressing me."

"Of course," Sally said, visibly gathering herself and giving Avery a beaming smile. "We have new stock in, shelves to fill, and I need to decorate the shop for the solstice! It's time for another witchy celebration in White Haven!"

"And I think it's also time for some pirate music," Dan said, quickly changing the track that had been playing.

Avery groaned as she heard the booming, jaunty words, "I am the very model of a modern major general."

"*The Pirates of Penzance*!" She looked at him, aghast. "In my shop!"

She tried to wrestle the controls from Dan, but he just laughed maniacally and scooted after Sally, tugging her hair and making her squeal as he did a silly jig. Despite her mood, Avery giggled, and once again thanked her lucky stars for her shop and her friends, because she was pretty sure the coming weeks were going to be hard.

✦ ❂ ⦿ ✦ ❂ ⦿ ✦ ❂ ⦿ ✦ ❂

Thanks for reading *Vengeful Magic*. Please make an author happy and leave a review at Happenstance Books.

I have also written a spinoff series called White Haven Hunters. The first book is called *Spirit of the Fallen*, and it's on sale now.

Newsletter

If you enjoyed this book and would like to read more of my stories, please subscribe to my newsletter at tjgreenauthor.com. You will get two free short stories, *Excalibur Rises* and *Jack's Encounter,* and will also receive free character sheets for all of the main White Haven witches.

By staying on my mailing list you'll receive free excerpts of my new books, as well as short stories, news of giveaways, and a chance to join my launch team. I'll also be sharing information about other books in this genre you might enjoy.

Ream

I have started my own subscription service called Happenstance Book Club. I know what you're thinking! What is Ream? It's a bit like Patreon, which you may be more familiar with, and it allows you to support me and read my books before anyone else.

There is a monthly fee for this, and a few different tiers, so you can choose what tier suits you. All tiers come with plenty of other bonuses, including merchandise, but the one thing common to all is that you can read my latest books while I'm writing them – so they're a rough draft. I will post a few chapters each week, and you can read them at your leisure, as well as comment in them. You can also choose to be a follower for free.

You can comment on my books, chat about spoilers, and be part of a community. I will also post polls, character art, share rituals and spells, share the background to the myths and legends in my books, and some of my earlier books are available to read for free.

Interested? Head to Happenstance Book Club.

https://reamstories.com/happenstancebookclub

Happenstance Book Shop

I also now have a fabulous online shop called Happenstance Books where you can buy eBooks, audiobooks, and paperbacks, many bundled up at great prices, as well as fabulous merchandise. I know that you'll love it! Check it out here: https://happenstancebookshop.com/

YouTube

If you love audiobooks, you can listen for free on YouTube, as I have uploaded all of my audiobooks there. Please subscribe if you do. Thank you. https://www.youtube.com/@tjgreenauthor

Read on for a list of my other books.

Author's Note

Thank you for reading *Vengeful Magic*, the eighth book in the White Haven Witches series.

I'm sure you've noticed that this book was told from multiple points of view. I was encouraged to do this by all of my fantastic readers who said they would love to have more insight into the other characters.

I must admit, I'd wanted to, especially after doing this with White Haven Hunters, but wondered how well this would be received, considering this is the eighth book! Hopefully you have loved the opportunity to get in the heads of the other witches, and of course Newton. I feel it's given the characters and stories a new lease of life, and I'm fizzing to get started on the next novel in the series.

I had a lot of fun writing about pirates. Cornwall is awash with pirate tales, and many of the places I refer to do exist, such as the Charlestown Shipwreck Treasure Museum and Jamaica Inn Smuggling Museum. Obviously the characters associated with them do not exist, and I'm sure there's no skulduggery among the archives! Wheal Droskyn in Perranporth exists too, and in fact there are hundreds of mines all across Cornwall.

Cruel Coppinger was a real pirate who landed on the north Cornish coast during a storm, and he became notorious for his cruelty. His story was embellished by the Reverend Robert Stephen Hawker, who collected legends. Zephaniah Job was also a real person who kept the financial records for pirates, and his ledgers were burnt following his death.

If you'd like to read a bit more background to the stories, please head to my website, tjgreenauthor.com, where I blog about the books I've read and the research I've done on the series. In fact, there's lots of stuff on there about my other series, Rise of the King, as well.

Now for the thanks I owe everyone who helped me produce this book.

I decided to run a competition in my newsletter and Facebook Inner Circle for a name for the parapsychologists. I had some fantastic suggestions and ended up narrowing it down to eight that had the final vote. Ghost OPS won by a big margin! Thank you Margaret Meyer for your awesome suggestion!

Thanks again to Fiona Jayde Media for my awesome cover, and thanks to Kyla Stein at Missed Period Editing for applying her fabulous editing skills.

Thanks also to my beta readers, glad you enjoyed it; your feedback, as always, is very helpful!

Finally, thank you to my launch team, who give valuable feedback on typos and are happy to review on release. It's lovely to hear from them—you know who you are! You're amazing! I also love hearing from all my readers, so I welcome you to get in touch.

If you'd like to read more of my writing please subscribe to my newsletter at www.tjgreenauthor.com. You can get a free short story called Jack's Encounter, describing how Jack met Fahey—a longer version of the prologue in Call of the King—by subscribing to my newsletter. You'll also get a free copy of Excalibur Rises, a short story prequel. You will also receive free character sheets on all of my main characters in White Haven Witches—exclusive to my email list!

By staying on my mailing list you'll receive free excerpts of my new books, updates on new releases, as well as short stories and news of giveaways. I'll also be sharing information about other books in this genre you might enjoy.

You can also follow my page, T J Green. I post there reasonably frequently. In addition, I have a Facebook group called TJ's Inner Circle. It's a fab little group where I run giveaways and post teasers, so come and join us.

About the Author

I was born in England, in the Black Country, but moved to New Zealand in 2006. I lived near Wellington with my partner Jase, and my cats Sacha and Leia. However, in April 2022 we moved again! Yes, I like making my life complicated... I'm now living in the Algarve in Portugal, and loving the fabulous weather and people. When I'm not busy writing I read lots, indulge in gardening and shopping, and I love yoga.

Confession time! I'm a Star Trek geek – old and new – and love urban fantasy and detective shows. Secret passion – Columbo! Favourite Star Trek film is the Wrath of Khan, the original! Other top films – Predator, the original, and Aliens.

In a previous life I was a singer in a band, and used to do some acting with a theatre company. For more on me, check out a couple of my blog posts. I'm an old grunge queen, so you can read about my love of that here. For more random news, read this.

Please follow me on social media to keep up to date with my news, or join my mailing list—I promise I don't spam!

f facebook.com/tjgreenauthor/

P pinterest.pt/tjgreenauthor/

♪ tiktok.com/@tjgreenauthor

▶ youtube.com/@tjgreenauthor

goodreads.com/author/show/15099365.T_J_Green

instagram.com/tjgreenauthor/

bookbub.com/authors/tj-green

https://reamstories.com/happenstancebookclub

Other Books by T J Green

Midwinter Magic #12
White Haven and The Lord of Misrule Novella

⭐ ✦ ✦ ⭐ ✦ ✦ ✴ ✦ ✦ ⭐ ✦

White Haven Hunters
The action-packed spin-off featuring Shadow and the Nephilim.
Spirit of the Fallen #1
Shadow's Edge #2
Dark Star #3
Hunter's Dawn #4
Midnight Fire #5
Immortal Dusk #6
Brotherhood of the Fallen #7

⭐ ✦ ✦ ⭐ ✦ ✦ ✴ ✦ ✦ ⭐ ✦

Storm Moon Shifters
Paranormal Mysteries set around the wolf shifter pack, Storm Moon.
Storm Moon Rising #1
Dark Heart #2

⭐ ✦ ✦ ⭐ ✦ ✦ ✴ ✦ ✦ ⭐ ✦

Moonfell Witches
This series features the mysterious and magical witches who live in Moonfell, the sprawling Gothic mansion in London. They first appeared in

Storm Moon Rising, Storm Moon Shifters Book 1, and then in Immortal Dusk, White Haven Hunters Book 6, and features characters from both series. However, this series can be read as a standalone.

If you love witches and magic, you will love the Moonfell Witches.

The First Yule: Novella

Triple Moon #1

52b8a877-c122-4701-b6ac-684d3869a3a1R01